TRUE BLEND

ALSO BY JOANNE DEMAIO

Snowflakes and Coffee Cakes

Blue Jeans and Coffee Beans

Whole Latte Life

For Mary, always

One

T HE WISHING FOUNTAIN SPRAYS SILVER water droplets arching high above it, looking like liquid stars. Grace wants to toss in a coin, eager to watch it loll back and forth down through the water until it settles with the other coins below. In that pool of shimmering wishes, small hopes and secrets are gathered together. Amy lifts her onto the low stone wall circling the fountain and wraps her arms around her daughter's waist. She bends, her mouth near Grace's ear, her breath tickling loose wisps of hair. Her fingers find Grace's palm and press a penny into it. "Make a wish," she softly says. There is only the sound of falling water then as Grace drops the penny in, silently captivated by its descent, and Amy wonders what she might wish for, if she even knows what a wish is.

They linger at the fountain, and Grace reaches up to touch the misty spray before Amy takes her small hand. Together they walk across Addison's town green to the library and find fairy tales and animal stories, each illustrated to bring the words to life.

"Can you give the lady your book, Grace?"

Her daughter lifts a storybook about kittens onto the counter, her fingers staying there, splayed lightly on the edge, waiting

1

for the book to be in her hands again. "Kittens," she says, turning back to Amy. "My kittens." She looks uncertain, and worried. This is something new: When anything she loves is out of her sight, out of her grasp, Grace comes close to tears until it is returned, until her arms hold it near. It's funny, what we keep from sadness, from loss. Grace only wants to hold her father again, Amy just knows it. She takes the new stack of books, part of the stack of stuff she uses to fill her daughter's life, and they leave. So grief whispers in again, like it does sometimes, until the library door opens onto the spring day and birdsong as they walk to the SUV outside.

"Swing? Want to swing," Grace says from her car seat.

"We will, sweetie. After the bank, I promise." Behind the wheel, Amy puts the key in the ignition and adjusts her denim skirt beneath her legs. A song is in her head, one about sunshine and happiness. Maybe she'll get a coffee-to-go after the bank and have it at the playground. The sand pail is in the back, in case Grace wants to play in the sandbox. It's good for her to be near other children, to socialize.

With a few minutes to spare, Amy takes the longer route, driving past the old stable and the pretty horses grazing; cruising by imposing historic colonials with potted purple and yellow pansies sitting on the stoops. Finally she drives into the bank parking lot early, like she does every Monday morning, pausing to listen to the end of an easy love song on the radio. "Come on, Gracie," she finally says as she puts her keys in her purse. "You can draw with the pencil now, okay? Julie will be waiting for you." She gets out and opens the back door, unlatches Grace and tightens one of her daughter's ponytails before lifting her out.

A driveway winding through a thicket of white pines sets the condominium complex far off the road. George Carbone checks his watch at the living room window. When his brother's gray sedan approaches, he slips into his windbreaker jacket, the glimmer of his father's ruby ring catching his eye. *Clothes make the man* his father always said, tugging the white cuffs of his shirt. Then he'd take George's mother in his arms and dance her around the room tenderly, the same way he loved her. He had set the bar high on marriage, on caring. George wears his father's ring today for luck.

"Ready to beat the odds?" Nate asks when he reaches across the front seat and clasps George's hand in a quick shake.

"To a point. What's with the gloves?"

"You like them?" Nate holds up a hand clad in a thin black leather sport glove. "Driving gloves. Everybody's wearing them."

"Yeah, they're all right." George sits back while Nate adjusts the rearview mirror. A bead of perspiration lines his brother's face. Morning rush hour has passed and traffic is light. George turns his father's ring on his pinky, thinking he'll risk a hundred on the slot machines. "We meeting the others for coffee first?"

"Not today," Nate answers, adjusting the rearview mirror again, tapping its angle.

"Why not? We always do."

Nate shakes his head. "I've got to run a quick errand so we're catching up with them at the casino. We can stop for coffee on the way." He unzips his black sweatshirt and shifts in the seat.

"What's the matter?" George asks. His brother's fingers drum incessantly while they wait at a red light. "You planning on dropping a barrel of money at the tables?"

"The usual. You know."

The light changes and Nate precedes every turn, every lane change with the proper signals. Every stop sign warrants a complete stop. The speed limit is respected. It is almost exaggerated, the care he takes driving early this May morning.

"But maybe it's time to up the ante today, take some chances," Nate adds. "What do you think?"

"Not me. I've got a couple hundred to lose, tops, and I'm done. Have a nice steak dinner and call it a day."

"Come on," Nate insists. "Live a little. You've got to loosen up sometimes."

A quick smile crosses George's face. "Loosen up? Cripe, you're the one wound up today." He looks out the window when Nate pulls into a local shopping plaza. "Hey, there's no coffee shop here. And nothing's open until ten, except the bank."

"That's where I'm going." Nate cruises down the sloping parking lot and stops the car near a small Italian restaurant and a fireplace accessory shop two storefronts beyond the bank.

"Why are you parking so far away? Get closer, let's get a move on."

Nate pauses, then reaches over to the back seat and hands George a black sweatshirt. "I'm blocking the view. Here, take this."

"Blocking the view. Of what?"

"Of witnesses."

George lifts the large hooded top before dropping it back in his lap. "What are you talking about? Witnesses?" His eyes stop then on a forty-five caliber gun his brother lifts from beside the seat. "Jesus Christ, Nate."

"Okay." A nondescript black vehicle drives slowly behind his parked car. "Look. We don't have much time. Something's going down here and I've got all the bases covered. Just go with me on this."

"What's wrong with you?" George asks.

"With me?" Nate looks long at him, as though gauging a decision. "Nothing," he says, then jumps when his cell phone rings. "Everything's good."

The cell rings again at the same time that an armored truck turns into the parking lot, heading directly to the front of the bank.

"She just pulled in?" Nate asks, glancing up toward the entranceway at the top of the sloped parking lot. "Okay, let me know." He slips his phone into his pocket and reaches beneath the seat, pulling out a handful of what looks like hosiery of some sort. "Shit. This is it."

"Whoa, whoa, what the hell?" George asks as Nate hands him leather gloves and a nine-millimeter handgun while rapidly reciting orders. Something about George being a show of strength, he only has to look the part and stand near the armored truck when they give him the word. Keep his face covered with those nylons. The gun is loaded, but don't worry. He only has to stand there. And don't talk, at all. Don't do anything that will identify him. George's mind reels as it puts together and resists what is happening. His eyes never leave the armored truck.

"So put the gloves on and get ready to pull those nylons over your head," Nate continues, his voice monotone. He's come under a spell, one George recognizes as Nate checks the mirrors and wipes his brow. He's seen it before when the pot grows large or the game slick and the gamble courses through his veins. "They're tight, but you get used to it. Your face always has to be covered, George."

George tries the door handle, joggling it roughly when it doesn't give. "Unlock the God damn doors."

But Nate's trying to keep up with the perspiration, swiping at his forehead. "There's no time. No time! We're taking down that truck and you'll be set for life. Do you hear me?"

"Is this a joke? What happened to the casino? Are you crazy?"

"The casino's happening, too. Later." He wipes his face, his eyes, the perspiration coming like tears. "Put on that sweatshirt. And the gloves, damn it, the gloves."

"Nate. *Nate.* Cut the shit now. I don't believe you. You're not doing this. Not you. I own a business. I'm in the Chamber of Commerce, for God's sake. I've got a good life. And so do you." He tosses the sweatshirt and hosiery on the floor, sets the nine-millimeter handgun on the seat and pulls and shoves at the locked door.

Nate looks up from stretching out the hosiery he is about to pull over his head. "Don't you get it? It's too late."

George follows his gaze to the black car, where two passengers sit in the front seat. "This is for real?"

The cell phone rings again.

"Leave it," George says so quickly, Nate pauses. "Just leave it. Let's get out of here. Now," he persists, still in disbelief. "It's not too late. We'll leave together. We can blow them off." He thinks he might convince him, that Nate wavers. His eyes change. George sees, in the flash of seconds, Nate travelling back in time to riding bicycles together with baseball cards clipped to the spokes; to tagging along with George in high school hallways; to paddling the old rowboat through the lagoon at Stony Point, a fishing line dropped in the salt water; to playing on the same baseball leagues during hot summers, dust rising around a stolen base. In those seconds, Nate will listen, he has to, and he'll start the car and take off with his big brother, maybe laugh about it when they get on the highway toward the casino, like they planned. A day playing cards and the slot machines with their poker friends. All he has to do is turn the key in the ignition. "Let's book."

When the cell phone rings again, George fumbles with the door lock, but Nate grabs his arm before he gets the door open.

"They won't let you go, George. Trust me." There is regret in the lowness of his voice, as though on some level Nate knows he has gotten in too deep and there's no climbing out.

George looks at his brother, trying to understand what happened to this day that started so normal, so mundane. They do it every few months, spend a day at a ballgame, or fishing, or at the casino, having a good meal, a few laughs. "No one gets away with a crime like this." He yanks his arm from his brother's grip.

"You'd be surprised," Nate says. "And those two won't let you walk away now."

"I can at least try. You coming with me?" He tosses the leather gloves aside and gets out of the car, then leans back—half in, half out, ready to bolt. An occasional car drives by far up on the street, unnoticing, distracted with cell phones and coffee and talk-radio. "You can't do this, Nate." But his brother is lowering the hosiery over his face. The distortion of his features, flattened and twisted beneath it, is appalling. George backs away.

"George!" Nate yells, his voice muffled through the nylon. "Just do it, man. Put on the sweatshirt and cover your face. It'll be okay. All you have to do is stand beside the truck, right against the gun port. That's it. If they see you walking away and messing this up, they won't like it. I told them you were game."

A motion catches George's eye. When a uniformed man steps out of the armored truck and walks to the door of the bank, it's clear that innocent people are connecting the dots of some crime about to happen. Some strange bullet's already been discharged and he's not sure he can stop it. He feels oddly cold and glances down at his shirt. It is soaked through.

And then it just happens, his legs begin backing away, his hand held up signaling he will not listen any longer. "Leave with me, Nate. Come on. Those guards will never give up that truck. They'll use their weapons before they turn it over. You know that, don't you?"

Nate leans across the seat, looking up at him through the open passenger door. "Not with the right bait, they won't."

"Bait?" They are moments away from some godforsaken act and George has no clear way out. He has to take a chance and walk. Maybe his brother will come to his senses and follow him, tag along like he used to, a step behind always. Start the car and pull up beside him to leave together. He turns, zips his light jacket and heads across the sloping parking lot toward the sidewalk up along the street as though he is nothing more than a passing pedestrian. Except there is no way a pedestrian hears his own heart beat the way he does.

"Just do it," Nate calls quietly. George turns as his brother releases the safety on the semiautomatic gun in his lap. "Come on. It's time," Nate insists, lurching with the force of the words. "Are you in?"

How many times has he heard that line? How many times has Nate called him to put together a poker night? *Are you in?* How many times has his brother dealt the cards, waiting for his call? *You in?* George looks back to the bank. A woman and her young daughter walk toward the door. His eyes drop closed for a moment when he whispers, "No, no."

If he leaves the scene and calls the police, is there time enough to stop what will happen in the parking lot? Because it's happening already, he's just not sure how. But it's all unfolding. So does he owe that woman and her child fair warning? Or is he wrong? Maybe they won't be a part of it. Maybe the worst thing he can do is yell and wave his arms at them to hide, to go inside the bank and stay there, to run, damn it.

His whole life comes down to this one moment, weighing the odds of surviving the crime as he helps the others right now, against the odds of leaving quietly and staying alive, calling for help once he's safely away from the scene. One moment, one decision.

———

When she's handed her deposit receipt and money, the teller asks Amy to count it. "Just to be sure," she says. So Amy quickly fingers through the bills, all the while hearing Julie make easy small talk with Grace sitting at her desk, squiggling a pencil across blank paper.

"Say bye-bye now," Amy says, looking over to her daughter as she puts away her money.

"She's such a good girl," Julie tells her with a smile. "You come and visit me anytime, Gracie. Next week, I'll have a lollipop for you."

An armored truck worker says hello to Grace as he walks past them on his way outside. He holds the door but Amy waves him off, stopping first at the self-service table and taking a handful of deposit slips. She opens her purse and neatly tucks them in beside the envelope of cash. Grace stands near her, touching her leg, holding her pencil drawing. They always touch, somehow. If not one, the other.

When they leave the bank, it is into a suffusion of clear morning sunlight. Amy pauses, letting its soft warmth rest on her face until Grace shifts beside her. Her fingers clasp tightly the small hand of her daughter. The child must still sense the loss of her father and shadows her constantly. Amy checks the time on her gold watch, the one Mark had given her for their first anniversary, having no idea those hands of time would count down a limited number of hours of their life together.

"Come on, Grace." Looking down at their daughter, Amy sees the rays of morning sun touch her honey-blonde ponytails. The light dances delicately through the fine wisps of her two-year-old tresses and Amy lets that light reach her own heart. "Let's go to the playground," she says as they walk off the curb. The step down is steep for Grace's legs. Amy carefully looks past the red armored truck parked there to be sure no cars approach in their path. Grace lags a step behind, her little legs working fast to keep up, so Amy slows and turns only to see a blur, a dark shadow sweeping toward her and pulling her daughter from her hand. There is sudden commotion, pressing unexpectedly close. Grace's pencil drawing flutters to the pavement.

Two

ARE YOU HURT?" THE DRIVER asks.

Amy shakes her head, watching the street where the armored truck drove off. "My God, they took her. They just grabbed her from me!" She is shaking and wraps her arms around herself. Arms that feel hollow and empty without Grace. She looks down at those arms and sees her gold watch. Three minutes have passed since she walked out of the bank holding her daughter's hand. Three minutes.

"Quick, let's get you inside," the other man from the truck says, taking her elbow to lead her to the bank. "Your legs are all cut, you sure you're okay?"

"Wait!" Amy cries. "I've got to get Grace." She digs into her handbag searching for car keys. "We'll follow them," she insists as her vision blurs behind tears. "If I can just find my keys." The purse drops to the ground and she crouches, desperately rummaging around her wallet and tissue and hand lotion and pens and her banking receipts, until the two armored truck workers take her by the arms and help her to stand.

"It's too late, they're gone already. They're gone! We've got to call for help right away." The uniformed man saying this pulls his cell phone from his pocket.

The driver, wearing only a dark T-shirt with his uniform pants, is insisting nonstop, "The police, call the police. Get the cops here." Perspiring and visibly shaken, he turns back to Amy. "Hurry now!"

"No, no." She takes a deep, shaking breath with tears lining her face. "No police."

"What?" both men ask at the same time.

"We have to wait," she explains, a hand pressing back a sob over her mouth. "They told me," she continues then, looking from one defeated face to the other. "The man with my daughter told me I had to wait an hour. One hour with no police contact," she barely says, her words choked back with crying. "One hour for my daughter."

"What? Jesus, that's too long! Your little girl—"

"Please," Amy pleads. "We have to listen to them."

"Take a deep breath and let's get inside where you can sit down," one of the men tells her, and she forces herself to breathe in. Her lungs can't seem to get enough oxygen though. The inhale is ragged and strained.

The men lead her into the bank, through the lobby to a small office where she sits, then promptly stands and circles the room. The bank manager rushes in behind them. "What's going on?" He looks at Amy and stops in his tracks. "What happened?"

"They have my daughter."

"Who has your daughter? Is she okay?" He looks out the window and when he does, Amy does too. In her mind, it is still happening, even though the parking lot is empty now. But to her, the man holding Grace is there still, his feet always moving, shifting his weight back and forth, back and forth, turning, jostling Grace in his grip, her ponytails swinging as he moves in shadow closer to the armored truck.

"What's going on?" the manager asks.

"They stole the truck!" the driver explains. "Didn't you see?"

"What? No. The truck's been stolen? You gave it to them?"

The driver nods rapidly. "Jesus, they took her girl to do it. They took her! Kidnapped her, right in broad daylight."

"What do you mean, they took her? You couldn't stop them?"

"No. Shit, it all happened so fast," the other guard says. "I was opening the back door on the truck and the next thing, someone's got me by the neck with a gun to my head, pushing me right inside. My God, I never saw him coming."

"I did what they said," the driver says, still shaking. "Man, they'd kill him otherwise. And the girl, they had her. So I did it, I called the dispatcher, just did what they said."

Amy turns to the bank manager. She holds out her arms, her right hand scraped raw, her fingers shaking. "They took Grace," she whispers. The bank goes silent, and with a few employees clustered in the doorway, listening, she explains. "He just grabbed her, and his feet, his feet, well they kept shifting." *A breath*, she thinks. *Breathe*. "Grace, her hair, her face. She was so afraid. And I couldn't see, in the sunlight." She closes her eyes against all the visuals that won't line up. "He kept moving closer to the truck. With my daughter." Finally, when she can only cry, the two armored truck guards fill in their details. Amy, her hand over her mouth, listens closely to each mention of a tone of voice, or type of weapon trained on them, or order given. They followed those orders; the driver lied and notified their dispatcher that they were leaving for their next scheduled stop for only one reason. It was all because Grace was in that man's arms.

"You couldn't use your weapons?" the bank manager asks, shaking his head no, like he already knows the answer. They all do.

"The girl. My God, if we did anything, they'd hurt her little girl. And as soon as they got her on the truck, that was it. We were out and they took off. They did it, man, they took her. They took everything—the truck, the girl, even my uniform shirt, man. Jesus."

"But there's a camera on the truck, right? Surveillance video? And GPS they can track?"

"GPS? You kidding me, man? That klunker's seven years old, we're lucky to have a working radio on it."

"But you called the police?" the bank manager asks.

"No, we can't yet," the driver explains.

"What? Jesus Christ." The manager lunges for a desk phone. "Christ, we need the cops, right now!"

"No!" Amy calls out. "No, we can't. Because he told me," she adds.

"Who told you?" the bank manager interrupts while picking up the phone.

"The man who took Grace. Oh God," she says, taking a long breath, remembering how he told her not to talk and to listen carefully. Remembering his one arm wrapped tight around Grace's torso and the contrast of his dark clothes against her pink jeans and blonde ponytails as he hoisted her up and shifted her weight. "He said they needed one hour. One hour with no police. And then I'd get my daughter back."

"So they took her hostage? Just so they could get away?"

Amy only nods, still crying.

"That's crazy," the manager says. "That's just crazy. We need the police here, right away."

"Please," Amy cries. "They said not to, and I'm too afraid they'll hurt her. Please don't call yet."

A quiet second passes. "All right," the manager finally relents as he sets the phone down. A lock of hair falls in his face; beads of perspiration line his forehead. "I don't like it, I really don't, but I'm not sure what to do. They say every minute counts. One hour for your daughter, I guess. That's it, though. I mean, that's *it*. And I'll keep the bank open so we don't raise any suspicions. But just an hour. Really."

Amy can't talk. An office window draws her closer to the outside and she moves to it, looking out at the street. Maybe they've dropped Grace off and she is wandering alone. They might do something like that. She could be walking in the road and a car might hit her. She can be cowering in a doorway.

The muted voices of the truck workers behind her repeat fresh details of the robbery. So she knows now. While she fell to her knees, while she squinted through glaring sunshine and harsh shadows, watching Grace hang limp—one ponytail askew, the powder blue hair ribbon flitting loose—another side of the crime played out on the armored truck, with weapons drawn, with lives threatened. All in three minutes time.

Now sixty more minutes must pass without Grace. Sixty minutes are the ransom for her daughter's life. No calls will come. They want no money from Amy. Sixty minutes to escape, in exchange for Grace.

Her only defense will be memory. So for the next hour, she must hear, see, touch, know every small detail that she can remember. The sweatshirt hoods and horrible hosiery masks, the two men outside the truck and the two others who overpowered the driver and deliveryman. Behind her closed eyes, she replays parts of the crime. She sees the man holding Grace turn abruptly to run onto the truck. As he turned sharply, Grace's legs swung with the jolt and a shoe flew off her foot. The small pink and white saddle

15

shoe skitted across the parking lot. Amy cried out before lunging for the shoe, for all she could have of her child. There was a race, suddenly, against mere seconds as a fourth man, a lone gunman who'd been standing beside the truck, swooped down at the same time. Her legs burned and stumbled, sliding her onto her knees while falling forward, the pavement gouging her skin, her eyes on the shoe. She grasped it and winced when the man's hand, a mere shadow behind, pressed firmly on top of hers.

"Let me have it," she pleaded. A prickling sensation grew on the back of her hand, beneath the breadth of his strong grip. Every bit of his calloused palm, the apprehension of his hold, the knot of a scar, pressed against her, skin to skin. The curve of his grasp, the ruby ring on his finger, all branded her deeply. She will never forget those etched details. Pure physical touch, her one human connection with the crime, became the focal point of the entire battle of wills. "Please," she insisted when he didn't relinquish his hold.

He shook his head no and that's when her gaze lifted to his. He wore a hood, and hosiery had been pulled over his face. Dark eyebrows splayed disparately beneath it, his nose pulled to the side beneath the hosiery strain, and his eyelids were shadowed slits from which he watched her. She recoiled from his startling appearance and recoils again now as well, quickly opening her eyes to the bright view outside the bank window.

———

George peels the black sweatshirt off from over his windbreaker, flings it and the weapon onto a padded bench in the armored truck then bends at the waist, pressing his hands into his knees and drawing in a breath. He blows out an exhale and stretches the hosiery away from his sweating face, trying to cool down and slow his heart. When he starts to remove the hosiery, a voice comes from the front of the truck.

"Leave it on. And where the hell are your goddamn gloves?"

George looks at his hands, then grabs up the sweatshirt and pulls the leather gloves from a pocket. He tugs them on while watching the man standing behind the driver, giving orders. "Who are you?" When the man turns back to the front of the truck, George moves closer to him. "I asked you who you are."

"Reid. Friend of your brother's."

Friend? No friend of Nate's would wrench a child from her mother, aggressively kidnapping her and subjecting the mother and child to such torment. So everything takes on a different meaning now. Friend, truth, instinct. He's got to look at details with that awareness. Both the driver and this Reid have removed the hosiery from their faces and cleaned up their appearances, with the driver having tossed the sweatshirt aside to wear the truck company's uniform shirt. George starts to lift the hosiery off his face again.

"Hey," Reid says quietly. "I told you already to leave that on. You'll be delivering the girl later and we can't have her identifying you."

"Later? You got the truck. Let her go, for God's sake. I'll get her back."

"And what's to stop them from calling the authorities then? If they have her, they'll call the police and we'll be surrounded in a minute. She's our safety net. With her on the truck, they're trapped, and they know it. They give us an hour, they get her back. No hour, no girl."

The girl. She sits in the rear seat, securely buckled in beneath a seat belt. Her feet hang idle, not reaching the floor. George lifts the sweatshirt he threw on the bench and pulls the saddle shoe from a

17

pocket. Could he have done more in the parking lot, more than try to reassure her mother? Or would it have made matters worse?

"Hey, look," the driver says. He points across the median to the far side of the four-lane road a mile from the bank. A serious car accident requires an ambulance and two police cars. "There's Jeremy," he says to Reid.

George looks out the side window. The ambulance and police cars are stopped, their lights flashing. Twisted metal is all that remains to one car's front end; the rear passenger door of a smaller car is crumpled like a piece of tin foil, the car itself resting against a telephone pole. A middle-aged man sits doubled over in the front seat of the smaller car while a younger man stands talking to a police officer, motioning various directions.

Reid glances over his shoulder at George. "He made a nice week's pay cracking up that car and keeping the officers very occupied this morning," he tells him.

All George fears when he looks out the window again is those police officers being radioed of the heist, then looking up from compiling their accident reports at the armored vehicle passing by. "What about these windows? Are they bulletproof?"

"Glass-clad polycarbonate. Nothing's getting through this," Reid answers, knocking on the passenger window.

"Well," George continues. "Don't the drivers of these trucks check in with dispatch? They must be waiting for his call."

Reid shakes his head. "The company has no idea they've been waylaid. The driver verbally completed his first stop to dispatch, confirmed the second and gave the route number, which is spelled out on this clipboard. It's the longer route, so the customer's not expecting him for a while. They do that. Vary their routes and their timing to throw off any robbery attempts." He considers George for a long second, squinting a little. "He was very cooperative with my guy Elliott, here." He nods to the driver. "Did whatever Elliott told him."

George sits then on the side bench behind the driver area, still breathing hard, knowing damn well the nightmare those truck guards just faced. Did Elliott direct their attention to the child Reid grabbed? Was her life negotiated in the orders? His gaze scans the truck's interior until it stops at the sight of the girl. He has to get her off this vehicle. "So you're following the truck's normal route," he continues to Reid, though watching the girl carefully and trying to figure a safe way out of this. "Nothing out of the ordinary?"

Nate walks in from the rear of the truck and sits with George. His gloved fingers drum on the seat. "That's how we're going to beat this," he says through the hosiery still on his face. "Just live normal, don't raise any suspicions. Elliott is keeping it real professional behind the wheel. And no one will know it was us because we're going back to our old lives after this. Back to our jobs, waxing the car, paying our bills. Like this never happened."

"What's wrong with you? It'll never work," George counters. "It's too much. Too big."

"There's no reason it can't work, George." Nate glances out the window. "Once we unload the money, we're all going back to our normal routines. Okay? You'll have your old life back soon enough. It's genius, man. We'll blend right in. No one will suspect a thing. That's our cover. Normal routine. Which is why we're going to the casino afterward and meeting the others, just like we planned."

"They're in on this too?"

"No. Shit, they don't know anything. And we're going to keep it that way, so stay calm, would you? One day you'll be glad you changed your mind and went with this."

George stares at his brother. "You don't get it, do you?"

"Get what?"

"I'm not here for the money. Screw the money." He lowers his voice. "The girl's the only reason I came back. Just that girl. You're all done, kidnapping a child like that."

Nate brushes him off. "She's a kid. She'll forget. And no one's going to hurt her, don't worry. That's not how we work."

"What's wrong with you?" George grabs a handful of his brother's sweatshirt. "Look at her. *Look at her.*"

Nate pulls out of George's grip.

"And what about your car?" George asks. "The authorities will trace it in a minute." He stands, grabs a ceiling-mounted handrail and studies his brother, trying to read his distorted face beneath the hosiery.

"Both cars at the bank were removed before we even got this truck off the lot. We have good help," Nate answers quietly. "And anyway, it wasn't even my car."

Little signs come back to George: the way Nate fumbled with the cooling controls and how he kept adjusting the mirror. They'd driven a stolen vehicle identical to Nate's. George sways with the moving truck; it's how his mind feels, swaying, reeling. Vehicles pass them on the highway now. He imagines the radios tuned to traffic reports, pictures the cups of coffee for the commute, the cell phone conversations. All the lives passing are intact. "Why couldn't you leave me out of this?" He picks up the nine-millimeter handgun off the bench. His fingers close around the barrel and he smashes the black handle against the goddamn polycarb window over Nate's head. "Damn it," he insists. "We're family, man. *Family.* What are you doing to me?"

Nate ducks when the gun hits the window. "Don't you remember? Last year at the casino, that night when we talked about the perfect gamble?"

How could he forget now? Over a glass of Scotch, they decided anyone knocking off an armored truck executed a real gamble, one with the highest risk and the highest financial gain. "The perfect heist," he whispers. "That was bullshit, Nate. Just talk, man."

"Not for your brother, it wasn't," Reid says from the front, still standing behind the driver. "And the only way to keep you quiet was to get you in that parking lot with a weapon in your hand. Talk and you'll do time."

He stares at his brother. "Get me out of this, Nate," he says, trying to drag a gloved hand through his matted, covered hair. Hosiery presses it flat. "Give me the girl and let us go."

"It's too late," Nate explains. "If I didn't bring you in, you'd put things together and say something to the feds. This way, you get a piece of it. You'll never have to worry about your liability insurance going up, or the rent in that plaza, taxes, nothing. I took care of you. You'll be living the dream."

Just like their father used to tell him when he played professional baseball. *You'll be living the dream, George.* Somehow it all got twisted up in Nate's mind; it got too extreme. There's some challenge to meet their father's expectations. He sits beside Nate again.

"Listen. I'll explain to the authorities that I was forced to participate."

"Doesn't matter, George," Nate answers. "Participation is guilt, regardless of how it happened. There's no going back, for any of us."

But there's always a way, a crack, a hole, something to get through. Leaning forward and resting his elbows on his knees, he hangs his head. The girl starts moving, trying to curl up in the rear seat. When he looks back, her eyes are closed, her ponytails in tatters as she sucks her thumb.

And her mother must be devastated. George looks at his gloved hand, remembering the feel of her hand beneath it. She wore a skirt and blouse, a delicate gold chain at her neck, and her eyes were desperate. Because she thought he was one of them. She thought he was evil. And all he could do was tell her to give them the one hour as she pulled away from his concealed face, as he took the saddle shoe in his hand.

He had no way to tell her how he walked away from Nate's car earlier while reaching for his cell phone to call for help. But then, well, then Nate said that thing about bait right when he noticed her and her daughter heading into the bank. And that was all he needed to see, because he knew it. He just knew it. They were the bait. And he couldn't tell her how he turned back to Nate's car, crouched low, bent inside the passenger door and pulled hosiery over his head before slipping the sweatshirt on over his jacket. In his rush, he couldn't maneuver his sweating fingers into the tight leather gloves and so shoved those gloves into the sweatshirt pocket instead. She had no way of knowing that he picked up the gun on the seat, joggled it, swore and threw it back down, then grabbed it again only to try to help. She never knew how he sweat profusely as he accepted that there was no other way to protect them. She'd never know that he couldn't live with himself if he'd kept walking.

She doesn't know still that he's on her side.

Time is a chameleon. It changes its skin, disguising mere moments beneath a forged eternity. Five minutes have passed. Amy's gaze shifts from the two armored truck guards standing outside the small office to the tellers in the lobby down the hall. She visually patrols, her eyes stopping on everyone to be sure the police are not being summoned. But are they doing the right thing? Minutes matter in cases like this. Do you follow the orders of a criminal mind?

"Would you like to freshen up, Mrs. Trewist? Your legs are cut up pretty bad." The bank manager motions to her knees. "I'll have one of the tellers help you."

Amy looks at her legs. Pavement grit is pressed into the raw scrapes and blood begins to cake on top of it all. She straightens her skirt, pressing out a wrinkle, and feels an injury on her hand. A deep, stinging scrape covers one side of her right palm, the hand that reached for Grace's shoe. "No. No, thank you." She squeezes her eyes shut and tips her head down for a moment. "Someone might call," she finally says. "I have to wait for her. Do you understand?" She needs to run to Grace when she sees her. She needs to bargain if the phone rings. "Do you? I can't be in the bathroom washing up. My daughter needs me to wait here."

Turning back to the window, she wills her love to Grace with one slow breath after the other until she hears only the deep whistle of air entering and exiting her body. Her lips form the few prayers she knows and when the driver of the armored truck offers her a chair, her body sinks into it.

Every time a telephone rings, her heart skips a beat. Is there a message about Grace? The last message she had was from the man who took her shoe, who spoke quietly to her. Her left hand rubs the back of her right, remembering his hold on it. She closes her eyes again, trying, trying to recall every single one of his words.

"Let them have the money." His voice sounded compressed beneath the stocking. It was like a voice coming from beneath a cheap Halloween mask, darkly hollow. "Your little girl," he said, crouching there, his hand on the shoe after she'd pulled back, shocked by his distorted face. "I'll do what I can to help her. Cripe, just give them the hour or, really, give them the hour or I don't know." He stood then, his head turning toward the armored truck while he backed away, as though checking to be sure it wouldn't leave without him.

And she noticed his hand again, the one holding Grace's pink saddle shoe, the hand with that ruby ring, reaching up to wipe the perspiration dripping down his face. She had never seen a hand tremble that much. It looked like the shoe would shake right out of his hold.

"Wait," she pleaded with him, sensing some shred of assurance in his words.

He turned and started to run toward the truck. But he stopped, and one last time he looked long at her. "Be strong."

Those were the last words, the last message about Grace. *Be strong.*

She looks out the bank window at the cars driving past, then down at her own hand. It shakes now much the way his did then.

———

George draws his hand over his masked face and looks back at the child. That's when he makes a silent vow that has him straighten the ruby ring on his pinky beneath the glove, then brings him to his feet. He walks to the front of the truck and bends low as Elliott continues driving. "The girl." There it is, the control. Finally. For her. His voice is quiet and steady. "If one hair is out of place on her head today ..." He pauses until Reid turns and looks at him. "I'll kill you. I don't care about the money, I don't care who you are."

With that, he turns and walks the length of the truck, past a built-in computer workstation, past a shelf holding two bomb-protection blankets beside two bullet-resistant vests. He sees it all, unwilling to believe that he is a part of the threat for which it is all intended.

The child doesn't respond to his presence. Kneeling near her, George tips his head down so that his concealed face won't frighten her. He keeps his touch gentle and carefully slips her stockinged foot back into the saddle shoe, ties the laces snug, then double ties the bow and leans against the wall beside her. In a few moments, he reaches into his windbreaker pocket and pulls out a candy. Loosening the wrapping, he holds it out. White snowflakes edge the bright green candy wrap.

"Here," he says softly. "Do you like candy?"

She doesn't move except to let her eyelids close, blacking out George and everything around him. Her hands hang limp, not responding to his offer.

"God help us," he whispers.

Three

THEY DRIVE IN SILENCE. GEORGE stands in the back with the child and Nate sits on the side bench as Elliott heads two towns east, following the prescribed route to the truck's next scheduled stop. Elliott detours briefly, though, pulling into a large shopping mall. He parks at a busy rear delivery entrance near a popular department store. A new wing is being added to this side of the mall and lumbering construction vehicles add to the parking lot commotion.

George isn't sure if the detour is part of the plan, or a move evading alerted authorities. Watching out a side window, he sees that Reid, who slipped out of the truck at the mall's main entrance, now maneuvers a plain white cargo van into the space behind the armored truck. The vehicles are parked back-to-back, with the armored truck obscuring the van rear entry with its own open rear doors. Heavy truck traffic passes through making noisy deliveries and crossing paths with construction vehicles. Reid arranges orange cones at the front corners of the van as though it's supposed to be there. He sets paint buckets and a sawhorse alongside it, waving hello at a passing truck driver as he does so. Horns blare, voices rise, scattered pedestrians hurry past and no one looks twice.

So there's the truth of it all: The best hiding place is in plain sight.

The money transfer starts right away. But as the one-hour window advances, their tense movements and low voices on edge, their thudding footsteps, all of it bothers the child. She twists in her seat as they pass bags and stacks of money from one vehicle to the other.

"Go, go!" Reid orders at any pause.

The motion of it all flows together in one wave of money. George doesn't know Reid or Elliott and cannot guess what they are capable of. He decides the best way to get the child safely out of this situation is to cooperate. And watch. And wait. So he works beside Reid on the truck, passing the money to Nate and Elliott on the van. He doesn't care where the van came from or how any of this has been arranged. It's imperative to just go with things, smooth, part of the wave.

The quandary, for him, is finding a fissure. There has to be one; there always is. Maybe it's the child, brought in to this as a guarantee but ultimately becoming the crime's flaw. Her fussing continues as she twists around beneath her seat belt. George takes two heavy parcels of banded bills that Reid set at his feet. Though the truck's rear doors are opened to the van, if he tries to slip off with the child, the others will stop him. He passes the parcels to his brother, all while keeping an eye on her. He is as much a hostage as she is.

When the girl's fussing grows louder and she begins crying, George glances over his shoulder at her, momentarily breaking the flow. When he does, Reid shoves a heavy package at him, throwing him off balance. Before Reid can turn to lift another clear bag of money, George takes him by his shirt and hurls him toward the front of the armored truck.

Maybe it's Reid, the fissure that will undo this crime. When Reid rises from the bench he'd fallen onto, Nate insinuates himself between the two men. "George," he says quietly, holding his brother back. He hitches his head toward the rear of the truck. "Give Elliott a hand on the van, why don't you?"

George eyes his brother, then turns back toward the child. Her ponytails are matted flat, tears soil her face. Rage and intent and emotional challenges and unspoken threat, her eyes have seen it all and her ears have heard it. She watches George approach and his life feels over for having a part in this. Completely over.

That's when he stops and turns back to Nate. "Go to hell," he whispers through the wet hosiery on his face. Elliott continues stacking heavy bundles in the van, each bundle landing with a dull thump. She hears that, too. That's what this is all about, that one noise. Money. "All of you, all right?" George meets each of their eyes. "I'm done."

Nate blocks Reid's attempt to confront George. "Let's finish this," Nate insists, "without messing up." Reid looks long at him before turning to transport the remaining cash.

George just walks away. He approaches the child, bends down and unstraps her from the seat belt. She watches his concealed face as he lifts her tenderly in his arms, holding her against his chest. One hand supports her weight, the other cradles her head when it drops on his shoulder. He carries her through the truck's open doors directly onto the windowless van and slowly paces with her.

"It's okay," he whispers, feeling her thin neck beneath his open palm. "Mommy's coming, Mommy's coming. Pretty soon now." He walks her to a side seat and sits her gently in it, crouching beside her and simply waiting.

In less than five minutes, as Nate moves the sweatshirts and weapons from the truck to the van, he fills George in on what's happening. "Elliott's taking the truck to the next bank on the schedule. It's only a mile away, so he'll be right on time." He straightens the stack of sweatshirts piled on one of the van's rear seats.

"That's crazy. Why not leave it here and be done with it?"

"The bank's expecting it. It's a way of buying more time, having that armored truck parked outside their building like it should be. Normal, man. If it doesn't show up, it'll draw more attention."

"Well what about surveillance cameras? They're everywhere now."

"And there are ways around them, it's all been taken care of. Elliott will park the truck in its usual place, put on a civilian jacket over his uniform shirt and slip out the side door unnoticed at the right opportunity."

"Just like that? Piece of cake?" George asks, picturing the distraction surely planned that will allow Elliott to do this. Some two-bit purse snatch, or a trip and fall. Something will happen to get any pedestrians' attention off Elliott exiting that truck.

"Hey. It's as simple as we make it. There's a little diner near there, he'll stop in and have himself a coffee, maybe a sunny-side up egg, and be one of the everyday people. All normal, all part of a busy Monday morning. Normal, man." Nate shakes his head, smiling. "It's genius, really. He'll walk away from the truck, never turn a head, and an empty car will be waiting for him, parked on the street, after his breakfast."

"And what about us?" George asks then. "Now what?"

"We're going to my place. Reid's driving us there."

"Your place? Cripe, are you crazy?"

"No, as a matter of fact. I get tile deliveries all the time. No one will think twice about a van making a delivery there. Normal, guy. Get it?" he asks as he turns and walks to the front passenger seat and takes the orange cones Reid had retrieved now that they're done.

JOANNE DeMAIO

George shakes his head, then looks to the girl sitting quietly. Eventually he pulls the candy from his pocket again and loosens the snowflake wrapping. She watches his gloved hands and when he offers her the candy, she takes it, her small fingers slowly pulling the chocolate from the paper. She holds the soft candy in her fingers for several moments before raising it to her mouth and taking a tiny nibble. Her other hand toys with the shiny plastic wrapping. As she crinkles the snowflake paper in her fingers, she starts to murmur, "Mumumum."

"She's coming," George tells her, glancing to the front of the van. "Pretty soon, sweetheart," he whispers.

———

Amy freezes. Even her breathing stops. Yes. There. She minutely tips her head. It's the wail of sirens growing louder. She spins then and catches the eye of one of the truck guards. He had given her a cool damp cloth to press onto her wounds while she sat at the window.

"It's okay," he reassures her. "We waited an extra ten minutes. To be sure." His reluctant smile tries to soothe her. "You know. For your daughter."

An extra ten minutes. She can't imagine holding on an extra ten seconds, not after surviving an eternal hour capable of pushing anyone to the brink. But when she stands to meet the uniformed police officers swarming the bank, the room fades. She reaches her arms out to balance herself, but her knees give out and she falls in a soft heap to the floor.

In an hour? Time changes shape again. A minute? His hand is over hers. She expects it to be ice cold. But it is warm. Careful not to hurt her hand beneath it. This isn't a hand that would pull a trigger. It seems more the working hand of a grown man, a capable hand that earns a living, that brushes hair, that raises a fork, that appreciates fine things with its touch, its maturity. It wears a beautiful ruby ring, the stone deep red, and suits his calming voice. *She'll be okay.* Amy strains to keep that voice familiar in her mind, to believe him. *Be strong.* But when she looks up at his face, those twisted features mock her.

"Mrs. Trewist," a voice says. She feels his hand still, warm and assuring. "Mrs. Trewist," the voice continues. The hand pats hers insistently and Amy opens her eyes to his mask. She turns quickly away.

"Amy, come on now," another paramedic encourages. He holds an oxygen mask to her face while another attendant rubs her arm, trying to revive her. "That's right, wake up now," he says as she pulls herself up and sucks in a deep breath of the clear oxygen. Someone's hand supports her neck and shoulders. Voices and uniformed officers blur around her; a paramedic helps her back into the chair. One voice grows clearer as it approaches, its authority quieting the others as he moves through the room and comes into focus.

"Mrs. Trewist, I'm Detective Hayes. I need to ask you some questions."

Amy nods and presses her hair off her face. "Have you found her? Is Grace okay?"

"No, I'm sorry. We haven't found her yet. Is there someone you would like us to call to be with you? Your husband? A friend?"

She looks at him, confused. What's real, what's not? Had Grace been kidnapped? Did Mark pass away the year before? "My husband?"

"Yes. If you'll give us his cell number. Or is there a work number where we can reach him?"

This is no dream. She hadn't gone through the five stages of grief for nothing. But the one stage she hadn't reached was removing her wedding ring. She touches it on her finger. They have no way of knowing that at thirty-three years old, she's already widowed. "My husband's been dead for nearly a year."

A beat of silence precedes their brief apologies. Their serious manner softens a little. But still, they need her to relive the trauma of her daughter being kidnapped as she repeats the story to these local police and once more to federal authorities. The details are already permanent fixtures in her mind, sights and noises that will never leave.

"Grace!" she called, feeling her daughter's hand wrenched out of hers. And the sounds of scuffling feet behind her, and Grace crying out once, only once in fear before going silent—they all seemed magnified. They were the only sounds that existed in that moment.

Then came the sound of that voice. "Don't say another word," the man holding Grace warned through the nylon pulled over his head. He shifted her limp child higher in his hold.

When she started to answer, when she begged, "Please," when she explained, "She's just a baby," he backed further away until she quieted. It was then, when her hand cupped her mouth, that his orders began while her daughter hung wilted beneath his curved arm. As he spoke, as she first heard the sound of words about needing one hour, her eyes never stopped recording everything: his expensive jacket, his leather shoes, a watch. Yes, there was a watch on the arm around Grace, where his jacket sleeve was raised. A heavy silver watch.

And the motion never stopped. For every step he took away from her, she stepped toward him in an eerie synchronized dance.

Everything blurred with the realization that she was about to lose her child.

"I didn't know what to do," she cries now. "If I talked, if I moved, I just didn't know what he'd do."

"Was he armed?" Detective Hayes asks.

Amy closes her eyes and draws a long breath. Her head vaguely nods. "Yes." And a new image takes a dark shape as the detective asks for details about the weapon. It's theoretically minutiae, specifics she'd seen and registered in a brief three-minute window.

The trembling begins again then, with details that aren't trivial at all. With firearm minutiae that are in her daughter's presence right now, affecting Amy physically as she looks at her shaking hands.

"Do you need a doctor, Mrs. Trewist?" an officer finally asks when the questioning winds down. "Or would you like to be examined at the hospital? There's an ambulance waiting."

"No." Where should she go now? Should she wait here at the bank, where her child's abductors last saw her? How are you to know? What are the rules? Or should she go home?

Home. Yes. The reporters will announce where she lives. They might have her daughter delivered home. Or they might call there with further instructions, or demands for more time. How long will Grace be their ticket to freedom? She has to be available to their communications. The image of her white farmhouse with gingerbread trim on the outskirts of Addison takes over her thoughts. Red rhododendrons bloom beside the front porch and a tall maple tree shades the side yard.

Home. The curve of the country lane leads to a lone farm where shoots of new corn recently broke through the plowed soil. Her closest friend lives on the same winding street, a road filled with history and a slower way of life. She needs to be near the barns and cornfields and weeping willow trees and peaked and rambling farmhouses, to see the old stone wall reaching down the length of the street. She and her husband bought their house and renovated it together before he died. She feels too that, in some way, he will be there, within the confines of the walls he helped restore.

"Can someone please take me home?"

———

George is fully aware that as a self-employed tile man, Nate sometimes accepts supplies of custom tile at his home, storing them in his cellar for a later installation in an exclusive foyer or state-of-the-art kitchen. So a van backed up to his garage is a common sight. Elliott safely meets them there as planned and once the packages on the van are moved to Nate's garage and basement, they stand just outside and arrange to get together again later to handle the money's distribution. But for now, everything is about returning to routine.

"What about the girl?" George asks from the rear seat of the van, where he's watched and waited the entire time with the child. Where his heart hasn't stopped racing and he's finding it hard to breathe. Her silence worries him. Mopping the perspiration off his still-concealed face, he approaches Reid who just got on the van and sits in the driver seat, waiting to leave with Elliott. "We've got to get her back. Cripe, there'll be a dragnet looking for her."

"It's all under control," Reid answers. His tone has changed, as though he knows now. George won't tolerate any threats. "You two just get yourselves to that casino so you won't be missed by your friends. Go inside here first and clean up. You're a wreck, Carbone."

It feels like physical exertion, the way George must force his thoughts to think one step ahead of Reid. "But how are we returning the girl? I'm not going anywhere unless she's safe."

"Listen, I can assure you that child will be well taken care of. Actually, her safety is paramount to keeping things running smoothly until she's returned. But we need you to spend a few hours gambling, having your face seen and building a credible alibi at the casino before that return can happen."

"What? And leave her alone with you? Where are you taking her?"

"Jesus, I can't tell you that, okay? The less you know, the better. All I can tell you is that she's safe. Don't you understand? I'm assuring you she'll be fine, that we only needed her to buy us the time. So the sooner you get going, the sooner we can release her."

George glances out at Nate and Elliott talking in the driveway, then steps behind Reid. "And exactly how is she getting back to her mother?"

When Reid looks up to the rearview mirror, George's eyes lock onto the reflection. "Relax, Carbone. I told you, *you're* the one who will deliver her later. We can't trust a stranger to do it, it's too risky. You'll be minding your own business running ordinary errands and shit will happen. We'll get the girl to you, nice friendly George Carbone who runs that happening delicatessen downtown. Everybody likes George, right? Who'd suspect anything?"

"It's all right, George," Elliott says, coming up behind him from the van's rear doors.

George turns back to Elliott. Can he trust him? And does he have to go along with more orders to protect the girl? When does that all end?

"I'll keep this guy in line," Elliott says. "The girl will be fine. The sooner we get her back, the better. Just get going with your brother and build that alibi so this isn't all pinned on you."

They're all standing at the edge of something, but George doesn't know what that edge is yet, or exactly where it is, so he can't cross anyone. He turns away again and pulls the hosiery completely off his head, pushing his hand back through his wet hair. It's not good, what this is doing to the child and her mother. "Just how am I supposed to return her after all that's gone down?"

"Hey," Reid says. "She hasn't seen your face. And you'll be freshly showered after a day at the slots, wearing clean clothes, acting concerned and all. She's what? Three, maybe? She'll never recognize you. Your brother will give you instructions on the way back from the casino. He knows what to do. And once the media catches wind of your part in the rescue, you'll be a God damn hero."

Reid's narrow eyes, the shadowed chin, a recent haircut, the composed demeanor, all of it becomes clear memory to George as he studies him. "So help me," he finally insists. "If any harm comes to her, if I suspect anything when I see her again, and I *will* see her again, you'll be all done. I'll use every cent I earned today to hunt you down." He puts a finger beneath Reid's chin and tips his face up until Reid slaps it away. "All this money will be for nothing," George continues, "because I'll put you through the meat grinder at my shop, piece by piece, if you so much as touch her."

Nate steps onto the van in time to hear the threat. He'd already removed the hosiery from his head and cleaned up his face. "Come on, guy," he says, grabbing George by the arm. "Let's cool off."

George wrenches out of Nate's hold and looks at the girl in the back of the van. Elliott is crouched near her, opening a box

36

brought in from the car he'd driven from the bank. A tiny kitten pokes its head through the flap and looks out wide-eyed. George shoves the hosiery from his face into his windbreaker pocket, then scoops up Reid's forty-five from the passenger seat. His only intent through all of this has been to return the girl safely. He's not too certain about much of this day, but is certain that one less weapon in her presence will help. He notices how easily he picked up the gun now. So that's certain, too, how he's already changed.

Four

HOURS LATER, CASINO LIGHTS AGGRAVATE George's headache. He leaves the others at the slot machines and goes to the race room, watching thoroughbreds run on the fifty-foot projection screen. Eventually his brother shows up there. Nate walks with a swagger suited to his fitted bomber jacket, jeans, sunglasses clipped to his shirtfront, and, George figures, to his new bankroll. He sinks into the chair beside him.

"Steve and Craig are at the tables. Let's play a hand of cards. Normal, you know?"

George knows; he gets it already. Normal means playing a few hands with their weekly poker night partners. But is it normal to not concentrate? He can't finish one complete thought; he can't get the girl out of his head.

"The eye in the sky's got to see us," Nate tells him.

"The what?"

Nate leans close. "Ceiling surveillance cameras. They're at all the tables. Come on, we've got to get filmed. It's our alibi."

Every angle's covered. Every defense considered. George goes along with the plan for a while longer, until his vision fails. No one knows it but him, the way it becomes impossible to read the dice or play a decent card hand. Under the threat of his own screw-ups drawing attention, he heads for the bar in a dark lounge.

"Jack and Coke," he tells the bartender.

In minutes, Nate slips into the chair beside him again. "It might help your alibi if you strike up a conversation with a woman, look friendly. Be seen, you know?"

Nothing will erase the image of the only woman on his mind. An afternoon is time enough to leave her child and a kitten in the care of Reid and Elliott. In one long swallow, he finishes his drink and turns to Nate.

"Either you're driving me back right now or I'll find my own way. We've got to get that girl to her mother."

Nate turns around and leans his back against the bar. "No. What we've got to do is act like we've got nowhere to go. You're taking a day off, remember?"

A news report on the television behind the bar interrupts them. They look up at the mounted set. "The sleepy town of Addison, Connecticut was rocked this morning by its worst crime in decades. Police are on the hunt for four men who orchestrated an armored truck heist from a local bank parking lot. Two armored truck employees were overpowered at gunpoint, while a child kidnap victim was taken hostage to secure the vehicle." The news reporter goes on to talk briefly with the bank manager while the camera pans first the community of well-kept homes, manicured lawns and parks, then the bank parking lot still roped off with yellow crime tape. "The suspects fled the bank location in the armored truck, which has since been located. This is a very active investigation, with Addison detectives still on the scene piecing together details, but two-year-old Grace Trewist has yet to be found," the reporter concludes. A recent photograph of the child fills the screen. "Her mother, Amy Trewist, has not come forward to speak, and the suspects are still at large and considered armed and dangerous."

George stands. Grace Trewist's mother is not physically able to speak publicly. They had seen to that when they disabled her in a few brief minutes. Completely undid her. He wrenches his brother from his seat and gives him a restrained shove, one that draws no notice from the staff, toward the Exit door.

———

At least one police officer waits in her kitchen; another two walk the perimeter of the farmhouse. Roadblocks keep the media off her street and Detective Hayes assures Amy they are following all leads to locate Grace. Everything takes time. But she can no longer watch the silent telephone, willing the kidnappers to call, cursing them in one breath, bargaining with the heavens in the next. She can no longer listen to updates from Hayes. The armored truck had been found abandoned at another bank, but with the public being unaware of the crime for the first critical hour, no one paid attention to its occupants. No clues are uncovered. The gunmen have tied every loose thread.

So she changes into blue jeans, a white oxford shirt and leather sandals, pulls her hair back in a low clip and goes out to her gown room where she always finds a certain peace. A stone rabbit doorstop holds the green wooden door open and sunlight warms the stone floor. The room had been tacked onto the rear of the farmhouse over the stone patio and was originally used as a garden room. But when she and Mark renovated, they transformed it into her bridal storage room. Tulle veils and satin sashes hang from vintage garden tool racks; beaded necklaces drape from a rustic rake head mounted on the wall; white gloves and an old bird's nest refurbished with lace scraps fill an antique birdbath; a small selection of secondhand gowns hangs on a metal rolling rack, waiting to be moved to her vintage bridal shop, Wedding Wishes, in town.

Today, though, the suggestion of dreams and happiness and love all seems illusory. Amy sits on the stool at her worktable covered with fabric remnants and a sewing machine. Outside, the green lawn slopes away from the doorway. Grace ran on that grass yesterday. If Amy looks hard enough, she can see that image. Not the image the throb of her bandaged hand brings to mind. No. Maple tree branches spread low in the yard and she decides she will hang the old-fashioned tire swing for Grace. Her husband brought the tire home last summer, but they never set it up. He had died two weeks later.

She stands and surveys the distant maple tree. Its strong branches will support her tire swing. "She's alive. She's breathing," Amy insists. Antique beaded handbags, gold and silver and cream, hang from a sunlit garden rack, the beads sparkling. She pulls a fox fur wrap from a low shelf below them. Everything about it is soft, from the pale silver fur to the silk lining. When Grace held it yesterday, her eyes dropped closed as she curled up with it. Amy puts the wrap to her face, a deep breath filling her lungs in an effort to inhale the same aged scent her daughter did. Some innate connection might help her through this. But the only connection she summons is a man's hand clasping hers in a silent struggle for the shoe. Shaking off the bristly sensation on her hand, she shoves the fur stole on a shelf and knocks an old mason jar filled with crystal beads to the floor. Its broken shards and beads glisten in the sunlight. "Oh, look what Mommy did," she says through tears, as though Grace is with her. Believing things, willing fate, it has to work, somehow. "Mommy made a mess now, didn't she?" she asks, bent over with a dustpan.

In this room filled with old wedding gowns, with aged lace and cream satin pulled from cedar chests, the vintage gowns hover like spirits, each one on the rack rustling a little, sending out some ethereal strength. Weddings are all about promise; the women who wore these gowns made vows. And he promised her, he *did*, Grace would be back after one hour. Her eyes scan the room before she runs outside to the tool shed. Flinging those doors open, sunlight floods the dark, musty space. Cobwebs and dust particles hang from the beams. She searches the wood shelves for a length of heavy rope and the old tire propped along the wall. Hefting her arm through the tire, she lugs that and the rope out to the maple tree.

"Mrs. Trewist," she hears as she stands beneath the branches. No one will stop her from hanging the tire. Grace wanted to swing. Today. *Swing, Mommy!* No one will bring bad news, not even the officer's deep approaching voice. Grace will come back. They'll spend the summer together here, swinging *every* day; Grace will play with old veils and sashes from the gown room; they'll walk and listen to birdsong. Every day. She drops the tire and tries to untangle the rope.

"Mrs. Trewist." A gentle grip takes her arm and turns her.

"No." Her desperate hands fumble with the rope and she's suddenly fumbling with her purse in the bank parking lot, frantic to find her keys. "I couldn't find them in time," she says as she looks up to a police officer's face. "They'd already left," she adds, holding back a sob.

"Mrs. Trewist. I understand. But there's someone here, a Celia Gray. She wants to see you," he says, then moves aside so that she can see Celia standing further behind, waiting.

Celia rushes closer and opens her arms to Amy. "Oh Amy, I just heard. How are you holding up?"

Amy lets her best friend hug her for a long moment before answering. "I'm not, Cee," she says softly, a length of rope hanging from her bandaged hand.

"Are your mom and dad coming?"

Amy nods, picturing the more than two-hour drive along desolate stretches of wooded highway from New Hampshire. Have they left yet? They had to pack a bag and close up their house. Will they stop in Massachusetts at a roadside diner for a quick rest stop? Time is endless now, every wait, eternal.

"Come on, let me make you a cup of tea inside, okay? I'll stay with you."

It feels good to give herself over to Celia's tending, the same way she wants to tend Grace. But the good feeling doesn't last because she can't help that she is unraveling. She's some ball of yarn and the kidnappers run with the leading strand. Leaving the rope and tire behind, the police officer escorts them through the backyard to the kitchen doorway at the rear of her house.

"Please tell me I did the right thing." Amy sits at her blue painted table, its wood finish distressed and weathered. Slats of late afternoon sunlight stream in through the paned kitchen window.

"Oh, Amy. Every decision you made was right and done out of love for Grace." Celia fills a pot with water. "Don't you doubt yourself." She sets two hand-painted teacups on the farm table.

"They told me, those men, that I couldn't call the police for one hour. So did I help Grace with my silence? She's not back, and he promised. Where is she?"

"Who promised, Amy? What did he promise?" Celia sits and takes Amy's shaking hands in her own. At first, Amy sees the sterling bracelet hanging on her friend's wrist, and sees her manicured nails. But feeling the touch on her hand, she is kneeling again in the parking lot on her scraped knees. His large hand covers hers.

Every detail is clear. His skin, his knuckles pressed over hers, the black cuff of his sweatshirt, the ruby ring.

"Give them the money, he told me. One hour. Like he was only a witness helping me. Be strong, he said." She lifts her gaze from their hands to Celia's face, seeing her straight auburn hair tucked behind her ears, her hazel eyes. She's home. She's in her kitchen with a friend. And something is so horribly wrong. "Strong?" she asks. "For God's sake, where *is* she? He promised," she cries, closing her eyes again and seeing his concealed face.

Celia turns in her seat and glances at the police officer who has entered the kitchen. "Amy," she says, turning back and pulling her chair close. "Let me call your doctor," she suggests. "He can give you something. Just to take the edge off and help you through this, okay?"

Amy looks long at Celia. "Nothing can help me now."

———

"Check your mailbox when I let you off," Nate instructs George when they are on the highway. "If any neighbors see you, wave hello, talk a little. They might have to vouch for your presence." He glances at the rearview mirror. "Then go inside and take a shower. And get into some clean clothes, like you normally would."

Normally. George listens in silence. It's ironic that normal no longer exists. They drive in silence for the next mile or two, passing an occasional car. "Jesus Christ," George whispers then.

"What's the matter?" Nate asks.

George hitches his head to the electronic highway sign flashing far ahead. "Is that an Amber Alert?"

"Damn it." Nate slows the vehicle as they near it and squints to read the words. "No, it's just construction announcements." He turns to give the sign a second look as they pass it. "I didn't think they'd issue an alert."

"Why not?"

"They need a vehicle to report, a car the girl might be in, or a license plate number to broadcast to these drivers. Some identifiable vehicle for them to watch out for." He adjusts his rearview mirror and sits back. "They've got nothing, nothing to locate."

George opens his passenger window a few inches and deeply inhales the outside air.

"Just take it easy, man. All you have to do once you're home is relax and watch the evening news for updates, then wait fifteen minutes in case a change of plans needs to be made. And don't tie up your phone. At seven-fifteen, drive over to your shop and give it a once-over. Like you always do when you take time off." Nate signals for the exit and leaves the highway. "We're almost there, home free." He lets out a whoop, then takes a long breath. "Okay. Okay, now when you're done at the shop, lock up and stop at Litner's Market, for a quart of milk or something."

George knows the place, the small convenience store not far from his home.

"Cars are always pulling in and out of there for a loaf of bread or paper towels. The commotion in the parking lot is all part of the cover, okay? You'll be an innocent bystander and shit will happen. You'll get her then."

"How will she be delivered? And what do I do with her?"

"I'm sorry, but if I tell you the details, it won't be spontaneous. It won't be credible." Nate turns into the long driveway leading to George's condominium. "You have to think like a witness in order to keep your cover. This way, not knowing, you will. Like a normal witness."

But normal witnesses don't bolt from the shower to vomit. Don't shake so much they cut their face shaving. Don't take a second shower after perspiring so badly.

At the end of the evening news, George sits silently in his living room. He glances at his father's ring still on his pinky. That's not something he can think about, his father. So that's gone now, the way he'd think easily of his dad. He stands and looks out the same living room window he looked out this morning and the memory brings him to tears.

Finally, it is time. Dim lights cast long shadows at The Main Course. Right on schedule, he steps in and locks the door behind him. Dean, his full-time butcher, ran the shop today. What George wishes is that he'd been here today too, filleting fish, making meatloaves to-go, been anywhere but where he had been. Walking through the shop, the countertops, the glass meat cases and the spice display racks, they all gleam. He has good help. In the back room, the equipment has been stripped down, cleaned and sanitized. He touches the blade on the commercial slicer and glances at the grinder. Fresh meats stock the refrigerator, with a stack of custom orders waiting for his attention in the morning. Satisfied, he locks up and leaves.

Lights come on in the old houses, the Tudors and stone-front capes set back on deep lawns. It is that dusky time of day when low sunlight and long shadows play tricks on your eyes. He is sure that even the lighting is part of the plan, casting subdued doubt on any witness' perception. That much precision went into the heist, that manipulation of memory using light to blur the lines of distinction.

He pulls into Litner's parking lot, picks a space not too far from the door and kills the engine. Should he wait in his pickup? Does he go inside? His heart drums in his chest as he looks around. Fluorescent lights flicker in the store window above handmade flyers advertising the week's specials, discounted sandwich bread and laundry detergent. In his rearview mirror, he checks the parking lot entrance. Perspiration covers his forehead when he finally gets out of the truck. He has to get out, just to take a deep breath.

It's amazing how he's acutely aware of every damn domino set in place. A teenaged girl exits the store and walks toward a red compact car at the very same time a dark sedan pulls into a space three away from George. Its headlights sweep the parking lot, adding to the mounting activity. An older minivan pulls in, loaded with loud kids in soccer gear. The girl leaving the store wears stereo headphones and so won't hear a thing. Is she a planned distraction? With two cars coming, the red car going and George locking his door, enough activity fills the parking lot to keep watching eyes off any one individual.

He turns toward the store entrance, noting the young kid running the cash register. An older man steps behind the counter, a store manager wearing a shirt and tie. His large stomach presses against the shirt as he turns back past the lottery tickets and cigarettes to answer a ringing telephone.

George knows. Even the phone call is planned, keeping the manager's attention off the parking lot. Nothing is what it seems, and never will be again.

"Hey, guy." Just steps away from the entrance, he hears the voice. If his every nerve ending hadn't been on edge, he would have missed it; it is that smooth. He bends his head down to get a better look while approaching the sedan parked beyond his truck. So they ditched the van. *Normal,* he whispers as he blows out a long breath.

"Could you give me directions?" Reid's voice calls.

George squints through the shadows looking for the girl. "Where you headed?" he asks, going along with the charade for the benefit of any witnesses. As he nears the vehicle, the rear passenger door opens and the child is set on the pavement. She turns back to the car and for the first time all day, he hears her speak.

"Kitty," her small voice calls out. It holds no fear, only fatigue and concern for a cat. So they haven't harmed her.

It comes then, the urge to run and scoop her up, to dash off in the other direction and never look back. George thinks he can run so fast, he'd beat the speed of time and bargain with the devil to change his fate. But then his stomach knots. He is the devil, as far as Amy Trewist is concerned.

"I just talked to your brother." George jumps at the voice coming from the driver's seat and looks back at Reid. "He's real pleased he took care of you today, financially. Took care of his family. It means a lot to him."

"Well I'm out," George answers quietly. "This is the end of it."

"You're never out." Reid's voice drops. "Lay low, George. For a good, long time. We'll be watching you, your shop, your life. One wrong move and, you know, accidents happen."

"Accidents? What are you talking about?"

"Just don't slip up." Reid shrugs. "Think twice. Always now."

George looks over at the girl. Her thumb is in her mouth while her pinky twists around a strand of her flattened ponytail. It looks like she just woke from a nap. Elliott sets a carton on the ground beside her.

Reid glances over at the child. "Even that Trewist lady," he says. "If you don't keep all this quiet, well hey, she lives alone, easy target."

But none of this matters anymore. George looks from the girl to Reid and doesn't wait to hear more bullshit. He's done. In one fell swoop, he turns and grabs the girl and the carton. With the child hoisted on his hip, he runs toward the store, jostling the carton as it nearly slips when he yanks the door open.

"Get off the phone!" he yells at the manager before the door even closes behind him. His pounding heart can't take much more and he struggles awkwardly to keep the cat carton upright. "Call 9-1-1, fast!" He looks over his shoulder and sees a glimpse of red taillights leaving the parking lot.

Five

AMY GIVES THE INVESTIGATORS PHOTOGRAPHS of her daughter, allows them to cull a set of fingerprints from Grace's room and relinquishes clothing samples enabling search dogs to pick up Grace's scent. With tongs, they lift select pieces and drop them in a plastic bag. Will the German Shepherds, noses to the ground, smell what Amy does? Will they pick up the scent of her daughter's soft clothing, dried in the spring breeze on the clothesline? Will they sense a trace of baby shampoo from her angel-soft hair? Will they recognize the waxy aroma of crayons from little fingers that color masterpieces?

Amy had felt she was helping, in some way, with all this. Now though, evening settles and the hunt intensifies outside her realm. Celia lit a fire in the stone fireplace and sits with her watching out the front windows. They speak little, instead listening for a knock on the door, a ringing telephone, any sign that Grace is alive. Pots rattle in the kitchen and the aroma of chicken soup fills the house, as though someone is ill. Along with her parents came the chicken, carrots, celery, onions and stewed tomatoes spilling from grocery bags. Her mother even brought ginger ale.

Finally Amy moves to the kitchen, picks up a knife and begins slicing celery at the counter. She slices only half a stalk before setting the knife down and turning to pull a bottle of Scotch from the high cabinet.

"Amy," Ellen Vance begins.

"Don't you dare. Just don't say anything, Mom." Amy fills a tumbler with the liquor, takes a long swallow and drops into a chair. "I need something, okay? If I can't have my Grace, really, I can't do anything else."

Ellen sits beside her and pours a splash of Scotch into a juice glass. "One drink. Just to remember a little. To talk about her while we wait."

So Amy tries to recall sweet thoughts of Grace. But every image torments without Grace here. It's such a struggle to merely choose thoughts. She searches her mother's face and catches the glimmer of heavy gold earrings. Her mother dressed for the trip. She wears a pale spring pantsuit, jewelry, a touch of make-up, though none of it masks the strain on her face.

"Why'd you dress?" Amy asks, her hand turning her whiskey glass.

"What?"

"When I called you this morning, you were working in the garden. Why'd you dress up?"

"Well. I was covered in dirt. Look." She lifts her hands, palm up, toward Amy. "I still can't get all the soil out."

Amy takes her mother's hand in hers and softly drags her own fingers over her mother's skin. Veins of dirt are imbedded in the fine lines of her mother's palms. "I touched his hand."

"Whose hand?"

"One of the kidnappers. I touched him, Mom. One of the men, he picked up Grace's shoe. It fell in the struggle." Amy looks up at her mother. "We reached for it at the same time and his hand covered mine." His hand must have touched her daughter's foot, too. Slipped on the shoe. She prays for a kind touch. "He's got Grace now." She drops her mother's hand and walks to the sink while peeling off her bandage. Running the water hot, she scrubs her own hands raw. "Why didn't I hold on or make him take me? Or reach for his gun and turn it on him?" Blotting her hands on a dishtowel, then hanging it over the back of a chair, none of it erases the thought of his touch. "Why didn't I do more?"

"Listen. You did all you could. It was a life or death situation."

Amy squeezes her eyes shut against the image of her tiny daughter jostled in the struggle.

"You did what you had to for Grace," her mother continues.

"But she's not back." She turns and listens to the evening sounds for a long moment before moving to the cutlery drawer. Handful by handful, she drops first forks, then spoons, into the sink. Water runs hot and soapy over them.

"What are you doing?" Ellen asks.

"I can't just stand here. I can't just think. It's driving me crazy." She picks up a dishcloth. "I have to clean up. I have to be busy, to do something."

Ellen steps behind her and embraces her, resting her head on Amy's shoulder. "I know," she whispers.

"Can we go look for her, Mom?" In the window over the sink, Amy's kitchen is reflected back in the glass. Antique china plates hang in a collage beside a heart-shaped twig wreath, a painted ceramic chicken sits on the far shelf and tiny blue hearts dot all the wallpaper. "Would you drive while I look?" she pleads to her mother's reflected face. "Maybe we can find her. You and me."

"Shh. No, Amy. We have to wait here. Everyone has to be able to reach you. The police. The kidnappers. They might call with instructions." Her mother adds a splash more Scotch to their glasses and puts Amy's beside the sink where she scrubs the cutlery. "We have to think positive. We have to believe she'll be back … That's why I dressed up." Ellen sips her drink. "Don't you remember? Gracie loves this jacket."

Amy looks at the paisley print swirling over the cream fabric.

"I dressed up for her," Ellen says, then reaches into the cabinet, lifts out clean plates and stacks them near the sink. From another cabinet, she sets a dozen coffee mugs beside the plates. "You wash, I'll dry."

Lowering her hands into the soapy dishwater, Amy sponges off a fork, rinses it and places it in the dish drainer. Her mother opens the cutlery drawer, picks up each piece Amy washes, carefully dries and neatly restacks them.

The sound of dropping cutlery strikes Amy as very lonely. Someone is putting away the silverware. A day is done. It is night. She silently slips the plates into the dishwater. The only sounds in the kitchen are her hands dipping into the water, the gentle stream of the tap rinsing the dishes, and the chink of forks and spoons. She has never known such long moments when words won't work and there is only sound.

An officer in the house intercepts all phone calls, fielding the media, taking messages from friends, keeping the line open as best he can. So when the phone rings, Amy turns off the faucet to hear the drone of his deep voice in the living room. Listening, she picks up a plate and silently drags the dishrag over it, her hand moving slowly until it finally stops.

"What's the matter?" Ellen asks.

Amy turns toward the living room. She has listened keenly to Officer Pine's unyielding voice all day and knows it well. It sounds different this time; its tone has changed. She drops the plate into the sink and runs through the kitchen to the living room.

The officer has disconnected the call and is nodding at Celia when Amy and her mother rush into the room. Celia stands and loops her arm around Amy's waist.

"Mrs. Trewist," Officer Pine says. "They've found your daughter and I'm happy to report that she appears to be fine and unharmed."

"Oh thank God," Ellen cries as she collapses in a hug with Amy.

"She's coming home," Celia says from behind tears. "Grace is okay."

"Where?" Amy asks. Her mother and Celia each hold one of her hands. "How did they find her?"

"Apparently Grace was dropped off in a grocery store parking lot and left with a passerby. He immediately called the police and she is in their custody as we speak."

"Yes!" Celia exclaims, punching the air. "Yes! Yes! She made it!"

"Please," Amy asks. "I have to see her. Can I go to her?"

"They're bringing her here, Mrs. Trewist."

Amy sinks into the couch with the realization of his words. Grace is safe and on her way home, home, home. Home to simmering chicken soup and her grandmother's favorite swirled jacket and a warm kitchen filled with hearts and love and laughter. Celia sits beside her as Ellen rushes to the front window. "An ambulance has also been dispatched here. She'll need to be examined at the hospital right away, once she's with you."

Amy nods. "And when will she be here?" She feels as though she has just emerged from beneath the sea, a sodden drowning victim given one last reprieve as she gasps in relief. The sound of sirens approaches.

"Well, I'd imagine that's her right now."

Grace sits in the back seat of a police van with George. The cardboard box is between them; a female officer sits across from them. "You're going to see your mommy now," she tells Grace softly.

Once George took Grace from Litner's parking lot, he wanted to stay with her until she was back in her mother's arms, so the officials allowed him to accompany her home. Grace doesn't recognize him from the morning. He reaches over now and checks the child's shoe. It is still double-tied snug. So that's what the day comes down to. Pink saddle shoes and dark weapons. One versus the other, for hours on end. The day shows in the child's weary face, in her misshapen blonde ponytails and lopsided hair ribbons. Elliott thought a kitten would keep her occupied while the day passed. Every now and again, the black and white kitten cries a soft mew from the box.

"She's okay?" George asks the officer, nodding at Grace.

"Seems to be. They'll be bringing her to the hospital to be sure."

Grace pops her thumb out of her mouth and looks at the carton. "Kitty there?" she asks.

"You can show the kitty to your mommy," George says. "Pretty soon, okay?" He tries to smile as Grace stares at him. The van slowly drives down a long side street, then pulls into a driveway crowded with official vehicles. "Look," George says, bending low to watch. "There's your house."

One steep peak crowns the farmhouse's white façade, an open porch hugs the front and a deep green trim outlines the structure. Lamplight spills from the windows in a warm yellow glow and a twig and forsythia wreath hangs on the wooden front door. A towering old maple tree reaches for the sky just beyond the house, and the lawn looks thick and jewel green. The blue flashing light casts distorted shadows on the plain detective sedans dotting the front driveway and the police cruisers lining the street.

When they pull into the long driveway, George doesn't recognize Amy Trewist waiting on the open front porch. He has to look again to be sure the woman standing there in fitted jeans and a white oxford blouse is, in fact, her. But he'd recognize those brown eyes anywhere after locking on to them that morning. It occurs to him that Amy might recognize him, but then it's apparent she is no longer in that morning moment. She runs down the steps, bending forward, straining to see her daughter. George and the police officers step out of the van, and he leans inside to lift Grace out to the driveway. Before he can turn back with the kitten in the carton, Grace is gone. As quickly as she had been ripped from her mother's grasp today, her mother has taken her back. She spins around, her arms wrapped tightly around her girl. A crowd of people swarms them, cheering and hugging little Grace. The entire time, Amy never lets her out of her embrace, her fingertips floating over the child's face, unable to stop touching her.

Through the blue strobe police lights, George watches from the sidelines. They are intermittently illuminated, over and over again, this mother and daughter who never deserved the day. He hands the kitten carton to one of the detectives.

"Come on, Carbone. They need you back at the station," the officer driving the van says.

George doesn't want Amy Trewist recognizing his voice, his eyes, while her memories are fresh. Grace is safe. They will have police protection for the time being, as well as plenty of family sticking close. One of those men must surely be her husband.

"All right, you leaving now?" George asks.

"Yeah, I'm ready to go. They're going to get the kid a drink of water and swing her by the hospital. Precautionary stuff, you know?" The officer starts the ignition and switches off the flashing light. "Nice to see a happy ending."

Several dark sedans sit at the curb. Maybe this will never have an ending. Hours pass before he finishes answering questions back at police headquarters. He repeats every detail of Grace's return in the parking lot, saying it was dark; he can't be sure how many men were in the car; no, he didn't get the license plate. Once he realized what was happening, he says, he rushed into the store with the girl, afraid for their lives. The reporters take pictures outside Addison's police department.

Reid was right. In the camera flashes that break the darkness, no one sees through his story, no one reads his thoughts, no one points an accusing finger. Instead, they make George Carbone a hero.

———

Night falls on the country road. An owl swoops from the big maple tree. Misty dew covers the distant cornfields. And it's all good, it's a peace that Amy wants surrounding her child. She tucks in the blankets around Grace. Earlier, when she had let detectives gently question her, Grace wouldn't talk, burying her face in Amy's shoulder instead. But to Amy, all that matters is this: The doctors issued a clean bill of health and she got to bring her home to cuddle with stuffed animals and to tuck under a soft blanket, wearing her spring jammies. Because home is love. At home, her daughter tastes love in a cup of warm chicken soup. She hears love in the tinkling notes of her wind-up music box and in her mother's words. She sees love in her colorful room and in the eyes of Amy and her parents, of Celia and her husband Ben. Especially, though, Grace feels a new love for the stray kitten curled against her in a tight ball. It is tiny, just a scrap of fur taken from its mother much too soon. Like Grace. Can it be anything more than a constant reminder of the worst day of their lives?

But Grace stroked the kitten gently and quietly spoke to it. Wherever she went, the kitten followed close behind, scampering along to keep up. They set down a saucer of warm milk and Grace waited on the floor, rubbing at her tired eyes as it lapped enough milk to fill its belly. Afterward, the two of them fell asleep together. What defines evil's existence is its contrast with good. Grace found the good in an evil day in a little kitten. The cat was like a guardian angel keeping her daughter's mind distracted from the danger around her. Now she's an angel in their home. They'll call her that. Angel.

Outside their home, police protection remains indefinitely. A cruiser sits at the curb.

"Mom," Amy whispers when Ellen walks into the room. "Did you make up the guest room for you and Dad?"

"I did. He's still at the Station, talking to the detectives."

"Well he is a constable, Mom. You know how that goes. The cop is always on in him."

"Especially when his beautiful granddaughter is involved. How is she?"

"Sound asleep. Would you sit here for a little bit?"

"Of course." Ellen bends over and leaves a kiss on Grace's face.

"I just need to do something," Amy says as she folds her daughter's clothes and sets them with her saddle shoes high on a closet shelf. She noticed earlier how the laces were tied in a double bow to keep the shoe snugly in place. The gunman had looked out for her.

Still, she feels hatred, directed at the man she came into contact with, the man who *could* have changed the day. Their hands and eyes had locked. And no amount of good, of caring for her daughter or encouraging words, can erase that he did not try to stop the crime.

But another man returned her daughter, a good Samaritan brought into this nightmare unwillingly. Someone who did the right thing from the very start. He scooped her daughter into his strong arms, grabbed the kitten and ran. What a difference between the two.

She slips a cardigan over her shoulders and walks outside to find Officer Pine sitting in his cruiser. He gets out of the car as she nears.

"Is everything okay, Mrs. Trewist?"

Amy nods, her arms wrapped around herself in the night's dampness. "I just want to ask you something. The man who phoned the police. The one from the grocery store parking lot. Do you know his name?"

"Oh sure. He's a great guy. George. George Carbone."

"Would you know how I can reach this George? I'd like to talk to him in the next few days and thank him."

"He owns the meat market down on the west side. It's in Sycamore Square."

Amy pictures the local plaza. A working windmill turns in a small pond in the center of the circle of shops. She recalls a jeweler, several clothing boutiques, and a clock and lamp shop. Sycamore trees line the long driveway leading to the plaza of cream-colored buildings. But she can't call to mind a fresh meat market.

"A butcher shop?" she asks.

"Well. If you want to call it that. George runs a nice place. The Main Course. Take a ride there some time. He'd be happy to see that you and your girl are doing fine."

Six

GEORGE WAKES TO THE SOUND of heavy rain the next morning. Lying in bed, he holds out his arms, turning them and studying the sinuous tendons. If only he'd followed his dream and become a professional baseball player all those years ago. He would be fresh out of spring training right now, traveling on the road with the team while Nate went criminal. Chasing infield ground balls while Nate sidestepped felonies. Seeing the cheering crowd as he rounded the bases instead of seeing pouring rain, thinking the water sluices over an armored truck, over a parking lot's pavement, washing away any lingering evidence.

No. Instead of fly balls exacting his eye-hand coordination, working with lethal blades does. His fresh meat and seafood market accommodates caterers, restaurants and a discerning public. And Nate's laid tiles in many of those customers' homes and businesses. They raised blue-collar trades to a new height. Nate is divorced, George never married, and neither one has kids. Which is exactly why George doesn't understand his brother's actions. Nate doesn't need the money. So they can return their share of it anonymously and restore the family honor. He'll tell Nate that. It's about family, after all, that's what Nate's been saying. Taking care of family. But in the meantime, he has to get ready for work, shower, make a pot of fresh coffee and read the front page of the paper.

His picture is plastered on it. And outside his window, two television vans are parked at the curb. So when the doorbell rings later, he fully expects a pack of reporters, microphones in hand, cameras flashing. But it's Nate who walks in carrying a toolbox and heavy carton of stone tile, his hooded sweatshirt covering his head from the rain.

"What's going on now?" George asks.

"Those tiles came in that you wanted. Thought I'd start on your wall here." Nate sets the box down and flips off his hood before pouring himself a cup of coffee. He wears his work clothes: blue jeans, a tight T-shirt revealing broad shoulders, and work boots. A loose denim shirt hangs past the leather tool belt on his hips.

"What's in the box, for real? I can't keep that cash here."

"Tile, George. Calm down." Nate pulls a box cutter from his belt and slits open the carton. He perspires even though it is cool; his voice drops even though they are alone.

George doesn't want their voices to drop. He doesn't want secrets. He just wants his footloose brother back in his own staid, workaholic life. "The hell with the tiles. We need to talk, Nate. I can't take this and we have to figure out how we're getting out of it."

"Don't worry," Nate tells him. "This is all part of the plan. Once your walls are redone, the safe will be invisible to the human eye."

"Safe? That's the plan to get out of this?"

Nate nods. "We're going about our normal lives, remember? You wanted to redo your kitchen wall and I'm taking care of it. Like we planned." He sips his coffee and eyes George's jeans and polo shirt. "Where's your work clothes? Don't you have to open up?"

"Dean's taking care of it. I'm not going in today."

"Why not?"

"You see those vans out there? I'm not about to deal with the media all day. That is definitely not normal, and don't you tell me it is."

"It is for you," Nate insists. "Now that you're a God damn hero. Didn't you read the paper? Heroes talk to reporters, build up the story, pump themselves up."

"I read it, all right." The paper ran a studio portrait of Amy Trewist and her daughter. She wore a simple sheath, her sandy blonde hair falling to her shoulders, her jewelry minimal. Glaringly apparent was the lack of a man. "Do you realize who you messed with yesterday?"

"We didn't mess with anybody. No one got hurt."

"Jesus, Nate, not that you can see, anyway. Didn't you read the articles? That lady is thirty-three and a widow already. She suffered enough without you screwing with her."

"Hey, she got her kid back. She'll recover." Nate returns the box cutter to his tool belt and pulls a heavy hammer from the beat up toolbox. He straightens his six-foot-one frame and taps the hammer head in his other hand. His eyes squint as he studies George. "Don't you start worrying about that dame now. Just get to work. Give the press the pictures and interviews they want and they'll get bored in no time. Your fifteen minutes of being a hero will be history in a week." He pulls out his measuring tape and checks a few numbers along the wall.

"Wait a minute, Nate. Screw those damn tiles." He grabs the tape from his brother's hand. "Listen, we have to turn ourselves in. We'll say we were threatened, something, I don't know."

"No. You listen." Nate grabs the measuring tape back. "This tile work's going to be fancy shit. I know you only wanted a backsplash, but this wall has to be extended. I need space behind it, you know what I mean?" He surmises the kitchen carefully. "We tallied it last night while you were bringing the girl back. Your wall will be worth close to a million. That's your cut."

It's the way Nate says it, his words coming as plainly as if he is talking measurements, fifteen and three-quarter inches by one million, that makes George pour his coffee down the drain. He can't drink, can't eat and he fought dry heaves once already. He can kick Nate out. Set his toolbox outside the door in the rain and lock the deadbolt. But yesterday is far from over. Until he figures something out, his brother will build a custom, hidden safe in his kitchen wall. And George has no doubt. The safe will be indecipherable from the tile under the influence of his skilled hands.

―――――

Amy no longer takes anyone at face value. When Hayes stops by her house on Thursday morning, she can plainly see that he is about fifty years old with very short light brown hair and a calm expression. But she knows there is more, unseen. There's a hand-gun on his body, strapped somewhere beneath his jacket. She works with him to quietly press Grace for simple details about her captors, but their attention distresses her. She gets even more quiet, sucking her thumb and withdrawing, not looking at either of them. So when Ellen puts on Grace's purple galoshes and takes her outside to splish-splash in puddles, Hayes turns to Amy. He asks her to describe the weapons that had been involved in the crime. Maybe they can be traced.

"Black as hell," Amy says, glancing out the kitchen window at her daughter walking in the light rain, before turning back to the detective. "The man holding Grace, his weapon seemed larger than the other's. Than the man who took her shoe."

Hayes tells her that the brain catalogues visions that, without prodding, the conscience remains unaware of. So he prods, and prods, asking for wording or insignias she might have seen, the finish of the grips, the presence of safety levers or any magazine protrusion. "The length of the barrels. Could you describe either one?" he asks.

Behind closed eyes, Amy pictures the man holding Grace beneath one arm, and holding a weapon in his other hand, keeping it pressed almost unnoticed along his leg. She hesitantly motions the length with her two hands.

"Maybe a four-inch barrel," the detective notes. "Did it look narrow? Wide?"

"Wide. Like there were two barrels together." She points to a picture from a selection he brought along, indicating traditional double action frames, and winces at the array of weaponry. "There are so many," Amy says, startled when Angel jumps from a kitchen chair up onto the table, stepping lightly across the images.

"Is that the cat from the kidnappers?" Detective Hayes asks.

"Yes. Angel." Amy scoops up the black and white kitten, and what she thinks is this: A couple pounds of soft, warm fur; a couple pounds of a cold, black gun. She shifts the cat's weight in her hand before setting her on the floor. "Too bad she can't talk. Imagine what she saw that day?"

"No kidding." Hayes turns back to the weapons and from what he repeats into a digital recorder, the guns involved seem to be a forty-five and a nine-millimeter.

If it weren't for the firearms violently imposed upon her life, she would still be happily ignorant to the ways of these weapons. She would be at work at her vintage bridal shop, scouting the Internet and flea markets for lace gowns with sweetheart necklines, for a white moiré silk, high-waisted dress a customer requested, for the elbow-length satin gloves she needed to pair with a 1950s sleeveless gown.

Instead she doesn't leave her home. Surrounded by an acre of tended land that the original farmer never relinquished to developers, the lawn and trees become her cocoon. The investigators, like Hayes, come to her, and Celia and Ellen run her errands around town. After walking blindly into Addison's worst crime ever, she doesn't trust herself to venture further than her own backyard and so it is with resistance that she finds herself in her shop later Thursday.

"I heard you again last night," Ellen says as she hangs a cupcake dress with a full skirt of lace and tulle, trimmed in ruffles, on a black dress form. "It's just like after Mark died. You're up half the night, Amy."

Amy sits on the gold settee, her hand skimming the brocade floral pattern. "Well of course I'm up. I can't stop seeing Grace being grabbed from my hands. Then I see that man's face, the one who took her shoe. He came so close to me. When I shut my eyes, he's right there. When I dream, he's there. So no, I can't sleep."

"It's not just sleep. You're not eating. You've been disorganized all week." Ellen lifts and drops the gown skirt, fluffing the ruffles. "You'd never even have come here today if I didn't put the gowns in your car and buckle Grace in the back seat. And you *love* fussing with the gowns."

Amy does. Her vintage bridal shop is all part of capturing her family history, a part of four generations of women woven together. A part of the art of her grandmother's intricate hand-stitched lace doilies and veils and table runners and even bracelets. A part of the sweet memories stopping at tag sales with her mother years ago, lifting lace treasures from old trunks or a chest of drawers. A part of the magic stories her mother spun about the lace. A part of standing together in the sunlight, her mother's hands lifting lace like butterfly wings for Amy to see, dust rising like fairy tale stardust. She feels a bit of that enchanted stardust in each lace gown she chooses and loves that she can share it with her own daughter now, too.

"You can't take another year to recover," Ellen is saying. When she lifts the gown skirt one more time, Angel scoots beneath it. "Be quick, for Grace's sake." Grace moves beside her, laughing at the little kitten's paw shooting out from beneath the gown, tapping at her foot. "I'll have to be getting back home to Dad eventually."

So there it is. Her father already returned to New Hampshire, to his waiting job on the force there. One day soon, her mother will leave her three hundred miles behind, too. Even though the police still check on her safety, she dreads being on her own again. Going out in public. Entering stores, walking through parking lots. Being responsible for herself and her daughter. Needing eyes on the back of her head.

"Maybe if you start dealing with people again, a little bit at a time."

"I don't trust people, Mom. I don't know how to anymore." She gets up off the settee and walks over to the counter, adjusting the bracelets on the jewelry holder there. The rain had stopped, and their gemstones and gold chains glimmer in the late afternoon sunlight shining through the front display window. All the while, her ears are tuned to Grace, waiting to hear words she might say.

"What about that George fellow? That would be a good way for you to get out a bit."

"Who?" She looks over at her mother.

"George. George Carbone. You were going to thank him for bringing Grace home safely."

Amy looked at his photographs in the paper all week, studying the face, the strong chin, the dark eyes. Yet he looked tense, or worried. Something. She cut out one picture and leaves it on her dresser mirror, thankful for his anonymous presence in their lives. But she hadn't reached out to him.

"You said you're afraid to trust anyone after this crazy ordeal," Ellen is saying as she wraps a fine-gauge crocheted bridal shawl around Grace's tiny shoulders. "Look how pretty! Do you want to see in the mirror?" Grace nods silently, and Ellen walks her to the full-length mirror. "But if there was ever someone you could trust," she says over her shoulder, "I think he would be the man."

Grace twirls around, holding the shawl in place, its tassels swinging. And Amy sees. Her mother has done it again, spinning magic with lace and beauty and gentleness, this time with Grace. Her daughter runs across the room laughing, calling Angel's name with the little kitten close on her tail, patting at the shawl tassels dragging behind her.

———

A lone piano captivates Amy with a single bar of music, followed by a familiar voice picking up the melody. Early Friday morning, she quietly closes the door behind her, listening to Sinatra. Looking around, words escape her. Dingy images of a butcher shop filled her mind during the car ride, which is why she left Grace at home with her mother. She pictured walking into a large, cold room lined with blood-smeared meat cases and industrial carving equipment. There would be men yelling over the sound of a meat grinder and bone saw, men wearing bloodied white aprons. A butcher shop.

Instead, gleaming glass meat cases meticulously display prime cuts of veal, beef and pork. Shelves of marinating sauces and spices line the walls, along with a recipe rack. Fresh seafood fills another glass case with catfish, swordfish, clams. Cheese and breads spill from a side shelf, and in a dinner-to-go case, seafood cakes and tuna kabobs with fresh vegetables entice the eye. Small round tables are clustered in the corner, a place to sit and have a sandwich, though all are empty at the moment. In fact, she is the only customer this early in the morning.

His back faces her, the broad shoulders pressed against a crisp white long sleeve shirt turned back at the cuffs, over which is tied a jet black apron. Those are the shoulders that lifted her child to safety. He's taller than she had imagined. And there is a slight movement; he seems lost in thought while working a substantial slicing knife. Reaching for the bell that hadn't rung when she slowly, carefully closed the door behind her, not that he would have heard it over the stereo, she reaches up and gives it a good jingle.

"Be right with you," he calls over his shoulder. He looks back again before walking over to the counter. "Hi there, what can I get you?"

"Mr. Carbone?" Amy asks.

He stares at her for a long moment, then squints briefly. "I know you." He steps closer, concerned. "Mrs. Trewist, right?"

"Amy. Please." She reaches out to shake his hand.

He holds his hands up, palms out. "Give me a second. Why don't you grab a seat over there while I wash up a little."

She glances over at the empty tables and hesitates, stepping back. "As long as I'm not keeping you?"

"Not at all." His gaze stays so steady on her, she glances toward the door, then walks to a table and sits down.

Oh, she had a picture conjured up just to her liking, one simple enough to make her life easy, one that let her quickly stop in at a butcher shop, issue her gratitude and escape amidst the mess and noise of meat cutting. George would be an ungainly, lumbering butcher, awkwardly accepting her thanks, guardedly declining her dinner invitation as he wiped his hands on a soiled, white apron.

"Welcome to the real world," she whispers, listening to the running tap water from the back. She searches for a mint in her bag.

"Can I bring you a coffee?" George calls out.

"That would be nice, thanks." Amy centers the napkin dispenser, brushes a crumb from the tabletop and straightens the opposite chair. Her hope of a quick and easy introduction fades when she notices the water stops running, Sinatra's volume has been lowered and the smell of fresh-brewed coffee fills the shop. She hasn't conversed socially, alone, with a man, since her husband died. Will this George see her vulnerability? Will he reach out and offer comfort? Or will he sense her newfound mistrust of people and think her visit is merely obligatory? She aches suddenly for the familiarity of her old marriage, for the easiness of the past. One damn day has taken her life and tipped it on edge.

———

George walks out into his shop and sets two coffee cups on the small table. "Let's try that again," he says, extending his cleaned hand for a shake. "It's very nice to see you, Mrs. Trewist. Amy." He takes her hand in his, feeling its soft suppleness when it's not fighting for her daughter's life. "I'm George."

"I meant to stop in sooner, but it's been a difficult week. I'm glad to finally meet you."

"How is your daughter?" He sits in the seat opposite her.

Amy stirs cream into her coffee. "She's doing okay, but she's very tired. Fatigued. So physically she's fine, as best as we could hope for anyway."

"But something else is wrong?"

"Well," she begins. "You were there."

"I was there?" He shifts in the chair, his coffee untouched.

"That night. At Litner's Market. The police told me you just grabbed her and ran. You didn't listen for any instructions once you realized it was Grace."

George sips his coffee then. He has to keep his story straight with what he told the authorities. "Nothing else really mattered at that point."

Amy reaches for his hand. "Thank you," she says. "I'm so grateful that you intervened like that. But I was wondering if you saw anything, oh, I don't know, anything I should know. If my daughter was upset, that sort of thing."

He pulls his hand away. "Not really. She seemed okay when they left her in the parking lot. Quiet, but concerned for the cat."

"Oh, her and that cat. They're inseparable. It's the quiet part that worries me though. Grace was such a chatterbox before and now I can barely get a word out of her. The kitten helps, the way she sometimes talks to it."

"She seemed pretty calm, given the situation. I'm sorry I don't know more and can't help you that way."

"That's why I'm here, actually. We'd like to thank you for how you did help. Grace and I. We'd like to have you over for dinner. On Tuesday, maybe? Around six?"

George leans back in his chair. "You've been through an awful lot. It really isn't necessary."

"But we owe you so much. And something you say might help get Grace to open up." She looks away, then back at him. "It would help me, too. It's better for me to keep busy."

"Let me take the two of you out, then. A restaurant Grace likes, maybe?"

"No. Oh no. I'm not taking her out yet. It's difficult even for *me* to be here." She takes a quick breath. "It's silly, I know, but I still get anxious away from home."

"I'm sorry. I had no idea."

"It's okay. I just feel better staying at home, where we're safe."

So there it is. The woman is living a nightmare every day. Afraid to go out. Afraid for her daughter's safety. Pictures of violence filling her idle time. "If it'll help, dinner would be nice, then." He hitches his head toward the meat case. "Can I offer you a dinner selection? A roast maybe? Or stuffed chicken cutlets?"

Amy walks to the meat case, passing the shelves of cheeses, cheddar and Monterey Jack and Parmesan he'd just restocked. Fresh loaves of bread are tucked in with the cheeses.

"Cranberry herb stuffing for the chicken? I make any request for my customers."

"It sounds wonderful," she says, turning to him. "But I need to keep busy. I'll cook something at home, if you don't mind."

"Of course. No problem then. Tuesday, it is. Six o'clock."

At the counter, she picks up one of the chocolates covered in colorful wrappers bordered by a snowflake print. "You put a lot of thought into your shop. After-dinner sweets?" She sets it back in the tray and pulls a pen and slip of paper from her purse.

"I try."

"I know you were there that night. But in case you've forgotten, with all the commotion, I'll leave you my address. My phone number's there too, if anything comes up."

George takes the paper and hands her a couple of dark chocolate truffles in return, which she slips into her purse. "Dinner will be under better circumstances," he assures her. He walks her to the door, holding it open, and she looks back at him. "Something wrong?" he asks.

"I just wondered if there is someone you would like to bring. Your wife, or a girlfriend?"

"It'll just be me."

"Okay, then." Amy pauses, then shakes his hand again before hurrying out the door.

Seven

CAN'T A FLASHBACK BE BEAUTIFUL? Can't a flashback remind us
of the pure goodness we cross paths with in life? Because even
though Dr. Berg is telling her that the violence she relives almost
daily now is, indeed, flashbacks, she thinks of the other kind
she knows. The bridal flashbacks. That's what she calls it when
a bride sets a veil on her head with just-the-right gown. Whether
the gown is a free-flowing layer of frills or beaded silk with a lace
bodice doesn't matter. The cue that evokes a childhood memory
is the veil of tulle or cascading lace, the moment it frames her
face. Suddenly all the pretend weddings and dreamt vows of a
young girl's play and dress-up show in the bride's thrilled expression when she looks in the mirror. Amy always thought of that
veil-inspired journey through time as a bridal flashback, one that
lingers until the bride says two small words leaving childhood
behind.

"I do," Amy says now when Dr. Berg asks if she has recurring
thoughts of the day of Grace's kidnapping. "Which is why I'm
here. They seem to be getting worse."

"How so?" he asks, jotting notes in a pad at his desk.

"The memories of that morning are usually vague. The details aren't clear. Except when these incidents occur and then it's like I'm right back in the bank parking lot."

"Flashbacks. They're vivid memories that come on suddenly, along with the emotions of the trauma. Sometimes they're so strong—"

"It's like I'm reliving it."

"Yes. They are very real, and usually triggered by something. A sound, a visual. Have you had headaches with them, or nausea?"

"No."

"Fainted or blacked-out?"

Amy stands and walks to the window. The glass muffles the noises outside, muting the cars driving past, the birds singing in the spring warmth. It mirrors the way she's been living, with the outside world muffled by the crime. "I wouldn't say blacked-out, not in the way you'd think. When they happen I'm awake, but completely back in the crime."

"That's a true flashback."

"Is there some way to treat them? My mother had to leave yesterday, so I'm alone with Grace again and need to manage this."

"First, give yourself time. It's been just over a week. And it is best that you stay around people so that if this happens when you're with Grace, they can step in. So since your mother had to leave, can you spend time at your parents' place? Because it's also really important not to withdraw, which is actually a post-traumatic stress symptom, too."

"And what would make someone do that?"

"Withdraw? Well, if a victim isn't strong enough to deal with their emotions, they might withdraw and avoid social situations."

"Is speech affected?" Amy asks.

"It can be. Conversations might lessen, or even stop completely."

"But in someone who hasn't fully developed socially, what happens?"

"Amy?" Dr. Berg sets down his pen and leans forward, resting his arms on the desk. "Are we talking about you now, or Grace?"

"Grace. It's Grace." She pauses, panicked to think of what her daughter's young mind is processing. "She barely talks now. Sometimes not at all."

"I had no idea," Dr. Berg says, shifting in his chair.

"She has this kitten," Amy explains. "She's so close to it. And she does talk to it, quietly."

"The cat from the kidnapping?" he asks. When she nods, he continues. "The cat was there, that day. You weren't. In her eyes, the kitten filled in for you, giving her comfort and security."

"So you're saying that even children experience PTSD?"

"Sometimes more so than adults," Dr. Berg explains. "That cat may be the only device keeping her talking. She's lived through a horrifying experience and without the cat, she could withdraw beyond your reach."

Beyond her reach. Again. Or still. She'd been taken from her that day and still is not fully back. She's still in the arms of a kidnapper. Still in the crime.

"Spend as much time with her as possible. Let her cling to you. Take her outside, too, so she can run around and get plenty of fresh air. Another thought is to keep paper and crayons on hand. Children sometimes communicate anxiety this way."

"Really. By coloring?"

"Yes. It's a form of release. Actually, you might want to keep a pencil and paper close at hand for yourself, too."

"For me?"

"Flashbacks are particularly clear, Amy. Write down any details you might see that you hadn't remembered. It could help the investigation."

———

It's okay, you know. Celia said it quietly as she manicured Amy's nails. The nail file scritched back and forth and her words slipped right in with its rhythm. Amy had told her she wasn't trying to impress anyone; she just didn't want people thinking she was coming undone, not taking care of herself. *You mean George? Listen. You can look. Smile. Have a nice time.* When she hugged Amy goodbye, she whispered it again. *It's okay, Amy. Enjoy the dinner.*

The funny thing is, Amy had started to think the same thing before Grace was kidnapped. She could look. She could consider the thought of having, some day, another man in her life. But since the kidnapping, she pulled those thoughts up short and kicked them right out of her head. Grace needs her undivided attention.

Returning now to the dining room after putting Grace to bed, the chandelier glowing over the cherry wood table, throwing soft light on the crystal and china, Celia's words return. *It's okay.* George stands in the dining room, hands clasped behind his back, looking at a large framed bride portrait hanging over the sideboard. He turns when Amy enters the room. "Is she sleeping?" he asks.

"Yes. I'm sorry she wasn't more sociable. But she loves the flowers. I had to leave the vase on her dresser, where she can see it. She's gotten so possessive since last week, of anything that's hers. Of me, the cat, and your flowers now, too."

All Amy saw when she opened the door earlier was the bouquet of flowers bursting into vivid color. It was so different from the sympathy arrangements from a year ago. These flowers were happy and light. Yellows and pinks and purples. Then she heard George say that they were for Grace. No one had ever brought her daughter flowers. When Grace later silently held out a piece of her sandwich for him, he took it. Then he made himself a peanut butter and jelly, sat with them and split it three ways. Grace was comfortable with her rescuer in the room.

George pours two glasses of wine now while Amy serves salad and the lasagna she'd baked.

"You were looking at my beautiful bride," Amy says, pushing her plate away after a few bites.

George helps himself to another slice of lasagna. "It's a striking portrait. Someone in your family?"

"No, actually. I found the painting at my friend Sara Beth's antique shop and loved it because of the lace gown she's wearing." Amy glances at the gold-framed painting. "I felt a connection to my grandmother, who was a lace-maker. I even added some of her handmade lace to my own wedding gown."

"That explains your line of work then, dealing with the vintage gowns."

"In a way." Amy sips her wine. "My grandmother told me that lace stitches lead us on a journey. They suggest a story, the way you see each tiny stitch create a larger visual. And in a wedding gown, that story is a love story, which I love to pass along to new brides." She looks at the painting again. "But I haven't opened up my bridal shop since the kidnapping. Grace is still too upset and I have to take care of her first."

"Is she showing any improvement?"

Amy shakes her head. "No. As a matter of fact, she seems to be getting worse. If you don't mind, I'm just going to run up and check on her." She stands, sets her napkin on the table and hurries off. In the living room, she switches on a brass lamp that casts a circle of pale light on a dark wood end table. Before walking up the stairs, she glances back to the dining room. It isn't George carefully stacking the china plates to bring into the kitchen that catches her eye. It isn't the continued small gestures of this man that speak volumes to his character. It is the way he turns and snatches up the silverware, as though he is angry at something, or someone.

———

George looks up from wiping off a plate when Amy returns a few minutes later. She gathers their napkins and pushes in one of the chairs. "Grace looks so peaceful sleeping, so I'm glad for that." She reaches for her wine glass, accidentally tipping it over on the table.

George lunges and quickly reaches past her to get hold of it, righting it carefully. "No damage done." He blots a small stain from the tablecloth. When he looks up, Amy is sitting, her eyes closed and her fingers pressed lightly to her forehead.

"Amy? Hey, are you okay?" One of her hands grips the table edge, so George dips a cloth napkin into a water goblet. "Here," he says, dabbing her face with the cool cloth. "You're perspiring." He touches it to her skin at her hairline, dampening fine wisps of hair.

At his touch, she opens her eyes.

"Are you okay?" he asks again. "Do you need a doctor?"

"I'll be fine," she answers, her voice quiet. "I'm really sorry. That happens sometimes."

"What happens?"

She closes her eyes briefly again. "I've been having flashbacks."

"You almost passed out, Amy." He opens a window behind them, letting in a stream of cool evening air before sitting and pulling his chair closer. So they inflicted this on her, too. "Do you need a drink of water?"

She reaches for her glass and what's left of her wine. "Maybe this is better. My nerves are so shot." She takes a long swallow of the liquor. "I try to get through a normal routine every day. Cooking, working on my gown inventory, tending to Grace. But these flashbacks just derail me."

"Maybe you should see a doctor."

"I did. My friend babysat Grace and I went this morning. He explained it all to me, how what I'm seeing are actual glimpses of memory."

Which means glimpses of him. George folds his arms on the table and leans close. "What exactly are you seeing?"

"My daughter, for one, in that monster's arm. And then," she pauses and reaches for the wine bottle, pouring a splash more into her glass. "Like this one, now. There was a struggle for Grace's shoe in the parking lot. In a horrifying moment right before she was gone, it flew off her foot. We both reached for it, me and one of those men. In the flashback, I see his hand reaching quickly right over mine. Then when I look up and his masked face is right in front of me, well, I can't even breathe."

So she sees his hand. *His.* A gentle breeze lifts the lace window curtain, letting the outside into the room to calm her, the air dew-laden this spring evening. And he knows now. Knows that while reaching over and quickly righting her spilled glass, his very hand had actually triggered her flashback tonight.

Eight

THE DUTCH COLONIAL NESTLED IN New Hampshire's hills looks like a watercolor painting when they round the bend in the road. Deep green shrubs frame her parents' house, and pink dogwoods and lavender lilacs hang heavy in bloom, their colors smudged beneath the late May blue sky.

Amy indulges her senses. The scent of spring floats in the fragrance of new blossoms and damp lawns, misting the air like cologne. A twig and berry wreath hangs on the wood plank front door, and inside, just past the foyer, dark paneling and floor-to-ceiling bookshelves line the family room walls. A worn oriental rug covers the dining room floor and framed family photographs sit on lace runners on living room end tables. But Amy spends her time at the oak table in the kitchen, staying beneath the security blanket of sound and aroma, of food baking, of tea and coffee simmering, of the clink of silverware to mugs. This is why you come home again, as simple as that. On their first night there, her father lights a fire in the kitchen fireplace and that's when she knows.

This is *her* old home, not Grace's. Which is exactly why her plan won't work. She has run home and run away from her own life. Withdrawn, just like Dr. Berg had warned. Even the little kitten is at odds here. She spends hours hiding beneath the sofa, much to Grace's dismay.

But Amy doesn't want to stay alone in Connecticut, either, so the next afternoon she takes Grace outside to her parents' backyard. Grace's legs step down the two deck stairs, coming to a full stop on each one. Cool weather flowers fill the deck planters. Pansies in yellows and purples tip their blossoms like happy faces.

Amy leans on the deck railing, watching her daughter look at her reflection in the blue gazing ball before poking through the strawberry patch. She'd pulled Grace's fine hair into two ponytails, just like on the day she was kidnapped. There's no getting around those little reminders. The sun shines as bright as it did that morning, too. So every sunny day has that potential to remind her. She steps off the deck and moves closer to Grace, toying with sunflower seeds in her jacket pocket that they'll plant together. Walking a few steps behind her in the garden, her ears strain to hear any words. This new radar runs between them as Grace continues to quiet. Her daughter's small voice comes back to her, softly, stopping her in place. "Cripe," she says.

No, there's no escaping that nightmare day. Not in New Hampshire, not in a beautiful garden on a May afternoon, not at home snuggled with stuffed animals and dolls and love. She hears Grace and thinks of the masked man walking away holding her shoe. His voice rings clear as she remembers his face, distorted beneath the hosiery. *Cripe, give them the hour.* He looked long at her. *Be strong.*

Grace pulls a fat red strawberry from the plant. "Cripe," she says again before putting the strawberry to her mouth. She licks it lightly before dropping it in her small basket. Where is she? Is she having her own flashback? Of what? How can Amy help her if she doesn't know what visions trap Grace's mind, visions from inside that armored truck? Her first instinct is to scold her daughter to not say that filthy word. Because that's what it feels like, filth. It crawls over her skin and makes her cringe. Instead, she takes Grace by the hand and leads her to a sunny spot near the fence, beside a stone garden bench.

"Come on, Gracie." All she can do is be a caring mother. And if that's the good that comes from her trip home, then it was worth it. She'll keep believing in this one way to help her daughter. Loving gestures and words versus flashbacks and memories. That's what it comes down to. Simple and powerful. Good versus evil.

"Want to plant sunflowers? They'll grow so, so big. Taller than me." She reaches a hand high above her head and prays that planting flowers will supplant whatever memory Grace relives right now. Kneeling in the afternoon's sun-warmed soil, she scoops out small holes in the dirt. Grace drops one sunflower seed in each of the holes. "These will look so beautiful, Grace. At the end of summer, they'll be like a wall of flowers!" Together they push the soil back on top of the seeds and very lightly tamp it down. The dirt is warm beneath their touch. Amy imagines the end of summer. September. Grace is a September baby. She will turn three and all the plans have changed. Nursery school might be put off. Summer is put off. Ease is put off. Her mother's garden is filled with baby plants, tomato and eggplant seedlings reaching to the sky. How will they ever get past spring?

———

When the white eyelet curtain dropped back into place, Amy knew her mother stood behind it watching them in the garden. She goes upstairs to the bedroom and stands silently in the doorway, her mother unaware of her presence as she thumbs through Amy's sketch pad.

The visuals her mother is seeing are not easy to take. The pencil drawings on the first pages, though raw in talent, depict appalling violence. A crude sketch of a gun covers one page. It is mostly black shadow, with lighter shadows pulling in detail like the double barrel and the checkered pattern of the magazine. Her mother flips that page to another view of a gun, its barrel more prominent because Amy had been closer to it in the shoe struggle. When her mother turns away, toward the window framed with lacy fabric, Amy understands why. It's hard to look at the reality of that day.

"Mom?"

Ellen jumps and turns to the doorway. "Where's Grace?" she asks. When Amy nods to the open window, she looks to see Grace outside with her grandfather, cutting lilacs from the unwieldy shrubs.

"Those are personal, Mom."

"I'm sorry. I only came in your room to open a window." Ellen sits on the bed with the pad in her lap, her other palm rubbing a circle on the hand-pieced quilt, over and over again.

How many stitches, tiny stitches of moments, hold our lives together? Amy thinks that every tiny stitch contributes to who we are. She sits beside her mother. This is one of them, now. The barrel of a gun is one.

"Oh all right," Ellen admits. "I was snooping, okay? What else can I do? You and Grace walk around shellshocked and there's no way for me to help. There's nothing I can do to fix it." She gives the sketch pad back to Amy. "So I looked in here to see if everything was in order. To see if I could iron a blouse or polish a pair of shoes. I don't know, something."

"You don't have to explain," Amy says. "I've learned some things can't be explained. You just ended up here. I get it. I ended up here, too. Back home with you. I'm just here."

"What *are* those?" Ellen asks as she nods at the sketch pad.

"Therapy." Amy opens the pad on her lap.

"Therapy? How can drawing horrible pictures help you?"

"They're more than pictures. They're images from my flashbacks."

"You're having flashbacks?"

"Sometimes. I didn't want to worry you, Mom. Dr. Berg told me to note down details and memories that I remember. The mind blocks painful stuff, but a flashback shows it." She turns to a sketch of Grace hanging in a man's arms. "Like this. It's a way to process the trauma, and I might see something that will help the investigation."

Ellen looks closely at the image, shaking her head.

"Mom?" Amy takes a long breath. "I think I made a mistake. Grace and I have to go home."

"What?" Her mother reaches for her hand. "You've only been here a couple days. I promise, no more snooping."

"It's not that. It's me. It's Grace. It's even Angel. You know how she hides under the sofa? That's kind of how I feel. Like we're hiding way under the big country house, far away where no one can reach us. And you know what good it's doing Angel?"

"None?"

"Right. And it's the same for me. I have to be home. And in my shop with all the gowns and brides and wedding plans. And well, home."

"But this is home, too."

Amy pats her mother's hand. "Not for Grace. Some bastard grabbed her from me, forced her on that truck and God knows where else. Then she comes home, *home*, and what do I do? I take her away? It's not good, Mom. I want her at home. Her home."

"I'll come with you then."

Amy shakes her head and sees the tears in her mother's eyes. "Dad needs you. And coming here did help me. I had time to think, and plan ways to help Grace. I'm rested. It helped me to go back alone. It's something I have to do."

"Well I'll make dinners for you to bring back and freeze. A meatloaf maybe? And some sauce and meatballs?"

"You don't have to do that."

"Yes, I do." Her mother hugs her then, her fingers toying with wisps of Amy's hair.

———

Because one perfectly normal day had been upended by a crime, Amy pays close attention to normal now. Things like the key clicking properly in the deadbolt lock when she arrives home the next day, as it should, give her a moment's peace.

And that the house feels a little stuffy, as it should, with the windows securely closed for the past few days, feels right. Her mailbox, too, is empty, thanks to Celia picking up her mail.

Once she has unpacked, fed the kitten and put Grace down for a nap, she checks her answering machine.

"Huh." There was a message blinking on it when she left, one saved until she could jot down the phone number. The light holds steady now. She taps the button.

"You have no messages," the electronic voice says.

"That's funny." She taps it again. Nothing. So she presses the Announcement button. The machine hums silently. Mark's voice, which she had left on it as a form of security leading callers to believe a man lived there, is gone. Then come two beeps alerting her to record a new announcement. "Come on," she insists, giving the machine a little tap before checking that the plug is secure and the volume turned on. But it doesn't matter; the Announcement plays only silence, then two beeps, again and again. So she tries turning on a lamp, wondering if a power outage messed up the recording while she was gone, her eyes first, imperceptibly, scanning the window locks.

Nine

Nate, you ever try knocking before you let yourself in?"
George walks into the kitchen finding tools spread out on the island countertop and his brother holding a three-foot level to the wall. George pours himself a cup of coffee from the pot Nate made before he started working. Nate does that, drinks coffee on the job all day. Now he studies the newly tiled wall without responding to George.

"Nate," George says again. His brother glances at him, gives a quick handshake, then presses the level back up against the wall. George doubts there are any flaws in the craftsmanship, just like there were none with the heist. Nate planned it, created it, built it up, perfected it, completed it, sewed up any loose ends and is wrapping it up now. Nothing out of line, no cracks.

"If this wall's not exactly vertical, I'm screwed," Nate says. "The slightest deviation will ruin the visual effect of the tile." He scrutinizes the bubble in the level.

"We have to talk," George continues. "It's been almost two weeks and I want answers, God damn it. I'm tired of you holding out on me."

"You see this crazing here?" Nate runs an open hand over the top three rows of stone tile.

"Crazing?"

"Fine cracks. Like a web in the glaze."

George looks closer, seeing tiny veins mapping some of the tile. "I see it."

"Damn, I'll have to replace them."

"The hell with the tiles. I'll break them all down if you don't start talking."

"Hey." Nate sets the level on the breakfast bar, swings a leg over one of the stools and faces George. "What's eating you?"

George leans against the counter. "What's eating me? You're kidding, right?"

"No."

"Except for the card game at Craig's, you've been keeping yourself scarce, and I want to know how it all happened. How you got involved, why the hell I'm involved, who those other guys are, what you're doing with the money, when this is going to end. Because I can't even think straight anymore." He shows Nate a nasty gash running across the side of his palm. "My hand practically went through the slicer yesterday."

"Whoa. You've got to be careful, George. All the time." Nate looks back at the tile wall as though it's still bothering him. "That's why we haven't talked. I'm being careful. It's part of the plan. Everything is. Even me laying low and not seeing you. Every minute is part of the plan."

"Listen, Nate." George swats a tile trowel off the granite countertop onto the floor. "I've about had it."

"No, you listen. The authorities are going to question you again once their leads get cold. And what you *don't* know can't hurt you. If I tell you how all this came about, you'd have to lie to them. This way, there's not much you can leak. You're home free." He leans over and picks up the trowel. "And rich, to boot."

"You think you're doing me a favor by not talking?"

"Pretty much." Nate stands and pours himself another mug of coffee, then puts a take-out egg and sausage sandwich into the microwave.

"You don't get it, do you? I want my life back, Nate." George holds out his hand, his thumb and finger spaced just so, rigid with resolve. "I'm this close to turning everybody in. I can't live like this."

"Calm down, George, and just think about it. If you talk, A—the feds will never believe you weren't in on it. So you'll do time because any participation is guilt. And B—Reid won't stand for it."

"Those two are a piece of work. You trust them with all this?"

"Reid? And Elliott? They got what they wanted. They're happy. Now we just have to keep it that way, understand? And you're the only one the cops are going to tap into, so you're better off unaware of the details."

"What about Amy? They'll talk to her, too."

"She doesn't know shit." Nate pulls his sandwich from the microwave and sets it on the island. "All she wanted was her baby back, and we did that."

"You did more than that. She can barely leave the house now on account of the flashbacks she's been having."

"Flashbacks? Now how would you know that?" He lifts the top off his steaming sandwich roll. "And give me your ketchup."

"I was there for dinner. She had me over to thank me for getting her daughter back to her."

"No shit."

George hands him the ketchup bottle from the fridge, then empties the rest of his coffee down the sink and checks his watch. "You staying here?"

"For a couple hours. I've got to fix that crazing." Nate eyes George's outfit, jeans and an old college tee. "You going in to work looking like that?"

"I'm actually stopping by Amy's house on the way."

"Again? For what?"

"I'm doing her a favor, helping out with something in the yard." From over a chair, he lifts a hanger holding black trousers topped with a white button-down shirt. "I'll change when I get to work."

"Jesus. All dressed up to cut meat," Nate says around a mouthful of egg sandwich. "Just like the old man. Always worried about your image."

"Don't even start about Dad, okay?"

"Fine. But it's not a good idea, George, seeing that woman. You'll slip up. I hope this isn't going to be a regular thing with you two now."

"Maybe it is, maybe it isn't. What's it to you?"

"You've got to leave her alone before she figures out you were there that day, somehow. Or her kid will. Just get back to your old life. I thought I told you that already."

"Do me a favor, will you? Quit thinking about me."

———

From the dark cloud that descended on Amy's life, the silver lining starts to emerge. It is the good that comes with the bad. The good is George stopping by to hang the tire swing on his way to work. The good is in Grace's bright smile as Amy pushes the swing gently beneath the shade of the tall maple tree. The good is in knowing she can swing her daughter every single day of the summer now, morning, noon and night, gently swaying her in the warm air, serenaded by robins and chickadees.

"I'm so glad you called yesterday. Grace loves the swing."

"Well when you didn't return my call, I worried."

"I don't know what happened to those messages while I was at my parents'. I guess that answering machine is so old, I really need a new one." Tiny yellow wildflowers spread through cracks in the old patio stones beside the maple tree. Red geraniums, vinca vines and spikes spill from two stone urns. George sits in an Adirondack chair there, leaning forward, his elbows on his knees. "So thanks for checking up on us. I appreciate that." She gives the tire swing a very slow spin.

"I'm glad. Because if seeing me brings back too many memories from that day, I'd understand."

"You don't bring any bad memories. You're the good in all this, George. We like having you visit."

George stands and pulls his keys from his pocket. "Well that's nice to hear."

Amy glances over at him. "I know that Grace and I aren't the easiest people to be with right now. We've got some issues going on, trust issues really. Especially in public places."

"I can understand why. But you trust me?"

"Yes, yes I do." She gives Grace another gentle push.

"Okay then." He looks at his watch. "I've got to get to the shop." He backs up a few steps toward his pickup truck, watching her. "Listen, there's a fair on The Green next weekend. It's nothing much, just pony rides, food booths, that sort of thing. Maybe you'd feel better about being out in public if you weren't alone. What do you think?"

"The Strawberry Festival? I thought about taking Grace to get her out a little."

"How about if I bring the two of you? For a couple hours? We'll make it an afternoon."

Amy hesitates. She looks out to the street, seeing the old stone wall running along the yards, the distant farm with rows of young corn plants lining its fields. It's so easy to not venture out, to stay right here. But still. "If things go well all week with Grace, then okay, that sounds nice. Maybe a fair would help her."

"All right then," George says, jangling his keys in his hand. "I'll call you later in the week to see if we're still on." He reaches for Grace on the swing and gives her foot a shake. "And to see if someone would like to ride a pony there."

Amy smiles. "And thanks again for the swing," she calls after him as he heads to his truck. He waves back at them, and Amy thinks it's more than a swing he's given her. It's a summer with her daughter, in the shade of an old tree.

———

When Detective Hayes calls later that morning wanting to stop by with further questions, Amy's long easy summer seems out of reach once again.

"Can I get you a cup of coffee, Detective?" she asks when he arrives.

"No, thanks. This won't take long." He sets a briefcase on her kitchen table, unsnaps two clips and opens the top. Papers and file folders are neatly stacked inside. He lifts out a pen and notepad. "I understand your reluctance to go out, so I hope you don't mind my stopping by. It's just that I like to check in to see how things are going."

"It hasn't been easy, that's for sure."

"I'm sure it hasn't, but time is critical and I do have a few questions, especially about Grace. Have you gotten any details from her at all?"

Amy sits down and crosses her hands on the blue table. "Nothing," she answers. "I've tried a few times, but she just clams up."

Detective Hayes snaps the case closed. He sets it on the floor and flips open his pad to a blank page. "That's understandable, she went through a lot. How about yourself? Any new details come to mind since we last talked?"

"No. Nothing of significance, anyway."

"Stop right there, Amy. Everything is significant. Every detail. The more we know, the better picture we get of the perpetrators. One random characteristic can tie everything together so it all makes sense. A tone of voice or accent, a brand of shoe, any little thing."

Amy watches him waiting, pen poised over his notebook. She stands and opens a kitchen drawer to retrieve her sketch pad. There's a moment of uncertainty when it feels as though the pad is her own diary, personal and difficult to relinquish. But she sets it on the table, nodding at him to open it. "I've been under a doctor's care," she begins. The detective studies her first handgun sketch. "I have flashbacks."

Hayes looks up at her. "A flashback can be just as good as a photograph." He lifts the page to the next picture, a second angle of the same gun.

"Dr. Berg advised me to keep a pad and put down, either in words or pictures, any new images that I saw." She sees the next sketch in the pad, one of Grace's upper body with a man's arm wrapped around it, his large watch visible. "He thought it might help me process the day. And that something might help the investigation."

"What is this?" Hayes asks when he sees the picture she drew just this morning, right after George left. It shows a man's hand covering hers, both hands slightly cupped.

Amy sits and slides her chair close to point out the details. "It's a hand of one of the gunmen. Remember I said there was a struggle for my daughter's shoe?"

"Yes."

"This image really bothers me. I guess it's because I was so near to him." The pencil sketch shows their hands atop the shoe. "We were inches apart," she explains. "I saw everything so close, I felt his grip, I heard his breath. And his hand, it was warm. That surprised me, that feeling." Finally she shakes her head in frustration and pulls the sketch pad closer. "There's something more, I *know* there is. And I'm not seeing it."

"But you got the shoe back?"

"Not until later. This was the man whose gun I witnessed up close. When we struggled for the shoe and I looked up at his face beneath that hosiery, I flinched. That's when he took the shoe and backed off."

"He took the shoe? What did he do with it?"

"I guess he put it on Grace's foot. When I got her back that night, she had on both her shoes."

"In your picture, he isn't wearing any gloves."

"No. No, he didn't have gloves on."

"That shoe should have been checked for prints."

"It wasn't. Grace had it on, and now I have it here, in her room."

"For Christ's sake. It's probably no good to us now, but can I see it?"

And just like that, suddenly, there's a new sliver of hope. Just a sliver, she feels it. A mountain. An ocean. A fingerprint. That might be all it takes to put an end to this. "That night of the kidnapping, I put her things in the closet and haven't touched them since. Her jeans, shirt, everything."

"Do you have a bag? A plastic bag, maybe?"

She retrieves a brown lunch bag from a drawer near the refrigerator. "How's this?"

"That'll work fine."

Upstairs, she points out the pink and white saddle shoes sitting on the top shelf of Grace's closet. Holding them by only the shoelace, Detective Hayes picks them up, one at a time, and drops them in the bag.

"I know it's difficult for you to go out still, but I'll need you to stop in at the station to be fingerprinted."

"Me?"

"Yes. These will be dusted and if we get clear prints, I'll need to differentiate yours from any others."

"All right, I can stop in. Do you think the kidnapper's prints can be deciphered too?"

"I don't know, Amy. At this point, I just don't know what we'll find."

The detective steps to the window and looks out to the yard where Celia is pushing Grace in her new swing and Amy can't help but wonder, while watching the small child, if he feels that ocean, too. That mountain. Hoping with one single set of fingerprints to end this, finding that same thrill as when the swing flies so high, it feels as though your feet will touch the sky.

———

There's something about that voice, that swagger in it, that gets his customers smiling, or tapping a foot as they consider the meat cases. Arranging a tray of boneless center cut pork chops in the display case, George hears only that, Sinatra's voice on the stereo system. But then another voice comes through, louder than Frank's.

"Mr. Carbone?"

He straightens and wipes his hands on his black apron. "What can I do for you?"

"Detective Hayes, Addison Police." Hayes shows his identification. "Do you have a few minutes?"

His brother was right. The leads must've run cold and they're back for more questions.

"Sure." George motions to a small office near the back workroom, turning down the music on his way there. A wooden desk, two file cabinets, an extra mismatched chair and a large bulletin board fill the space. "Have a seat, Detective. How can I help you?" George leans up against the desk front, his arms folded in front of him. Years of playing poker count for something. Though he feels a nagging prickle of perspiration, he wears his poker face. Reveal nothing, show nothing.

Detective Hayes lifts a briefcase to his lap. "Well, Mr. Carbone."

"George. Call me George."

"Okay, George." He glances over his shoulder. "What a business you run. Been here long?"

"Just over ten years. Took it over from my father."

"Nice place, definitely. Food looks great." Hayes opens his briefcase. "So listen, I like to check in with my witnesses periodically and see how they're doing. If anything new has come to mind."

"Sounds reasonable."

"All right then." Hayes pulls his notepad from the briefcase and jots down a few lines of information. "There's something I wanted to verify with you, Mr. Carbone. George."

"Shoot."

"When the Trewist girl was given to you at the market, you didn't notice any weapons in the kidnappers' possession. Is that right?"

"Yes it is. It was kind of dark out, though."

"But you were called over to a car. And the girl, Grace, was put in the parking lot from the back seat of that car?"

"Correct."

"And when that happened, the car's door must have been open."

"It was."

"So the car's interior light would have come on, with the door open."

George pauses, watching the detective. Nate is right again. His best defense is ignorance. "It may or may not have been illuminated. I really don't remember."

"Nothing comes to mind? An interior seat color? A person's hair as they set the girl out? A fabric of clothing, a sleeve maybe?"

George knows damn well exactly who sat in the car, what they were wearing, what they looked like. He also knows damn well that he can straight-up confess right here, right now. He considers the detective waiting, pen poised. "No. Nothing," he answers. "Do you have a suspect in mind?"

"Just doing a little fishing." Hayes makes a note in the pad. "How about on the car seats? Maybe they got careless and left a nine-millimeter in view? You wouldn't have noticed anything by any chance, papers, a weapon, a cell phone in the dim light?"

George lets out a low whistle while his heart pounds in his chest. "Oh you're wrong there. Weapons I would have noticed."

"Seems they covered their bases pretty well."

George shrugs. "People make mistakes. You've got to follow through, I guess."

"Anything else you might recall in that low light?"

"No, nothing more than I've already reported."

The detective flips his notepad closed and sets it in the briefcase. "You okay?" he asks when he looks over at George.

"Yeah. Why?" George asks, shifting his position.

"You must handle a lot of raw meat in here." Hayes tips back his chair and looks out at the work area behind him. Meat grinders and a bone saw are readily visible on a long countertop. "You've got the air temperature pretty low."

"Have to. Health regulations."

"That's what I figured." He points to George's face. "You're sweating."

"Jesus." George quickly brings his hand to his forehead.

"It's tough, I know," Hayes adds, snapping the case closed. "Being involved in a crime does funny things." He stands then, the briefcase hanging from his grip. "Listen, if you think of anything, give me a call, would you?" Hayes reaches into his pocket and hands him a business card.

"Sure." George walks him out into the showroom while tucking Hayes' card in his pocket. "You, too."

"What's that?" Detective Hayes turns toward George.

"If you catch those guys, let me know. We'll all rest easier."

"Oh, you'll know about it. You're an eyewitness. I'm hoping you could identify a voice at least." He extends his hand for a shake. "We'll be in touch."

George shakes the detective's hand and watches him leave, waiting at the door until he is long out of sight.

Ten

*I*T MIGHT HELP HER TO *have an emotional release.* The child psychologist saw right through Grace's growing silence to the source of it. *At our next appointment, we'll try play-acting, association cards, that sort of thing. Her fear is bottled up inside her and she needs to rid the feelings from her system, to get mad, to cry,* Dr. Brina had said.

Are there association cards for adults? What would elicit a response from Amy? Because she needs it too, to get mad, to purge the rage from her system. Slamming her hand on the steering wheel while driving isn't cutting it. Wouldn't she love to go face-to-face with the men who subjected her child to this? To lean in like a drill sergeant and spew her thoughts at them?

By the time she gets home and unbuckles Grace from the car seat, she's still too mad to get afraid of the voices coming from the house. How can someone be inside? If anything, it makes her even angrier, this violation of her home, this thought of what else can go wrong. She and Grace walk the flagstone path from the driveway to the back door and hear conversing, arguing even, in her kitchen. She turns to Grace and holds a stern finger to her pursed lips, shushing her firmly. Standing off to the side, she peers through the paned windows on the farm-style door but sees nothing out of place. It's only when she turns the key in the lock does she realize the voices come from a talk show on the radio.

But still, something's not right. Something that has her set the keys lightly on the kitchen table and silently tug Grace's jacket from her arms. Something that keeps her ears tuned as she shuts off the countertop radio and walks through the rooms.

Something that makes her question what she thought she knew, that she shut the radio off before they left earlier.

———

George cuts off a stretch of butcher's twine. He slides it beneath the pork loin, pulls the twine tightly around one end and makes a square knot, leaving a long length on one side of the knot. Laying the twine along the length of the roast, his thumb holds the knot firmly in place as he wraps the string around the meat. A quick visual check confirms the tension is just right as very little of the juices seep out. He lifts the loop at his thumb and passes the end of the twine underneath, then pulls the twine upward to tighten it around the roast.

Dean serves the lunch customers out front and has switched the stereo from Sinatra to a midday news report. The armored truck heist manhunt has been expanded from the eastern seaboard to the west coast. Reward amounts spiral as authorities suggest that professional, lifelong criminals played a hand in Addison's headlines.

Played a hand. George stands at the counter in his black apron and continues wrapping and tying the pork loin in one-inch increments until the entire length has been tied. If only they knew how *playing a hand* spiked the crime. It's like paging through some old photo album in his mind, the images he remembers of Nate always playing a hand with fate. There he is climbing trees unfit for climbing, staying in the water until lightning strikes close, flirting with fast cars and bikes, skiing precipitous black-diamond slopes and walking blindly into an early volatile marriage. Moving back home after his divorce, he seemed to regroup. But after their father died, the gamble took different shapes as it escalated from weekly poker games to horse racing to the slots, each one strung together somehow, with Nate incrementally increasing the tension and tightening the knot of risk.

George manipulates the roast, checking for tautness. He tightens each tie, then wraps the string around the meat lengthwise, bringing it back to the original knot. Too much pressure on the twine will misshape the roast. He pulls just tight enough, then ties one last knot in the string to secure the work he has done.

Just like Nate did, perfectly securing his work. He tied him up hand and foot in his ultimate gamble until George can't make a single move without feeling those strings pull.

———

"Now don't get mad at me," Celia says when she turns her car into the driveway of a small ranch house and parks in the shade of an oak tree. They had gotten cones to-go on the way, and she bites into the last of hers before wiping her fingers on a napkin. "The listing agent needs me to stage this for an open house, but I wanted to ask you something first."

"I won't get mad, Cee," Amy answers, holding a double-scoop, fudge-swirled vanilla cone. "What's up?"

"For starters, what do you think of this house?"

Amy glances out the passenger window, aware of Grace behind her in the car seat, spooning her strawberry ice cream from a small cup. The neighborhood is one with older homes pressed close together on shaded lots. "It's pretty," she says of the cream and brick-front ranch.

"It's got new siding and a new roof, too. Move-in condition." Celia steps out, opens the car's back door and lifts Grace up, ice cream and all. Together they walk to the front entranceway where a garden bench and antique milk can sit on the stoop. Celia holds Grace on her hip and shifts a notepad and pen from one hand to the other. A realtor's lock box hangs from the front door handle. "Do me a favor?" she asks Amy. "Punch my password on the keypad and get the key out."

"What's the code?" Amy tips up the lock box, waiting.

"Twelve fifteen. My birthday."

Amy presses the numbers, one, two, one, five and the lock releases.

"Go ahead and open it up," Celia says around Grace in her arms. She strokes the girl's hair as they step inside, where the living room leads to a small dining room with sliders to a deck. "Okay," she says, setting Grace and her ice cream down before taking a quick breath. "Now for my real question. I'm just going to put it out there."

"Celia. What is it already?"

"It's just that ... Well I'm wondering if you would consider buying this house."

"Wait. You want *me* to buy it?"

Celia nods. "When it came on the market, I thought of you right away."

"Why?" They walk through to the kitchen, finding sleek modern cabinets and countertops, an island with pendant lights and stainless steel appliances. Amy sits at a stool at the breakfast bar and hands Celia her cone so she can lift Grace and her ice cream cup. "Upsy-daisy," she says, settling her daughter on her lap.

Celia sits on a stool beside Amy and gives her the cone back. "It's just that you're all alone in that big old farmhouse now and I get worried."

"But I'm not alone. I've got Grace and you're right down the street. My parents are a phone call away. Even Mark's things are still there," she adds while licking around the fudge-swirled scoop. "My life's in that house, Celia."

"But it's a big place to take care of alone. This house is small, the yard work is next to nothing, so upkeep is easy. And hey, it's really close to your shop and to the school. You and Grace can walk together in a few years."

Amy shakes her head no while biting into the cone.

"I thought it was something I could do to help. You know. That maybe you'd feel safer in a nice, small place?"

"With a concrete countertop and subway tile backsplash? Seriously?" Amy takes Grace's plastic spoon and helps her fill it with strawberry ice cream from her cup.

"I know," Celia says. "Your kitchen, that beautiful country kitchen. The knotty pine cabinets, that awesome blue farm table, your hearts and roosters everywhere. And the food, the coffee, the life that happens in that gorgeous room. Okay, what was I thinking? Even *my* heart would break if you parted with it."

Amy stuffs the last of her cone into her mouth and pulls a paper napkin from her purse. "Wait," she says around the ice cream. "You tricked me, didn't you?"

"What do you mean?"

"Taking me and Grace out for ice cream was all a ruse. Just to get us here, wasn't it?"

Celia shrugs. "It worked."

"Oh you owe me one. Seriously. Like, right now. Because I could definitely go for another scoop. How about you, Gracie.

Hm?" Grace scrapes her spoon around the empty cup that Amy holds. "Want more ice cream?" So this is new, the way she always presses Grace to respond now. It scares her that her words are fewer and fewer each day.

"I thought it might distract Grace, too. Get some smiles going on," Celia adds quietly.

"Thanks." Amy wipes a dribble of ice cream from Grace's chin, then lightly tickles her cheek.

"Okay then, so no to this house. But would you at least get a security system? Or even a dog?" Celia asks.

"We'll see. I'll think about it, anyway."

Celia gives her a smile and a quick hug. "If you ever change your mind though, you let me know."

From Amy's lap, Grace reaches her open arms up for a hug, too. "You're such a sweetie!" Celia bends and hugs her close. "After a hug like that, one more ice cream coming up, ladies. Let me just take some quick notes on lighting and furniture groupings here, first."

Amy glances back into the empty dining room. "It amazes me how you transform these houses, Cee. How do you even know where to begin?"

"If there's one thing I've learned staging homes, it's this. Buyers love picturing themselves in staged homes. But the secret, for me, is not to show them the lives they already have. A house sells every time I show them the lives they *want* to have."

As she walks away jotting down design notes, all Amy can think is this: If Celia could somehow stage this house with the life she *used* to have, one without fear, one where Grace's happy voice filled the rooms again, one where she didn't do a double take at every shadow or turn at every noise or see a bank parking lot every night before falling asleep, she'd buy this house in a heartbeat.

Eleven

NIGHTMARES COME TO LIFE WITH strangers. George knows that going out in public still frightens Amy. At the Strawberry Festival, people mill about, coming up from behind, turning corners in front of them like looming reflections in a crowded house of mirrors. He stays close, linking his arm through hers, talking and pointing out the sights.

"Look," he says. "Maybe Grace would like that?" Two young women paint strawberries high on the children's cheeks. Amy lifts Grace onto the bench and keeps her hands on her daughter's shoulders the entire time. Grace tips her head down as the paintbrush strokes her face and the painter speaks softly, telling her how pretty she is, asking her age.

Afterward they walk slowly around Addison's Green. Craft booths line one end, selling twig wreaths, sterling jewelry, handmade rag dolls and driftwood paintings. At the Women's Club booth, Amy buys Grace a sweatshirt screen-printed with smiling strawberries. She ties it around her daughter's waist.

"Do they come in adult sizes?" George asks the attendant.

"Oh sure," she answers. "They're all the rage today."

He looks at Amy, sizing her up. "Give me an adult small," he says, pulling his wallet from his pocket. He drapes the sweatshirt over her back, tying the sleeves loosely around her shoulders.

Food booths selling sausage sandwiches and foot-long hotdogs and cotton candy crowd the center of The Green. They walk past to a midway where a half dozen game tents boast stuffed animals and fuzzy stuffed strawberries as prizes.

"Do you want to play something?" Amy asks.

"Well. It's been a long time, I might be a little rusty." He steers them over to the games and tries his hand at tossing Ping-Pong balls into clustered fish bowls, consistently missing his target. But it doesn't matter. What matters is the way Amy hoists Grace up to see, the way they laugh together. They move on and pick the wrong numbers in the big spinning wheel of chance.

"Three baseballs, three tries! Win a prize!" a caller yells out.

George turns to see six clay bottles stacked pyramid-like on a table. "Now we're talking," he says. "The midway meets its match."

"Knock them all down in three shots, you win a keychain," the caller explains. "You've got a pretty good arm, so do it in two shots for the fuzzy strawberry. One shot, you hit the jackpot."

George takes three baseballs in his open hand. He sets two down, turns sideways and eyes the towering bottles. It all comes back to him: the weight of the ball in his palm, the eye-hand coordination, the focus of the game. But something else is there, too. He turns and scans the midway crowd, sensing that someone is following him, watching his every move.

"What are you doing?" Amy asks. "Eyeing the runner back to first?"

He looks long at Amy, certain the odd game of hide and seek continues behind them. "He wanted to steal second," George tells her. "Now. Here's the pitch." He joggles the ball and follows through with a strong shot, clearing the tower from the table in one loud clatter. The caller presses a button setting off whistles and whoops so that people passing by stop and look.

"Here you go," George says when he bends down to Grace. She opens her arms to a teddy bear the color of honey. When she looks back up at George, he winks at her. "Say hi to Bear."

"Bear?" She pulls the stuffed animal close and presses her cheek against its soft fur.

"Thank you," Amy whispers before taking Grace's hand and leading them to the hansom cabs circling The Green. When Grace reaches out to touch one of the horses, George lifts her up onto his shoulders to give her a good view of the animals. He holds her ankles as she leans close to touch the fur, laughing when a horse's skin quivers beneath her tentative touch.

"Which one do you like best?" he asks Grace, and she points to a jet-black horse pulling a white carriage with red leather seats. So he pays for a double ride around the festivities, lifts Grace off his shoulders and sits her on the seat, Bear in her lap. He and Amy sit across from her beneath the carriage canopy, out of the sun and away from the crowds.

"How are you doing with all this?" he asks Amy.

"We're having a great time. It actually feels good to be out for a change."

George sits back beside her. Sawhorses barricade car traffic from the streets surrounding The Green, leaving only the horses and buggies making their rounds. Big carriage wheels turn on the gritty pavement and the horse hooves clop in a slow, easy rhythm. Many of the surrounding colonial homes are registered with the Historical Society. Widows' walks top some roofs closer to the cove. George pictures captains' wives keeping a lookout for their husbands' ships returning from sea trade back in the eighteenth century.

Tall oaks looking to be as old as the homes, their towering limbs stretching far over the street, throw large pools of shade below.

All the while he never stops being aware of Amy beside him, their bodies shifting slightly with the carriage ride. After the first trip around The Green, the swaying motion lulls Grace. Amy reaches across to lift her and Bear onto the seat beside her, and Grace sleeps curled in the corner. If only he could reassure Amy, if he could tell her that her daughter was fed that day, and had a blanket. Elliott told Nate she watched a cartoon movie and napped. She played and talked with Angel. Any guns were put away once their purpose was met in obtaining the truck.

But he can only pick up the pieces from here. The carriage veers onto Main Street and heads toward the cove, passing a large old barn and historic homes gracing the entranceway to the serene inlet off the Connecticut River. Clusters of wildflowers grow from gaps in a colonial-era stone wall fencing off surrounding woods; old maple trees shade weathered picnic tables; sailboats drift on the calm, silver water, their sails sun-bleached white. The carriage wheels crunch over the stones in the packed dirt parking area.

"Is he supposed to drive down here?" Amy asks.

"Only under special circumstances."

"And I'm guessing you convinced him this was special?"

"Yes, I did. There's something soothing about the water. An old beach friend once told me it cures what ails you."

Amy looks out at the little harbor. "I haven't been here in a while," she says as the carriage slows. "Grace and I like to have a picnic lunch under the trees and feed the ducks."

Their driver pulls up on the reins, sets the brake and steps off the carriage. "Okay, folks. You've got a few minutes."

The horse shifts its weight while the driver stays close by, skimming a few stones on the water. A brown timber barn, the old Christmas Barn gift shop, stands on a gentle hill beyond the cove's far shore. Someone hung a large flag covered with painted strawberries over its doorway for the festival. The water stretches before them reflecting the blue sky on its surface, its ripples catching sparkles from the high afternoon sun.

"Why can't it just be this?" Amy asks.

The scent of flowers and dew and spring fill the air. Grace sleeps deeply in the sweet warmth, beneath the shade of the carriage's white walls. And so George wonders what more Amy is seeing, or feeling. "What do you mean?" he asks.

"This spring day … It's beautiful. But so was that day at the bank," she continues softly. "So peacefulness is deceptive. The sun and sky looked just like this. Everything seemed perfect, but it wasn't."

"Well today it is. It really is, Amy," George assures her. "I know it's hard for you to trust it, but it's all how you choose to see it." His arm reaches around her shoulder and she closes her eyes with his touch. "Don't block it out," he says. "Look at me."

Amy does, then looks away, out at the lapping water. They sit silently and it only makes him more aware of her, of her breathing, of her anxiety, of the strawberry sweatshirt draped over her back, of why he's a part of her life, of the moment their hands met in a bank parking lot. The lengthening silence intensifies every truth in his mind and so he tries to change it. His fingers graze her cheek, turning her face back to him. "You can find the good. You have so much already, but can't see it clearly right now."

She still doesn't talk, but this time, she doesn't look away. This time, they closely watch each other until his fingers light on her cheek and he leans closer, pressing his lips to hers. Just for a moment, just lightly. Just until he realizes that if he's being watched, this kiss brings the crime to an entirely new territory.

One that Reid, Elliott and his brother will never accept. And so he closes his eyes, raises his other hand to Amy's face and cups it as his kiss deepens for only a moment longer, long enough to feel her hair against his hands, long enough to feel her breath catch as she kisses him back, long enough for his inhale to be regretful when he pulls away, his hands still holding her face as she whispers his name. She takes one of those hands and sits back watching him until the horse nickers and stamps its foot, the driver turning back to them then.

———

They eat sweet sausage sandwiches and pink cotton candy, listen to a local swing band and ride the carousel. Later they run into Celia and her husband Ben, so Amy introduces them over strawberry shortcake and coffee together, with Ben and George talking up the latest baseball stats. George doesn't take her and Grace home until Amy uses all the stimulation she can from the festival, keeping her daughter awake and alert until the end of the day. She fears that Grace's new tendency to sleep stems from her inability to process the crime. Dr. Brina's comment has stuck. Grace hasn't cried at all, hasn't screamed or even had a temper tantrum. Is it all bottled up inside her little body, tiring her?

Relieved to finally be back in her farmhouse, Amy puts Grace to bed before sitting on the living room sofa and pouring two iced teas. George's voice comes to her from the kitchen, where he checks in with Dean on her telephone. She sips her drink and walks to the front windows, looking out at the evening. A violet horizon hangs over the western sky, beyond the old farm at the end of the street.

"I need to tie up three roasts tomorrow?" George asks. "Okay, I'll stop in tonight and pull them from the freezer."

The resonance of his voice reaches her. She listens closely and finds comfort in its sound. Maybe it is because of the perfect day he arranged. Or maybe it is the sunset and the coming summer with its possibilities.

"How about the flank steaks? Did the sale move those?"

Amy touches the cold glass to her cheek, listening, feeling the very idea of him. She hears his intonations with crystal clarity, imagining that this must be what is meant by a blind person's acute hearing compensating for their loss of vision. His solitary voice, and the assurance of it, has grown familiar now.

"No wonder. It's a good barbecue weekend."

There are quiet pauses when he listens to Dean. She thinks of his kiss at the cove, and listening to his voice feels intimate now.

"Cripe, not again," George says from the kitchen. "Damn it, that machine's got to go."

And just like that, every heightened sense stands on red alert. Setting her glass down on the table, she hugs her arms around her waist and reminds herself what she has come to realize through all this.

Nothing is what it seems. Nothing. It is *George* standing in the kitchen, George Carbone, *not* one of the kidnappers. She stays at the window and listens to hear his voice again, to hear George. Not the man she had confronted in the parking lot.

"Amy? Is something wrong?" George slowly turns her away from the window.

She hesitates, shaking her head. "It's nothing, really."

"What do you mean? You seem upset."

She reaches the back of her hand to his face, to know it's him, and he folds his hand over it. "I guess I'm still having a hard time with this."

"With this." After a pause, he asks, "With us?"

"No."

"Okay." He gently releases her hand and walks to the sofa, watching her.

"I heard you talking," she admits.

"To Dean?"

"Yes." She turns to the window again, her arms still folded around her. "It's silly, really. It's something you said."

"Me?"

She glances at him as he lifts his iced tea. He looks tired. Warm June air brings out a wave in his dark hair while the dim lighting shadows his face. "George," she says as she moves to the sofa. She sits beside him, remembering that she's sitting safe in her own home, on her acre of land with a new tire swing hung outside waiting for beautiful moments with her daughter. It isn't fair to think of George, the kind man for whom she finds herself caring, in the same thought as the man who struggled for Grace's shoe. "I'm sorry."

"Don't be sorry. Just tell me what's bothering you."

Amy stares at him. "Cripe."

A long moment comes between them, as though he is waiting for more. "I don't get it," he finally responds.

"Cripe. You said it on the phone. And one of the kidnappers said that same word to me."

"If it makes you feel any better, I was talking with Dean about an old meat grinder. It's on the fritz."

Angel scampers across the living room floor, a scrap of fur alive with energy. "Apparently the kidnapper said it in front of Grace, too," Amy tells him. "I hear her say it sometimes."

"Grace says it?"

She nods and takes his hands in hers, running her thumb over his calloused skin. "It's okay. You didn't know."

"Are you sure that's the word?"

"I remember everything he said, George. I've heard it a thousand times in my head since then. But it's how he said it, like he was trying to help me. *Cripe, just give them the hour.* As though that's all it would take and then everything would be over." She closes her eyes and feels her knees scraped raw, feels that day. "I don't know if giving them the hour was a bargain with the devil or with God, but sometimes, like right now, there are moments when it feels like the bargain will never end."

Twelve

Detective Hayes tries to link the pieces. Somewhere, beneath a clip or in a handwritten margin note or in the shadow of a photograph, an implication waits to spring out at him. When Officer Pine leans against the door jamb to the closet-sized office, Hayes looks up from the folders, papers, photographs and scribbled notes, clipped and labeled and filed and stapled in neat piles.

"What do you have?" Pine asks.

"One of two things."

"Number one?"

"Nothing."

"Nothing?"

"Right. A crime transpired in mere minutes in an empty parking lot. There are no witnesses other than the victims. I have a stolen armored truck loaded with four million dollars because the banks were stacking the vaults that day. The truck proceeded on its merry way to its next scheduled stop so as not to attract any attention. Successfully, too, I might add. Currently being rechecked for prints and any hair, fabric threads, fingernails. Anything. I have four perpetrators, faces brilliantly concealed, though all appeared to be Caucasian, as best as can be deciphered, maybe thirty to fifty in age."

"Well now. That narrows things down."

"The weapons are a real help, too," Hayes adds. "Forty-fives and nine-millimeters. As common as peppermint gum. And I have an unaccounted-for block of time between the robbery and the return of the kid. No clues, no witnesses, no evidence. They just vanished. And don't forget the victims. Two armed truck employees, the driver and the hopper, dismantled in less than sixty seconds. Not enough time to garner details. I have a distraught young mother, widowed, with unclear memory except for flashbacks. I have a butcher who stumbled upon the kid in a shady parking lot at dusk. Minimal to zilch visibility. Oh. And I have a two-and-a-half-year-old child hostage who has stopped talking."

"Okay. Nothing. What's the second possibility?"

"Perfection. They pulled off the perfect crime. A heist in an empty parking lot with no witnesses, knowledge of the armored truck schedule that buys them time, perfect masks, typical clothes every other guy out there is walking around in, a stricken widow, a hostage drop in the worst light of day, and oh yeah, my best witness can't talk."

"Don't forget the cat."

"Right. Which the humane society and local shelters have no record of."

"So how's it perfection?"

"It's the domino effect," Hayes explains. "Every vague, indistinct fact, from the use of a child to the lighting of the day, was intentional, falling right into place and bumping the creeps to their destination, probably on a tropical island right about now. I'm sure there are dominoes that I'm not seeing, but the ones that I do see flipped down and around, up and down like magic, every single one moving the crime unimpeded along its path."

"I guess we need to find more dominoes."

"Yeah." Hayes turns to glance out the window behind him when a motorcycle thunders past outside. "One that twisted a little when it fell."

Amy gathers her purse, stands and straightens her skirt. She's heard enough. She stopped in at the police department on a whim, hoping to inquire about any progress in the investigation since she'd been fingerprinted over a week ago. When the receptionist sat her in this empty office adjoining Hayes' until he was free, Amy had no idea she would hear the full truth laid out. When the motorcycle blows past, she takes a resigned breath, walks out of the office, down the hallway, and out the Exit door without saying a word to Hayes. There would be no point in hearing the stacks of paper rifled through again, no point in photographs being unclipped from forms, no point in hearing another version of the same explanation that they've got nothing.

———

George knows without looking. Summer sounds from the hills outside come through his windows. Robins' song and a distant lawn mower blend with the June air. On Wednesdays, Dean opens up the shop and grinds the hamburger or debones chicken thighs, and George uses the morning to run errands or finish paperwork or get a haircut. Today a noise stops him, and he knows. It silences the robins and drowns out the distant mower.

Nate has bought a bike. He bought into the dream. Two brothers, two Harley Davidsons. And what the sound of that approaching bike engine does is trigger hearing another sound, that of baseball cards clipped to their bicycle spokes. Looking out at the long drive, he sees Nate, nine-years-old and pedaling furiously to keep up with him, flying down the neighborhood streets on simmering summer days. Nate's voice carried to him, mixing in with the wind and the rat-a-tat-tat of the baseball cards, planning their routes, coasting down hills, dreaming of bigger bikes. Later, in a dark lounge, how many times did his brother's voice beguile with that same dream? It never stopped, Nate's way of envisioning the adventure of cruising the open road together on real motorcycles, sans the baseball cards.

George steps out his front door and waits in the warm sunshine for his brother to pull up, because he just knows it's him. Nate is still bent on shaping his dreams into real life. The heist went down. So will the bike trip. Those childhood baseball cards meant something. Pretend doesn't exist in Nate's mind. Maybe it never has.

The Harley pulls up alongside the curb, its chrome-spoked wheels spinning to a slow stop. Nate wears dark sunglasses, jeans, black tee and leather boots. "Get on," he yells over the idle, hitching his chin toward the seat behind him.

George considers the bike, knowing he'll get on. Nate will believe he's giving in to his grin that asks *What's the big deal? Let's just go for it, man. Feel good.*

But that isn't what has him step closer. It's that now he has to keep tabs on how his brother orchestrates his own world, his own laws. And the only way to get inside Nate's head is to go along with him and observe. To hike his leg over the seat and settle in behind him.

Then it's just the two of them moving through Addison's back roads on a Harley Davidson. This time they don't end up in a bank parking lot. This time there are no armored trucks or kidnapped girls. This is a good high, meant to bring George back for more.

Railroad tracks run dead-center through town, one side of the tracks more rural with old homes with varying roof peaks and gingerbread trim, the other side more congested with tended houses on precise, manicured yards, grocery stores and banks nearby. Nate drives over the railroad tracks, through town to the Turnpike where he weaves in and out of car back-ups, cruising the highway until exiting and coasting around The Green. He parks the bike in front of Joel's Bar and Grille.

"You're fucking crazy," George says. He drags a hand back through his hair and shifts in the booth. Except for where the entrance door is propped open, not much sunlight reaches into the neighborhood bar. The hum of passing cars and pedestrian voices comes in piecemeal.

"No I'm not." Nate fills two glasses from the pitcher on the table between them.

"What would you call it then?"

Nate throws back a long swallow. "Buying a bike? Taking advantage of the situation. There's one with your name on it waiting for you. Jump in."

George lifts his glass, watching his brother closely. "Water's fine?"

"Something like that."

"I thought we weren't supposed to spend the cash."

"Not so anyone will notice. What's the big deal with a bike?" Nate turns in the booth, stretching his legs out. "We had plans, remember? The call of the open road."

"That was talk, Nate. Bullshit."

"No it wasn't."

"Dreams, then."

"Yours for the taking."

"Not now. That dream was for when we were older. Kids grown, no obligations."

"You got any now?"

George doesn't answer.

"What?" Nate asks.

"Nothing."

"What are you holding out on me?"

"Nothing, I said." He takes another drink of the beer, setting the mug in front of him.

"It's that woman, isn't it?"

George glances toward the door. How did he end up here, sitting in a local bar at ten-thirty on a Wednesday morning, downing a brew with the rising sun, an illegal millionaire keeping a cautious eye on his dubious brother? What the hell happened? His father would turn in his grave. "Her name's Amy."

Nate shakes his head. "Now you see? I'm not the one who's fucking crazy."

"Why don't you shut up?"

"What are you doing messing around with that dame?" Nate reins his long legs back in and leans his elbows on the table.

George considers his brother. "I've got an obligation."

"The hell you do."

"The hell I don't."

"You're going to screw up, George. The guys won't like it."

"Do you realize what's happened because of that day? Her girl stopped talking after what we put her through."

"We didn't do anything. She was taken care of."

"Right. Ripped out of her mother's arms, stolen away, guns and crazy bullshit going down all around her. Christ, Nate. She's not even three-years-old."

Nate blows out a long breath and tops off his glass. "All right. But you've got to be careful. That Amy, she could figure things out."

"Like what? My face was concealed."

"What about the girl? She might recognize you from being on the truck."

"She was in shock on that truck. I doubt she's going to match me up to the crime."

Nate takes a long swallow of his beer and eyes George. "So what are you doing? You *seeing* her, you know, or just checking up on her?"

George thinks of the day he spent with Amy and her daughter on The Green, right outside the bar he sits in now. He looks from the doorway, from cars passing and kids wheeling by on bicycles, to his brother's face, contemplating how much his brother should, or already knows. "I'm seeing her."

"Damn it. What are you, a martyr? Making things up to her?"

"What if I am? What's your beef with it?"

"You'll slip, George. You'll say something, or she'll wonder about your cash flow, or the girl will somehow remember you."

"Stop right there." George drops his voice. "First of all, there is no cash flow. That money's a frozen asset. Somehow, someway, it's all going back, even if it's dumped off in the middle of the night. I can't live with that bank account in my kitchen."

"You better get used to living with it." Nate leans back in the booth. He points at George, keeping his voice low. "You start screwing around with returning the cash, you'll leave a trail of crumbs leading right back to us. I beat the freaking house that day and you're not going to take me down with some lousy guilt trip."

"What? You took *me* down with that heist, screwed up my whole life, Nate."

"I *fixed* your life. After ten years of walking in Dad's shoes cutting meat instead of playing ball, you're finally set. That's major league cash, man, you can live any dream now. And we worked real hard for it. Someday you'll appreciate it. Just let that money sit for now. That's all you have to do. Forget it and resume your normal life. Can't you get that through your head?"

"I did. It's only *normal* that I see Amy. No one would think twice about how that came about. Fate brought us together when I returned her daughter." He stands up and looks down at Nate. "So you see, I do have an obligation. There won't be any new Harleys parked at my home. I'm not going anywhere and I'm not going to stop seeing Amy. You don't control me, Nate."

Nate squints up at him. "Reid won't like it."

George looks at the ceiling with a deep breath. "If he's got a problem with my life, he can come see me at the shop, okay? Where's he hiding himself anyway?" He imagines one day walking into town hall and seeing Elliott on the town council, or going to buy a new car and Reid's the sales manager.

"I can't tell you, man. And you're still being watched."

George sits again. "I figured as much. By who?"

Nate shakes his head. "Listen, when the Feds keep coming up empty with who took that truck, they'll go back to what they do have and pick it apart. And they have you, George. You. Until that trail is ice cold, you don't know where Reid is, how we planned it, where we all met, how much of that day was planned months in advance, how much was fucking coincidence and who's watching who. All you know is that you spent the day at the casino. With me." Nate leans across the table. "Got it? You're my alibi. I took care of you, guy. You're set for life. Now you've got to take care of me. Like always, you know? We look out for each other."

"You think that's all there is to this? Family taking care of each other?"

"That's right." Nate stands and clasps George's hand with both of his in a shake. "That's right."

———

Does color mean anything? Grace lies on her stomach on the kitchen floor, a rainbow of crayons spread before her. Angel bats the magenta beneath the table, then sits under a chair and watches it roll. Grace carefully selects her colors, her fingers coming to light on first one, then another, as though with artistic thought before she wraps her hand around it. Then she slowly covers page after page of her doodle pad with scribbles and squiggles. Some pages bear what looks like no more than a handful of commas; others are nearly filled with a solid block of color as her arm moves round and round, stopping only to select a new crayon before filling in every white space with thick red or green or blue.

Do they mean anything, the colors and changing hand pressure on the pages? Do they express her daughter's confusion? Anger? Fear? Amy wants to take a few pages herself, pick up the crayons and scream her hand arbitrarily across the paper. She imagines a real scream emanating with the crayon motion. When she looks at Grace, she hopes for it. Any noise, any word or sound coming from her baby's lungs can release that day.

Amy pulls her own sketch pad from the kitchen drawer, lifts the cover and sees the black gun and her daughter's stunned expression. *Come on, Gracie*, she thinks. *Just let it out. Scream, for God's sake. Scream.* But nothing, nothing ever comes.

So she folds the pages of her pad back to a clean page. Then she gets down on her knees beside Grace and sets her pad on the wide-plank wood floor. Angel walks over, stepping lightly. She stops and curls her feet beneath her, watching as Amy shifts her legs and lies flat beside her daughter. She reaches for a brown crayon and presses hard on her own page, her arm moving in slow and angry circles.

———

Once Nate drops him back home, George changes into the same white shirt and black pants he insists his help wears. Before leaving, he picks up his mail, setting the bills on the kitchen counter. Nate's tiled wall rises before him, looking like a panoramic view of a stormy sky, dark gray stone tiles marbled with streaks of cream. He reaches a hand around the side and slides out the fifth stone up from the floor. His fingers find the release beneath the tile, allowing him to pull out a drawer from the wall, a drawer concealed by Nate's craftsmanship. A drawer deep and wide enough to hold two large black duffel bags.

Two black duffel bags that weigh on him always, even as he walks past the wildflower beds and up the green-painted stairs to the front porch of Amy's farmhouse on his way to work. A pot of geraniums sits on a bistro table between two white wicker chairs. The inside door is open and he sees into the house but hears no noise. No chatting voices or rattling pots from the country kitchen with decorative baskets hanging on the heart-dotted wallpaper. No romantic tunes playing on the radio, no telephone ringing in the room where a red ceramic rooster and pewter creamer sit on top of an old wooden potato bin. From the cool shade of the porch, he knocks on the screen door just as Amy rounds the corner.

"Well hi there," she says, walking over and unlocking the latch. "What a nice surprise."

"Hey, Amy," he says. "I hope you don't mind, I thought I'd swing by on my way to work."

"No, not at all," she says, smiling. "Come on in."

She holds the screen door open for him as he steps inside, turns back to her and hesitates for only a moment before raising his hands to her arms, leaning in and kissing her lightly. Her hand rises to his face and he takes it in his, asking "How are you today? Everything's good?"

She leads him through to the kitchen, talking as she does. "We're doing all right. Grace is napping right now." When he leans against the counter, she crouches down and picks up crayons from the floor. George bends and scoops up the last few, setting them on the table. Amy pulls out a chair and sits. "Did you have lunch?" she asks. "I'll make you a sandwich?"

"No, thanks." He still stands, watching her set one crayon at a time in the empty box.

"Grace was doing some coloring." Amy sets the crayon box in a drawer, then goes to the sink and squeezes a dab of dish detergent onto a sponge and washes and rinses the few lunch dishes in the sink, not saying anything, as though he's not there.

"Did you go out anywhere this morning?"

"Just for a quick errand." She turns to the blue farm table and wipes sandwich crumbs into her hand, then reaches for the coffee decanter, fills it with water, sets it back and turns on the coffee maker.

And what George notices is that she's not talking at all while she doesn't stop moving: drying her hands on the dish towel, rehanging it on a chair back, reaching for white coffee mugs from the cabinet, pulling out spoons from the silverware drawer, straightening the forks while she's at it. Doing anything, anything,

anything, but talk. He finally steps behind her at the cutlery and reaches around, taking both her hands in one of his and closing the drawer with the other. They stand there like that, motionless, until he hears her whisper.

"She won't talk, George."

He turns her to him, pressing a strand of blonde hair from her face, waiting for her to say more.

"I don't know what to do," she continues. "Every day she's more and more quiet."

"Listen." He pulls out a chair for her to sit. "Have you been to your bridal shop at all?" he asks as he gets the coffee and pours their cups.

"No. I can't think about gowns and brides right now."

"Maybe that's the problem," he answers, setting their coffee down on the table and sitting with her. "Maybe Grace has to see normal again. You know. Doing things you love. Gowns and lace and happy brides. She has to get past that day."

"But I try, George. I take her outside, on the swing. I had her coloring this morning. We take little walks. I coax her words, begging her to speak."

George is shaking his head, no.

"What?" Amy asks.

"Maybe she's not getting past it because you're not. Amy, even if you have to pretend, it doesn't matter. It's for Grace's sake. Hang veils, order gowns, stop at your friend's antique shop that you told me about."

"Sara Beth."

"Right. Maybe she has some vintage wedding things you can use."

"I don't get it. How would that help Grace?"

"You're all she has, Amy. Just you. And if you're still in that day, she's with you. But if you leave it behind, she'll follow you. *Show* her how."

Thirteen

PLAY HERE ISN'T JUST PRETEND, isn't just fun. The next day, that is especially clear to Amy when they move from the playroom, with its low tables, small chairs and puffy clouds painted on a sky blue wall, to the doctor's office with mahogany furniture and laden medical bookcases. Play is a mirror to her child's mind.

"She's withdrawn even further this week, Dr. Brina."

"Does the regressive behavior persist all day?"

"It's starting to." Grace sits in her lap with her arm around Bear. "I try to engage her as much as I can. The bear is from the Strawberry Festival, which she loved with all the food and sounds, and the horses." She strokes Grace's hair. "Remember the pretty horses?"

"So the stimulation lessens the regression."

"Only when it's almost over the top. And then she sleeps really deeply afterward. But I can't stimulate nonstop. I'm a single mother and have to get back to work. A couple employees open Wedding Wishes for a few hours each day because shipments come in and brides are stopping by, but it's time for me to be back there."

"Of course. It's best for both of you to resume some sense of normal routine." Dr. Brina writes notes in Grace's folder. "But what really worries me is that Grace still hasn't expressed any emotion," the doctor says, glancing up at Amy.

"No she hasn't," Amy answers, almost in fear. "No crying, no anger. Nothing."

"It would help her tremendously to have that release. If you can visualize it, the bad feelings from that day will start to dissipate."

"Is there any way I can help bring that on? To break through this wall?"

"You just keep doing what you're doing. Your role is comforter and you need to remain calm, thoughtful and really connected. Does she still talk to Angel?"

"All the time," Amy answers. "They're thick as thieves, those two. I even bring the cat to my shop when we're there, to keep Grace engaged and talking."

"Good, good," Dr. Brina says as she stands to walk them out. "She'll come around, won't you, Grace? She'll be back to normal soon. You'll see. It just takes time."

But what is normal? When they get home, Amy first brings her daughter into the gown room on the back of the old farmhouse. Two gowns hang on a rolling rack, one tea-length, the tulle stirring in the fresh summer air as though a bride just walked past, her vows whispered softy. But she's been anxious to see another gown that arrived, this one a silver silk brocade from the mid-1920s that she bid for on eBay. Unwrapping the tissue from the fabric, the soft color shimmers beneath her touch.

"See the pretty silver gown, Grace?" Maybe George is right. Maybe if she gets on with her life, Grace will too. She has to try. "Help Mommy hang it up, okay?"

Grace climbs onto a stool beside her and touches the swirled fabric, tracing a finger along the floral brocade. "Do you like it,

Gracie? Hm?" Amy will take anything, any response, as talking. But nothing comes, so she reaches for a padded hanger and lets her daughter hold that while she slips the gown onto it. "It looks like pretty stardust, doesn't it?" she asks as she holds it up and the silver threads glint in the sunlight.

The contrast between this silver gown and a white lace gown hanging on the black dress form will be striking in her shop display window. Two variations of normal, Amy thinks, because it wasn't until shortly after this silver gown had been worn in the 1920s that white became the accepted norm for bridal gowns. So normal changes, then.

Without Angel in the gown room with them, Grace is quiet. She stands in front of the painted shelves for a moment before lifting off a birdcage veil and moving it as though it's living and talking to her. But still, no sound. So has normal changed for them? Is it normal now for Grace to talk to a cat, but not to her? Is scribbling slashes of crayon color on paper, but not verbalizing slashes of emotion, something she'll take for granted now? That's what she'd like to ask Dr. Brina at their next appointment. To define normal.

After putting Grace in for a nap, she goes to make a cup of coffee and stops short in the kitchen. She'd had a coffee this morning, but two cups sit in the sink now, hers and Mark's. It's just like after Mark died; she'd sometimes pour two cups of coffee without thinking as though longing to hear his voice, to feel him close again. Her doctor assured her then that it was part of grief, reenacting old rituals in an effort to hold on to someone gone, particularly with the suddenness of his death.

So does she need him again, now? Would it help to hear what he'd say about their daughter's silent suffering? Why else would his blue mug be sitting in the sink, a ring of dark liquid pooling in the bottom? She empties out the cold coffee, rinses and dries the mug and sets it back up on the shelf, all the while trying to visualize herself pouring coffee into it earlier that morning.

———

How do you know when it's the end? When something's over. When it's the last time you'll see a face. The last time you'll hear a voice, left only with a memory bringing it back, often on the wings of regret. Regret for what you didn't say. Or did. How do you know when you'll never be somewhere again, that you've had your last glimpse of the sea, your last breath of its salt air? Would you cherish it any more, knowing? How do you know when it's the last foul ball you'll catch, the last time your bat will send a fastball into a line drive bringing you to second? The last time you'll feel the summer sun on your face, the touch of a hand in yours. Would knowing make it sweeter, or sadder?

Years ago, George had spent the morning following his father's funeral walking along the high tide line, making peace with a decision. The sea, and its rhythms, and salt air, and deep blue sky meeting the water at the horizon, it all spoke to him. Standing at the edge of the sea had a way of stripping life down to what mattered. And what mattered was his father. He'd never dreamt their phone call the week before would be their last.

He walked back to the cottage then and cleaned up the yard, raking up the winter debris, leaves and twigs that had accumulated over the cold months. His arms, arms that would make something else of his life now, worked with a gentleness as the rake pulled over the grass. Because it was scraping over the last place his father had walked; the last place on earth that he had set his feet; the place where EMTs carefully lifted him onto the stretcher as he took his final breaths. Maybe he'd plant something in this spot. A flowering shrub, or the beach grass his father loved, tall thin blades swaying in the slightest hint of a sea breeze, whispering fleeting memories in their sound.

Afterward, he pulled his two overnight bags from the car and set them on the enclosed front porch. The cottage was musty still. Nate and their father had been there for just that reason, to open it up for the summer. And so George opened all the porch windows to finish what they weren't able to and warm air drifted in with birdsong, carrying a sense of voices on its ethereal wings. That's what life asks of us sometimes, he knew, to step up to the plate and take your place. He went out on the back deck then and sat for several hours on one of the Adirondack chairs facing the lagoon, letting the day unfold on its own as he just let things be, let life be, at the sea. Let the blue heron stand still, the minnows swim, the grasses sway, the tides change. Until Nate's car pulled into the stone driveway.

"George," Nate said, stopping in his tracks when he came out the back screen door.

He didn't answer. He didn't even look at him. Instead his eyes closed with a long breath as the sea life that had hung in limbo for the past few hours suddenly resumed.

"George. What are you doing here?" Nate glanced back into the cottage as though there was an answer there, then back at George. "I thought you left for the airport."

"I'm not going."

"What?"

"I'm not going back. It's all done."

"What are you talking about? You made the cut. You're this close to being called up to the major leagues. George." Nate stepped closer, watching him carefully.

George shook his head. "My decision's made. I can't do it, Nate. I've got to stay here now."

"Here?" Nate crouched down beside his chair. "Bullshit. Those your bags on the porch?" he asked, hitching his head in that direction. "We've got time. I'll get you to the airport."

"Drop it, Nate. I'm staying. I'll go to the shop in a couple days and keep things going for Dad."

"The Main Course? Are you crazy? Dad's gone, George. Let it go. You don't belong there, twenty-five years old and cutting meat."

"Yes I do."

"The hell you do. Your team needs you. After the spring you've been having? You're at the top of your game." Nate stood, pacing the deck, throwing a stone in the still water. "It's baseball, man. It's your thing. You're living the dream."

"We can't let that shop close, Nate. That was Dad's dream. You know that."

"Not for you, it wasn't. His dream for you was playing ball. You're just grieving, George. The funeral was only yesterday. Shit, give yourself time before you decide, you'll see. It's what you've worked for. Don't blow it because of this. You belong on the field."

"Maybe once I did. But not now. I'm staying, like it or not. For Dad."

"I won't let you." Nate looked long at him, then turned on his heels and walked inside.

George could just picture him rushing through the cottage to his bags on the front porch, picking up one in each hand. It would be easy to come under his sway, to let his kid brother's insistence, his kid brother's vision of a baseball dream, get him to change his mind. He could stand, hesitate, then lock up the cottage, convincing himself that it was the right thing to do. But there was the catch. The right thing never needed convincing.

Minutes later, Nate hit the screen door handle with his elbow, then kicked the back door open and headed through the side yard to his car, carrying George's bags. "Let's go, George," he called over his shoulder.

George didn't move. He just sat there in the misty salt air hovering over the marsh, late day sunlight turning the grasses golden, Long Island Sound out beyond the marsh, where he knew gulls swooped and sailboats drifted in the gentle breeze. And he knew what he was leaving behind, could picture clearly exactly how he left it all in the locker room. His mitt, the batting gloves, uniform, a couple favorite bats. The guys on the team. The line drives, the stolen bases, the workouts. But life came down to choices, and whether it was to steal a base or take over your father's business, the one thing baseball had taught him was that once you made that choice, you didn't look back.

"George," Nate called out from his car.

George knew without watching. He heard every bit of the sound on this quiet afternoon at the beach cottage. He heard Nate's keys jangle as he opened the trunk. He heard the thud of his overnight bags being heaved inside, followed by the slam of the trunk. He heard Nate's footsteps on the stone driveway and it made him think that his father's feet made the same sound a few short days ago, at this place he loved. It wasn't until there was a silence, a long minute of it, that George actually turned and saw Nate standing beside the cottage where their father died, tears streaming down his face.

George stood then and their eyes locked on to each other's.

"I didn't mean for it to happen," Nate said, his words nearly choked back by a sob. "It was an accident. Just an accident. Don't quit baseball because of it. Don't walk out on your dream."

George squinted, his throat tight as he fought his own emotion.

"I tried to save him. I did the CPR thing, but it wouldn't work. I couldn't get him back." Nate's face twisted in grief, and in remorse for whatever happened a few days earlier between their father and him. "Don't let baseball die, too, George. You're so close to the majors." He checked his watch and opened the screen door, going in to close up quickly. "We have an hour," he said through the screen. "I'll get you to the airport. Come on, we have time."

As George turned and sat in the white chair again, he heard his brother call out his name once more. Just once. *George!* It carried through the cottage on the sea breeze and kept going, reaching out over the breaking waves, echoing up to the skies above the sea.

———

Standing in front of the bedroom mirror now, after more than a decade had passed since that day, he sees his father looking back at him. It's there less and less now, that glimpse of recognition in his dark eyes, that familiarity in his gaze, the same strong hand rubbing the set of his jaw. And unless he does something to fix his life, and Amy's, his fear is that one of these times, it will be the last time he sees his father this way. Because the more that crime changes him, the more unrecognizable his reflection becomes.

"George!" Nate calls out again from the living room. The poker game had broken up and the other guys had left. Only Nate stayed behind, eating one of the leftover grinders and watching the Yankees on the television. "Come on, you're missing the game."

George walks out to the living room, slipping his arms into a long-sleeve shirt loose over his tee. "I'm going by Amy's for a while."

"What? Now? It's almost nine," Nate says from the couch.

George picks up the remote and shuts off the television. "Get out."

"Okay, okay." Nate stands. "She talk much about that day?"

"Sometimes."

His brother squints at him. "Just be careful, all right?"

"What are you talking about?" George shrugs into the shirt shoulders and heads for the door.

"I'm just thinking about you. You've got a good life with your shop and all now. Real good. Maybe some day you'll enjoy some of that extra money and start living the dream. Is she worth losing it all?"

"Move it," George tells him, holding the door open to the night, watching his brother pass by.

———

When he gets to Amy's, he's a little surprised to see her windows closed up tight, the shades drawn. Summer's in the air and it seems she would want to hear the whisper of it in the leaves, feel the breeze puffing her lace curtains, maybe sit on the front porch, the scent of flowers and dew rising in the evening.

"She's upstairs, checking on Grace," Celia tells him after he knocks. When he steps inside, she continues quietly, "She didn't have such a good day. Maybe you can cheer her up?"

"I'll try," he answers, turning to see Amy coming down the stairs. "Hi there," he says, studying her closely. She wears a long sundress with cowboy boots, her hair down, a turquoise bangle on her wrist.

"George, hey. No card game tonight?" she asks.

"It broke up early. One of the guys, Craig, he and his wife are splitting up. After he told us, the game kind of died. How about here? Everything okay?"

"Celia and I were having movie night."

"Could you get me a soda, Amy?" Celia calls out from the living room over the banter of Danny Zuko and Sandy, and the music of *Grease*.

George takes Amy's hand and leads her into the kitchen, where she pulls the ice tray from the freezer and fills a tall glass with cubes. "How's Grace today?" he asks.

She glances up from pouring soda into the glass. "She's fine, but still not talking."

A quick smile passes over her face, trying, trying to stay strong always for her daughter. He sees it more than she does, and so takes the glass from her hand. "You hold your thought." He brings Celia her drink and returns with Amy's denim jacket. When he holds out the sleeves, she turns and slips into it.

"What are you doing?" she asks.

"I'm taking you out for a drink."

"But Grace—"

"Celia says she'll stay as long as you want. The house is closed up tight, your daughter is safe. Come on, sweetheart." George moves in front of her and takes her hands in his, his voice quiet. "Do this for yourself. The weather's good, your friend is here, the house is locked, bring your cell." He glances at her boots, then moves his hands up her arms to her shoulders. "And do you happen to have a cowboy hat?"

"Yes, actually," she answers, stepping back. "Grace and I have matching hats."

"Bring it," he says with a wink, jangling his car keys and turning to head outside.

———

"No way." Amy glances out at the flashing neon cowboy in the window as George parks his pickup truck at Joel's Bar and Grille. "Line dancing?"

He reaches over and tugs at her cowboy hat. "You know how?"

"Well, yes. But—"

"Oh no," he says, swinging his door open. "No buts about it. Thursday is Line Dancing night and you need to stomp a little fun into your day. Come on."

Inside the bar, the music is loud, the talk and laughter raucous, and a chorus of boot kicking stomps keeps the beat on the wooden dance floor. George takes her elbow and leads her right into the thick of it, leaving no time for hesitation, no seconds for resistance, no moments to think as she hooks her hands on her hips and step-touches her way through a song about breaking hearts. And she wonders if there's any better way to shake off a breaking heart, hers included, than to stomp it off.

George must be thinking the same thing because when she laughs and starts to leave the dance floor after the first song, he shakes his head no, takes her arm and gets her to shuffling and tapping, strolling and swaying through the next two songs, putting her worried heart on hold with honkytonk words of rocking cowboys and good times and footloose attitude. When she takes off her hat and bends into a low bow after the third song, he finally leads her to a small table in the back.

"One drink," she says, breathless. "Really, George. One drink, then I have to go."

"Let's make a deal," he answers, reaching across the table and moving a strand of hair behind her ear. "One drink and one more dance."

Sometimes, like right now, there's just no arguing especially if you've already been swayed. She glances over to the crowded dance floor, then back to him with a grin. "Okay," she finally says. "Deal."

He orders them each a draft beer and she likes that, the way he has them become a part of the whole night at Joel's, completely. When the waitress sets down their drinks, Amy takes a sip, watching him. "Tell me about yourself, George."

George sits back and shifts in his chair. "What do you want to know?"

She tips her head and eyes him. "Tell me about your family."

George looks away and rolls his shoulder.

"Loaded question?" she asks.

He laughs. "No. Well, maybe a little. My parents are both gone. But I've got a younger brother. Nate. He's thirty-six and a little rough around the edges, but he polishes up okay. He's the family risk-taker. The greater the risk, the more determined he gets. Typical kid brother stuff."

"You don't take risks?"

George hesitates. "No," he says then. "I'm not a gambling man."

"But you play cards."

"It's a social thing, not really gambling. It's what happens while we're playing that counts. You know. The talk, the laughs. I play mostly for my brother, as a way to stay in touch. We do things like that. A hand of poker, a ballgame."

"You never married, George?"

He looks at her for a long second. "No."

"A guy like you? You must have had some close calls." She glances over at the almost fluid lines of dancers stomping through another love-gone-wrong song. "No achy breaky line dancing song that suits you?"

He winks and picks up her cowboy hat from the table, setting it on an angle on her head. "Not really. I was seeing someone for a few years, but it didn't work out. My father convinced me we get one shot to do it right, do love right, the way he did with my mother. If it's not love, the marriage won't stand up to life. So it's actually the ultimate risk."

"Marriage? A risk?"

"To be sure you get it right. I mean, we're talking love, and emotion, and two-stepping with the right cowgirl off into the sunset." He raises his drink in a toast to the dancers electric sliding across the floor. "Serious stuff. That's why my brother's divorced. He likes risk, win or lose. He jumped in to a wrong marriage at twenty-one and lost. They broke up in a year. Me? I've had a few chances, once or twice. But I'm also somewhat of a workaholic. So I give most of my time to the shop. It's been in the family a long time and means a lot to me."

"Oh, you're one of those then," Amy says from beneath her hat brim, pulling it down low and eyeing him cautiously. "Married to the job."

"Something like that. I took over the business when my father died."

"Now that's very honorable. And before then?"

141

"Baseball. I was in the minors, Triple-A. And had some good times there. But then there was an accident and it changed everything. Nate and my father were at our summer cottage at Stony Point and Nate had my old man doing work he was probably too old to handle. Things happened, an unfortunate fall from a ladder. And a heart attack. Which came first, we don't really know. Did the heart attack cause the fall, or the other way around? To this day, my brother still feels the blame."

"Oh, I'm so sorry to hear that. It couldn't have been easy, for any of you then. Life deals difficult cards sometimes."

"Isn't that the truth." George takes a long drink of his draft. "Now tell me about yours, Amy."

"About my life?"

"No. About the cards life dealt you today. Celia said you weren't having a good Thursday."

"It's nothing, really."

George raises an eyebrow. "Let me be the judge of that." He reaches across the table, takes her hands in his, and waits.

And she tells him about the nothing behind silent, hang-up phone calls. The nothing overcoming her when she found Mark's coffee cup in the sink. And mostly the nothing that came out of her sweet child's mouth today. "It's all either nothing, or it's my whole life. Sometimes I can't tell which."

George looks past her when the line dancing breaks up and the music shifts to a slow country number about driving and love and destinations in the heart. He stands, gently takes her cowboy hat off her head and sets it on the table, lifts her hands and tells her, "We had a deal. One more."

When Amy stands, he puts an arm around her waist and walks her to the dance floor. She turns and he takes her in his arms, and when he leans close, she hears his words in her ear.

"I was wondering," he begins. "Has Grace ever been to the beach?"

She shakes her head no, nearly moved to tears by the lightness he brings into her life.

"It's the best medicine, you know. The salt air. Why don't we go Sunday? We'll stop at my family's cottage at Stony Point, spend a few hours on the beach, right at the sea."

Amy pulls back and smiles at him. "That sounds beautiful," she says. Her fingers move to the side of his face and when they do, he slips his hand around her neck, tangles it in her hair and presses his mouth to hers and the kiss becomes part of it, the moment when she closes her eyes and imagines the sun reaching the sea in a thousand sparkles, its warmth touching her face, the salt air reaching deep into her lungs, the waves breaking close.

George pulls away then, stroking her cheek before pressing her head against his shoulder. "We'll have a good time. But right now, don't think, don't plan." His arms hold her closer and his body moves with hers. "Just dance."

Fourteen

D O GLIMMERING MOTHER-OF-PEARL PAILLETTES COUNT as wishing stars? Because if the wonder of those star-like vintage sequins could grant a wish right now, Amy has a few she'd like to make. And so she sends a silent wish out to the heavens when the bride-to-be walks out of the dressing room wearing a gown meant somehow just for her. This Princess-line cream silk gown drapes elegantly on the woman. Silver beads and those iridescent paillettes shimmer like stars in the sky.

"It's been close to a year since I saw this," the customer tells her. "My sister Eva and I were passing by and saw it in your window. I'm so glad you still have it," she says while turning on the raised pedestal in front of the full-length mirror.

"She's a designer, a denim designer," Eva tells Amy. "And she incorporates stars in her work."

"Well then, you couldn't custom order a more perfect dress." Amy adjusts the gown's small train. "This one's from the early 1970s and I've seen variations of stars on wedding gowns, but the hand-worked beading on this one is really special. It may even be a couture gown. If you give me your name, I can hold it for you until you decide."

"Maris. Maris Carrington. And you'll only have to hold it for an hour while we shop a little more. I'm so buying this gown today."

"Yes!" Eva exclaims. "She's getting married right on the beach. An evening wedding in August."

"That sounds beautiful. Imagine if a few early stars are out in the sky during the vows?"

"That's what we're hoping," Maris says, pulling her brown hair back off her face as she continues to study the wedding gown. "I'll be wearing my sister's veil for my Something Borrowed."

Amy turns to her daughter sitting on the settee with Bear and a small doll. "Grace, would you get Mommy the flowers please?"

"What a great assistant you have," Eva says, turning to watch Grace retrieve a small bouquet from a low shelf. Grace walks quietly to Maris, stopping a few steps shy.

"Come on, sweetie," Amy says quietly.

Maris bends low and smiles at her, reaching out her hand. In a moment, Grace stretches out her arm and relinquishes the bouquet laced with ribbons.

"Thank you," Maris tells her. "You're a great helper to your Mommy. And the flowers are as pretty as you are."

"Remember," Amy says as Maris turns back to the mirror. She places a very simple veil on her head to complete the look. "When you're choosing your flowers, the shorter the veil, the smaller the bouquet."

"Wow," Eva exclaims quietly at Maris' reflection in the mirror. "Jason's going to love seeing you in this gown."

Amy thinks of Maris as she buckles Grace into her car seat at lunchtime. The idea of getting married right on the beach with the sea and sky spread before you seems almost magical. She hopes for some of that wonder in Grace's life this weekend, when

George takes them to the beach. The sea breeze will lift her hair, the endless blue Long Island Sound fill her vision, the cries of swooping gulls reach her ears, the salt water waves play tag with her toes as she laughs and runs from them. The beach will leave no room for silence.

But for now, the words to gentle love songs come easily to Amy. She'd closed up Wedding Wishes for this lunch hour excursion to buy new bathing suits, playing the radio softly on the drive to the mall. She serenades Grace while driving to the rear entrance of Macy's, where the steel grid work of a new mall wing rises and construction vehicles lumber past.

Once Grace is settled in her stroller, Amy glances behind them often, checks parallel traffic lanes and keeps an eye on the passing trucks while walking to the store. No one would realize, seeing this young mother dressed in black skinnies and a sleeveless peplum blouse, a large handbag looped over her shoulder, that the sheer lunacy of masked gunmen has her so alert. That firearms once aimed directly at her elicit tentative steps.

"V-3," she says to Grace when she notices the square sign mounted high on a lamppost. She bends forward to see her daughter's face, hoping her words are an invisible lifeline. They keep coming, her words, one on top of the other, to keep Grace from going under. "It's busy here. We have to remember that Mommy parked in row V-3, halfway up." She approaches the entrance door, just to the right of the row in which she parked. "V-3, V-3," she repeats, committing it to memory.

George is in two places at once. He ties on his black apron and stands in front of the meat grinder at The Main Course. The beef has to be ground first, while the machine is still cold. He knows this without thinking. Bits of bone have a tendency to break warm gears or chip warm knives. But today his heart isn't in preparing the comfort foods for his clientele in this small plaza of shops. Because part of him is still sitting in Detective Hayes' office, where he had been summoned before work, glancing at the shoulder holster holding the detective's department-issued firearm. Could George have used the gun he had held? Should he have turned it on Reid and put a stop to that whole day? Brought it to an end with a bullet?

He maneuvers the meat into the grinder. The sound of Dean's voice talking with lunch customers up front reaches him the same way Detective Hayes' message on his voicemail did, asking him to stop in before work. "Coffee?" Hayes asked when George sat earlier in the wooden chair beside the desk. George waved him off. What he'd like to do is wave his whole life off. Just take enough of the damn money and go. Pack a bag, board a plane and disappear into the skies, leaving the mess of his life in the white vapor trail behind the jet, evaporating with each passing day. But he can't. He won't leave Amy behind, alone.

Curls of meat exit the chopper as he continues to feed in more.

"The FBI completed an analysis of the psychological profiles of our suspects. Our intention now is to mesh different angles of thinking with the profiles. It's a method of drawing out their identities and estimating their movements following the crime."

"Okay. Makes sense," George answered, resting an arm on the desktop and studying the detective's face. Hayes was clean-shaven, his light brown hair combed back and his heavyset frame in pretty good shape. The casual clothes and composure indicated a learned patience. But his holster fit as well as his shirt, leaving George no doubt that Hayes knew precisely the quickest route to slipping his weapon from its place and aiming it at someone's head. He must have spent days at target practices during his years on the force. Maneuvers had been mastered, situations predicted. George had lifted the forty-five from his dresser drawer last night after bringing Amy home, laid it on his kitchen table and familiarized himself with its eight-round magazine, its rounded trigger guard, its four-inch barrel.

Did he fit the psychological profile? Did the profile suggest that the suspect never once pulled a gun trigger? That the suspect protected the life of a child? That the suspect just last night aimed the loaded gun at his reflection to try to feel what Amy had felt? Until he saw his father looking back at him in shame? He removes the overflowing plate of ground beef now and starts on a second round.

"One scenario we've devised is that every single aspect of that day was painstakingly planned to manipulate our thinking and investigating. It isn't pure dumb luck that left us with a cold trail. And if this idea holds any water, then you are clearly part of the plan, George. They would have observed you recently and specifically selected you as their accomplice, if you will, without your knowledge."

George eases up on the pressure when the meat starts to back up. Damn right it was without his knowledge. Would that count for anything, if he started talking right then and there? If he came clean with the detective? If he drove him to his home, released the latch behind the kitchen tiles, pulled out the hidden safe, separated the zippers on the duffel bags and opened the flaps to banded stacks of currency, the scent of ink and paper rising to meet them?

"They knew there was a dragnet in place searching for them and couldn't risk losing four million by accidentally handing the girl over to an undercover guy in a parking lot. They insured that bankroll with total premeditated control. Nothing was left to chance—not their freedom, not the welfare of the child. Her well-being was put into a familiar, upstanding citizen's hands to ensure no assault or murder charges. Your hands."

George spoons the two full plates of ground beef into a display tray, pressing the edges with the spoon back. "Got it. They researched me and trusted I'd take care of her."

"In which case, you would have been tailed that entire day. They couldn't lose you before finishing the crime as planned. And that explains why they held the kid so long. That unaccounted-for block of time's been a thorn in my side. But they were waiting for *you* to get back from the casino."

George still wavers between the two places at once. He takes the grinder apart and washes each piece with soap and hot water before setting them out to air dry. The knife and plate stay together because they wear to fit each other during grinder use and can't be interchanged with others. This, too, he knows without thinking. His movements are rote, including the visual inspection ensuring no food is drying on the surfaces, so rote his mind is still in Detective Hayes' office.

"So I'm looking for your itinerary," Hayes said. "Start to finish. I know you came from the casino, but I need exact times, names of who accompanied you, any stops along the way for coffee, food, the tables you played, who you talked to, ETAs, ETDs."

George sets a thinner plate and knife on the grinder and tightens the adjustment ring. He needs to prepare breadcrumbs for the cranberry herb stuffing. It didn't take him long to relinquish Nate's, Steve's and Craig's names. Normal. That's what he told the detective. It was a normal day, four friends spending it at the casino.

He picks up a knife, hacks a chunk of bread off a day-old loaf and feeds it slowly into the chopper. Too much at once will jam the gears. He knows that, too, without thinking.

One more thing he knows: Distractions cause accidents while working the knives—he's got the scars to prove it. So with worries about Amy coming at him from one direction, and the authorities from another, and his brother from a third, he knows to stay away from the combination of razor-sharp boning knives and slippery sinew and bones. Instead he sticks with the breaded stuffing, leaving the chicken thighs for Dean to debone.

All while picturing Detective Hayes picking up the phone, calling the casino and requesting the surveillance video, completely unaware that he is hot on the right trail.

——

"Will this be on your credit card?"

"No. Cash today." Amy sets a royal blue tankini and a pair of tropical flip-flops on the counter.

"It's going to be a nice weekend for the beach," the sales associate, Susan, says.

"I know, we can't wait to get there." Grace sits in the stroller, stretching and pressing against the safety strap, restless after an hour of trying on swimsuits and cover-ups. And Amy's glad. Any expression of emotion, including agitation, is welcome. Grace twists back and looks up at her as she pulls her wallet from her handbag.

"Don't you love this style?" Susan folds the swimsuit into white tissue paper and slips it into a shopping bag, then counts back the change. "And remember to bring sunscreen, too!"

Amy agrees and loops the shopping bag handle over the stroller handle. When she approaches the Exit door near the Children's Department, she hears a voice calling out *Miss! Oh Miss?* and turns to see Susan hurrying over.

"I'm so glad I caught you." She waves Bear in front of her. "Look who was on the floor near the rack of flip-flops," she says, placing Bear in Grace's open arms.

"What do we say to the nice lady?" Amy asks, bending forward to coax words from Grace's lips. *Come on,* her mind pleads. *You know this one. Say it,* she thinks as Grace buries her face in the stuffed animal's fur. "Thank you. We say thank you, Grace."

"That's okay." Susan smiles at Grace. "You hold him close now."

Outside, Amy reaches into her purse for her aviators. "V-3," she says, slipping on the glasses and lowering the stroller onto the pavement. The parking lot is still busy with shoppers rushing in on their lunch hour and the strangers pass close, walking with clipped steps, keeping her vigilant. She walks half the length of parking row V-3 before slowing to a stop. Her maroon SUV is nowhere in sight, not in the spaces ahead, not behind her. With her flustered turning around, one of the shopping bags slips from the stroller handle, spilling onto the pavement. She bends over to scoop the flip-flops back in and upon straightening, feels lightheaded. She tips her head into her hand, then backtracks a few car-lengths to get a clear view of the large square sign mounted on the lamppost.

"V-3," she reads aloud, squinting back down the long row of parked vehicles. Every space is taken. It just doesn't make sense. Double-checking the store entrance doors to be sure they are the same ones they entered through earlier, she wheels Grace through them again, back into the store, circles around and exits once more.

"Well this is ridiculous," she says. "I must have walked right past it." Again she steps into the parking lot and walks the entire length of the row of vehicles. There are no maroon SUVs parked in row V-3. Can someone have stolen hers? At the end of the row, she cuts a sharp right into row V-4 and examines the cars packed tight into each space. Maybe the sun is playing tricks on her. By the time she tips the stroller up onto the sidewalk, her heart is pounding and her face is flush with perspiration. Grace squirms in the stroller, stretches her legs out straight and sinks down low in the seat, thumping her Velcro sandals on the sidewalk in a one-two beat.

Amy wheels over to a wooden bench and unbuckles her daughter, sitting her on the bench while stacking the two shopping bags and Bear into the stroller seat. Grace slips off the bench, reaches her hands up on the stroller handles and starts to push it. Its wheels waggle sideways before straightening.

"Grace! Hold Mommy's hand!" Amy lifts one of Grace's small hands from the stroller and folds her own hand over it. Together they maneuver the stroller up row V-3 once more. Now her mouth has gone dry and she blinks her vision back into focus. "Calm down," she tells herself. They can't be victims of yet another crime; it's just implausible. Grace pulls her hand away right as she turns to scan the cars in the adjacent rows, and just as suddenly the vehicles melt into the color of gray, dissolving into one large pool of gritty pavement until no cars remain. Only the armored truck. Her hand feels painfully empty again, trying to squeeze her fingers around her daughter's fist. When she spins around, the gunman climbs the steps into the armored vehicle, her daughter's shoe in his pocket. They have the truck, for God's sake. Why can't he relinquish her daughter and leave? Why does it have to come to this? The ground slowly comes up to cradle her as she sinks into a crouch, the warm pavement turning liquid, swallowing her legs. She drops her head low.

"Please." The whispered plea begs for her daughter while from behind sunglasses, her eyes watch the armored truck. A voice reaches her ears; its deep inflections sound distant. Muffled, as though on the other side of a mask.

"Excuse me," it calls out, drawing nearer. His shadow falls on her and she flinches. "Are you okay?" he asks, extending a hand down.

Amy raises her eyes and sees Grace in the arms of a stranger. He has taken off his hideous hosiery mask and returned her daughter. She knew all along that he was good; she heard it in his voice.

"Grace," she says through tears, taking the stranger's hand and pulling herself to her feet. He has gotten her daughter off the armored truck.

"I saw her wander off with the stroller when you lost your balance. She could've gotten hurt."

Amy takes a breath, letting oxygen reach deep into her lungs. The stroller. Shopping bags spill from the seat. She nearly loses her balance with the realization they are at the mall. "Thank you," she says to the man. Does he hear her heart slamming inside her? "I just got really dizzy suddenly," she lies. "The sun's so bright."

"Maybe you need to sit down?" he asks as he places Grace into her arms.

She notices it right away and is stricken with sadness. Grace's body has gone limp. She shut down in fear when a man's arms lifted her up. Amy hugs her close and gently rubs her back.

"There's a bench near the door." The man lifts the stroller with one hand and takes Amy's arm with the other, walking them slowly through the parking lot.

And all the while she knows. Her car is gone. There's no sense in looking further. She hears a noise and embraces Grace's head to her neck. "Mumumum" comes softly to her ear.

"Can I call someone for you?" the stranger asks. He is in his forties and dressed in a business suit, apparently on his lunch hour. "You probably shouldn't be driving."

Amy sits on the bench, the warm sun causing her to perspire even more. Does she look the mess she feels? "Thank you. I'll be fine." When the man pauses, watching her cautiously, she insists. "Really. I'm feeling better now." She reaches for her cell phone in her purse. "I'll call a friend to help me."

"Okay then." He glances at his watch. "I'll wait to be sure they can come for you," he says and Amy can't argue as he stands beside the bench keeping an eye on Grace.

With her daughter slack in her lap, one arm cradles her while with the other, her fingers carefully press the correct digits she had programmed into her cell weeks ago. She waits through three rings, shifting Grace and imagining George's shop. Imagining the sun shining through the windows, a few people sitting at the small tables with a roast beef sandwich. Imagining the sound of the telephone lost in the sound of Sinatra. She closes her eyes and sees George, with his dark hair and white shirt, setting down a sharp silver boning knife, wiping his hands on his black apron before picking up the telephone. Finally she hears his voice. A beat of silence passes as she collects herself, strokes Grace's hair and takes a breath.

"George?"

Fifteen

IN THE SILENT BREATH BEFORE she says his name, George senses something is wrong. He leaves The Main Course and drives to the mall, knowing exactly the entrance Amy is waiting near. Remembering exactly the commotion of construction vehicles and sawhorses and steel girders distracting wary eyes from an armored truck.

"Are you sure it was V-3?" he asks after his hands lightly stroke the length of her arms twice, coming to a stop holding her hands. When she nods and sits slowly, George sits beside her on the bench. He realizes then that he still has on his black apron and pulls it over his head. "We'll double-check."

"George," she says so quietly. Grace holds Bear beside her, fidgeting and pulling her knees up, straightening them, turning backward on the bench.

"What's the matter?" George hooks a finger beneath Amy's chin and turns her head. Her skin is warm and perspiring. "You can replace the car."

"I had a flashback."

"Here?" His gaze moves from her eyes, to Grace, and back to her again.

"In the parking lot."

That was what he heard in her whispered voice on the telephone. Exhaustion. She depleted her energy fighting off a flashback.

"A very nice man helped us and waited while I called you."

He leans over in front of Amy and pats Grace's knee, his eyes locked onto Amy's. "She's okay?"

Amy looks at her daughter, her eyes filling with quick tears. "She could've been hurt, George. I'm scared now."

George did his own research on flashbacks and post-traumatic stress. Much of it boils down to a loss of control and the debilitating vulnerability that follows. Amy needs to be out of this place now. She needs to be home, in her country kitchen with a cup of coffee, making lunch for Grace, filling Angel's water dish, opening a window, controlling the small things. First they have to call the police to report her vehicle stolen. He surveys the parking lot now.

"Could it have been parked in B-3? Or D-3?" he asks, taking her hand in his.

"No. No! I distinctly checked twice to be certain that I parked in V-3. It's V-3!"

"I understand. I'm just wondering if the flashback might've confused you. Let's take a another look around before we call the police." He straightens her shopping bags in the stroller, folding his apron into one of them. "We'll put these in my truck first, okay?"

Amy scoops up Grace and walks beside George as he heads left, in the direction of his parked vehicle. Pushing the stroller, he suggests they walk up and down a few rows, just to be absolutely sure she isn't mistaken. They pass two similar SUVs, one white and one bright red. Five rows over from V-3, halfway down on the right hand side, a maroon SUV is parked.

"It's not mine, George. I didn't park this far away from the door."

"What's your license plate number?" he asks as they near the vehicle.

Amy's eyes drop to the plate and her feet stop moving. She leans heavily into him and he knows that the vehicle parked in row V-8 is hers.

———

Amy wants to go home. She wants to go home and stay home and never leave her property again. She wants to putter in her gown room, repair vintage veils and dresses, order antique purses and necklaces, then push Grace in the swing and read books in the sunshine on her stone patio before falling deep asleep in her bed. Then she wants to wake up, tomorrow or the next day, have a cup of coffee and call her mother and tell her all about this unbearable mall dream from which she has just woken.

George drives her SUV with one hand on the steering wheel, the other holding her hand the entire way. "I'll call my brother," he says when they stop at the railroad crossing, waiting for the gate to rise after a train speeds by. "He'll give me a ride back to get my truck later."

She hears the train pass and hears George's words, hears the near vibrations of his voice within her air-conditioned vehicle, hears Grace's silence, and closes her eyes.

"You're just tired, Amy. That's what brought it on. You've been through a tough time with Grace. Worry takes a lot out of you."

It isn't fatigue. One fine morning walking out of the bank, a stranger ripped her daughter from her hand. And it wasn't only

Grace who was kidnapped. In a way, Amy was too. Kidnapped into that moment as it replays any time she closes her eyes. Any time the sun shines in just the right way or she turns quickly at a sound. Any time Grace won't speak. Her life's been abducted, held still in the one moment that, try as she might, she can't get past.

———

"What's going on?" Nate asks as George gets in the car idling in Amy's driveway.

George pulls the car door closed and scans the house. The farmhouse doors are shut and locked, as are the downstairs windows. The twig wreath and wicker porch chairs, the hydrangea bushes and the dogwood tree throwing a pool of shade on the green lawn, all belie the troubles behind the front door.

"Let's go. I'm running late."

Nate leans low and scans the white clapboard and green gingerbread trim outlining the peaked front. A cultivated bed of wildflowers edges the front yard. "Nice place she's got here. She takes care of all this by herself?"

"She manages. Let's move it."

"Where is she? I'd like to meet her."

George looks at his brother. He called Nate at a job site and he wears dusty jeans, a T-shirt and construction boots. "After what you put her through that day? Go to hell."

"Hey. If you're going to be seeing her, eventually we'll have to meet."

"Not today, you're not."

Nate slips the car in reverse and backs out of the driveway. "What's going on?"

"She had a problem with her car at the mall and called me for a ride."

"Couldn't you follow her home in your car?"

"It's a long story. Just step on it, would you?"

At the mall, Nate cruises by the construction area of the parking lot where they had transferred the money into the van. Dirt and stone clutter the pavement and steel girders reach up from the ground. The men wear hard hats and drive massive equipment.

"Brings back memories, doesn't it?" Nate asks, glancing from George beside him back to the spot where the armored truck had been parked. "What a high that was."

"Amy had a flashback."

"A what?"

"A flashback, in the parking lot. She got disoriented and couldn't find her car."

"You mean a real flashback? When you're really out of it?"

"That's right. It was a flashback of that morning in the bank parking lot. Of that *high*."

"Hey, I'm sorry. I didn't know." He turns his car into the row George indicates and pulls into a space three over from the pickup truck.

"She's really upset by it. Her daughter was with her when it happened."

"Shit. That's pretty tough."

George gets out of the car and stands in the bright sunlight. "She'll be all right."

Nate gets out too and closes his door behind him. He walks around to the trunk and leans up against it with his arms folded across his chest. "You all set now? I've got to get back."

"Yeah, I'm good." George pulls his keys from his pocket and walks toward his truck. As he unlocks the door, a small paper beneath his windshield wiper catches his eye. He lifts the wiper, expecting a flyer for pizza delivery or a financial services seminar. And so at first he doesn't recognize just what he is seeing and almost tosses it. But when he turns away from the glare of the sun and looks again, he squints closely.

Amy had an audience. The grainy photograph captured her terrified and sinking into a crouch in the parking lot. Beyond her Grace wheels the stroller unattended. He turns and walks toward his brother's car. Nate has gotten back in behind the wheel and George raps on the window. "Is this your idea of a fucking high?"

Nate rolls down the window and takes the picture from George. "Jesus Christ." He stares longer. "Is this what I think it is?"

George scans the other windshields around them, half expecting to see a square paper beneath each wiper.

"Someone's playing a serious game with you," Nate says.

"No shit. And you say no one got hurt? This is what the hell your scheme's done. What good is your million if someone's got to live like this?" George grabs the picture back and looks at it again. "Where's Reid keeping himself?"

"Reid? Why?"

"He warned me, that day when he dropped off Grace at Litner's Market. Told me to lay low or shit might happen to people, including Amy."

"Like what?"

"I didn't stick around to hear. Just tell him to call off his dogs. She doesn't deserve this." He turns and walks toward the parked cars, looking from the pavement to the storefronts, trying to place where the photographer had stood.

Nate swings open his car door. "Hang on. I'll come with you."

George has had enough of his kid brother. "Back off already." He grabs a handful of Nate's shirt and gives a shove. "Get the hell out of here before I turn you and your fucking bankroll in to Hayes. I should've turned that lousy gun on *you* that day. This is your fault, man, *yours*, and I'm sick of it. All because of your God damned need to take down the house and pay me back for some lost dream. You're taking good people down."

Nate straightens his shirt. "What do you mean, pay you back?"

"You know damn well what I mean. It's not your fault I quit baseball to run the shop after Dad died. That was *my* choice. So you can stop trying to make up for what I might've lost. Drop it already."

"All right, all right." Nate drags his hand through his hair. "At least let me help you now."

"Even if it means turning on Reid?" He watches his brother's expression, still uncertain how pivotal a part Reid played in the heist and how much sway he holds over Nate. "Tell me right now." He steps closer. "Straight up. You with *me* on this or not?"

"Yeah, I'm in. Someone's screwing with your head, George. And Amy's, too." Nate takes off his sunglasses and wipes the back of his hand across his brow. "I'm in."

George walks quickly through the parking lot with Nate following. "Let's go, then."

"You think whoever did this actually moved her car and set her up to get upset?"

"I don't know what to think, other than I'll kill him. If he doesn't leave her alone, I swear I'll kill whoever did this or go to the authorities and put a real quick end to all of it."

"Cool down." Nate catches up with him. "Go to the authorities and this gets worse. Don't worry about Reid. I'll help you keep an eye out and we'll take care of this together."

They turn left at row V-3 and George points out where Amy said she had parked. In the photo, it all matches up. Someone moved her SUV, played with her head and then caught her at her absolute weakest. They walk to Amy's space and stand there, uncertain of just what to look for. Nate turns back to face Macy's and George cuffs his white shirtsleeves beneath the hot sun, then pulls the photograph from his shirt pocket. They study it and try to place any of the cars around them.

George is doing something else, too. Someone gave this a lot of thought. Someone figured where to hurt him most. So what he's doing now is getting the message. If he doesn't stop seeing Amy, thereby putting his identity along with four million dollars at risk, they won't stop seeing her either.

Sixteen

ONE YEAR AGO AT THIS time, Mark was still alive. He had brushed a coat of white paint on the paned kitchen door that morning. After lunch, he geared up to go mountain-bike riding with a friend. No one ever foresaw that a steep trail would end his full life; that his loss of control on a wide curve would throw him off the bike; that he'd hit the ground wrong. That by four-thirty that afternoon, he'd be dead. His life had completed its span, bridging over a winding river of days and events and emotions. Even though this is not a happy anniversary, Amy had hoped to commemorate surviving a difficult year. After all, she had shaped a new life raising Grace alone, keeping their farmhouse and evolving her bridal shop into specialty vintage gowns. She never dreamt that on this day she would be calling Dr. Berg for help.

Celia arrives at the moment she hangs up, standing at the door with a tray holding two cups of coffee and a box of doughnuts. Later, Sara Beth is meeting them for lunch at a new outdoor café near the cove, bringing a 1950s veil she found while buying a set of old china teacups for her antique shop. She thought the veil would perfectly pair with a shorter-skirt bridal dress Amy bought at a neighbor's tag sale. Everyone tries to help her on this sad day.

Her mother already called twice, sent a bouquet of flowers and wanted to drive down for the weekend. But Amy told her she was spending the next day at the beach with George. Sitting seaside will be a nice change. She and Grace both need it.

"Do you want a doughnut, Grace?" Amy asks her daughter.

Grace kneels on a kitchen chair and reaches into the colorful doughnut box. "Which one do you like?" Celia asks her. "Does one look especially good?" She glances at Amy, and Amy knows. She's trying to nudge any word from her mouth. "Is there a certain one you want?" Celia continues. "Yes or no?" Her hand softly brushes over Grace's blonde hair.

"Nothing works," Amy whispers, shaking her head slowly. Grace silently lifts out a strawberry-frosted. "Can you say thank you to Celia?"

Celia sits across from Amy at the blue kitchen table and peels the lid from her steaming coffee cup. "Doesn't that look yummy?" she asks Grace.

Grace glances over at Celia and nods, then scoots off the kitchen chair, gingerly holding the doughnut in her small fingers.

Amy pulls a paper towel from the roll. "Wait, honey," she says, trailing Grace heading toward the living room and the television. "Put this on the table with your snickie-snack." She tickles her back and elicits a happy squeal from her. "Okay," she says, turning back to the kitchen, wiping powdered doughnut sugar from her hands on her shorts. "Well that's something." She takes a satisfied breath. Little victories mean everything now. "I just got off the phone with Dr. Berg," she says to Celia then.

"Your doctor? What's up?"

"Yesterday's up. I can't be having any more flashbacks like I did at the mall and needed advice. He told me that flashback triggers are activated by things related to the trauma." She picks up the notepad where she wrote a bulleted column. "Locations, smells, sights, sounds, people, touch. The brain remembers in a lot of ways."

"Okay. Makes sense." Celia bites into a chocolate frosted doughnut.

"Some triggers can be as vague as time of day, or if I'm in the right frame of mind, even a certain touch can stimulate a flashback."

"But you'll be facing triggers all the time," Celia answers around the mouthful of food, sucking a glob of sugar from her manicured finger. "So how do you stay in control?"

"Practice. I really have to manage the flashbacks." She lifts the page to the listed controls and slides the pad to Celia. "If you know these too, you can help me if it ever happens while I'm with you?"

"Maybe." A quick smile comes and goes, one that says she is sorry Amy's life has come to this. Celia pulls her chair in close. "Let's practice now." With a long sip of coffee, her eyes scan the page. "So these are what you can do if you feel a flashback coming on?" she asks.

Amy nods, waiting to start.

"All right. First. Breathe slowly and deeply. Focus totally on the act of breathing."

Amy fills her lungs with a long breath of air and exhales. The sunny window over the kitchen sink faces her and she closes her eyes against its image, paying attention only to the feeling of deep breathing. Focusing like this makes her aware of the effort necessary to breathe in a slow manner, reducing her heart rate as well. With the next breath, she slows the process even further.

"Good. Now visualization. Mentally travel to a safe spot. Or use spirituality. Turning to your faith helps those who are religious."

New Hampshire is ever her place of safety, sitting in her parents' kitchen. Something cooks beneath the lid of a big pot on the stove. Her mother moves between the sink and the table, and her father stokes the old stone fireplace. Sitting in the plaid-cushioned wooden chairs feels like sitting in a pew. The same peace is found there as in a dimly lit church. "I'm with Mom," she whispers.

Celia smiles and looks down at the pad. "Next. Plant yourself, setting both feet flat on the ground. Try to slip out of your shoes and do this barefoot. You want the sensation of being solidly grounded, right where you actually are."

And not in the flashback, goes unsaid. So Amy stands in her denim board shorts and pink tee, pressing her bare soles into the cool wide-planked kitchen floor, committing the steps to memory by physically doing them now before any anxiety strikes. *I'm home*, she thinks from behind closed eyes. *I'm in control.* The grained wood planks meet her skin.

"That's it? Just simple things like that?" Celia asks.

Amy hesitates, then turns and picks up the prescription bottle from the kitchen counter. "There's this, too. It's a mild tranquilizer. If a situation upsets me, or if I feel I'm losing a sense of control, I can take one as needed."

"They're not too strong?"

"No. Just enough to take the edge off my nerves." She sits beside Celia and they read the label together, Celia's fingertip following the lines of print. "They might help," Amy adds quietly. "Especially if they keep me calm with Grace. Because what happened yesterday at the mall absolutely cannot happen again. Ever."

That's what this all boils down to. Grace.

The kidnappers, weeks later, still, even now, continue to take her child further from her. Because if she flashbacks in public and risks Grace's safety again, Amy knows her daughter could be removed from her custody. One sunny day, four men took Grace, and really? She glances into the living room. She still hasn't gotten her back yet.

———

Each day at three o'clock, the church bells ring on Main Street. When he hears them chime today, George turns up the flight of granite steps, pulling open the heavy door and sitting in a rear pew. Sunshine streams in through the stained glass windows, casting an unfamiliar illumination to the space. In the echoing quiet of a church at midday, he feels like everything has turned unfamiliar. Nothing makes sense. Several parishioners walk in, pause, step behind pleated curtains into the confessional and walk out again. The thick velvet curtains hang in heavy deep red folds, the soft pleats falling in refinement right down to the floor.

As each penitent lifts the drape, George wonders about their sins. A man in his mid-sixties, a young woman who looks no older than twenty-one, a nicely dressed middle-aged couple. What can their sins be? Do their digressions compare to his? Do their sins keep them awake late at night, or open the Scotch for a long drink at three in the morning, or clamp their stomachs down against food? One by one they emerge, briefly kneel and depart. After an hour, when the church empties, he sidesteps out of the pew, walks down the aisle, lifts the velvet curtain and kneels.

The small dark space embraces him and he shifts his shoulders as though he has to fit into it before pulling the photograph from his pocket and squinting at the grainy details. His finger traces over Amy's troubled face. The photograph is what brings him to his knees. There is nowhere else in the world to turn for guidance.

He slips the photograph back into his pocket and bows his head, waiting. Following a long pause, the wooden window before him slides open in dark shadow.

George straightens. "Bless me Father," he murmurs, the words carrying the full grave weight of every word, look and thought that contributed to Amy's trauma. He glances at the shadowed outline before him and shifts on the kneeler, feeling the cushion below his knees, his peripheral vision sensing the velvet curtain folds beside him keeping out the light. After dropping his head for a long moment, he looks up again. The priest waits silently for George to go on, leaving him feeling like he is falling into a dark chasm, the wind rushing past as the fall quickens.

"Father, I need help."

The priest raises his hand in the sign of a cross and begins with a quiet blessing. The low voice sounds fluid, a deep brook flowing over stones, the intonations rising and falling easily. George can't be sure if the solemn words are spoken in English or Latin, reaching far back into the faith for credence.

"What's troubling you?" the priest then asks.

George hears every small sound within the confessional, including his own long breath drawing behind his clasped hands. He hears that the priest's voice is not young and hears the rustle of black fabric as he brings an arm up and leans his forehead on his closed hand.

"Father. Before I begin this, I need to ask you a question. I'm not really sure how to ask, but what I need to know is what your obligation is in hearing confessions."

"As a confessor," the priest slowly begins, "I am bound to be both a judge and healer. So my obligation works in two ways, devoted both to the salvation of souls as well as to the honor of God."

"No. That's not what I meant." George clears his throat. "What is your responsibility to the information you hear in a confession? Is it confidential?"

The priest lifts his head but keeps his gaze down. "The sacramental seal is inviolable. Canon Law prohibits me from disclosing your sins, for any reason at all, in any possible way. I am also forbidden to share the knowledge about any sin learned from hearing a confession with civil authorities, or for any purpose of external governance." He assures him quietly, "You are very safe here. Would you like to continue your confession?"

"Father, the fact is I have a difficult decision to make, but I'm not sure that I'm really here for a confession." George's voice is low. Is it a sin that he protected Grace? "I have to right a wrong that's been done, and I don't know how to do it without hurting someone."

"Sometimes it helps to go back and look carefully at the path that brought you to this point. What started all this?" the priest asks. "What does your being here stem from?"

"A crime."

"Is that why you're here? To seek absolution from the crime?"

"No. I'm not ready to do that."

"Maybe it will help in your decision to turn that corner and seek absolution as a starting point."

Burning tears sting his eyes. What the hell is happening to him? He can't think straight, can't sleep, can't work. He wants nothing more than deliverance from the evil stacks of currency in his tiled kitchen wall, the evil in the semiautomatic weapon in his dresser drawer, the evil that is yet to come.

"I don't know." He bows his head on his clasped hands. "Right now I'm afraid at how my life, and something I did, is hurting someone else." When did he stop being a good person, deserving of pride and respect? He doesn't want to be this other person. "I've got to come clean with someone I love."

"Why not start here?"

George watches the priest's dark silhouette long enough to see him breathe. To see him live without trepidation. To live the life he's chosen.

"I want you to know that I didn't choose to end up in this situation," George whispers defensively. "Maybe this isn't right. Maybe I shouldn't even be here." He half rises before sinking back to his knees. Here he has an ally. Here his story stays safe behind the velvet curtains. Here this priest can carefully sort out God's plan for George in all of this. He will remind him that Grace is alive.

"Okay, Father," he whispers. "How do I begin this thing?" The priest drops his head and purely listens. No one takes notes, his voice is not being recorded, and reporters won't wait outside afterward as he tells the story. Some day, he will have to repeat these same words to a man who *will* take notes. Detective Hayes will record every nuance and the reporters will be waiting everywhere he turns.

For now, his words blur into a low monotone that will forever hum through his memory. He closes his eyes for most of the talk, being aware of only his breathing and his low voice.

Astute questions occasionally come at him through the dark, at which point he hesitates and hears his mouth swallow. A slight ringing fills his ears in the pause before he answers the priest's questions, his dry tongue thickening the syllables of kidnapping and stalking and fear.

"You have to tell her."

"Tell her?" George asks. "Just like that?"

"Yes, at least that she is being followed. She deserves that much. In God's abundant love," the priest explains, "He wishes for us not only to seek His pardon, but to seek His likeness as well. In my counsel, I urge you to tell Amy of the imminent danger facing her and her child. The truth can only open her heart later to compassion, when you one day must tell her the rest of the truth."

"She needs to know for her own safety."

"Of course. But it's more than that. Saint Boniface said that the church is like a ship. But I see life, too, like a ship, with the waves of personal challenges pounding its hull, tossing it on the sea of our days. And in the words of Saint Boniface as well as the Father's intent, your duty is not to abandon the ship, but to keep her on her course."

The coincidence is uncanny. George feels like his own father is speaking to him, twisting his love of the sea and Stony Point and the beach into his guidance. After a long silence, he hears an exhortation to make an act of contrition, then the familiar rhythm of the words of general absolution. It is done. Through his relieved exhaustion, the language grows indecipherable again. But he listens and welcomes the benediction in the spoken rhythm of his faith.

"Are you okay now?" the priest asks. He looks directly through the screen at George.

"I think so."

"I'm Father Rossi. Let me know, please, at any time, if you need help. You have a long road to travel."

"Thank you, Father," George answers, seeing the priest nod in shadow. He stands then, presses the velvet curtain aside and walks out into the church. Doing so, he remembers the lightness that filled his step emerging from a confessional as a child and is ashamed at the difference.

Who would have predicted back then the words he whispered today? His shoulders feel the burden depicted in the old arched walls, the stained glass windows and solemn statues. Those statues seem to watch him now, shaking their heads in disappointment as he steps into a rear pew and kneels, his body doubled over in prayer. The priest gives him privacy, waiting behind in the confessional while George collects himself.

This absolution is only the first. More difficult ones will follow, one day. He drops his head over his clasped hands, unsure of how much time passes before he looks up at the looming altar, presses his hands on the pew back in front of him and pushes himself up to leave.

Seventeen

W HEN HER EYES OPENED IN the still-dark room early this morning, she pulled the sketch pad off her nightstand. The dream had come again and sitting up in bed, all that mattered was transferring the image from her mind, through her arm, and out to the paper. Her hand worked methodically to define the details, the large hand over hers, the curve of a wrist. She outlined her fingers extending beyond his grip, feeling Grace's shoe beneath her hand, and something else atop.

"What?" she asks as she continues working on the sketch with her morning coffee. As she cross-hatches light pencil lines over the entire page, seeing the hands the same way they appeared in her dream. Obscure. Vague.

The shoe beneath, his hand atop. Her fingers struggle to draw a sensation, the pencil wavering over the page. There was a hard lump of some sort, a ridge of a scar, pressing against her hand in his grasp. But her dream hinted at something more behind the veil of sleep and its soft silk netting of drowsiness. The eternal battle of that moment reaching for Grace's shoe will return again and again until she deciphers what is missing.

Her pencil-shading continues until Grace runs barefoot and laughing into the kitchen, with Angel scampering quick at her heels.

"Whoa, whoa, look at you," Amy says, setting down her pencil and watching the two of them. Grace wears her new plum colored ruffled bathing suit and a short bouffant-style wedding veil sits lopsided on her head. The billow of white tulle puffs out like a summer cloud. "Have you been in Mommy's things again?" she asks.

Her daughter stops short and smiles at Amy through the lacy fabric, then scoops up the kitten in her hands. The layer of the tulle veil floating in front of her face hangs to her knees.

"Sara Beth gave that to Mommy to sell in the shop. We can't play with it, Gracie." The thing is, she finds it hard to deny her daughter any pleasure now. "But first, I guess you want to get married?"

Grace nods at her, but no words come. Angel lolls like a dish-rag in her arms.

"Okay," Amy says, walking over to them. "I can marry you two. Stand nice and straight." She reaches down and adjusts the veil on Grace's head. "Ready?" she asks, hoping for an answer. Waiting. Smiling, expectant.

Grace shifts her feet and silently takes a step closer.

"Well now," Amy tells her. Even though her heart tells her no words will come, she can't let go of the hope. "You have to promise your love and friendship to the kitten. So here we go. Okay?" After a quiet moment, the kitten still lying limp across Grace's arms, her paws hanging down, Amy continues. "Do you, Grace, take this kitten Angel, to be your faithful friend for life?"

Grace looks at the kitten, then up at Amy. Her mouth forms no syllables, her breath carries no sounds.

174

Amy lets out a frustrated breath. "I'll take that as an *I do*. And now," she continues as she lifts the veil back over Grace's face so that the cloud of tulle towers over her head, "By the power vested in me, I pronounce you the very best of friends, for richer and for poorer, forever and ever. Now go turn off the TV and get ready to go to the beach." She raises the veil off her daughter and sets it on the table. "And find me your flip-flops, missy. George will be here pretty soon."

Grace sets the cat on the floor and runs around the table, heading finally for the living room where her dollhouse is set up, the television is on, and her flip-flops and a lime green sand pail sit on the couch. Amy turns to the table, finishes the last drops of her coffee and glances again at her sketch pad. A layer of the veil covers her new drawing and she sees her image through the fine, lacy fabric.

Veiled. The same way it appeared in her dream, the shoe skittering across the pavement followed by a mad rush to claim it, a blur of motion and weapon and hands. The delicate pattern of the veil fabric obscures the sketched image much the same way the dream did, yet hints at detail behind the tulle. The intent of a bridal veil, when all is said and done, is to lift it. This puff of tulle once concealed a bride's young face; the guests had to wait to see clearly the spark in her eyes, her emotion, until the veil was lifted.

Amy slowly lifts the tulle back off her sketch, knowing that some veil in her memory has yet to do the same.

———

"Which one is your house key?" George lightly jangles Amy's key ring as she buckles Grace into her car seat.

"My house key? Why?"

"I need a drink of water before we leave. I'll just be a minute."
It isn't completely true, but true enough. What he really needs is to
check every downstairs door and window, quickly, to be sure the
house is secure while they're gone. But he can't tell her that yet. He
wants, at the very least, for Amy and Grace to have this day at the
beach simply for what it is.

And so that's what he makes it into. Driving Amy's SUV, he
stops at a shore town close to Stony Point, pulling off the main
road onto a busy beach road lined with tiny cottages stacked too
close together, a video game arcade crowded with teens, and sea-
sonal stores selling penny candy and overpriced beach umbrellas. He parks at one of the shops and leaves them waiting in the
vehicle until he returns with two inflated tubes, one a duck swim-
ring for Grace.

"Oh. I almost forgot," he says before backing out of their parking space. He reaches into one of his cargo short pockets for a small
bag. "We've got to make a beach bum out of your daughter today."

Amy pulls a plastic pair of purple heart-shaped sunglasses
from the bag and laughs. She twists around and sets them on
Grace's nose. "Don't you look cute!" she says, stroking her cheek
in a feather touch. "Now what do we say to George?"

"Amy." George shakes his head. "Don't."

"Why not? She might say thank you," she insists. "You never
know if she'll talk, even a little."

"No. No strings today. No fishing for words, no pressure. Just
let her be at the sea, however she wants to be. Okay?"

Amy relinquishes a smile and reaches back to give Grace's foot
a quick squeeze. "Deal. I kind of like that idea, actually. We'll let
the sea work its magic."

They drive a few miles more, turning off the main road beneath
a railroad trestle, driving past cedar-shingled cottages and bungalows

painted sunshine yellow and ocean blue, porch windows opened to the sea breezes, flower boxes brimming with geraniums and cascading petunias. Stony Point is one of those rare places frozen in time, and for that George is grateful. His only wish today is to take them all back in time, for a while, to a day before the heist.

"My folks had a cottage here so Dad could be at the water. He loved the beach more than anything. Nate and I rent it out every now and then, and keep it maintained, you know, keep the yard trimmed, the cottage clean, but we haven't used it in years. We'll park there and walk to the beach."

The cottage sits pretty on a side road, nestled in large shrubs of beach grass, its backyard facing the lagoon. George always liked this marsh area where the inlets winding through the grasses gently rise and fall with the tides. It's been a good place to contemplate summers, to ruminate life. The cottage's cedar shingles have weathered to a silver-gray over the years, some edged with black now, and the white trim could use a fresh coat of paint.

"Well isn't this beautiful," Amy says when he pulls into the stone driveway.

"We can sit out back on the deck later. Grace will like it there, it's very peaceful. And maybe the swans will swim by."

"George." Amy steps out of the SUV and looks out at the view of the lagoon and the deep green grasses curving through it, a great blue heron standing still on the banks. The sky beyond has that vastness that comes from only being over the sea. She turns back to him and says the words he'd hoped to hear. "It's like our own fairy tale, this little shingled gingerbread cottage, swans and the sea. What a perfect place."

But every fairy tale has an element of wickedness, a dark shadow hovering behind the storyline. George opens the back of her SUV and lifts out their canvas beach bags and sand chairs. All he wants to do is put as much distance as he can between any evil and this place, this day.

———

Every hour of the afternoon passes like she's turning the page of a photo album, each hour filled with its own beautiful images. It would be the type of album that becomes its own treasure: large and worn from many days spent poring over it, from your finger lightly passing over a cherished image on the beach, or your eyes tearing with the fleeting sweet memories.

Amy can picture it, the page filled with images of George on his knees, the June sun burning his shoulders, three sand pails scattered close by as he drizzles sea water on the turrets and towers of the castle he builds with Grace at the water's edge. Amy knows, oh she just knows that his low voice is talking and making up some fantasy story about princesses and gentle dragons to go along with the castle. And she sees the image of Grace picking up small white seashells and ever so carefully placing them on the castle walls as George finishes digging out the moat.

And there are the sunshine glistening images of Amy floating in her tube, her fingers skimming the salt water, the sway of the sea beneath her while Grace stands knee-high in the Sound with her duck swim-ring around her waist. George stands near Grace and so, so gently occasionally lifts her beneath her arms and swings her legs through the water, eliciting a happy squeal, her head tipped up, her smile frozen in sunlight.

And there is the precious hour he gives them, just her and Grace alone at the edge of the sea, when he heads back to his family's cottage. Forever she'll have the images from those solitary minutes with her daughter as they walk along the high tide line holding hands, stopping now and then to pick up seashells, sea glass and pretty stones, dropping them into the sand pail. They find a conch shell near the pier at the far end of the beach and Amy holds it to her daughter's ear so that she can hear the sound of the sea in it. The waves lap at their toes and the sun lingers high in the sky just for them, it seems, glistening diamonds on the water surface. She bends close to point them out to Grace and tells her they look like tiny, sparkling stars ... perfect for summer wishes.

"You're too good to be true," Amy says when George returns holding a bag with two ice cream bars and one vanilla-chocolate sundae cup from the ice cream truck parked nearby. He steps out of his docksiders right into the sand, pulls off his New York Yankees tee and hangs it over the back of his sand chair.

"Was that your team?" Amy asks as she peels the cover off Grace's ice cream cup.

"Almost." George slides his chair beside hers.

And she doesn't say more, because what can she say, really?

"Oh, I brought something for Grace. It was in the old toy trunk in the cottage." George takes a plastic horse from the bag. It's brick red in color and a little dusty and worn around the hooves. "Because every castle needs a grand horse to patrol it."

The small horse stands on the blanket beside Grace, where she sits spooning her ice cream, a few vanilla drops dribbling down her hand. The waves break close at their feet, the sun warms their skin and Amy closes her eyes behind her sunglasses. If she could stop the clock, this is the moment, right now, where the minutes would pause. She eventually takes George's hand in hers.

"Look," George quietly says, tipping his head close to her ear.

She opens her eyes to see Grace lifting small spoons of sand and showing them to the horse propped beside her before tipping them out on the castle towers. George's hand is still in hers and her thumb idly strokes his skin. "His hand was scarred like yours," she says after a moment, her words almost lost in the sound of waves and a sea breeze. She turns her face toward his, leaning back on the sun-bleached chair, her thumb feeling the ridge of a scar from his work. "But your hands carried Grace to safety."

He entwines his hand around hers and kisses her fingers.

Later, they linger on the deck at George's cottage; the soft lagoon grasses whisper ancient secrets of the sea, with schools of minnows occasionally ruffling the marsh water's calm surface. Inside his cottage, comfortable upholstered pieces and painted wood tables furnish the living room, everything kept neat and tidy. In her life that had spun out of control, she likes the feeling of chaos being kept outside the door here. Even in the sunny kitchen, the chrome chairs are tucked evenly up to the Formica table and artificial peaches spill from a big ceramic bowl on the very center of the polished tabletop.

Wearing their swimsuits and cover-ups, they stop for a take-out clam dinner and eat at a wooden table beneath a big patio umbrella. When they pick up the highway and head home, George tunes the radio to her favorite station, playing sentimental love songs that she hums along with while Grace toys with her seashells and horse in the back seat. Amy feels the beaches and the cottages getting smaller and smaller behind her. Just for a few miles, she still hears a sense of the lapping, lapping waves and the wind and the seagulls' cry, as though that beautiful conch shell presses against her ear. He gave her this.

———

Something else happens, too. Driving home, sensations mount in the fluid sound of their voices, in the charge of their touch. The sensations trigger a vague memory and it feels as though a flash-back threatens. Once they arrive at her farmhouse, those sensa-tions build and she thinks of the ways to block triggers. But still, when she gives Grace a quick bath and puts her to bed, her skin prickles with anticipation. Never before has a flashback taken this long to arrive. Dr. Berg warned that an accumulation of triggers that alone are harmless can elicit a strong flashback in their very accrual.

The evening air feels cool, so she slips an oxford blouse on over her bathing suit. With the sun setting, dew rises on the grass. It's difficult to be discreet trying to control the triggers as George pours a glass of wine outside on her stone patio. One long, slow breath follows another.

"Look at that." Twilight fades into darkness and nature paints the moon low in the sky, spilling silver light on the distant corn-field. A smudge of scattered stars shows through the dark violet sky. But it is his deep voice that elicits a response when its quiet vibration tickles down her spine. "It looks like a painting," he says, "the way the moonlight shines on the fields."

Amy tries desperately to push away the impending flashback. Her eyes close for a moment, using visualization to travel back to the beach, the golden sand, the sound of the waves. But it's not enough. She steps out of her sandals and grounds herself, pressing her bare feet hard into the warm stone patio beneath them. The sensations scarcely subside.

"The whole day felt like a painting," she says quietly in the dusky light. Shadowed silhouettes of maple trees frame the view of the cornfields beyond her yard.

"How so?" George asks.

She listens to the night's sounds, a lone robin call, the lingering cicadas, trying to focus on anything to help her through this as she takes a long breath, considering the day and considering the sensations she feels. "Being at Stony Point? It all felt like beautiful beach colors and ocean sounds swept across some sort of life canvas. The sea breeze and salt air, the seagulls, that gorgeous summer sky over the water." George moves close behind her, his arms wrapping beneath the loose blouse, around her waist, as he bends close to listen. She takes his hands in hers and leans back into him. "It was a watercolor kind of day, all about the sea and waves, and your amazing lagoon." He leaves a soft kiss on her cheek and she turns back to the night, seeing the sunny images from the edge of the sea instead. "It all spread into a beautiful day. And I'll always remember it, George."

His hand runs along the length of her arm and Amy's breathing deepens while her heart beats faster. She thinks again of Dr. Berg's suggestions to manage flashbacks and inhales another slow breath. The last thing she wants is to worry George on this perfect day. But when he turns her around and his hands cradle her face, she is almost panic-stricken—visualizing the sea, the boardwalk, anything, anything at all, to stall what is coming straight at her. His eyes meet hers as he moves a wisp of hair from her cheek, and she hopes he doesn't notice how, wordlessly, she is trying to stop the flashback building with each touch of his hand on her skin. When he tips her face up and leans close, when she feels his mouth on hers, his breath near, hears him whisper her name, the flashback wins. It starts at her toes, tingling, no matter how hard her bare feet press into the ground.

It's important to know that the brain remembers in many ways. Just a certain touch can stimulate a trigger. And so she lets it happen; there is no use fighting it as this persistent flashback completely overwhelms her. It has taken all day, a constant back-and-forth struggle that has become too strong to resist. Finally, finally she fills with the flashback that comes with his every touch, fills with the bittersweet memory she lost a year ago, a flashback of being in love.

———

George lies in the dark room and senses the night just outside Amy's bedroom window. His arm holds her close and he kisses the top of her head while she sleeps. A soft breeze reaches in through the open window and he looks toward the sky through a shadow of swag lace curtains framing the windowpanes, the dark outside pale with moonlight. He takes her hand and cups it in his, to his chest, while she sleeps. Their bodies are still now, hers pressed to his beneath the sheet on this summer night.

He closes his eyes, thinking of the past hour and loving her even more, yet fearing what that might mean. Fearing the crime drawing even closer. The curtain moves again with a slight breeze. A rustling of tree leaves murmurs in the dark.

But there is something else he hears, not recognizing it for a long moment. Amy stirs and his hand strokes her hair.

He knows then, with that touch, with her so fully in his life now, what it is he hears. The crickets' song, the night owl call, all sounds of the countryside have stopped. The life outside the window, in Amy's yard and out past the farm fields, pauses with a long silence, the way it will when a predator is in the midst.

Eighteen

A MY AWAKENS TO A SOFT sound, one reassuring and puzzling. Its high pitch seems like the happy squeal of young children, a sweet vibrato. She closes her eyes and allows herself the luxury of picturing Grace at the beach the day before. Her beautiful laugh still rings clear in memory. But while lying in bed with only a cool sheet covering her, she recognizes the other sound she's hearing. It's her teakettle. The steamy whistle reaches from the kitchen and spreads through the upstairs like a wispy cloud.

It must be George. He must be in the kitchen cooking something for breakfast or setting the table. Earlier, in her sleep, she felt his kiss on her lips when he bent over and said *Good morning* before he left the room. He'd been up with the sun, needing to stop home and get to his shop early. She sits up, wanting to see him now, before he leaves. Wanting to still feel his arms around her, to hear his whispered words that came in the dark the night before.

But the sun shines too bright for daybreak. With a quick glance at the clock, she tosses back the sheet and gets her robe from the closet. It is almost nine. George would have left hours ago.

The insistent teakettle whistle brings an alarming image to mind of the stove flame licking at her daughter's summer pajamas, sparks flickering up to her fine blonde hair as Grace swats at the burning fabric. But her daughter knows not to play with the stove. She slips into her bathrobe and pulls the sash tight around her waist while hurrying to Grace's bedroom, finding her still asleep, her sheets bunched at her feet, Bear lying on the floor.

And Amy's heart drops with the realization of her own fragmented frame of mind. Did she sleepwalk with a flashback, returning to bed after lighting the flame on a kettle of water? She can't continue to jeopardize her daughter like this, so she returns to her bedroom, picks up the telephone on her nightstand and dials The Main Course. Maybe George knows.

———

George sits at his office desk placing orders with meat vendors. School let out and the barbecues will be firing up at backyard graduation parties. He rose at dawn, stopped home only to shower and change into his black and white work clothes, and left right away for his shop, buying a bagel on the way. Now the aroma of fresh-brewed coffee and the sounds of Sinatra fill his office as he hangs up with one of the vendors. The phone rings as soon as he sets it down and he nearly topples his coffee in his quick reach for it.

"George?"

"Well good morning," he says to Amy while blotting the puddle of coffee with a napkin. He pictures her sleepy, beginning her day in the kitchen, the sun streaming in the paned windows, Angel at her feet waiting to be fed, Grace sitting with a bowl of cereal at the blue table.

"Good morning," she says quickly, sounding distracted. "I'm glad I caught you."

"What's the matter?" He crumples the soiled napkin into a ball.

"It's probably nothing, but I wanted to check with you first. Listen, did you happen to make a coffee here this morning?"

"At your place? No."

"You didn't put the water on and maybe forget about it?"

"Amy. What's going on?"

"Well, it's the funniest thing. It's nothing, really, except that I was in bed and a noise woke me up. At first I thought it was you, downstairs."

"What kind of noise?"

"The teakettle. It's whistling. You didn't heat water for an instant coffee?"

"Have you gone downstairs?"

"Not yet. It's still whistling, but I wanted to call you first. George?" Her voice lowers to a hush. "I don't remember going downstairs. Do you think—"

"Where's Grace?" he asks, not letting her blame the odd morning on herself, just like she blamed her misplaced car on herself. Someone is at it again.

"She's still in bed."

"Get her, Amy. Get her now and wait upstairs until I get there."

"Oh don't be silly. I'll go shut it off and be done with it."

"No, don't. And get Grace right now. Do you understand? Now."

"George, you're scaring me. Do you think someone's downstairs?"

"Just sit tight. I'll be there in no time." He hangs up knowing damn well now that someone *was* in her yard last night. Dean isn't due in until one o'clock, so he has to close everything up. He double-checks the meat grinders and bone saw and quickly puts a tray of Cornish hens back into the freezer before dropping a couple knives into the wash water. As he shuts off the coffee pot, Sinatra continues to play on the stereo and it's like his father is there with him. The music's always been a bridge like that; his father speaks to him through the lyrics. If he were still alive, George would snatch up the phone now and call him. His father would talk him through this, would tell him what to do, what to say to Amy.

And while Sinatra keeps singing of sacrificing everything for love, George knows. He'd tell his father that, too. That he finally gets it, gets how you know when someone is the right person. And he can just hear what his father would say, with a satisfied look on his face.

Well, George. Now do you understand why I never explained it to you?

"Yeah, Dad," George answers as he rushes into the cutting room while lifting off his apron. "I get it. Because there are no words."

That's right. And that's why my ring is so important to me.

George hangs the apron on a wall hook. "The ring?"

Sure. The ring says it all. Sinatra wore one, too. All the time. But it's not like mine. His had the family crest. Mine? With that ruby? Don't you know what that is? It's your mother's heart. That's how you know when it's right.

"Someone has your heart," George says as he locks up the door and runs out to his pickup truck.

———

She looks a little disheveled waiting at the painted porch railing, barefoot in a floral tank and denim cutoffs, her hair in a ponytail.

"Hi sweetheart," George says, climbing the steps and looking beyond into the house. "Where's Grace?"

"In the kitchen." Amy holds the door open for him.

George walks in and scans the living room, his eyes stopping on each window, already searching for the breached location. "I told you to wait upstairs," he says.

"I thought the pot might burn if the water evaporated. And I didn't want to hear it anymore. George, I can't keep doing this, blacking out and forgetting. I'm afraid one of these times Grace will get hurt." She turns away and moves toward the kitchen. "I've already put in a call to my doctor about it."

George grabs her arm. "Amy. Listen to me." He pulls her in close, holding tight. "Nothing's wrong with you. You have to believe me. What if someone had broken into your house? There could have been a confrontation."

She covers his hand with her own. "Don't you think you're overreacting? Why would someone want to break in and turn on the teakettle? Seriously? I mean, nothing's stolen, nothing's out of place. It was me, George, don't you see?"

"No, sweetheart, I don't." He releases her arm and moves into the kitchen. Angel sits straight on the floor in front of the refrigerator, her radar ears turning to every sound while Grace spoons a mouthful of cereal at the table, still in her pajamas and swinging her legs beneath her. The green sand pail and red horse are beside her bowl. "Hi there, Gracie," he says, patting her head before turning to the stove.

Amy comes up behind him. "I turned off the flame a few minutes ago."

George sets the blue kettle on the cool front burner and lifts the silver cover. A couple inches of hot water remain, so whoever had gotten into the house did so not too long ago. He jiggles the back door handle against the deadbolt and the door doesn't budge;

all the glass is intact in its small panes. Over the kitchen sink, the blue and white checked curtains are pushed aside, the windows looking out to the backyard. "Were these open all night?"

"No. I just opened them now. It's so warm today."

He moves into the dining room and immediately notices not so much the window, which is closed, but the screen that is jimmied off the frame and hanging slightly askew. So it's starting to happen. The cracks from one day, from the crime, begin to show.

Amy stands at the kitchen sink, her back to George. She tips her head up with a long swallow of water before he notices there's a prescription bottle in her hand. "What are you doing?" he asks.

"Dr. Berg prescribed these. They're a mild tranquilizer." She leans against the sink and wraps her arms around herself. "I have to stay calm with Grace. I can't risk her safety. Look what happened at the mall when I lost control."

"How many did you take?" George asks. Because anything goes now, anything, and he has no way of knowing if the pills had been tampered with this morning.

"Just one."

"Are you feeling okay?"

"No. I'm not. I don't remember doing any of this. How can I forget moving my car at the mall or turning on the teakettle? I could've burned down the house, for God's sake." Angel walks between her feet and so she pulls the cat food from the cabinet and adds more to the bowl, handing it to Grace to set on the floor. "Will I forget in ten minutes that I fed the cat? That I made the beds?" She sinks into a kitchen chair. Grace hooks the pail of shells on her arm and climbs into her lap.

George sits beside her. "We have to talk, sweetheart."

"You know something. I've done something else, haven't I?"

"No. You haven't done any of this. That's why we have to talk." He takes Grace's hand and winks at her, not wanting to upset her with his urgency. "Is Celia home?"

"I doubt it. She's on deadline with a few houses to stage this week."

George checks his watch. "Listen. I've got to stop at Dean's place and see if he can open up the shop. Then I'm coming back here. In the meantime, get Grace dressed, have something to eat. Pull everything together for me. Can you do that?"

"I don't think I'm liking this, George."

He looks long at her, loving her to pieces, his heart breaking into as many. "Me either. Just trust me, please Amy. We'll talk as soon as I get back."

"But I'm going in to work this morning, so many gowns came in. Grace and Angel were coming too. Really, George, I just can't—"

"You'll go later. Lock up behind me and leave it locked."

Amy sets Grace on the chair and follows him to the front door. When he steps outside, he turns back and kisses her quickly.

"George? Are Grace and I safe?"

He nods. A stalker moved closer to his victim right in step with George, right into her house after he spent the night. The game rules have been laid out. The closer George gets to Amy, the closer the stalker gets, too. "Lock the door, though."

Amy closes the heavy wooden door. When he hears the dead-bolt turn, he hurries off the front porch and around to the dining room window to right the screen before she has a chance to notice it. Try as he might, George finds no other cracks, nothing else out of place.

Amy dresses Grace in blue shorts and a flowered top, then puts two ponytails in her hair. Never before did she have to stop mid-ponytail and clasp one hand inside the other to stop the trembling. Will she turn around and find the television on or a faucet running, not remembering going through the motions? What's next? Will she forget she dressed Grace and reach into her closet for another outfit?

"No, no," she says as she slips a butterfly barrette in front of Grace's ponytails. One day can't keep taking pieces of voice, of memory, erasing everything in a different kind of kidnapping. Amy sits Grace and her green sand pail on the bed and slips her matching butterfly sandals on her small feet.

"There. You're all dressed. You look so pretty, now I could never forget that," she says while lifting Grace off the bed and standing her on the floor. "We're twins today, wearing the same outfits."

Grace lifts her beach pail and the seashells clatter as she pours them out onto her bed. Angel jumps up and walks slowly between clam and mollusk shells, whiskers stiff, eyes wide. She's never smelled the sea before.

"George says we have to stick together, you and me." Amy crouches beside Grace. "He must be pretty smart, because he knows I'll always stay with you. Always, always." She hooks a finger beneath Grace's chin and lifts her face. Morning sunlight coming through the lace curtain touches wisps of her ponytails. "You know that, right? You always stay with Mommy. Even if Mommy is upset and you feel afraid. Do you know Mommy loves you?" She looks directly at Grace's mouth, willing words to form. "Answer me, honey. Please," she whispers. "Just a little bit. Do you know I love you? Say yes, Grace. Tell Mommy yes." Her hands frame Grace's face while her thumb strokes her lips. "Come on.

Try to say it. Yesss. Hear Mommy make silly sounds?" Her thumb presses at Grace's mouth. "Ssss. Like a sssilly sssnake." Tears rise in Amy's eyes as she wills her daughter to speak. One spills down her cheek and Grace's eyes follow it. "Now Mommy's crying tears. Tearsss."

Grace lifts her finger to Amy's mouth and touches it to her bottom teeth as Amy hisses. Amy tries to do the same to her, moving Grace's bottom lip and touching her little pearl teeth. "Knock-knock." She taps lightly on a tooth, waiting.

It doesn't work. Nothing works. Grace turns to her scattered shells. Some are chipped, some still damp with the sea, most are sandy. The scent of tangy salt catches in their intricate whorls. After a second, Amy stands up and her hand moves to bless herself in one sudden, fluid motion.

———

When she walked onto the front porch holding Grace's hand, he knew the sight of Celia would silence her. She'd figure if he went out of his way to find her friend at work staging some remodeled colonial or three-bedroom cape just to watch Grace for a while, things are bad.

George takes her hand after Celia and Grace leave and walks her to the backyard. "My mother called," Amy tells him. Two dragonflies hover over the grass; a robin doesn't stop toodling; the sky is hazy with the day's heat; Amy walks barefoot in her denim shorts and a pretty tank top. So all should be easy, he thinks, just like this summer day. "She wants to visit in a couple of weeks."

"That sounds like a good idea," George says. He feels that perspiration has dampened his white shirt to his back.

"She still worries about me. First it was because I was widowed. Then when I decided to keep the house, she worried if I could take care of the property. Then after Grace was kidnapped, she worried about everything. She wanted me to move back home until they caught the men who, well, you know. I haven't heard from Detective Hayes for a few days. Do you think he's made progress with the investigation? If he had anything to report, I'm sure he'd call. I guess the more time goes by, the colder the trail gets. Sometimes I wonder if they'll ever catch them. I think my mother wonders, too. That's why she wants to spend time with me."

"Amy." They had walked to the tire swing the whole time Amy prattled on. She pushes the tire gently as though it holds her daughter.

"Grace is her only grandchild, you know. I really don't mind indulging her."

"Sweetheart," George says quietly.

She turns to him with angry tears in her eyes. "Mom can help me in my boutique. I need to put out more summer dresses. I have a Starlight Special going on, for the summer evening weddings. Celia helped me decorate the shop for the sale, with twinkly lights everywhere. Just like stars."

"Shh." George sits in the shade beneath the tall maple and tugs her hand to sit, too.

"It's not fair," Amy says.

"What isn't?"

"Do you know the signs that someone is emerging from grief? Well I'll tell you." She takes a quick breath. "First. Reinvesting in other people's lives. Like I did in Grace's." She looks up at the blue sky, fighting back those tears. "That's why I decided to keep this house alone, for her. What a beautiful home my daughter has.

And having new dreams and goals, that's a good sign. And I did, I reinvented my bridal shop with the vintage angle, decorating it with stars. Because what bride doesn't go into a marriage full of wishes? But the strongest sign of emerging from grief?"

George waits for a quiet second. "Tell me."

"I know that one, George. I reached it. Feeling a sense of joy with life. Coming out of grief feels like a budding spring that follows a long, nasty winter. Like a rose unfolding to the sun."

"You'll get there."

"But I already did!" she insists. "I felt all those things. Every one of them. On the morning when I walked out of that bank ... I had new goals, I was reinvesting in life and I felt so happy. Then a monster took it all away from me."

"Amy, stop."

"No. No, listen. Because then? Then I got it all back again."

She looks straight ahead, down over the gentle sloping hill to her farmhouse. But George knows she isn't seeing her small garden off to the side of the yard. She isn't seeing the zinnias growing taller in front of the fence. She isn't seeing the closed-up gown room with June sunshine reaching in its window, waiting for her to get back to the business of brides. Because the silent tears streaming down her face tell him that she knows. She knows his next words will change everything.

"I got it all back with you," she explains. "This weekend. I was reinvesting in *us*." She turns to him then, her eyes welling. "Last night, joy came spilling back into my life. I never thought I could trust again, but then? Then I trusted you. Did I tell you what a perfect night I had? That I'm so happy you came into my life? And you're going to change that now, aren't you? You're going to scare me and take it all away. That's how it goes. I take a baby step forward and life sends me a giant step way, way back, until I just can't move anymore."

George takes her hand. "Nothing's going to change last night, do you understand? Nothing. We'll get through this together. And it is scary, but it's more dangerous for you not to know."

"Dangerous?"

"I hoped it would blow over, that it was all just a prank. But when you called me this morning, I knew someone had been in your house when you were sleeping. It wasn't a flashback, Amy. It wasn't you who turned on the stove. And you *did* park your car in V-3 last week. I didn't know until now what I should do with this." He pulls the photograph from his shirt pocket. "When I saw you taking tranquilizers, I knew I had to tell you. You don't need the pills, your mental health is fine, and you're *not* blacking out and losing your memory. Grace is very safe with you. You're a wonderful mother to her."

"Then what is it?"

He looks at the picture of Amy crouched in the mall parking lot and hands it to her. "I think you're being stalked."

Nineteen

S OMEONE TOOK A PICTURE OF me that day?"

"Apparently. All the little things that you thought were memory lapses? They're not. They're stalking, Amy."

She looks up from the photograph. "George, you're scaring me. Are you sure about this? Because memory problems *are* a symptom of PTSD."

George reaches over and traces a soft line around her face. The day is summer still, with only the buzz of cicadas and the call of a blue jay moving through the warmth. "Your memory's fine. You're a good mother to Grace."

"But why would someone just take out Mark's coffee cup, or leave my radio on? And the teakettle? I don't get it."

"It's complicated. They seem like simple things, but they aren't. Someone's playing a serious mind game by trying to undermine your confidence. It's not getting into your home that matters to them, it's getting into your head."

"Why though? What have I done?"

"Nothing, sweetheart. It's got to all be connected to the heist, somehow."

Amy studies the photograph again, then hands it back to George. "Do you really think that's it?"

"I don't know. If they're setting things up to make it seem like Grace is in jeopardy in your care, then that throws you off the heist trail and on to something else. It takes the heat off."

"Oh my God. I've got to tell Hayes."

George folds up the photograph. "Let's think this through, first."

"What do you mean, think it through? I need to report this, George. This is serious."

"Of course it is. But when you tell Hayes, he has to see you're on top of things. He can't see the situation the way a stalker might like him to."

"Which is?"

He presses the back of his hand to his perspiring forehead and squints into the early summer sunshine. "As though you're coming undone by things."

"So what do I do?"

"Okay. First we need a written log of everything. Of every incident that's happened." *To buy me time to get to the bottom of this,* he thinks.

"I can do that."

"And you need evidence that you've taken precautions since the crime. That you installed security lights, changed your locks, that I cut the shrubs back from your windows, anything to ensure Grace's safety." *I need to ensure that if this is Reid, he stops.*

"If you're right about this, I mean, should I get a dog?" She takes the picture from him and unfolds it again. "After Mark died and I stayed on here, my father said I needed a gun. He thought I was too isolated on this property. I didn't get one, but I did apply for my permit. So do I need that gun now?"

"Amy, Amy." George tips her chin up. "Slow down. Let's plan this one step at a time. I'll stay with you for a while, okay? I'll move in here or you and Grace can move in with me. Because you cannot be alone."

Amy shakes her head no with a sad smile and stands then. "I have to be, George. I need to keep working with Grace." When she starts back toward her house, he quickly catches up to her. "With any more upheaval," she tells him, "I'll lose her once and for all to the damn silence. I love what you're trying to do. And I promise I'll be very careful, but I have to think of Grace first. It's up to only me to hold things together here."

George looks out toward the distant cornfields shimmering with heat waves, then back at her ready to argue.

"No," she insists quietly, shaking her head as she opens the back screen door into the kitchen. "I can't have you move in and disrupt her routine. It's too risky."

Risk, that's what it's all about, no matter what he does. He leans against the kitchen counter, his arms crossed, knowing she won't budge on her decision. Instead she's already got the sink filled with soapy water and has dropped in the breakfast dishes, trying to control the small stuff of her life, scrubbing forks and spoons first, then a breakfast plate, a pretty dish edged with blue flowers, for all she's worth. Her shoulders move with the motion and no doubt she's crying at the same time. He steps behind her, puts his hands on those shoulders and turns her to him. The plate drips in her grip and he hugs her, plate and all, for a long moment.

———

Since she gave voice to two particular words, she can't get them out of her head. Saying them made the reality of the stalking situation stark. When she walks over to Celia's house to get Grace, Celia has a tall glass of ice water waiting in the midday heat and Amy quaffs it down in long gulps. She paces back and forth on her friend's deck watching the little golden retriever follow Grace with her green sand pail around the yard. The puppy steps with happy, loopy ease. Okay, so maybe a dog isn't a bad idea. It would alert her to danger around her home. The two words keep alternating in her mind. Gun. Dog. Semiautomatic nine-millimeter handgun. German shepherd.

"Do you think it's a good idea to go to your shop alone?"

"What?" Amy's gaze turns slowly to Celia sitting at her patio table beneath the navy umbrella.

"If George is right and someone is following you, then you're not safe even there."

"Well now. Isn't that nice? Then they won, didn't they? I'll just stay home and put bars on my windows and padlocks on my doors."

"You know what I mean, Amy. I'm afraid someone can get to you there alone."

Amy walks off the deck to the spigot on the back of the house. She tips her glass beneath it and turns the handle, letting cold water spit over her ice cubes. Sasha stands beside her cautiously watching the water flow, inching closer until she finally laps the running water. Her pink tongue curls around the stream. When Grace laughs, the noise surprises Amy and she turns to see her daughter behind her.

"Sasha's drinking," Grace squeals, grinning widely.

"That's right," Amy answers. Why can't she be happy to hear her daughter's words? She should repeat them and rhyme them and take Grace's hands and do a dance and draw out a song of words. Why does there have to be this rage that she can't even direct? When Sasha turns away and lies down in a shady spot near a gnarled lilac bush, Amy sets her water glass down. Cupping her hands together beneath the faucet, clear water fills them and she presses her perspiring face into the liquid. Again she does it, splashing the water up into her hair. As she turns off the water, Grace's little hand reaches from behind her. Amy softens the flow and Grace moves her fingers into the water, then dabs her dripping fingertips on Amy's cheeks. Her fingers are feathers, the sensation on her skin as good as words. Amy sinks to Grace's height and her tears mix with the spigot water. Is her stalker watching this intimate moment? She won't give whoever's intruded into her life the satisfaction of looking around to see.

When Grace takes her wet fingers to the shade to cool Sasha, Amy returns to the deck and to Celia still sitting at the patio table. "I know why you worry, Celia. You think this nut will grab me off the street while I'm hauling gowns into my shop."

"That's right," Celia says clearly, squinting up at her in the bright sunshine. "I do. Why take chances?"

"But don't you see? I can't stop living because of this. I have to keep moving forward with Grace. We keep busy with the gowns and playing and gardening and walks. Simple things that keep her engaged. That keep reeling her back to me. Because it seems like she's getting worse and I can't let her see a *new* fear. She can't be afraid to live. So *I* have to keep living."

"And I don't have to like it. If it were up to me, I'd keep you both inside with those bars on the windows where I know you'd be safe."

Amy leans on the railing, watching Grace in the yard.

"At least you have George. He was worried sick when he tracked me down at that little Tudor out on Old Willow Road. You and Grace mean the world to him."

200

"He wants to move in with us so we won't be alone."

"Don't tell me you said no."

Amy reels around and eyes her friend. "Don't *you* tell me how to live, Celia. Please. Did you lose your husband, your income and your child? I've hardly been able to open my shop these past weeks. And for God's sake, you don't even have a child. You have a dog. You really aren't in a position to tell me how to live my life."

"I'm not telling you how."

"Aren't you though? Don't work alone. Stay home. Padlock your doors. Live with George. Come on, already!"

"Listen. You have to be really careful with this stalking now. And whether you like it or not, I care and I intend to check up on you all the time." With tears running down her cheeks, Celia looks out at Grace and Sasha in the shade, then back at Amy. "You're my best friend, who I love very much, and I really don't want anything more happening to you. Okay?"

"I'm sorry." Amy sits in the chair beside Celia. "I didn't mean what I said. I just get so darn mad at all of this."

"I know," Celia agrees, swiping her tears. "We're all on edge. It's only because we're worried." She squeezes Amy's hand, then. "About *you.*"

The sensation comes again, *again*, with the feeling of someone's hand pressing around hers. She collects Grace and her sand pail and heads home to her sketch pad to draw the feeling into an image. Her pencil shapes the scene as viewed from above. Two hands, the pressure, the warmth, and what? What? The lead pencil point shades his knuckles with short hatched lines, clearly defining the hand. Fading lines, scars, dark lines, all shaping something apparent but not visible yet. She uses a tissue to blend the hatched shading, studying the hand on top of hers as she does. Something is lodged in her memory, some silent detail that screams to be remembered.

———

"What happens now?" George asks Detective Hayes. He hadn't told Amy that the detective called him earlier to stop in for fingerprints. One issue to handle was enough.

Hayes opens a folder on his desk. "Routine stuff. They'll be scanned and digitally encoded. But since the girl's shoes came back with clear prints, we need to compare them with the prints of anyone who came in contact with the evidence. We're coordinating a separate fingerprint file on the case. The FBI is, too. Everyone's got a hand in this one."

"And my prints will be a part of the file?"

"You returned Grace that day. If the prints on the shoes aren't yours, or her mother's, they may be solid evidence in a future conviction."

"And how accurate is this computer search stuff?"

"If the suspects have a criminal record, ninety-eight to one hundred percent. No two people have identical prints, so we're looking at a high degree of consistency. Your prints will be keeping company with the best, George. An FBI database stores digital images of millions of people along with their criminal history." He looks from a copy of the prints to George. "If they have one. Some records are in the system temporarily, like yours. And Amy's. As part of an investigation. They'll be deleted once this is done."

George holds out an open hand. "What about scars on the prints?"

Detective Hayes turns the fingerprint images toward him. "See the white line? Scars are the easiest patterns to decipher in a print. But they change over time; they thicken, they heal, so they're unreliable as a source of identification. It's the ridge pattern on your skin that stays the same. The computer creates a spatial map of your ridge pattern and converts it into a binary code. When it's scanned in, the entire system can be searched for identical prints. And if they match the print lifted from the shoe, that avenue is closed."

"You mean to tell me that the guys who pulled this off left prints? Wouldn't they wear gloves?"

"You'd think so, but after twenty years of doing this, I can tell you one thing for certain. Someone always slips up."

———

"I know what you're doing," Amy says when he walks into her kitchen later that evening.

"You do?"

"Yes." She takes the DVDs from George's hand. "Bugs Bunny cartoons?"

"For Grace."

Amy looks at George and smiles. "Thanks." She holds up the next. "Runaway Bride?"

"Chick flick. You know, with bride stuff. For you."

"And Marty?"

"Have you seen it?"

"No." She reads the back of the movie box. "Ernest Borgnine?"

"He plays a butcher. Lives in New York with his mother." George waits until Amy looks up at him. "All his brothers and sisters are married, you know? And his customers come into the shop, and his friends, and they always ask him *Marty, when you getting married? Your brother just had a nice wedding. When you going to find a girl?* And this Marty, he's a little overweight, in his thirties, and one day he comes home from work and his mother tells him he should go dancing at the Stardust Ballroom. She says her nephew told her they've got a lot of nice tomatoes there."

"Tomatoes?" Amy walks into the living room and slips the Bugs Bunny disk into the DVD player.

"Sure. You know." George follows her and sits in the club chair. "And he meets a nice girl there. She's a little plain, kind of shy. And they hit it off. But then everyone panics about him being involved with a girl. His friends feel deserted and tell him he found a real dog. His mother's afraid she'll have to live in an apartment with a new daughter-in-law and says she doesn't like the girl. And poor Marty, he starts to listen to everyone. Until finally, well, never mind."

"What? What happens?"

George picks up the newspaper. "Never mind, I said. You'll have to watch and see. Now sit with Grace and Bugs Bunny, would you?"

"George." Amy crouches beside him in the club chair and speaks quietly while Bugs Bunny hatches a scheme. "I do know what you're doing."

"What am I doing?"

"You're bringing all these movies so you'll have to stay with me half the night watching them. You don't want to leave me and Grace alone."

"So?"

"We're okay. I can take care of myself and Grace."

"I don't doubt that for a minute. But I can take care of you, too. And I like to watch movies. It would help if you'd subscribe to a movie service, though. My DVD options are getting limited."

"Oh, you did all right." Amy watches the rascally rabbit dancing across the television screen. Grace and Bear and a pail of seashells line the sofa. "Tomatoes?" she asks after a moment, still crouched beside the chair.

George just looks back, not saying a word before leaning over and kissing her mouth.

"What's the matter, George?" she asks when she pulls back a little, her hand rising to his face, stroking his cheek.

"You're kind of cute," he whispers. "That's all. Now go sit with Grace."

Amy does, curling her legs beneath her on the sofa, and George lifts the newspaper. But he can't read a word. He can't leave Amy. Beneath the reading lamp, behind the open newspaper, he shakes his head. He can't stop loving her.

Twenty

AMY TURNS THE PISTOL IN her hand and draws a finger along the barrel. A week passed since she learned someone is stalking her. Like an old-fashioned scale, her mind has gauged a gun against a dog, back and forth, one side sinking lower in favor, then rising as the other's benefits weighed heavier. During that week, Grace, Celia, George, and her walking-partner Sara Beth all kept her occupied. Her parents phoned daily. Someone is always with her, but in the end, that type of personal protection will stop. In the end, everyone has to live their own lives. In the end, she needs something she can count on, right away. She can count on a gun.

"The nine-millimeter is our most popular handgun, even though it's not the best manstopper," the salesman explains. "If you're looking to use it for self-defense, you might want to use jacketed hollow point ammunition."

"Jacketed hollow point?"

"Right. It mushrooms upon impact. You'll get less penetration but it does greater tissue damage because of the larger diameter of the expanded bullet. Commonly used for self-defense."

"I see." Amy's slender fingers tuck her layered blonde hair behind an ear and what she sees is this: a jacketed hollow point pumped into the men who assaulted her and Grace one fine morning. Her hatred for them grows as Grace's silence lengthens. Would the day have gone differently if she had been armed? If she slipped her hand into her purse and pulled out a nine-millimeter semiautomatic and trained it on the man holding her daughter? Or took her own hostage, her gun holding prisoner the man who reached for Grace's shoe? Would she have won a show of wills then? But Detective Hayes mentioned the kidnapper holding a forty-five caliber weapon. "Do you think I need something larger?"

The salesman points out forty-fives in the case. "You really shouldn't overpower yourself with more gun than you can comfortably handle. The nine-millimeter is a good choice. With the right ammunition, it'll have sufficient knockdown power. You can always trade up in the future."

Will this never end? Will she always be trading up, considering gun models, taking lessons? Will she need a weapon concealed on each floor of her home? What would be effective to store in the pantry? The basement? Will Grace need to be trained in weapon use one day? Will she come to carry a gun as easily as a cell phone?

Amy glances around the shop, the pistol in her grip following her gaze. Bob, her salesman, is reaching into the case and pulling out various nine-millimeter handguns. Bob. Such an innocuous name. Friendly. Approachable. Bob sells weapons that disrupt and impair the blood supply carrying oxygen to the brain. That disrupt the central nervous system. That break bones and the skeletal structure. That cause neural shock.

"Now, Amy, is it?"

"Yes. Bob."

He sets four different nine-millimeters on top of the display cabinet. All the shop's weapons are visible behind glass, much like the precious gems at a jewelry store. They spin out before her on tiers of enclosed, softly illuminated shelves. Lethal guns lie at a precise angle, muzzle to handgrip, in a circular case that gives the optical illusion of infinity. A full array of black and silver and brown wood winds across the shelves. Her eye returns to the blacks. Black looks serious; it holds no fancy allure, no shiny details, no mistaken intention.

Bob slides a gun closer to her. "Keep in mind a couple things as you narrow down your selection. These are all nine-millimeters. Since you're thinking about self-protection, consider the circumstances under which you might discharge it. In a violent confrontation, you *won't* be cool, calm and collected. Stress and fear screw up your motor skills and it's damn easy to fumble with too many controls."

"Well. There are more controls on some of these than on my microwave. What do they all do?"

Bob's hands move in sync with his words, pointing out the various knobs and levers and slides. "You've got a magazine release, slide release, safety levers, takedown levers. And on models like this one," he sets a black and silver gun in her hand, "the controls are ambidextrous. One of each on each side."

"It's a little confusing."

"The one you started with has only the magazine and slide release. It's very simple to operate under duress."

Amy reaches for that gun.

"One more thing. Position yourself with it as though you were going to shoot. We have to check the trigger reach."

"Like trying on a pair of gloves? See if my fingers fit?"

"Pretty much. Go ahead and reach your finger to the trigger."

Amy wraps her fingers around the weapon and tentatively holds her arms straight out. "How can you tell if it fits?"

Bob takes her hand in his and turns her arm for a better look at her fingers curled around the weapon. "Not bad. If the first pad on your finger engages the face of the trigger, the fit's good."

Amy tips her head, checking the fit. "I'll take it."

"You don't want to try any others?"

"No. I want this one." She sets it down and pulls her Connecticut Pistol Permit from her purse. "I need the gun and anything else necessary. Ammunition, a gun safe, maybe a holster of some kind, cleaning supplies."

"Okay, I just have a couple forms you need to complete. And what about training?"

She pulls a pen from her purse. "Where would I do that?"

He slides a glossy brochure across the counter. "The indoor firing range is down the street. You'd want a combination of classroom and live firing instruction. I'd advise a basic safety course followed by a defensive handgun course. Some of the classes pack a lot of punch in a few hours."

Without basic training, the weapon is no good to her. Amy turns it over in her hand. The pad of her thumb runs over the dotted black polymer grip. Sara Beth is babysitting Grace and so she needs to get back home, under the pretense of returning from a special therapy session. There are all kinds of therapy, after all. Physical, psychological, social. She considers the gun, needing to control it physically first. Psychologically, too. So the defensive lessons on the firing range will be her therapy now. Therapy preparing her so that next time, she'll be ready.

"I can sign you up for the lessons here. We're part of the same facility."

"Okay, Bob. That will work out just fine."

"I hate doing this, but I need as many eyes on her as possible." George pulls the pencil from behind his ear and rips a piece of meat wrapping paper from a roll. He writes Amy's address on the paper and hands it to Nate standing on the other side of the deli case, sunglasses perched on top of his head.

"Why do you hate me helping?"

"You bullshitting me?" George asks. "This is all your damn fault to begin with, and now I'm asking for your help?"

"Yeah. Well. I know the house. I picked you up after the mall thing." Nate folds the paper in half and tucks it into his jeans pocket. "I still don't get why you hooked up with her. If she figures things out, you're screwed."

"Quit worrying about me."

"It's not just you I'm worried about." Nate checks his watch. "I'm coming around back to make a sandwich."

"Not with those clothes on, you're not." A film of white dust coats Nate's jeans and the long sleeve denim work shirt he just slipped out of. He wears heavy work boots and a T-shirt revealing seriously strong arms. Tile work does that, the same way throwing baseballs did, developing the biceps and triceps fully. "You'll contaminate the place."

Nate walks in a long stride to the round tables in the corner and hangs his shirt over his seat back. "Make me a sandwich then, would you? Got any roast beef?"

George returns with two roast beef sandwiches on hard rolls, two cups of his shop's house blend coffee and a jar of horseradish. He sits across from his brother. "And don't be going by her place until I talk to her."

"I won't," Nate says around a mouthful of sandwich. "You've got the cash, George. Why don't you hire someone to watch her and find out who's doing this shit? I mean, stalking? That's pretty serious."

"How many times do I have to tell you I'm not touching that money? It's not ours to spend. Let's just return it and the hell with it." He picks up his sandwich and sets it back down, untouched. "Forget the day ever happened."

Nate finishes chewing and washes the food down with a swallow of black coffee. He opens what is left of his roll and slathers horseradish on the pink roast beef. "Hey, it was all insured. No one's really lost anything. If we play our cards right, we'll be set for life with that cash. Like right now, it can find who's stalking Amy. It opens doors."

"Like shit it does."

"No, really. Let's say it's your birthday. Now I can buy you season tickets to the Yankees if I want. I could never swing that before."

"What do I want with season tickets? I'm not driving to the Bronx more than once or twice a year."

"It was almost your team, George. It's my way of paying you back."

"Will you get over it, once and for all? I don't want to hear for the rest of my life that you fucked up my shot at the majors that day at the cottage. Dad died when he did. It is what it is, Nate. Drop it already."

"Oh, cool off. I'm just saying you earned it, man, if you spend a little on yourself. Kind of like a sweat equity." Nate tips back in his chair and eyes George. "Sweet Jesus, we did sweat that day, didn't we? So enjoy the payoff. We can take that bike trip any time now. Go out to the west coast. You're looking stressed, George. It'd do you good to get away. Just the open road ahead of us, blue skies and all." He presses what's left of his sandwich into his mouth. "We can even fix up that rat trap at the beach now," he says around the food. "Hell, we can remodel it into a seaside resort."

The bell over the door rings when a young working couple stops in on their lunch hour. They consider the meals-to-go case. "Hold your thought," George says as he goes to take their order. They buy seafood cakes and two porterhouse steaks before leaving. When George sits across from Nate again, he picks up his sandwich. "And we're not doing any beach remodeling either, so don't get any ideas. I like that little cottage just fine the way it is. The same way I liked my life the way it was. It was *my* life." When the bell above the door rings again, George sets his sandwich down and shoves the plate to the side, nearly whispering, "For all the money in the world, I don't own it anymore."

"George?"

They both look back to the doorway. George glares at Nate, then pushes back his chair and wipes his hands on his black apron before walking quickly to the door. His eyes never leave her, never leave the deep gold gypsy skirt and fitted black tank, never leave the face that looks relaxed for the first time in a week. The therapy must have helped. And he doesn't stop hearing his own heartbeat, as he's unsure as to what Amy might have heard.

"Hey," he says, kissing her full on the mouth. "This is a nice surprise, what are you doing here?"

"I thought I'd stop in and say hello. I have a few minutes."

"How about a bite to eat?"

"No, George. Just a visit." She hitches her head toward Nate. "Did I interrupt something?" she asks.

George looks over his shoulder, hesitates, then takes Amy's hand. "It's just my brother. Come on."

Nate pulls the sunglasses off the top of his head, slips them in the pocket of the shirt on the chair back and slides a third chair over to the table.

"Nate. I'd like you to meet Amy Trewist. Amy, my brother Nate Carbone."

"Nate," she says, smiling.

Nate stands and takes her hand. "Amy, nice to meet you. Grab a seat."

George pulls out her chair. "Coffee?"

"No, thanks," Amy says, squeezing his hand. "Sara Beth's babysitting Grace. We're going out for lunch and ice cream."

"How'd the therapy go this morning? Did it help much?"

"Definitely. I'm making good progress," Amy assures him.

"I'm sorry to hear what's happened to you, Amy," Nate says. "I told George if there's any way I can help, I'd like to."

Amy's gaze moves between the two brothers. "I'm okay," she insists. "These things have a way of working themselves out."

"Well until they do," George adds, "I told Nate about the stalking."

She turns to Nate. "It's nothing, really. George is very protective."

"With good reason," Nate agrees. He sips his coffee, watching her over the rim.

"We thought that when Nate's in your part of town, he'll swing by your house," George lets her know. "To be sure no one's there that shouldn't be."

"You really don't have to. I could never impose on you like that, Nate."

"It's no problem."

"The more people around you right now, the better," George insists.

"You guys," she says. "You make it sound like I'm some damsel in distress. I am very careful. And nothing's happened for a few days. Maybe he's losing interest."

"Maybe. Or maybe he's gearing up for the next round," George says. "In the meantime, I'll feel better knowing my brother's around, too. And you won't mistake him when he swings by. That's his motorcycle parked outside."

"Well now that I've got my Carbone bodyguards lined up … thank you, Nate. For Grace's sake, I won't argue further."

"Your daughter?" Nate asks.

"Yes, and she's my first priority."

"I'm sure she is." Nate reaches for George's plate with the still untouched sandwich and pulls it in front of him.

"Don't you have to get to work?" George asks, pulling the plate back across the table.

"What do you do, Nate?" Amy asks.

"I lay tile. A lot of commercial work, some specialty residential jobs."

"You're an artisan, then."

"I'm not sure that's the word I'd use," George says, never breaking eye contact with his brother.

Nate reaches over and clasps his hand. "Thanks for lunch. And Amy," he says, standing. "It's been a pleasure. I'll be glad to swing by, it's no problem. Anything for George."

"Don't forget your shirt," George calls after him.

Nate turns back and lifts his work shirt off the chair. "Thanks."

"He really doesn't mind driving by?" Amy asks once Nate walks out to his bike. "Things seemed a little tense when I came in."

"He can be a pain in the ass." George watches him start the bike outside. "Ever since we were kids, he always tagged along, trying to impress me so he could hang with his big brother, you know? To this day, he's forever planning something with me, even more so since the accident with my father. A ballgame. One-on-one on the basketball court. Stops in here twice a week just to have lunch. So he can get a little overbearing, too, and then I need some space." George sips his coffee, watching as Nate maneuvers into traffic. "And he never lets me forget his big dream, which is for me to buy a Harley and take a road trip with him. Two brothers on the open road, riding off into the sunset out west, or something like that. You get the picture."

"Sounds kind of nice. You're lucky to have him."

"Yeah." A quick smile passes over his face as he looks out to Nate's now empty parking space. If you'd call it luck, he's not so sure.

———

Amy *had* been in the neighborhood when she stopped in to see George. She had been killing time before the appointment she'd scheduled with Detective Hayes.

"Maybe I'm crazy, I don't know," she says once she sits beside his desk. "But I think I'm being stalked." There. She said it. For a week she thought about doing this and finally decided that if she was buying a gun, it was damn real. The incidents are valid. She needs all the protection she can get, so the police need to know.

"Stalked. What's happening?" Detective Hayes asks.

She tells him everything, starting with her tampered answering machine and ending with her whistling teakettle. "They're kind of insignificant. I mean, I haven't been threatened in any way."

"Oh, I think you have," he interrupts. "Non-violent threats are still threats. And they can escalate."

"So you don't think it's just me? Forgetting things with the stress I've been under?"

215

"No, I don't. And I'm glad you're telling me. Sometimes victims think the stalking is harmless or will resolve itself. And that's not often the case."

"Well now. This keeps getting better."

"Anyone got a beef with you? Agitated neighbor? Family quarrel?" When she shakes her head no, he goes on. "Didn't think so. What I'm inclined to think is it's all tied in with the heist. I'm just not sure how, yet. Or why."

"Me, either."

"I'm going to need you to do a few things to help us out. You've taken all security precautions?"

"Lights, locks, that sort of thing, yes," she assures him.

"Good. Lock your garage, too. And document everything: phone messages, letters, email, mysterious gifts. It's all evidence. And keep your cell phone charged. You know, in case anything happens to your landline."

"I hadn't thought of that."

"And if you're in your car and think you're being followed, drive directly here."

"You're not taking any chances, Detective."

"We absolutely can't. The thing with stalking is that there's not much the police can do about it at this stage. Of course, with what you've been through, I'm documenting it all as part of the same crime."

"Which means I'll have police protection?"

"We can't stake someone at your house around the clock, it's really not feasible. That's why I need you to be vigilant. But I'll have a cruiser swing by regularly. Don't worry, we'll keep an eye on you."

Something about the day has a Christmas feel to it. It is the secrecy. No one knows that she talked to Detective Hayes. No one knows she bought a nine-millimeter handgun. Not even George. This is her life, her decisions. Her daughter that she needs to protect. The package remains in her SUV trunk like a hidden Christmas present. As she spoons vanilla ice cream dripping with hot fudge into her mouth, she knows she can reach the weapon within seconds, if necessary. She can stop someone dead.

And all the while Amy smiles and converses with Sara Beth as they plan their next walking route. Grace sits beside her, and Bear sits beside Grace. A string of seashells form a necklace around Grace's neck. But will Grace indicate which ice cream she prefers? No. Will she laugh and call Amy silly when Amy leaves a dot of ice cream on the tip of her nose? No. Will she sing along with Sara Beth when she softly sings a nursery rhyme? No. Her daughter has nothing to add about grandfather clocks striking one and mice running down and hickory dickory dock. And so Amy is thrilled to know she can stop any bastard who steals these little pleasures from her child again. That is the good that comes from being stalked. It's empowered her.

It does something else, too. She and George grow even closer. When he isn't at work, he is with her. If he can't be with her, he phones or sends quick emails about their weekend plans, or quotes a Sinatra song. He calms her through her flashbacks, holding her and talking softly. He often brings dinner from The Main Course so that she can spend more time with Grace, taking little walks with her, pushing her in the swing, keeping her at ease. He doesn't complain when Amy sits quietly beside him night after night watching old movies with her ear tuned to the shadows outside.

And he listens carefully when she explains the police cruiser parked on her street that evening.

"Are they keeping a cruiser here round the clock?" he'd asked.

"No," she explained. "Just every now and then."

So she isn't surprised when her phone rings shortly after she falls asleep that night. George uses any reason to phone: an idea to help Grace talk, a suggestion for the next night's movie, mostly to be sure she's okay. Amy sits up in the dark, disoriented from sleep. George had brought only one movie that night: *Gone With the Wind*. He sat with her for four hours, keeping her and Grace safe. Half asleep now, she smiles and reaches for the bedside phone, realizing when she hears the dial tone that it isn't the phone ringing. It is the doorbell. So she slips into her robe and ties it while hurrying to the front door. The bell rings again. Lamplight from her bedroom dimly falls onto the staircase. She hits the switch for the outside light and opens the front door fully expecting to see George.

But nobody is there. And the outside light has not turned on. "George?" she asks through the screen, trying to see past the dark porch while her hand flips the light switch repeatedly up and down to no avail.

No one stands on her porch. No car is parked in the driveway, its warm engine clicking and cooling. No police cruiser sits guard at this hour. It is just quietly dark. So was the doorbell part of a dream? Or real? What Amy does know is this: It's time to open her early Christmas present. She bolts the door, returns upstairs to her bedroom and pulls the padlocked box from her closet shelf. The thing is, unlatching the lock and slowly opening the lid brings the same thrill as opening a gift. She lifts the gun, presses in the magazine clip and turns off the lamp, sitting in the dark on her bed for the next hour. Not moving, merely listening. With a knot in her stomach, she silently dares, and curses, her stalker's next move.

Twenty-One

Dɪᴅ ᴛʜᴇ ᴅᴏᴏʀʙᴇʟʟ ʀᴇᴀʟʟʏ ʀɪɴɢ? She lies still, looking at the ceiling. Or had she been in a half-sleep state, thinking of George and imagining him calling, or returning? And just because the porch bulb burned out doesn't mean she is being stalked. When sunlight filters through her lace curtains, she sits up and opens her nightstand drawer, reaching far back. Her hand finds the weapon, which she immediately returns to the safe in her closet.

"I put it away," she reminds herself. "I put the gun safely out of reach, out of reach." The drill, over and over, is meant to stop any panic during her morning shower. If only the pelting water could wash her doubts away. Did she unplug the toaster? Did she close the garage door?

Celia checks in with a quick phone call while Grace is still asleep.

"I'm not going to work this morning, Cee."

"Why not? It's time to change up the summer display. You have those new gowns for the mannequins. Plus it's a nice day to get out."

"I'm a little tired today."

"What's the matter?"

"Nothing, really."

"Yeah. Right. Something's keeping you from those gowns. Do you have coffee on?"

"Yes."

"Food?"

"Cranberry muffins."

"I'll be right there," Celia says, hanging up before Amy can argue. Before she even has a chance to wake Grace, Celia walks in her back kitchen door looking around the room for stalkers and shadows keeping her awake at night. She wears a seersucker pantsuit, her auburn hair is pulled back in a messy bun, thin silver hoops hang from her ears and a leather portfolio is pressed beneath her arm.

"Here." Amy sets a steaming mug of coffee on the table. She slices open a muffin, spreads a pat of butter in the center and warms it in the microwave. "I'm okay, Celia. Really. You'll be late for work."

Celia picks up the white mug when Amy sets the muffin on her plate. "Well how did I know that someone wasn't here holding a gun to your head making you cancel your gown plans?"

"Oh, come on." Amy sits across from her.

"Come on? What are you saying? That it couldn't happen? Like Grace couldn't be kidnapped? And you can't be stalked?"

"Maybe I just don't want to believe it anymore."

Celia raises a concerned eyebrow. "Listen. I talked to Ben last night." She adds a dollop of cream to her coffee, stirs it and taps her spoon on the cup. "We both want you to consider something. And don't answer me until you've given the question serious thought." She pushes half the muffin into her mouth, chews and chases it down with coffee.

Amy motions to the portfolio between them. "It's not about that little ranch you showed me, is it?"

"Partly." Her fingers lace around the mug. "It could be the perfect home for you. The owners moved out last weekend, so it's empty now. And they've dropped the price. Just consider it, okay? Being that it's not so isolated, and it's easier to take care of than this place."

"I don't know. I really don't want to move."

"Well think about it. Ben and I are worried about you here in this big old house alone and we also want you to consider spending *only* the nights with us. For a while." She holds her hand up straight when Amy opens her mouth to speak. "No. Don't answer me now. Talk to George about it. And maybe your parents. We've got room for you and Grace and hey, we've got a dog, too."

"You know how I feel about taking care of myself. It's something I have to do."

"Right." Celia slides her cup aside. "Except these are extraordinary circumstances you're living under. The standard rules don't apply this summer." She stands to leave, taking first another long swallow of coffee, then nudging the ranch house specs closer to Amy. "Stalking doesn't just go away. It gets worse. If you're going to be responsible for Grace, you can't keep your head in the sand. Remember, forewarned is forearmed."

Amy watches silently as Celia picks her keys up off the table, backing away while tipping the last of her coffee into her mouth. "I'm running late, but please think about it for me?"

"I bought a gun." Celia's eyes close and Amy waits quietly for them to open, for Celia to process *that* information. "So I am forearmed now."

Celia sinks back into her chair and checks her watch. "Does George know this?"

Amy shakes her head no. "I didn't want to be talked out of it."

"Damn it," Celia says, stamping her foot. "You see how it's escalating already?"

"No, it's not. Dad told me I should have a gun after Mark died. So I got a gun."

"That's different and you know it." She takes an exasperated breath and another glance at her watch. "I have an appointment I really can't miss. But you and I have some serious talking to do. When's a good time? And I won't take no for *that* answer, because I'm sure all your others will be no."

"Tomorrow, okay? There's a gown at an estate sale I want to check out. Come with me and Grace, and we'll talk afterward."

It felt good to commit to Celia and to her shop again. She'd been away from the tulle and lace and veils, and, well, and happiness, for too long. The gowns will be in her life again tomorrow. So she feels better waking Grace and giving her breakfast, saying small phrases to her over her cereal. She feels better pulling the stepladder from the pantry and opening it on the front porch. Her doctor had mentioned that after what she'd been through, it's not uncommon to have exaggerated startle reactions. So the bulb was nothing, just a burnt-out bulb and she'd ridiculously panicked and gotten out her gun. Because any little thing can get her jumpy. She reaches for the light switch and flicks it to be sure it's turned off before removing the old bulb. Then flicks it again.

Okay, so maybe her reaction last night wasn't exaggerated. Because when the old, burnt-out bulb illuminates, she knows someone *had* been on her porch the night before. Maybe now more than ever, she needs to trust herself.

TRUE BLEND

Since she had taken the reins of control back by buying a gun and reporting the stalking to the police, Amy sees that to keep control, she has to pull back tight on the bit. That afternoon, she watches from the opposite side of a mirrored wall as Dr. Brina works with Grace, trying to trigger a response without Amy in the room. It's like watching a silent movie, the doctor going through the muted motions on the other side of the wall. She shows her daughter pictures, encourages Grace to color, tries in vain to invoke anger, fear or sadness. Dr. Brina instructs Grace to hammer square blocks into square holes and Amy whispers "Whack it!" from behind the wall, wringing her hands together. "Get mad, Grace."

When Dr. Brina suggests that a speech therapist might be able to cull verbal sounds from her small patient, Amy makes an instant decision. Walking with Grace in the bright sunshine out to her SUV, she checks the door handles and looks inside, front and back, in her new security routine. Once Grace is buckled into her car seat, Amy carefully drives through the parking lot toward the exit, frequently checking the rearview mirror to see if anyone follows them. But the closer she gets to her destination, the less she thinks of stalkers. It's the kidnappers who take over her mind.

She'd never found it in her heart to return to the bank and subject Grace to any frightening memories there, but now she drives into the very parking lot where the kidnapping happened. Except she isn't here to bank and she isn't here for herself. She's here to get her daughter to speak.

Dr. Berg told her weeks ago that disturbing memories need to be processed and the crime put into proper perspective in the subconscious mind. Otherwise avoidance symptoms can lead to

223

complete withdrawal. Grace is steps away from isolation. Angel is now her only link to this world.

"Come on, honey," Amy murmurs as she unbuckles Grace. She walks slowly past two stores, approaching the bank while holding Grace's hand the same way she did that morning. Her fingers curl around her daughter's small fingers and she says soft, encouraging words. The sun shines bright; the similarities between the two days are strong. In Amy's mind, she pictures yellow crime tape wrapped around the parking lot. In her mind, she also pictures breaking through that tape and bringing Grace back, finally, once and for all.

Grace walks quietly beside her and Amy feels when it starts, when her daughter resists, her feet slowing.

———

George closes up The Main Course and cleans the meat grinders. With a special wrench, he removes the nuts and bolts that hold the auger housing in place and sanitizes, rinses and sets out each piece to dry. He takes no chances. Just like he told Amy. Risk isn't for him. He prefers the sure thing. Scrupulous attention to his specialty meat shop brings him steady business.

As he goes through the careful motions of sanitizing the equipment, his thoughts are free to start planning the next day, considering what he needs to order, what special cuts he needs to prepare. Who will come into the shop? That thought is new. He recognizes the regulars. They talk about their kids, their golf swings, car trouble. "What's good today, George?" they ask, trusting him to suggest only the best, from hamburger patties to the finest steaks. "What's the special?"

Then there are the folks he doesn't recognize. He never used to think twice about them. Now he watches them differently, wondering if Reid sends them to keep tabs on him. A woman in her late twenties stopped in that afternoon. "I'd like four of the stuffed peppers," she said, pointing to the meals-to-go case. Her accent had him look twice. It placed her from an eastern European country, maybe Ukraine or Poland. Is she a nanny? Or is she working undercover, watching him? Is she a live-in health aide here on a temporary visa to earn money to bring back home? Or is she a resident transplanted from the old country? Does she like it here? In the past, those interested questions would have been asked. Today, he didn't want to know. He just made note of her fair skin, the light brown hair, the voice.

After stopping at his condominium, taking a quick shower and putting on jeans and a casual tee, the woman's face passes through his thoughts again. And again after he walks from his pickup along Amy's driveway, up the stone path to her kitchen door in the back. When he knocks, finds no answer and the door unlocked, he walks in. Could her stalker be an eastern European woman?

"Hello?" he calls out. A white coffee cup sits on the blue table. The cup is full, but the mug cool to the touch. "Amy?" He looks out the kitchen window, thinking she might be at the tire swing with Grace. But she would have heard him come in if she was in the yard.

In the living room, pillows neatly line the sofa; a cotton throw is draped over a chair back; the lamps and framed photographs of Grace all stand precisely in place. There are no signs of a struggle. He stands at the bottom of the stairs with a hand on the banister, listening. After a second, he takes the stairs two at a time.

Grace's bedroom door is ajar. "Amy?" he asks, opening the door and squinting to adjust to the darkness behind it. Amy sits in a chair pulled close to the bed. She shakes her head back and forth without speaking. "What's wrong?" he whispers, his hand on her shoulder. The curtains are drawn and Grace sleeps soundly with Angel curled against her leg. "Did something happen?"

She stands and pushes past him to the bathroom out in the hallway, locking the door behind her. He turns and follows, trying the bathroom doorknob, jiggling it and pressing his ear to the door. The noise from the other side is muffled and sounds as though she's sick. "Amy. Are you all right? Open the door."

The toilet flushes and tap water runs in the sink, but still no word from her. As soon as he hears the door unlock, he opens it and sees she's splashed water on her face and neck. But more than that, he's shocked to feel the weight of her when she walks into his arms.

"What have I done?" Amy asks. They sit on the couch and George hands her a tall glass of water. "It seemed to make perfect sense at the time. We want Grace to speak. To react. So I brought her to the place we want her to react to." She takes a long, shaking breath. "What was I thinking? That I could play God?"

"Don't be so hard on yourself. Grace is slipping further away each day. Any mother would try to reach out like that."

"Not *my* mother. Why didn't I just make her soup? Or read to her and hold her?" She sips the water, barely swallowing a mouthful. George sits beside her and tucks a strand of hair behind her ear. "What's wrong with me?" she asks.

"What exactly happened, Amy? What did Grace do?"

"I brought her to the bank, thinking it's the one place that can get a reaction from her, even if it's a bad one. But then, oh George, it was terrible." Her eyes fill up again. "She tried to pull away, but I didn't let her and kept walking to the bank. And then?" She stifles a cry, raising her hand to her mouth.

"What? What happened?"

"Her legs stopped working. Just like that. She crumpled to her knees on the parking lot pavement." Tears stream down her face and George gets tissues from the kitchen, returning and blotting her cheeks. "My poor Grace," she cries into her hands.

"It's okay, she'll be all right. Don't worry."

"No. No she won't. I did her in. She couldn't walk, George. I actually had to pick her up and carry her and she just hung limp in my arms. And I could see, oh God I could see, she wasn't with me at all. I pushed her over some edge I didn't know was so close."

Amy stands and goes to the living room window, looking out toward the red barn down the street. The corn crops are tall enough now to rustle in the breeze. A stone wall runs along the street to the farmland. The sun is shining bright on Celia's yellow bungalow. All these pretty sights, and this. She turns to George. "I put her to bed and she hasn't even moved in all these hours. She's just gone, deep asleep."

"Why don't you wake her up now? Easy, talk softly to her like nothing's happened."

"I'm afraid to."

"Afraid of what?"

She returns to the couch and sits beside George. "I'm afraid of what I did. The way her legs stopped working, it's like I paralyzed her. And if I wake her up, I'll know. What if she doesn't walk? What will I do? What will I tell the doctors? That I took her therapy into my own hands? I'll lose her, George. They'll say I'm under too much stress. They'll take her away from me."

"No they won't. If she doesn't walk, we'll call Dr. Brina. She'll understand. She'll tell you what to do." He looks around the room.

"It's awfully warm in here. Let's get these windows opened and get some air in here first."

Amy watches him unlatch the new brass locks and lift the paned windows. He opens the front door and late day sunshine spills into the living room along with summer noise. Chickadees and robins serenade the evening. And it feels like she is watching an old home movie, remembering with aching fondness a life she once knew. A lawn mower moves in even paths across someone's jewel green lawn. A car drives by, a neighbor coming home from work at the end of the day. Somewhere down the street a dog barks, wanting to come in and be with the people. And the same birdsong that reaches Amy's ears reaches upstairs to Grace's. It is a life she used to have before she waited for Grace to speak.

She lies down on the couch, closes her eyes and purely listens. Is this what it feels like to lose a child? Life seeming like a home movie? A time past? George walks by her, lightly stroking her arm as he does. They say no pain compares to the loss of a child. Would you even call it pain? She lies absolutely still, eyes closed, trying to feel where it hurts.

Eventually she hears George talking, not sure exactly what he is saying behind her closed eyes. It is more the deep tone of his voice that reaches her. He always understands. He always tries his best to make her life better. With her eyes still closed, she can't picture him not being in her life.

"Come on," he says quietly, his voice distant. "Look who's waiting for you."

Amy's eyes open to see George coming down the stairs holding Grace. At the bottom step, he sets her standing on the living room floor and crouches beside her. Her arm curls around Bear, her ponytails are flattened from sleep, her cheeks flush with summer warmth. And her legs stand straight and strong.

"Go see Mommy now," George says. He looks over at Amy and winks.

Grace toddles over to her mother. Even though all Amy wants to do is fly off the couch and sweep her child up in her arms, she waits, lying on her side, her arms open to her daughter. Grace climbs up and snuggles against her, Angel jumping up right behind her.

He's done it again, Amy just knows. Grace curls right into her body. He's given her their normal back. "Thank you," she whispers over to him.

"Don't thank me," he answers, standing at the foot of the staircase still. "You need to take a lesson from your daughter. Move past it. What's done is done."

Twenty-Two

I T'S AMAZING THAT THIS TYPE of thing happens daily, throughout the country. Lawyers and housewives and cashiers and pharmacists and librarians, people from all walks of life, learn, eagerly too, how to kill. Looking at the six other faces with her, Amy would never dream this of them if she bumped into them in the grocery store buying bread and orange juice.

"Okay, people. I know you're ready to learn to shoot. But at the same time, you have to know how to defend yourself. We've got twenty minutes left and a little more material to cover. Next class will have an hour of gun time."

The students sit scattered at two wooden tables in a small room at the firing range facility. Their serious expressions don't waver as they learn how to defend their bodies from lethal bullets. Lenny, an insurance adjuster of about fifty, dressed in a business suit, raises his hand. "So we should bring our equipment next week?"

"Yes. A handgun, ammunition. Eye and ear protection, if you have it. If not, we'll provide. I'll cover defensive tactics for a half hour, then we'll move into the firing range. Now," their instructor Ron says, walking to the chalkboard and drawing stick figures and arrows, "anyone can stand in a doorway and empty their bullets into an aggressor." Ron has square shoulders and a wide girth. His blond hair is buzz cut and his voice grows raspier the more he talks. Amy notices the shoulder holster beneath his sport jacket when he tips up a water bottle. "But death is not instantaneous," he continues. "Your attacker might get one shot at you before he drops. So all the training on how to fire that weapon is futile if you're standing exposed in a doorway and his shot hits its mark. You're both dead. That's why you have to know defensive tactics as well, and find cover. Cover goes hand in hand with discharging your weapon."

As he speaks, he walks to his desk, swigs the water and gives a handout to each student. "It's important to know the difference between concealment and cover. Concealment hides you but it won't protect you from a bullet. Draperies. A chair." He knocks on the hollow core door to the classroom. "Think that's going to stop a bullet? Hardly." He clasps his hands behind his back and walks to the center of the room. "Concealment."

Pencils move along the handouts, labeling and note taking. The students, four men and two other women, study the diagrams. Amy knows they are picturing themselves finding pleated drapes to hide their bulk, or a wingback chair wide enough to conceal their bodies.

"Cover is something you can get behind that will either stop or deflect bullets. Try for cover rather than concealment. Any ideas?"

The young woman who Amy had seen pencil in *college student* on her information card raises her hand. Ron nods at her. "A refrigerator?"

"Good," Ron answers. "Defense strategies in the home exist. A washer and dryer. Even a heavy mattress will work. Cover. Try to place something thick or hard, preferably both, between yourself and the attacker. The handout lists more suggestions." He looks at his watch. "Quick review, then we'll adjourn until next week."

Amy straightens her papers, knowing that most of what's on them is common sense, which flies right out the window in dangerous situations. She could hardly think at all when Grace was kidnapped.

"Defensive tactic options. Consider a dog. Big or small, doesn't matter, although a hundred-pound canine is a good deterrent. Either way, any size dog will alert you to approaching danger before it's actually on your premises. The bark alone may change an intruder's mind." As the instructor paces the class, he leafs through the yellow information cards each student filled out, listing names, occupations, reason for attending and the handgun they own.

"A cell phone. Mandatory defensive tactic." The students' pencils pause as they listen for explanation. "Why?" he asks. "Trewist?"

"In case the attacker cuts the landline before entering the home."

"Right. He's trying to prevent any 9-1-1 calls. He cannot disable your cell phone however. So you've got dogs, secure deadbolt locks, cell phones. And you've got cover and concealment for initial defensive actions. Any questions?"

"Yes." Amy raises her hand. "What about children? Young children. Can they be taught anything that might help?"

The instructor's voice softens, as though he recognizes her. As though her question draws the connection between the young widow and small child and recent kidnapping still headlining the daily news.

"How old is your daughter?" he asks, though she'd not identified the child as male or female.

"Almost three. In a few months."

"Three." Ron rubs his chin and expels a long breath of air. "Teach her a good place to hide."

In her mind, a roving camera scans the old farmhouse, moving through each room with his suggestion. It passes her living room, her growing collection of antique tables and lamps backlit by sunshine reaching through the paned windows. Should she skirt one of the tables with a heavy fabric? The camera glances in her dining room, seeing the hutch filled with vintage china and a collection of crystal goblets leaving no room for a child's body. It moves into the country kitchen, cozy with cushioned chairs and a distressed blue table and plenty of cabinets where she can carve out a child-sized space. She pictures Grace cowering behind a cabinet door, knowing if life ever comes to that, her child will never talk again.

———

Replica of Jacqueline Kennedy dress worn at wedding to Onassis. Silk crepe-de-chine cream color wedding dress with lace inserts. Funnel collar and long lace sleeves.

She'd almost missed the gown mentioned in the estate sale listing of Queen Anne end tables and mahogany dressers and an extensive record collection and a twelve-place-setting china set. Amy's grandmother always told her that lace stitches lead us on a journey the same way moments do, stitched together to make a life. Could Amy find answers in the lace stitches of Kennedy's dress? How did Jacqueline continue on after the nightmare day of JFK's assassination? Amy had to see it, to be certain this Valentino reproduction was an exact copy of the Kennedy dress. Because an exact replica will have a secret within those stitches, one that might help her.

She pulls her SUV up to the curb behind Celia's car and looks out at the stone colonial house with a wraparound porch. Several cars are parked in the driveway already. She gets out and notices the close humid weather before lifting Grace from the car seat.

"Hey guys," Celia says, walking up to them. "Wow, what a turnout. They must have lots of good stuff up for grabs."

"Well all I want is that dress. Ready to go in?"

"First I have to say hello to this cupcake." Celia bends down low to Grace. "Hi there, pretty," she says, leaving a quick kiss on Grace's cheek. "You ready to gown shop with the big ladies?"

Grace nods slightly and reaches for Amy's hand. They start up the shaded walkway toward the arched front door. "How's Ben?" Amy asks. She keeps an eye on a few shoppers hurrying ahead of them, particularly one who glanced back her way. Her brown hair is shoulder length and she wears denim shorts, a tank top and brown leather sandals. Another defensive tactic she learned is to be aware of your surroundings. Always. Would a stalker be this close, a shadow brushing past her at a private estate sale?

"He's taking Sasha to Puppy Kindergarten tonight." Celia bends down toward Grace. "Sasha's going to doggy school."

"Thanks, Celia. For trying," Amy says softly, her concerned gaze moving from the woman ahead of them to her daughter. "Don't give up on her."

"Never," Celia answers, squeezing Amy's hand. "Hey, check out the old wicker chairs. Those would look great on my porch."

"On the way out, Cee. I've got to see that wedding dress before someone beats me to it." Amy steps inside the house and notices the cool dank, first, the way you will when a home hasn't been lived in and has been closed up for a while. She stops at a folding table in the foyer manned by family members collecting fees for any items bought. "Can you steer me to the wedding dress you advertised?"

A woman in jeans and an old college tee rifles through papers and hands her a printout with a copied photograph on it. "That's my mom. She borrowed a little Jackie style and wore the dress in 1970. Isn't she beautiful?"

"She is." Amy studies the woman who married over forty years ago now. Stitches, stitches, decades of moments stitched together for this bride and groom, with a look inspired by Jackie. One person's moments have a way of rippling into others sometimes. "Can I keep this?" she asks the bride's daughter.

"Oh sure. I've got plenty here. The dress is upstairs, second room on the right. It's been folded up in a cedar chest all these years, so it's wrinkled. But it should hang out just fine, if you're interested."

As she's talking, a woman passes too closely from behind and turns left into an elaborately wallpapered dining room. Amy notices it's the same woman who brushed against her outside on the walk. She looks back at the photograph then. "So it's not an authentic Valentino?"

"Believe me, if it were I'd be selling it at Sotheby's instead of here. But it's really clean, no stains, no rips. Worn only once. She and my dad were married for forty years. He passed a few years before Mom."

"I'm sorry to hear that. It's a beautiful dress with a lovely story then."

She turns to find Celia and Grace together in the living room. Celia is showing Grace an oak mantle clock. *Tick-tock, tick-tock,* Amy hears her whispering to her daughter.

Upstairs, the two-piece wedding dress is laid out on the top of a bed, its white chenille bedspread accentuating the rich cream color of the satin and lace. "Oh my," Amy says under her breath. She knows from one look it's in pristine condition.

Celia comes up behind her. "Can't you just see Jackie in that outfit?"

"Can I ever." She lifts the top by the shoulders and holds it up at arm's length. Stitches, stitches. What motivated Jacqueline to choose this particular Valentino dress for her wedding to Onassis? What story is stitched behind that decision? Bands of cream silk alternate with bands of floral-detailed lace, the scalloped lace over a pleated skirt giving it Jackie flair. Her new post-Kennedy identity weaves itself into the design. Amy lowers the dress for Grace to see. "Isn't it pretty? You can help me hang it in the shop window."

Grace reaches out to touch the lace before Amy folds the ensemble into the pale blue box it came in and heads toward the staircase. As she's about to step down, that same brunette is coming up the stairs, their gaze meeting long enough for Amy to notice her brown eyes are small, her nose tipped. Once she passes, Amy continues down to purchase the dress.

"I see you're asking two hundred. Would you take one?"

"Well. It *is* a Valentino knock-off. How about one-fifty?"

"One twenty-five, cash?"

"Deal."

She turns to Celia behind her. "Cee, did you want to look at those wicker chairs?"

"No. Actually Grace and I are going to browse for a minute. I'm going to treat her to something." She reaches down and takes Grace's hand. "We'll meet you outside."

When they walk out a little while later, Grace is holding up a doll for Amy to see. "It's wearing a tulle wedding gown, just like your brides," Celia says. "I think it's an old cake-topper. She spotted it in a curio case and I bought it for her. And this is for you."

She pulls a necklace from a brown bag. "If anyone needs a wish right now, you do. So maybe you can wish on this star."

Amy takes the sterling necklace from her, touching the oval camphor stone set in an ornate silver setting, a silver star set in the stone. Her eyes tear as she looks up at Celia.

"It's from the 1900s. So I'm thinking it's got lots of good wish juju." She winks at Amy and takes Grace's hand again. "Now how about we stop at Whole Latte Life for a coffee, and an ice cream for Miss Grace here. And I want to hear about that g-u-n, like you promised."

"Ice cream for three, Cee." She presses her forehead with the back of her hand. "It's way too hot for coffee."

———

"What?" Amy asks, smiling uncomfortably. She'd gone from talking about lace wedding gowns to whispering about black semiautomatic weapons, all in ten minutes time.

"You look the same, that's all. And yet there's this change," Celia says over her hot fudge sundae. "Your thinking's different."

"It has to be now." Amy leans close. "I had my first defensive handgun lesson today."

"No way. When I called, Sara Beth said she was watching Grace while you were at therapy."

"Yup." She turns to Grace and wipes a dribble of chocolate ice cream from her chin. "That's my therapy."

"You know, some people shop for therapy, Amy."

Amy looks over at the door when a woman walks in, that same brunette with denim shorts, tank top and brown leather sandals. "Well Cee, if anyone thinks about coming into my home again … Let's just say this therapy prepares me. Forewarned is forearmed, remember?" She nods in the direction of the brunette standing at the take-out counter. "Every time I turn around, I see her," she whispers. "Is she following us?"

Celia glances over at the woman. "I think you just have an overactive imagination right now. Addison's a small town. I've bumped into people too, shopping, going out to eat. It happens."

So is every stranger a threat now? Will every familiar face put her on edge like this? Once she's back home and Grace is in bed, she locks the deadbolts on the doors and heads to the kitchen to make a cup of tea. First, though, she checks her email on the laptop, so glad to see one from George. It's brief and a little mysterious, saying only that he hopes she enjoys listening to her favorite radio station tonight. "What are you up to?" she whispers before putting on the stereo softly and finding the lite station. How many times has he teased her that she is a hopeless romantic, listening to the sappy songs dedicated to lovelorn hearts? Then he serenades her with a line or two from an old standard.

"Join me in bringing friends and lovers together tonight, taking your requests on the love line." The disc jockey's voice pours forth like smooth syrup, his silken words tying the songs together with declarations of romance and sweet nothings. Amy listens as she brings her tea and laptop into the living room. The DJ tells someone named Sal that Laura misses him terribly and will be home soon, then plays *What a Wonderful World*. She wonders about Laura. Is she nearby? At work? Or far away on a trip, emailing her request to the local station. No matter what happens, love is always in the air. That's why she listens to this station, she told George. Through any tragedy, any distance, the airwaves shimmer with it.

A breeze drifts in through the open windows and the day's summer heat lingers into the evening. Amy searches online for Jackie Kennedy's Onassis-wedding dress. She wants to design a placard to place next to it in the shop, giving her brides a sense of history with the gown.

"Pick up the phone and join the love line that stretches from here to there, bringing hearts and lovers together." Crickets chirp lazy in the heat, and in the glimpse of night sky visible through the window, it's easy to imagine a crisscrossing network of love reaching across the skies, stars glimmering at each connection. "Lovers like George and Amy."

She spins around, staring at the small stereo on the bookcase.

"Amy, George is sending a special message. He wants to let you know that he finally got it right. He's certain of it. He loves you and is missing you tonight, Amy."

Lyrics about finding the right someone, the only one who thrills, wind through the quiet room then, the brush sweeping across the drum, the piano light, the tempo slow. And it's as though George is there, telling her *It Had to Be You.* She pictures him sitting alone in his office catching up on paperwork, paying bills, his hands moving over the calculator. The meat cutting equipment beyond gleams after his routine wash-down. Only his brass lamp throws a circle of illumination on his cluttered desk as he bends over his work, the computer screen before him.

And he tuned to her radio station, to her lovesick program. He had picked up the telephone in his hushed office and talked to the DJ about her. His black apron hangs on a wall hook, his white shirtsleeves are turned back and he needs a shave at this late hour. She imagines the rough feel of his face, imagines pressing her fingers against it and George taking her hand in his and kissing it. And his voice, his voice. Quiet. She walks to the window open to the distant cornfields and the vast summer night sky above. And somehow, in the still heat, through the song lyrics, she hears his voice, too.

Twenty-Three

GEORGE LOOKS IN THE MIRROR and his father looks back at him. He stands tall, his dark hair neatly combed. There is more heft to his carriage than to George's. Maybe it comes with age. Gray creeps into his hair at the temples. The image appears more tired than George remembers his father looking. Did he do this to him? Did worry age him? His father stares back with familiar eyes. But is it really his father, or do the shadows of the room deceive him?

"Dad?" George asks.

The reflection looks down and adjusts crisp white shirt cuffs before slipping into a tailored black suit jacket and shrugging the shoulders perfectly into place. Lastly, he slips on the ring, ruby set in gold. Then his eyes lift and meet George's. There is disappointment in them, but it softens with the connection.

"You raised the bet," the reflection says.

"What?" George misses that voice and aches to hear more. To have his father back.

"You told her you love her. She's a good girl, George. I'm proud of you." His brow furrows. "But how will you protect her now? You raised the bet."

"What bet?" George drags his hand across his eyes, rubbing away the uncertainty of the conversation. Is it really his father or is he only seeing features in his own face reminding him of the man? He touches his hair and watches the mirror carefully.

"You're forcing the stalker's hand. He moves with you. When you're idle, he is. When you make a move, he does. Telling her you love her is a big move. Just be careful, son."

George looks from his father's ruby ring up to the white shirt and black jacket before looking down at his own white work shirt and black trousers. His mind has to be playing tricks on him. Isn't it him in the mirror?

"I had to tell her. I love her and don't want to lose her. But she doesn't know what I did." When his gaze returns to his face, Nate brushes tile dust off his hands while keeping an eye on George. "Nate?" George shakes his head.

"Don't you see? You're the one putting her at risk. You're putting everyone at risk, including yourself. And now Dad's upset. I was trying to look out for you now that he's gone. You know, to keep the family together. You and me. Like always. Why the hell'd you let it get this far with her?"

"Get this far?"

"In the game. Your hand's not strong enough. You're looking at a bad beat." He deals George five quick cards.

George catches the cards in his hand, noticing the ruby ring on his own pinky now. The stone glimmers like a small pool of fresh blood. "I've got to protect my hand, Nate. I've got to protect Amy. You dragged her into this mess and I swore I'd get her out. I never meant to fall in love with her."

"You should've folded. He'll raise you, you know," Nate says from behind the cards fanned in front of his face. "That stalker."

Perspiration beads on George's forehead. "He's bluffing. I'll snap him off."

"I don't know if you've got it in you, brother."

"What do you mean?" George tugs on his white shirt cuffs the same way his father did. He tucks the shirt neatly into his black trousers.

"It's your image, you know?" George hears a familiar noise. Nate has released the safety on a forty-five. When George looks up, hosiery presses against his brother's face. Or is it his own, his nose pulled to the side beneath the hosiery strain, his skin flattened abnormally, his eyes slits. "It's all about image."

George looks away.

"You've got to dress the part, George," his father says, and so Nate is gone now. Darkness embraces him and he shifts his shoulders in the space closing in. Velvet drapes hang beside him. Finally, after a long silence, he raises his eyes.

"Clothes make the man." Father Rossi looks closely at him from behind his black shirt and white clerical collar. "In God's abundant love, He does forgive. Though you must not only seek His pardon, but His likeness as well."

Perspiration covers his body. The priest's words from confession come to him often now; suggestions of compassion and truth always skirt his thoughts. Amy needs to know that truth. He pulls his shirttails from his trousers and unbuttons the shirt. The fabric is soaked through and his lungs drag in air.

"You let me down, George," he hears his own father say. "You were such a good kid. I thought you'd keep Nathan in line. He always liked to play games. Still does." George's eyes refuse to open. The shame of the past weeks humiliates him in his father's eyes. "How'd you ever get involved in that scheme of his? Fix it, George. You should've *stopped* him. I would never put your mother

242

in that situation. Do right by Amy. You can't live like this. It'll destroy you."

"But what is right?" George asks.

"Maybe it will help to seek absolution," the priest answers quietly.

"Tell her, George," his father adds.

"If you really want her safe, George, break up with her," Nate says. "Then the threat's gone."

The voices grow louder with each sentence running into the next. *Call or raise the bet. Clothes make the man, but it's still about character. Seek absolution. You let me down, George. Seek the Father's likeness. Character counts.George.Play your hand.Tell her.*

George extends his arms and tries to back out of their web. A new voice fights for his attention. It is a voice he respects as much as he dreads. "Your prints will be keeping company with the best. Though I'm sure the trail has been wiped clean," Detective Hayes says. "You're sweating, George." He twists out of his white shirt, careful to keep the inky pads of his fingerprinted fingers from touching the fabric. *You're sweating, George.George.George.*

The alarm clock on the bedside table sounds loudly. He reaches over to silence it and falls back on the mattress, catching his breath.

"Jesus Christ. Leave me alone. All of you." He swings his arm over his eyes and tries to get back to sleep. Once he came home from the shop last night, he had poured himself a drink, called Amy, and at three in the morning looked at the clock again over a second glass of Scotch. Maybe the liquor brought on the dreams. Or maybe he needs to eat something. But when he thinks about everything the dreams alluded to, his stomach turns on it all.

That's what his life has come to. Drinking alone on an empty stomach, exhausted and afraid for Amy and her daughter. He'll see

Nate today at the summer poker barbecue. It's time for answers. Reid or Elliott has to be behind the stalking threats. Maybe he can buy them off through Nate. He'll dump half the cash in their laps if it'll secure any guarantees.

Still, something is wrong. He sits up, feeling the weight of the air pressing against his damp skin. But the air is too warm. And it is moving, puffing the curtain slightly. He slides his legs out of bed, walks to the window and holds his open palm over the radiator. Someone turned on the heat.

———

The lace on her vintage gowns brings back sweet memories. Amy stands on her back step, sets down a basket of clothespins and thinks of her grandmother, of her hands tatting lace, of the art of the old country. As she clips a frilled chiffon wedding dress from the 1980s to the clothesline and wheels it out into the sun, she wonders if her grandmother ever missed her home. If she flashbacked to Europe the way Amy flashbacks to the bank parking lot. Were her grandmother's memories vivid flashes of rolling farmland and blue sky? After passing through Ellis Island, when she looked out her New York tenement window onto another brick building and dingy clothing and sheets hanging from a maze of rope strung between the buildings, did the old country flicker in her eyes? Maybe that's why Amy loves her farmhouse and her life in Addison. She looks out on what her ancestor had once seen and loved and left behind across the sea. Open land and clear sky.

There is a noise behind her and it becomes, just like that, a shoe sliding across pavement. A footstep. And so her training kicks in with a long, slow breath filling her abdomen before exhaling to ward off the flashback. Then she turns to see Grace in the doorway, watching her hang the gowns to get the wrinkles out and freshen them in the sun.

"Well hi there," Amy says, opening the side door. "Coming out?" The flashback evaporates and Angel runs by, a scrap of black and white fluff rolling past like a ball.

Sometimes she has to rebuild in small victories, like warding off a flashback, especially after George's dedication last night. She wants to be strong for him; to have something left inside, some strength to share with him. Grace follows the kitten down the two steps onto the green grass and together they sit facing Amy, beneath July's warm morning sunlight.

Will Grace remember this, the way she hangs newly-acquired wedding gowns in the summer sunshine? The way the lacy gowns look, strung out across the lawn as though they're dancing their first dance, swaying in a gentle breeze? The delicate silk and tulle of the gowns ripple with gentle movement, come to life again. Is it a pleasant memory able to supplant the violence of being pulled from her mother's hands? She has to fill Grace's senses with simple times like this: a summer morning with long white gowns wafting in the hazy sky. Maybe this will work better than play-acting and association cards. Maybe those tactics bring back pain.

Amy looks down at her daughter in the grass. How was trauma handled before analysis and child psychologists and medication? What would her grandmother do in her shoes? She reaches for the Onassis dress and a handful of clothespins from the basket. "Grace. Come here, honey."

Her daughter's need for affection and words and connection hasn't lessened like her voice has. Grace climbs the steps. "Help Mommy, please. Hold the clothespins." She drops a few pins into Grace's tiny, outstretched hands and plucks one out to pin the cream dress on the line. "That's much better," she says, keeping easy, undemanding words flowing between them, even if they are only her words. "You're a big help."

As she wheels the rope out and clips a short bouffant veil on the line, Grace's voice stops her mid-clip. "What?" Amy asks, every sense drawn like a magnet to the child.

"Angel help," Grace nearly shouts. She bends down, looking like she'll topple right over, the sunlight catching on her wispy ponytails, and one at a time, sets two clothespins at the kitten's paws.

Hope, that elusive feeling of hope, touches her. Amy can't help wondering if she pushed her daughter past a breaking point at the bank the other day. If her two words now are the beginning; that Grace has hit bottom, turned a corner and will rebuild her vocabulary one word at a time. She says nothing more, and so Amy finishes clipping the tulle veil on the rope and wheels out the clothesline, the gowns shimmering and waltzing in the sun.

———

George turns his pickup into Amy's long driveway while listening to the tail end of a radio news update on the heist. The report confirms that the heist was *not* an inside job of the armored truck company. Upon stepping out of the air-conditioned cab, the thick summer heat reminds him of the furnace heat he'd woken to. Reminds him of drinking alone last night. Of the havoc indecision wreaks on his life. Of the nightmare voices calling out to him. Of hurling his Scotch tumbler at the fireplace in a rage directed at Nate and Reid and Elliott and an illicit bankroll.

Amy watches him from behind the kitchen screen door. She wears a fitted sleeveless denim dress with a V-neck and a gold initial pendant around her neck. Still feeling his father's shame, right now she is everything he isn't. He doesn't know how to deserve her.

"You're early," Amy says through the screen. "Do you want a coffee?"

"No, thanks." He stops right outside the door. "Where's Grace?"

She glances over her shoulder. "In the living room with the cat. The TV's on."

"Come here." George opens the screen door, holding one hand behind his back. "I've got something for you."

"You do?" She smiles and steps out into the sunshine. "What is it?"

He takes her hand, walks her a few steps away from the doorway and backs her up against the house. "This," he says, handing her a small milk glass vase with a sprig of baby's breath and one single, salmon-colored rose in it. She takes it, and his hands hold her waist then, feeling the faded denim fabric beneath his touch.

"George, it's beautiful," she whispers. "But what's the matter? You're quiet."

He raises his hands to her face, bends and kisses her. She feels delicate to his touch, her hair pure silk, her lips sweet. George deepens the kiss before ending it slowly, pulling away, reluctant to stop, his fingers skimming her face. He searches her eyes. "I love you." His voice is low. "I love you, Amy." He needs to say it again and again to drown out the other voices. *Seek absolution.* "I wanted to tell you that before we got to my brother's barbecue."

"I know you do." Her fingers light on the rose petals. "I heard your dedication last night, remember?"

"You liked it?"

"It was perfect."

247

"Good." *Do right by her, George.* They stand inches apart. "I meant it." He kisses her again.

"Is everything okay?" she asks.

If you really want her safe, George, you've got to break up with her. "Yes. Why?"

"You look pale today. Something on your mind?"

"Well." He looks past her to the gowns hanging in the breeze, then back at her brown eyes. "Only you."

She touches his cheek.

"Maybe we'll cut out early and come back here later," he says. "You better get Grace. Oh, and I brought her something too." He pulls a grape lollipop from his cargo shorts pocket.

"You spoil her," Amy says when she opens the screen door, glancing at him over her shoulder. "And she loves it. Come on in. I've just got to get her into her new polka dot sundress. My mother sent it for a summertime gift."

The screen door squeaks closed behind them. Walking though her country kitchen, seeing the pine cabinets and blue painted table, wicker baskets and dried flower arrangements, vintage china plates displayed on a stenciled wall shelf, he knows that this is all that matters. He has to insure this life for Amy and her daughter. And he can't insure it if he isn't here.

———

Since the kidnapping, scenes like this have become as fragile as a tottering house of cards. Amy leans forward and studies the yard as George parks in front of Nate's house. Geraniums spill from a large window box on the stone front cape. The American flag hangs from the flagpole, cars line the wide driveway and noise rises from the backyard. Good noise. Adult voices talk and laugh, competing with a radio announcing the Yankees game alongside children's voices rising in play.

Good noise, good sights, goodness all around. Amy lifts Grace onto her hip and George carries a cooler of fresh steaks and hamburger patties. They walk past well-pruned hydrangea bushes to the backyard and a sea of guests dressed brightly in shorts and polo shirts, tank tops and sandals. A plastic wading pool is filled with clear water for the young children and a badminton volley is heating up. The picnic table overflows with guests and food.

It is easy to recognize the friends George had described for her. His poker partners Steve and Craig man one of the smoking grills, Steve tall and thin, Craig heavyset. Already she feels affection for most of these people. They are George's life. They are his closest friends and their wives, his old neighbors, his long-time acquaintances. They mean the world to him and from their greetings, their hugs and smiles and enthusiastic handshakes, the feeling is mutual. Those greetings spill over to her and Grace as they move through the yard.

"How nice to finally meet you. How are you, dear? Doing well?"

"You're prettier than George described you."

"We saw you on the news. So glad you're both okay."

"And who's this little doll?" some ask of Grace.

"My sister's getting married. George says you sell beautiful gowns."

"You'll sit with us at the table, okay?"

Time passes easily, the way you remember sweet summer days passing beneath glints of sunlight, in the shade of leafy trees with a cool lemonade in hand. Amy drifts in and out of several conversations; at other times she quietly soaks up the sun and good feelings, walking with Grace's hand in hers. George sits at the picnic table with them, filling their plates with burgers and potato salad and devilled eggs. When he can, he steals Amy away from the women and makes the rounds with his friends, introducing her, bringing her into his world. Then, just as suddenly, the friends' wives Nan and Melissa nudge her elbow and lead her away to meet Chelsea, Melissa's high school daughter. Later Amy sits in a chair at the wading pool, dipping her bare feet in while Grace kneels in her polka dot dress and drags her hands through the cool water. Across the yard, George talks intently to Nate. He leans in seriously until he takes his brother's arm and gives a shove toward the house. His face is dark and Amy turns to watch, but then Melissa hands her a piece of watermelon.

"Thanks," she says, lifting her feet from the pool and taking Grace by the hand. There is still a twinge whenever she does that, her eyes scanning the crowd for any danger that might pull Grace's hand from hers again. Caution has become its own limb now. Amy moves to a chair in the sun and holds the watermelon slice while Grace takes a sloppy bite. She dabs at the juice on her daughter's chin when Nate comes up behind them.

"Hi Amy. We haven't had a chance to talk all afternoon."

"Nate." She squints up at him in the sunlight, wondering what riled his brother. "Hey. Where's George?"

"Over at the grills."

"Oh."

Grace keeps her eyes on Nate and begins to back up, bumping into Chelsea. "Come on, Gracie." Chelsea extends her fingers. "Let's go blow bubbles." Grace takes her hand and moves close to her new friend, standing behind her legs. "Do you mind, Amy? I'll keep an eye on her."

"That's fine, Chelsea. She'd like that." Amy watches them go, then turns back to Nate. His light brown hair looks a little longer than when they first met. He wears cargo shorts, a polo shirt and leather Docksiders. "It's good to see you again, Nate."

He crouches beside her in the lawn chair and plucks a few blades of grass. "Same here. How are things going?"

"Pretty good, thanks."

"George says you're doing okay. No more stalking issues?"

She looks over at him and shakes her head. "All's been quiet. Knock on wood."

"Yeah, seriously."

She wishes then that George would head her way. It feels strained with Nate quiet beside her. "So hey," Amy says after a few moments. "What a great day for a barbecue."

"Sure is. We get together with the gang every summer." He scans the people in his yard and quiet comes between them, again.

"Well you have a lovely place," Amy finally says.

"It's home," he answers. "George and I grew up here, you know. My parents left all this to us. All our history is here."

"That's pretty amazing, to hold on to the family home like that. It's what I want for Grace, too. A nice home, fond memories of summer days. Especially after what she's been through."

"George tells me you've got a beautiful farmhouse. Lots of character in those old places."

"We love it there."

"You and George?"

She looks at Nate, uncertain of what he means. "Grace and I," she clarifies.

"Right." He looks across the yard at Grace. "She's a sweet kid. We're going to roast marshmallows in a while, so she'll like that. The coals are red hot on the grill."

"Sounds fun." Amy turns toward the grill and sees Grace running ahead of Chelsea, blowing bubbles as she goes, her smile delighted, her blonde ponytails flyaway. And in that second, she gauges the distance between her daughter watching the bubbles rise and the *red hot* grill. Chelsea laughs behind her and Grace glances over her shoulder, not watching where her legs are taking her.

Suddenly George moves into view, Amy sees this. He's talking to Nan, but he's distracted by Grace. Her eyes shift to Grace then, still moving toward that darn grill, Chelsea beside her waving her arm so that a stream of clear bubbles blows from the wand.

Images, images, all frozen in her mind as she starts to rise from the lawn chair. Grace laughing and running pell-mell with her bubble bottle, her face tipped up to the summer sky. Amy knows, she just knows as she glances quickly back at Nate before loping across the lawn. "Amy?" she hears Nate call out. She knows Grace is headed straight toward that simmering grill. Images, images.

Grace's ponytails bouncing with each step, the wispy locks catching the late afternoon sunlight, her polka dot sundress fluttering.

George moving past Nan, his arms pressing her aside as he begins to run in slow strides. Just in case, Amy knows, it's just in case, as he closes the distance between himself and Grace.

Chelsea laughing, calling for Grace to look up at all the bubbles.

Grace turning while running, her smile wide, then fading as she senses George closing in behind her.

A glare of sunlight momentarily blinds Amy. When she catches sight of Grace, her expression has changed. The grill is steps ahead of her and George runs faster. He stumbles, his hand touching ground as he regains his footing and rushes up from behind, a dangerous shadow and footsteps. Grace is in the bank parking lot again, Amy can see by the look on her face. She's flash-backed. A madman is about to swoop her up in his hold.

"Grace!" Amy calls out, trying to get her daughter to stop. Or turn. Or fall, even. Anything but run head-on into that flaming hot grill.

George, his arms reaching out, lurches forward, grabs Grace around the waist and lifts her high, swinging her around to safety. It's actually physical, the relief that hits Amy. It comes in an instant sob, knowing full well what George just averted. Time stops right there, stops her in her tracks, a hand cupped over her mouth, tears in her eyes. But it's what happens next that gets her moving, that starts slow steps to Grace. A sound she hasn't heard in over a month, not since before the kidnapping, draws her. Grace's little lungs let forth a scream right as George lifted her and her voice hasn't stopped. He turns around, searching out Amy. Holding Grace in his arms, his hand gently cups her head close. Amy imagines his voice, deep and warm. *Here's Mommy. Mommy's coming. Mommy's coming. Shh.* And his eyes stay locked onto Amy's as she moves faster while trying to hear George over the crying.

"She's talking," George tells her.

"What?" Her eyes move to her daughter's face as she takes her from George and cradles her.

"Mumumum." The voice doesn't stop, repeating it over and over again.

"She's talking, sweetheart," George says as he stands very near and puts an arm around her and Grace. "She's going to be okay."

Amy looks at her daughter in disbelief, wipes tears from Grace's face with her thumb, kisses her and lightly rests her fingers over her mouth. They feel her daughter's breath and lips and jaw shaping words. She never imagined what it would take to end Grace's silence—that her daughter would have to relive moments of the crime to do so. Because that's what just happened: George grabbing Grace up in a second of distress mimicked the kidnapping in the bank parking lot, bringing it all back to her. Except this time, Amy was able to save her. It's as though Grace waited in her silence, for all these weeks, for her mother's arms to sweep her to safety. And finally, finally, she did.

George moves behind her and leans down close to her ear. "Let's take Grace over into the shade. We'll get her something to drink."

Melissa, Chelsea and Nan hurry over. "Is she okay?" Nan asks. "Did she touch the hot grill?"

"I'm really sorry, Amy," Chelsea says. "We were just having fun with the bubbles."

"Not to worry. She's fine," Amy says, hoisting Grace up higher. "She's perfectly fine, aren't you Gracie?"

Grace stops crying then and looks directly from Amy to Chelsea. "Want to go in the water," she says while hiccupping her sobs still.

Amy laughs, then looks back at George. He's the only one who knows what this means. The only one who fully realizes what impenetrable wall has just been broken through. He takes her arm and leads them over to the wading pool where two chairs sit side-by-side. Amy sits with Grace in her lap and hugs her close. When Nate approaches with a huge bowl of chocolate ice cream and rainbow sprinkles, she's a little surprised when George steps in front of him. She can't hear what the brothers say, but George takes the ice cream and stands there until Nate turns and heads back inside.

"Here you go," George says then, crouching beside them and giving Grace the bowl. She digs in and lifts a dripping spoonful to her mouth. When she lifts the next spoonful to Amy to taste, she thinks it has to be the very best ice cream she's ever had.

"Amy," George says quietly. "Do you think Grace is all right? You okay here?"

She nods, leaning around Grace to slip off her sandals. "Couldn't be better," she whispers to George. Then she hugs her daughter again. "Love you, Grace. Love you."

"Love you, too," Grace answers before slipping off her lap and taking a high barefoot step over the edge of the plastic pool into the water, Chelsea kneeling close by, reaching into the pool, her fingers making gentle splashes beneath glints of sunlight, in the shade of the leafy tree.

Twenty-Four

AMY LIFTS THE SUV'S REAR door, visually calculating how many trips she'll have to make between the car and the house. Her parents are arriving tonight and she wants the kitchen stocked. Spilling out of grocery bags are half gallons of ice cream, wafer cones, fresh coffee grounds, cake ingredients, peaches and plums, hamburgers and hot dogs. Gone are the carrots, celery, onions and soup chickens. She's had enough of those sad foods to last a good long while. This visit is different. Celebrating is in order.

As a town constable, her father has to get back to New Hampshire the next day, but she's so happy her mother is staying on for a couple weeks. All Amy wants to do is sit on the summer grass with her, Grace chattering in her swing, sharing ice cream as she tells Grace's brave story. That's all. Three generations of women connecting easily beneath the shade of an old tree. Or sit with her mother late in the evening with a slice of cake and a cup of decaf.

A return to normal. It's started. A day has passed since Grace found her voice. She is getting better and Amy's optimism leaves her thinking that maybe the stalking can be explained too; maybe it isn't what it appears to be. She lifts two bags and positions the house key in her hand so that she can easily unlock the door. "Come on, Grace. Let's get these things put away before Grandma and Grandpa get here."

"Want to swing, Mommy," Grace says, pointing to the tire swing beneath the maple tree.

The screaming of the day before strained Grace's throat, leaving her voice hoarse. Amy nursed her with cool juices and ice-pops and now she hates to deny that voice's request. "Later, honey," she says gently, walking up the driveway to the back of the house before the heavy bags slip from her grip. "When Grandma gets here." She finagles the kitchen screen door open and positions the key between her fingers. "Hold the door for Mommy, okay?" she asks, tipping her foot against the screen door so that it won't close on Grace.

"Want to swing," Grace says again as she holds the door.

Amy smiles, still not used to the sound of her daughter. "Let's find Angel first. You have to take a nap with kitty before Grandma and Grandpa see you." She hefts a bag that slips lower and carefully presses the key into the deadbolt lock. Before the key is fully inserted, the kitchen door falls open with only her touch. Every sense is heightened as she remembers locking and double checking the deadbolt before she left earlier. Remembers turning the doorknob and pushing on the door to be sure, before turning away and brushing lint off her white board shorts.

She nudges the door further open and stands on the threshold. Someone has been, or still *is* in, her house. From the doorway, her eyes sweep the kitchen and a glimpse of the hallway and living room. Everything stands stock still in the summer heat: the kitchen chairs tucked to the table, the telephone on the wall, the rose from George in the vase. She turns and scans the countertop, the stove, the sink. There are no whistling teapots, no soiled coffee cups. No noises.

"Angel," Grace cries, running past Amy when the kitten sashays across the kitchen floor.

"Grace!" Amy yells in a harsh whisper. She sets the bags on the floor and nearly falls over her crouched daughter as she rushes to lift her up onto her hip. "Shh." The order is stern and unmistakable. "We must be very quiet." Grace's surprised eyes are riveted to her face. Even the kitten freezes at her sudden distress. "Shh," she warns again, clutching her daughter tightly, turning silently and inching toward the living room. If an intruder is in her home, she wants the advantage of surprise.

Each step is cautious. Grace's arms clamp around Amy's neck. Does she feel her pounding heart, too? In the living room, there is a sense of déjà vu. She's done this before, this standing in place, observing the room. She already scrutinized the furniture and her growing collection of antique tables and lamps backlit by sunshine reaching through the paned windows. Sitting at a table in a weapon safety classroom, she considered skirting one of the tables with a heavy fabric.

Teach her a good place to hide.

She has to hide Grace and turns again to hurry back into the kitchen. The room is big and warm and full of padded chairs and a blue farm table and plenty of cabinets where she can carve out a child-sized space. Bending while holding Grace, Amy opens one lower cabinet after another. The pots and pans littering them will make too much noise to brush aside. And can she really close her daughter behind a cabinet door, her legs folded up to fit the space, without her Bear or seashells or bubbles, snuffing her words again? She shifts Grace on her hip. It would kill her to put her in there.

Amy looks at the ceiling because that's where her gun is. Upstairs. She walks through the living room, slips out of her sandals and climbs the stairs barefoot. "Shh," she reminds Grace, a hand poised to cup over her child's mouth if necessary. A drop of perspiration trickles along her temple. At the top of the stairs, she can't be sure if she hears a noise. They edge along the wall and fold into her bedroom doorway. "Oh God," she whispers. Her bare feet press quietly over the carpet to her closet. She stands Grace beside her and pulls the gun case off the high shelf, unlocks the combination on the second try and touches the weapon. Her hand jumps back.

Every touch, every noise is a gun going off on her nerves. Grace wraps an arm around her leg. "See Mommy's pretty dress?" Amy pushes clothes aside on their hangers to clear a space beside a silky black dress. "I want you to stand there next to the dress." She takes her daughter by the shoulders and guides her backward. Grace resists, stumbling a step. *Teach her a good place to hide.* Folds of long skirts and tunic tops hang like veils around her shoulders. "You have to stay right there until I get you," she orders, her hands holding Grace's arms firmly. "Please Grace. Please don't move."

There is a low noise then, and Amy abruptly straightens to decipher it. Someone is moving the sliding closet door in the far bedroom. The door unmistakably rumbles as it glides along its track.

"Dear God," she whispers, her hands shaking uncontrollably. She sets the gun case on the bed and presses a magazine into the grip. This isn't happening. It can't be. There had been so much happiness this morning. Grace was tired, but talking. Softly, but repeatedly. Hope returned, mounting with each spoken phrase building her delicate house of cards.

Another noise, then. Amy spins toward her doorway at the sound of a dresser drawer being pulled out. It is an old Shaker style bureau from a flea market: stripped, sanded and painted white. The wooden drawers have no runners. Are her stalker's slick hands reaching into the drawer, sweeping through the space? She wants to run into the spare room, screaming: *What do you want? Just get out of here! Go now!*

Well they'll get nothing, she decides, picturing Grace being snatched away at the bank. Never again. She tries to swallow, but her throat closes up with what's coming. She presses the handgun discreetly to her side and turns to Grace. Her daughter steps forward, her pinky curled around a swatch of the silky black floral dress fabric while she sucks her thumb. Amy conceals the gun behind her back. "No sweetie," she whispers. It's horrendous, the way the kidnapping forces her to do things she does not want to do, never wanted to do in her life—moving Grace into a closet, bending and hugging her close with her free hand, pressing her face to hers, kissing her cheek—all while holding a gun behind her own back. "Let's make a little tent," she suggests, quickly framing skirts and pants around her child. "This is like hide and seek, Gracie. You stay right there until I find you. Show Mommy how very brave you are, okay?" She drapes the hanging clothes around Grace's body. "I'm going to close this door a little bit. You stay right there." As she says the words, her eyes hold Grace's, unblinking, willing unconditional obedience. "Shh now."

Satisfied that she understands, Amy turns around and moves to the doorway, her eyes darting between the bedroom down the hall and the gun in front of her. *Stress and fear screw up your motor skills and it's damn easy to fumble with too many controls on a gun.* She brings her other hand to the gun, gripping it tightly and feeling the shake of her own nerves. Her body has its own mind now and it's telling every one of those nerves to stand on edge. She moves out into the hallway, glancing back at her closet before closing her bedroom door. Her steps are sure but silent as her bare feet inch along the landing with her back to the wall, her eyes never leaving the spare bedroom. There will be no mistakes this time. A dresser drawer slides open. Her breath stops. Quick footsteps move through the far room, but the door is nearly closed, blocking Amy's view.

Cover. Try to place something thick or hard, preferably both, between yourself and the attacker.

Amy disagrees. She presses her back firm against the hallway wall, lifts her two arms gripping the gun and trains it on the spare bedroom. Shafts of sunlight come in through the hall window, catching swirling dust particles and shining on the handgun like a spotlight. She has the advantage; her presence isn't known. Whoever leaves that room will have two choices coming face-to-face with her nine-millimeter. Either they will follow her order to pick up the telephone, call the police themselves and wait to be arrested with her weapon fixed on them, or they will take a jacketed hollow point. No negotiating. No questions. She owes Grace this protection.

In a violent confrontation, you won't be cool, calm and collected.

Her outstretched arms waver, guessing at a moving target's path, and her finger, held back from the trigger, quivers. Oddly, the tremor is startling and she stares at the vibrating motion of her finger. No one warned her about this damn shaking. No one advised her how to stop it. She slowly forces her finger in, fitting the pad of it lightly above the trigger, afraid those shaking nerves alone can discharge the gun once the safety is released.

She lifts her sight then to the doorway, blinking away a bead of perspiration that rolls into her eye. Her thumb releases the safety lever. Ready.

The door opens and Amy lifts her arms higher. Aim. "Don't *move!*" she shouts as the intruder appears before quickly stepping backward, her hand to her heart. "Oh Jesus Christ," Amy cries, her weapon trained on her mother's shocked face. Her finger wavers, adrenaline making it unsure of its next move. "What the hell are you doing here?"

Her mother's open hand presses against her chest as she ducks behind the door.

"You scared me half to death!" Amy stamps her foot. A sob interrupts her words. "Jesus, Mom, damn it!" she says, resetting the safety before forcefully lowering her stiff arms to her side and slumping against the wall. "I almost *killed* you." She sinks into a crouch and wraps her aching arms around her legs, the gun hanging in her grip, her head bowed onto her knees.

"Amy?" Ellen asks from behind the door. "What's happening? Can I come out?"

"*Yes.* Why didn't you *say* something? You're not supposed to be here until *tonight.*" Amy yells as her mother blurs behind her tears, liquefying in a nautical striped shirt and denim capris. "What if I had pulled the trigger?"

"I didn't even hear you come in. Am I safe? Is that a gun?"

"What do you think it is? Why didn't you just wait for me downstairs? And where's Dad? I didn't see his car."

Ellen walks carefully to Amy's side, still catching her breath. "We decided to come early. With the stalking going on, I didn't want you to be alone anymore." Her words sound fragmented, responding to facing down a gun barrel. "When you weren't home, we let—" She gasps. "Oh God. We came in. You sent me a new key, remember? And I came upstairs to unpack while Dad went to gas up the car." She reaches over and tentatively raises Amy's hand to take a look at the gun. "I wanted to be done packing so I could spend time with Grace."

"Grace." Amy pushes herself up off the floor and runs into the bedroom. She shakes the gun out of her hand onto the dresser top and yanks the closet door open. It's empty, the black dress hanging alone. She pulls the chain for the light and swipes hangers randomly to the side. Her hand tangles in airy fabrics meant to be worn on carefree summer days, not meant to hide a child. Grace is pressed far against the back wall behind a long bathrobe, her thumb in her mouth, her head tipped down. "Mumumum," she says softly around her thumb without looking up.

"Oh, Grace." Amy scoops her into her arms and takes a shaking breath. "It's okay, honey, it's okay. Mommy found you," she says, the back of her fingers caressing Grace's soft face. "And look who's here," she whispers excitedly, turning to Ellen. Seeing her mother standing there brings it all back. "I'm so, so sorry, Mom," she cries. "I didn't know it was you. If I only knew."

Ellen sits on the bed, still visibly shaken. "What is going on here today? I don't understand."

"I aimed a gun at you, Mom. God, I don't believe it."

Her mother looks from Grace's face to hers and Amy knows she looks like a madwoman. Tears streak her perspiration; circles rim her eyes; she's lost weight. "Mom. I have so much to tell you. About our therapy. And the gun. And the stalking. And George."

"Amy. Amy, slow down. Take a deep breath."

"Grandma," Grace says, leaning toward Ellen with outstretched arms. "Swing me now?"

"What?" Ellen asks.

"I had to tell you that, too. She's better, Mom. Grace is talking again." Grace squirms out of Amy's arms and scrambles to the bed. Amy follows behind her, crying at what almost happened out in the hallway moments ago. "I am so glad you're here."

———

"Do you want to sit inside or take Grace out to the swing?" Amy asks the following evening. The heat of the day lingers after supper. It is that perfect hour when colors have cooled, the greens of the maples, the blue of the sky. Robins sing clear falsettos in the lengthening shadows. She presses a scoop of cookie dough ice cream into a cone. The ache in her arms throbs from the tension of holding her gun the day before.

"Wherever you want," Ellen answers. She dabs a paper napkin to her forehead. They sit at the kitchen table, having just washed the dinner dishes. George's white vase with the rose in it sits in the center of the blue wooden table.

Amy looks over her shoulder toward the window. "I don't know. There's nowhere to sit at the swing. But it'll be nice and cool beneath the tree."

"We can bring a blanket."

"Maybe. You're not tired of pushing her in the swing?"

"No." Ellen takes the cone Amy holds out.

"We could sit on the Adirondack chairs on the patio if you want." Amy starts to fill a second cone. In between scoops, she samples a spoonful loaded with chunks of cookie dough.

"That would be fine, too. Whatever you want to do."

The cone in her hand cracks as she presses in more ice cream. Amy furrows her brow and digs in for another scoop. "We could bring the lawn chairs out to the swing. I don't know, though, because Grace likes to sit on the blanket with Angel and Bear."

"Well, Amy. Where do *you* want to have the ice cream?"

"I can't decide. Okay?" She presses the scoop on top of the loaded cone and it splits open in her hand, blossoming like the petals of a flower. "God damn it."

Ellen sets her cone in the sink and grabs a handful of paper towels. "What do you mean you can't decide?" She leans past Amy and swipes up the mess, dumping it in the sink and returning with a damp cloth to wipe the table. "You can't decide where to *sit?*"

"That's right, okay? Look what happens when I make decisions. I almost killed you, Mom."

Ellen stops wiping and sits beside her. "I know."

Every conversation they had today wound its way back to her holding a loaded gun on her mother. Amy holds up her hand in front of her face. "I couldn't *force* my finger to shake right now, the way it did yesterday, even if I wanted to. I was at the mercy of my nerves. Control is such an illusion."

"No it isn't. Don't ever believe that. I'm still here, aren't I? You have more control than you realize. So don't be afraid to trust yourself and just live, Amy. And always remember that sometimes … How does that saying go?"

"What saying?"

"I saw it on a bumper sticker. Shit happens?"

"*Mom.*" Amy stares at her mother. "Your language."

"Well sugar happens doesn't quite say the same thing."

"Mom." Amy pauses, then whispers, "Seriously."

"What?"

She gets up and goes to the kitchen window, looking out at the yard. "I get so afraid sometimes."

"Of what?"

"Of what's happening. It's like that armored truck came right at *me* and knocked me off my feet. My life's unraveling. This isn't me, this worried, indecisive woman. I can't focus anymore, I'm nervous, I'm losing sleep."

Ellen finishes wiping the ice cream off the blue table without comment. "Where's George?" She comes up behind Amy at the window.

"George? What's George got to do with this?"

They both look out at the yard, Amy leaning her hands on the countertop, Ellen holding soggy paper towels. "Maybe everything." Amy throws her a glance. "Come on, dear," Ellen explains. "It's been almost two months since that day at the bank. Grace is talking again, the police are still investigating the crime. You've got new deadbolts, a gun, a self-defense class and therapy. I'm staying as long as I can so you're not alone with the stalking issue. You've gotten back to your bridal shop, part-time. You're handling the effects of the kidnapping just fine. Better than fine." She steps beside Amy, watching her face. "Maybe something else is careening right at you. Maybe some*one* is knocking you off your feet."

"George?"

Ellen raises an eyebrow.

Amy turns around, leaning against the sink. "He wanted me to have time alone with you. Which I almost effectively ended, I might add. I still don't want to believe it, Mom. But I can't get it out of my head. What if I pulled that trigger? I came so close."

"You're changing the subject. Why don't you call him?"

Amy sits at the table again, lightly touching a petal of the pink rose. "He's got a Chamber of Commerce meeting tonight."

Ellen watches her for a moment. "You miss him."

"He's the best thing that's come out of all this. It's so strange to think that if that horrible morning hadn't happened, I wouldn't know him. I can't even imagine that." Angel jumps onto the kitchen table and sniffs at the ice cream. A melting dot clings to one of her whiskers, drooping it down. "I'll see him tomorrow. He's coming over for dinner."

"But call him later."

"Why the sudden interest?" Amy asks while lifting the cat off the table.

"Listen," Ellen begins. "It took a whole year for you to get back on your feet after Mark died. Then, you're right, another terrible day came through your life. But when the dust finally settled, who was left there? George."

Amy watches her mother, waiting for her to finish the thought she knows is coming.

"The kidnapping is behind you, but you're telling me you're afraid of what's happening."

"So?"

"Maybe it's a man you're afraid of."

"Oh, come on. You're saying my falling apart isn't post-traumatic stress?"

"Not anymore." Ellen looks straight into her eyes. "You've got that ordeal under control. I think you're afraid of what's next."

"Afraid? Of George?"

"No, of course not. But of loving him." An easy smile comes to her face. "Being unable to decide where to eat your ice cream is not post-trauma stuff. It's jitters, dear. Because I believe you've gone and fallen in love."

Twenty-Five

M RS. TREWIST, PLEASE HAVE A seat," Detective Hayes says as he leads her through his office door. "Can I get you a coffee? Water?"

"No, thank you." Amy sets her straw tote on the floor beside the chair. The office is cramped and the detective seems to fill all the space. A computer monitor hums on his desk, ringing telephones and muffled voices leach in through the closed door.

"Is everything okay?" he asks as he pulls in his chair. "Any more stalking incidents?"

She tells him about the porch light. "So was it stalking or just a fickle light bulb? Either way, it scared me just the same."

"I understand. We'll definitely keep the patrols coming around."

"And I really appreciate it." She presses a wrinkle from her black tank dress and folds her hands in her lap. "But the reason I'm here is that I haven't heard anything about the investigation and I wanted to touch base."

"Of course," Hayes answers, pulling a thick manila folder from his desk drawer. He opens it flat in front of him. "Let's look at the developments and see where we're going with this."

Words, words, words. Nothing to hold on to, to clench, to celebrate. To quell her fear. He reviews the psychological profiles, explains how they tracked George's movements that day in an effort to duplicate the perpetrators' trail, how no suspects could be deciphered on the casino surveillance videos, how the fingerprints on Grace's shoe have been definitively identified as hers and George's.

"George did rescue Grace at Litner's Market," Hayes adds. "And from the few prints lifted, we could only match yours and his." He folds his hands over the open folder and looks at her. "A few leads also came in when the updates made the headlines. Our next move is to up the reward money."

"Money talks?"

"It's amazing how much. We're also cross-referencing the evidence with similar crimes nationwide to flesh out our leads."

"But what you're telling me is that right now, you have nothing."

"No. We do. But only up to a point. Then everything seems to drop off the map."

"Great."

"*Seems to*, Amy. Trails don't evaporate like that. We just haven't sniffed it out yet. I know it's discouraging, but keep in mind that there is good to be found here. In many crimes of this nature, some sort of critical injury is inflicted. We're thankful that you and your daughter, as well as the armored truck employees, came out of it unscathed."

Amy stands and walks to the window. Waves of heat rise from the street outside. "Have you seen Grace's medical records? Would you like to see the therapy appointments blocked off on my calendar? Or how about my prescription tranquilizers? And what about flashbacks, Detective? Have you ever had one and nearly fainted afterward? Have you?"

Hayes shakes his head. "No, I haven't, and I'm sorry. I didn't mean that you haven't suffered. I just meant that no guns were fired. I meant you're all lucky to be alive, and I'm not just saying that. You really are."

Amy takes her seat with a deep breath, scanning the papers in the folder. "Listen. I brought my sketch pad." She leans over for her tote and pulls it out. "I've been coming back again and again to the one incident when Grace lost her shoe."

The detective opens the pad to the latest sketches.

"I'm not sure why, but there's something about that part of the ordeal I seem to be missing and my mind won't let go of it. Most of my flashbacks center around it." She points out the last two sketches, the curve of the cross-hatched hand covering hers, the shadow of a scar, the gritty pavement penciled beneath. "Something's missing, I just know it. Some detail that I feel could help the investigation."

"The details in these are very astute, especially the gun sketches, and as accurate as could be expected, so I'm not sure what it might be. Something with his hand, maybe? Or a detail on his sleeve?" When he glances at her, she shrugs in frustration. "Well definitely let me know if it comes to you." He slides the pad back her way. "I'm expecting an update from the FBI. We do this weekly conference call thing. I'm sure they'll have something more."

It must be hard to admit that all your efforts are ineffective. That your professional training, your investigative techniques, your psychological analyses, they all come up empty. That the evidence, the vehicles, the fingerprints, the eyewitnesses, the victims, they all amount to nothing unless you put a spin on it. These thieves are smooth. Amy reaches into her tote and pulls out a candy wrapper.

"I was moving the outfit Grace wore when they kidnapped her and found this in her jeans' pocket." She hands him a green plastic wrapper covered by white snowflakes, knowing full well it once covered a chocolate truffle, the same chocolates George carries in his shop. "Is it possible that the men who did this are local?"

Hayes takes the wrapper. "Doubtful."

"But I see this type of chocolate in different shops around town." Could the kidnappers have bought some while George wrapped two pounds of pork chops for them, Sinatra crooning on the stereo? "I know it's only a candy wrapper, but can't this mean there's a chance they're from around here?"

Hayes toys with the paper wrapper, turning it over. "If they were, their absence would be noted. See, they wouldn't be expected to stick around with that type of bankroll. They'd hit the islands or set up brand new lives somewhere else. Family members, employers, neighbors, someone would notice their sudden absence. It's more likely that they were pros moving in and out of the area just for the duration."

———

Still, Amy can't help but wonder. In the grocery store, she watches the produce stocker with renewed interest. What did a man who spends his Tuesday afternoon stacking hundreds of one-pound bags of carrots, being careful not to start a carrot landslide, have to lose? Isn't picking bruised peaches from a summer display shelf, or sweeping spilled blueberries off the floor, enough motivation to consider another way?

She pushes her cart through the aisles, half watching the other shoppers while she looks at the stocked shelves. Someone has to stack all these cans of tomato paste. Every day. Or at least rearrange them, pulling the inventory forward, turning dented cans. She sets four cans in her cart, along with a large can of whole peeled tomatoes. Who notices when it is time to reorder the paste? When inventories are low? Is tracking cans of tomato paste enough to push someone over the edge? Will it drive that person to hold a kidnapped child hostage? How much resentment leads to showing a forty-five to keep the mother back? What makes it worth it?

A shopper leaves his carriage smack in the middle of the aisle as he studies the mayonnaise. He looks old enough to have grown children entering college, his mortgage only half paid off, his house needing a new roof, his car three years old already. What is he? An electrician, maybe? An accountant? Did he sit in his den at night, papers spread over the coffee table, carefully planning a May morning outside the local bank? A bank with which he is familiar because it holds his accounts? Did his neighbor, maybe a state employee, help with visions of a new driveway, new vinyl siding on his Garrison colonial? Then the two families could take a week at Disney World?

"Excuse me," she says, waiting to pass.

"Oh. Sorry," he answers, barely moving the carriage out of her way.

Amy winds around to the specialty cheese case. She picks a chunk of Parmesan and adds it to her carriage. Her heart pounds as she turns to the registers.

Shoppers' faces loom close, their features distort. Has the kidnapper been in her midst all along, blending right in? What better cover than normal routine? She checks her gold watch and bumps a rack of sale toothpaste, knocking half a dozen boxes to the floor to disguise her panic. No one needs to know that she *has* to bend over just to catch a breath, bending her head to her knees to merely breathe.

—

"Amy. What's wrong?" George asks.

Does he mean besides rising with the sun, hanging two gowns on the clothesline before going in to work to revamp her tired window display? Besides suspecting the poor produce guy of kidnapping Grace? Besides pressing Hayes for answers? Besides wondering if George actually spoke with the perpetrators in his shop? Besides holding at arm's length, all day, her mother's words? *You're afraid of what's next. Of love.* Amy stands at George's door. Is that what this is all about, that she's afraid of love? All day, her body resisted the idea, running any which way it could until there was nowhere left to go. There is only here.

"Nothing's wrong."

George steps outside into the sunshine and takes the grocery bags from her arms. "I just wasn't expecting you. Are you sure you're okay?"

"Yes." She looks at this man who worries about her. At his dark hair still damp from showering after work. At the casualness of a pair of jeans, black tee and brown leather running shoes. At the heavy watch on his wrist and at the jaw that hasn't been shaved. At anything but the eyes that love her. "No. Well, I don't know."

George tips his head down, trying to catch her eye. "Is it Grace?"

"No. No, she's fine. She's home with my mom." She takes a quick breath. "George. Would you mind if we had dinner here tonight?"

"Here? You and me?" He shifts the bags to one arm and lifts her chin up.

"I brought some food."

"By all means." He holds the door open and she feels a rush of cool air-conditioned air pressing outside into the heat. "Come on in."

She's never been in his home before. If her mother saw her hesitate, she'd say *There! See how you did that? You're holding back.* She shakes her head, wondering if all women have these silent talks with absent mothers, and follows George into the kitchen. He sets the bags on the dark granite counter and she moves beside him, carefully pulling out lettuce, tomatoes, carrots and cucumber. Control is what it is all about. Yes. Controlling everything except what stands beside her.

"We should probably get this started," she says without looking at him. "The sauce will have to simmer. Can I just use the phone to call my mom first?"

George motions to the cordless. "Go ahead." He steps out of the room while she talks. Afterward he sets a large pot on the stainless steel stove, pulls olive oil and spices from the cabinet and opens two cans of paste while Amy chops the sauce tomatoes. She feels him working close beside her, handing her a sharp knife, their fingers touching in the exchange, their words quiet. All the while, he watches her.

"What did you do today?" he asks. He rinsed and shredded the lettuce and reaches over for her knife.

"Not too much." Beside her, his arm rhythmically slices tomatoes for the salad. "Worked with my gowns this morning, changed the mannequin displays, added flowers and summer decorations to the window. You know." She pours olive oil in the pot and fusses with the sauce, adding garlic, stirring in water and adjusting the flame. "Ran errands this afternoon and my feet are killing me now." She slips off her wedge sandals and turns then to the salad ingredients, shaving carrots and slicing cucumber, dropping the pieces into the wooden salad bowl George already filled with lettuce. With that done, she reaches for the chunk of Parmesan.

"Do you have a grater?" she asks, waiting for a moment before closing her eyes when there is no response, when she has to admit he'd left the kitchen. Every nerve ending senses his absence. Eventually she turns and walks barefoot out of the room, seeing for the first time his home. It is all a part of him: the sloppy pile of books on the coffee table, the painting of a thoroughbred horse, a sweatshirt tossed on the dark furniture. This is all new, her eyes touching upon small details.

She sees him before he sees her. Or at least before he acknowledges her. He sits alone at his dining room table. The leaf is still in place since his last poker game with the guys, but instead of poker chips and cards and ashtrays and liquor glasses covering the tabletop, a calculator and neat piles of invoices and quarterly statements from his shop take their place. An empty coffee cup sits amidst it. She sees scraps of his life when she keeps her eyes from his.

George sits at the far end of the table beside the sliding glass door, looking out at the warm summer evening, a half-full wine glass before him, the bottle of Chianti beside it. Behind him, there is the large living room, a stone fireplace on the far wall.

A lone bird still sings outside and a mourning dove perches on the edge of a birdbath, burying its beak in the clear water before tipping its head skyward. George watches it flap off in a flurry and its sudden flight seems to release him. He lifts the wine bottle and fills another glass, for her.

"Talk to me," he says.

"George." He looks from Amy's hands gripping the chair back, to the faded denim vest over her black tank dress, to her eyes. That's when her small smile stops and she takes a seat at the far end of the table. "It's been a crazy summer," she begins, waiting when he stands and picks up her wine glass, depositing it on the table in front of her before returning to his seat. She takes a long sip and he is certain that she came here to break up. It's all been too much, too fast. Their relationship can't work. She isn't ready.

"And a difficult one," she continues. "My thoughts have gone in so many directions. And my emotions? They've been all over the map."

"Don't patronize me."

"What?"

"You heard me. We both deserve better than you going around in circles."

"I'm just trying to explain why I'm here."

George looks out the slider, finishing his wine. He refills his glass, glancing at her. "You know I love you, Amy. Now I'm going to tell you one more time." He sips the red wine. "Talk to me."

She closes her eyes for a moment. "I'm afraid."

"That's better." He takes a long breath.

"I don't know if I can continue to see you."

The smell of spaghetti sauce fills the room, carrying the ironic idea of dinner, and wine, and intimacy. When in actuality, she's giving him an out without even realizing it. "What are you afraid of?"

Her eyes widen in an effort to stave off tears. "You," she whispers.

He gives a short laugh and drags a hand through his hair. "You're afraid of me."

"No." She shakes her head.

"Well what is it then?" he asks, his voice rising with impatience.

"Of us. I'm afraid of what we have, George. You don't know what my life's been like this past year. The two people I loved with all my heart were suddenly taken as though they weren't mine to begin with. One minute they were there, the next they were gone. Just gone."

"Grace."

"Yes. And Mark. And each time, it felt like a physical blow to my body. It just doubled me over."

George brings his elbows to the table, lacing his fingers together and pressing them to his mouth. He isn't sure what she is getting at. Has Grace given a verbal indication as to his identity? Or did Amy put pieces of her memory together and recognize him from the parking lot? Is she turning him in gently?

"I love you, George. I do. Okay?"

He looks across the length of the table at her, at her blonde hair tucked behind her ears, at her initial pendant hanging from a gold chain. Her face is flush with the day's warmth even though he's set the central air to chill the place.

"I want to be with you. I want you in my life. But my God, if anything should happen to you, if Grace and I were to lose you, I don't think I could take it."

"So you're breaking up with me because you love me?"

She presses a finger beneath her eye to stem the tears. "That's how scary the thought of loving again has become since that day at the bank. It's why I get nervous when we get close, why I can't make decisions. Oh, I guess it's why my silverware is really shining these days. If I lose you, George, if you stop loving me, or leave me, or die, I don't think I'll be able to breathe."

George stands and looks out the slider at the dark shadows of twilight. "There are no guarantees in life. There are just odds. None of us knows what's around the corner."

"I'm sorry," she whispers. "I just don't know how to get past this."

"Don't be sorry," he answers. "You're very right. It *has* been a crazy summer. Every time you get on your feet, a wave comes up behind you and knocks you down again." He walks to her and sits close. "You need life to be slow and sweet and predictable right now."

"I do."

After a moment, George sets his elbows on his knees and takes her hands in his. "Are you saying you don't want to see me?"

She shakes her head no, tears rising. "Please don't hate me. I'm just saying that after everything I've been through, I don't know *how* to let myself do this again."

"What about that night after the beach? I felt something then."

"I know. But that was before. Before the stalking or whatever the hell it is. Before I got so scared again, of *everything*. Even of us."

"What did you think?" he asks, leaning close, their faces nearly touching, their voices barely audible. "Did you think I'd let you go without a fight?" His thumb catches a tear on her cheek. "Did you think I wouldn't try to fix it for you?"

"I can't leave you. It's just that I love you and that really scares me." She smiles through her tears. "Sometimes I wake up and I don't know what's real. Only for a second, because of all that's happened. When I'm lying there, I wonder if it's real that you brought Grace back to me. And then I *do* know. And I think of you at work, maybe, and you're listening to Sinatra, or talking to your customers. And my heart feels so happy, George. And then," she pauses, "I just get afraid."

"Don't." He tips his forehead to hers, still holding her hands. "I would never hurt you."

"I know."

George brings a hand to her face, his thumb stroking her cheek. "Hey," he says softly as an image of his father comes to mind. *Do right by her, George,* he said in the dream. *Make me proud.* He isn't sure if this is right, but something tells him to try. It worked for his father all his life. "When's the last time anyone took you dancing? Not line dancing. I mean really dancing."

"Oh George." Amy smiles into his hand.

"Do you know we've never been on a real date, you and me? You can't break up with me if we've never even gone out. Let me take you out dancing."

"Somewhere like The Stardust Ballroom?"

George tucks a lock of hair behind her ear. "For you, sweetheart? I'll have it built. You find a beautiful dress, wear it and I'll take you dancing. How about Thursday? Keep Thursday night open for me." He puts his other hand on her face and kisses her. "Then I'll take you to the movies on our second date, next week. We'll have popcorn and Raisinets." He helps her to her feet, holding her in his arms and slow dancing beside the table. "Then, for another date, we'll go out for a long dinner. Take-out seafood on the river. We'll drink coffee afterward and stay up half the night watching the boats. It'll be a slow and easy summer."

"Sounds wonderful," Amy says, her arms circling his waist while they sway in a slow, silent waltz in the dining room.

"It can be." Whispers change into kisses as he traces her face; kisses change into touch as he feels her hands and mouth collect sensations, slowly, reaching beneath his shirt, moving over his skin, believing that she can do this. That she can love him.

George kisses her longer, slow dancing her into the living room. His fingers wrap around all of hers, folding her hands in his as he backs her up beside the fireplace, raising her arms and pressing them to the wall. She closes her eyes briefly, thinking of the sketch she drew earlier. It's always the same, always the same. The image never changes, and yet. And yet it's unfinished. George's grip on hers is strong and she can't fight the memory of another grip in the bank parking lot. But his insistence now distracts her, the way his hands move to her shoulders, slipping her denim vest off before cradling her face as she leans back against the wall, his arms blocking her in.

"You have to know," he says, looking down at her. The room is shadowy, the outside light fading at dusk.

"Know what?" she murmurs back, her hands touching his shoulders, his arms, slipping around his back, pulling him closer.

"That I'm not leaving you." He bends then and kisses her as though he's on one long inhale, that the kiss is necessary to live. With his hands still holding her face, with the kiss growing deeper, he walks her over to the sofa, lowering a hand behind her back as he lays her there, her arms pulling him down with her. In the darkening room, his presence is a mere shadow, a closeness that can't be denied. But it's the strength of his insistence, of the way his hands roughly get her clothes where they need to be, that has her breath quicken, has her kiss him deeper still, pulling him nearer, as if that were possible. Amy takes his hand in hers, entwining their fingers as his mouth moves to her neck, her throat, her shoulder.

And she thinks that being with George in the dark, with no illumination in the unfamiliar room, is the same as trying, trying to remember the missing details of one day; she was there, yet still searches. Like now, with the weight of him moving over her, she feels enough of his strength to know him, to love him, and yet the darkness covers something, somehow. He pulls his hand away then and takes her arms, pressing them up on the sofa beside her head, and raises himself over her. When she starts to reach for his shoulder, his hands quickly slide up to her wrists, holding her arms down.

And when he lowers his mouth to the soft of her neck, not releasing her arms, she knows that all of life is like that damn sketch. Love is sketched in too, in the moment she says she loves him, in the seconds after he loosens his hold when she moves her hand over his heart and he stills, in the memory she has of his thumb tracing over her lips before his fingers cover them when she starts to talk. It's never really complete, the lines of love and worry and doubts and love yet again all crossing the other, sketching, sketching further with each breath we take, each touch we give.

⸺

When Amy's fingers entwine with his again, he gets angry. Not at her, but angry that the thought has to be there at all, the thought that she'll recognize him from the mere feel of his God damn hand. That one memory can bring the realization of exactly who he is at any moment, even right now as he moves over her. And so George takes her hands, and with his anger, clenches them, gets them away from the scene of the crime once and for all when he raises them higher and presses them into the sofa. And he's mad, too, that he couldn't do it, he couldn't take the out she offered. When she arrived earlier, it was the perfect window through which he could escape, leaving this all behind. He could've told her he understood her doubts and that it would be best if they went their separate ways. That their history was too painful for this to work.

Instead he feels every bit of the length and curve of her body beneath him now, every molecule of her skin and soul pressing against his, his every touch sparked with that anger still. Because why couldn't he just buy that bike and hightail it out of Addison for a while, at the very least, taking off with Nate and choosing a different way of living. One without Amy Trewist tormenting a part of every day, every thought.

And so it's all there—the anger at a bankroll behind tiles in the next room, at a brother who dragged him into this, at a father who instilled in him a conscience, at a priest telling him to seek absolution as if he God damn knows. At a beautiful woman who crossed paths with him one fine spring morning and changed the direction of every single thing he does, so that whatever he does now puts her at more risk. And *that* gets him mad, that he can't love her freely. And so his hands tell her *this* is how it'll be, pinning her bare arms down, pushing his hand beneath her back, lifting her to him until he's brought to tears that this is how love came to him, on someone else's terms, and so tonight, one time, that love is on his terms, physically, and he's sure she knows it.

Afterward, she lies silent beside him. And he has to look away, to shift his position, raising his arm so that it crosses over his eyes. Time passes, a minute or ten, it doesn't matter. What matters is that it passes in her silence, and he's also damn sure she'll leave in another few. Just pick her dress and denim vest up off the floor and quietly slip away to be done with him after what he just did. Maybe it's what he wanted, to give her an out too, with the force of his touch. Instead her hand eventually rises, again, to his heart, feeling the beat of it, he knows.

As soft and gentle a touch he's ever felt. And his breath releases, slowly leaving his lungs and leaving him depleted.

"George," she whispers in the dark now, so very close beside him on the couch, her legs against his. "Before, I didn't mean—" she begins, but he reaches over and presses back her blonde hair, his fingers sliding along her gold chain to her initial pendant, and shakes his head, no. "What?" she asks.

"Don't," he says, his hand reaching behind her neck, her skin damp with perspiration, his mouth kissing hers gently. "It's okay. Don't talk, don't explain." He shifts on his side and kisses her again. "We both understand this night for what it is."

She looks at him and her own fingers trail along his face, drop to his shoulder and pull him closer so that they make love once more, certain now. At least he is. Certain that they're both in this, come what may, no matter what hand they're dealt. Later they have dinner beneath a dim light near the slider, which he opens so they sit at the edge of a night that's cooled little outside.

"You know, George, I never want to feel again what I felt before."

"And what's that?" he asks, sipping a glass of wine, thinking that she's referring to his own contention earlier on the sofa. Warm July air drifts in beside them, the crickets chirp lazy.

"That feeling that I can't eat. That's what happened. I was so afraid I'd lose you, I couldn't eat." She spears a forkful of spaghetti and he nudges her salad closer. "Aren't you hungry?" she asks, motioning her fork to his full plate.

He looks down and moves it aside. "I had a late lunch. I'll pick later." Though he knows he won't. Every damn voice in his head has ratcheted up the volume now.

When they have coffee, they sit out on the deck in the velvet black night. Not a breeze stirs any leaves; the heat hangs heavy; a distant train whistle winds through the quiet. And things have changed between them, he feels it and thinks she does, too. She's looking up at the night sky.

"There are no stars tonight, George. Look."

He does. No stars glimmer above; no silver moonlight falls on the earth. "Amy," he says then. He had an out earlier, one that's long gone now. She tips her head, waiting. He waits, too. Has been all summer long. He shifts his position in the deck chair, looking up at the sky above for a long moment. "They're out there. We just can't always see them."

Twenty-Six

Amy walks through her showroom at Wedding Wishes with two long gowns draped over her arm. Everything about the day feels perfect. The sunshine after a morning shower makes things sparkle; twinkling lights in her shop hint at stars; returning to working with her gowns brings in two morning consultations. Sometimes life is just as it should be.

"I love this one," the bride-to-be stepping out of the dressing room tells her. Embroidered lace netting overlays a satin underslip on the sleeveless sheath gown.

"It's perfect," her sister says from the velvet settee where she sits with their mother.

"Are you sure?" Amy asks. One look at the mother-of-the-bride's misty eyes tells her that yes, this is the dress. The tears give it away every time. "I've got a Victorian that might work. The sleeves are long, but they're lace so you wouldn't be too warm." She hangs the two gowns on a nearby rack.

"Oh no. I'm getting married in the heart of summer. This gown is it."

"When's the date?" Amy steps behind the bride and fans out the brush train.

"The end of August," she says. "In my backyard. We're keeping it simple. We've got a gazebo and my mom's flower garden will be in full bloom."

The sheath gown with its straight neckline is sublime in its simplicity. "A garden wedding! Sleeveless really caught on in the 1970s, so you picked a great era to choose from." Amy steps back and studies the way the gown falls along her body. "A few alterations and you'll be good to go. Do you have a tailor?"

"We do," the mom answers. "And what about a veil?"

"I think a birdcage, to keep that light, elegant look," Amy suggests as the bride turns on the raised pedestal. "Maybe anchored with a special flower from Mom's garden?"

They all tear up again just as the door to the shop opens and a copious bouquet of summer blossoms, of dahlias and hydrangea and larkspur and calla lily, is delivered by a florist from the next town over. "Is there an Amy Trewist here?" the deliveryman asks.

"Oh! That's me." Amy steps forward and takes the large arrangement. "Wow, these are gorgeous."

"Can you sign please?"

"Yes, of course." She dips her face close to the flowers, then sets the arrangement on the checkout counter and takes the clipboard. "Thank you so much."

"Have a nice day," he tells her as he walks out.

Amy turns to see the three women in her shop watching her with smiles on their faces.

"Hm," the bride muses. "Maybe you'll be looking for a gown for yourself soon?"

"Me? Oh no. We're just dating," Amy answers with a laugh. The bride looks from the flowers to Amy with a raised eyebrow. "Really," she insists.

When the appointment ends and the bride lifts her gown, all wrapped and zipped in a garment bag, Amy stops her. "Wait," she says as she pulls a pink and yellow dahlia from her bouquet. She sets it in a sprig of baby's breath and entwines it all in a silver barrette, then pins it in the bride's hair. "You'll have a beautiful day, I'm sure. And don't forget to add your wedding wish to a star on the Wish Wall before you leave. Then after the wedding, bring me a photograph and I'll replace your wish with it. Everyone loves seeing the wishes come true."

With the wish posted, the women head out to Whole Latte Life, intending to celebrate in the coffee shop with lots of coffee and plenty of cake. Amy closes the door behind them and finally has a moment to call George at work. Listening to the ring, she knows he is walking to the wall phone, wiping his hands on his black apron before picking up. Strains of Sinatra meet her ear before his voice does. "Main Course," George answers.

"George?"

"Well hello, sweetheart. How are you today?"

"Even better now," Amy tells him. "Is it busy there?"

"Little bit. Dean's up front. How about you? Feeling good this morning?"

"Yes," Amy says, smiling. "I just sold a gown, too, and wanted to thank you before my next appointment gets here."

"Thank me?"

"For last night, and for the flowers. They're very beautiful."

There is a long moment then with only Sinatra in the background singing of the moon and stars, his voice lifting you there.

"George?"

"When did they arrive?"

"Just now. Really, you didn't have to."

"I didn't."

"What?"

"I didn't send flowers, Amy. They're not from me."

"But the card—"

"Did you read it right? Could they be from someone else? For a birthday, or a thank-you from a bride, maybe?"

"No." She pulls the card from the center of the bouquet. "It clearly has your name on it." Suddenly all she wants to do is grab the bouquet and fly actually, the same way Sinatra is singing about flying. Except instead of flying to the moon, she'd fly out her shop's door, chase down the delivery van and refuse them. She'd throw the whole thing back inside the van, fling it with all her might, snapping the stems and destroying the pretty blossoms.

"Amy."

"God damn it, he even signed your name."

"I'll be right over."

"Wait," she says, turning and looking out the shop window onto The Green across the street. People stroll past, wooden barrels overflow with geraniums and summer vines, the wishing fountain spews water high into the sky. Everything here is fine. But is Grace okay at home, rearranging her refrigerator magnets, her tiny voice bringing the plastic pieces to life and not vanishing in the grasp of a kidnapper's arm? Did someone send the flowers to get her on the phone with George, to get her vigilant eyes and ears and thoughts off of her child? To distract her?

"I'll just be a few minutes," George says.

"No." She pauses, thinking quickly. "That's okay. I'll be fine. I'm *not* missing my next consultation. The bride is so excited to see the new dresses that came in."

"Amy."

"No, George. What I'm going to do is act like this never happened. I think that's best. Whoever is behind this will see that I'm not playing. I'm staying in my shop and women will be trying on gowns all morning, exactly like I planned. And then I've got a therapy session scheduled later. I've got to live my life and not let this stop me."

"Your mother is home with Grace?"

"Yes. I'll call her right now and check on them."

"Nate's stopping here for lunch. I'll tell him to drive by on his way back to work, just to be sure everything's fine."

"Okay. And I'll let Detective Hayes know, too. George?"

"What is it?"

"Do you think the flower shop has a record of who did this?" She hears him take a long breath. "No," she answers herself. "No, I guess they wouldn't."

"I'm sure he covered his tracks. But give me the name of the florist and I'll look into it. And be very careful for me today, okay?"

———

George waits to hear her disconnect the call before slamming the handset onto the phone cradle on the wall. It bounces right off, clattering to the floor before he picks it up and throws it against the wall, the impact neatly cracking it in two.

"Son of a bitch," he says under his breath.

Dean looks into the back room. "What the hell's going on here?"

"Don't ask."

"What'd you do to the phone?"

"I said, don't ask." He grabs up the broken phone, storms into his office and closes the door behind him. Then, nothing. Because what is there to do? And doesn't someone know it, that he's tied up in knots with the whole damn thing. He lifts his black apron over his head and tosses it over the hook on the back of the door. Isn't it enough that he followed their orders on the day of the heist? Because the words from a dark confessional have been growing louder lately. He can't seek only His pardon, but His likeness as well. But doesn't the good he *has* done count for anything? He folds back his shirt cuffs and sits down at his desk when someone knocks at the door.

"Later," he yells out.

The knock repeats before the door slowly opens.

"I said *later*!"

"Hey," Nate says. "It's me. Dean said you're all wound up back here." He slips out of his denim work shirt and drapes it over a chair. "We doing lunch?"

"We'll grab something out. I've got to run an errand."

Nate picks up the broken phone from the desk. "Nice work, George. What's going on?"

"Long story. Come on, let's get out of here."

"Where we going?"

"I need a new phone. And I've got to stop at the florist."

"Florist?"

"I'll tell you about it on the way." George lifts his keys off the top of the file cabinet beside his desk. He pulls Nate's shirt off the chair, too. "Don't forget your God damn shirt." He throws it to his brother.

"What happened? Someone bother Amy again?" Nate shifts into his shirt sleeves.

George opens his office door and tosses the cracked phone in the trash. If he could find the son of a bitch, there would be a head cracked open, too. He turns around and throws his keys to Nate. "You don't know the half of it. You better drive. I'm not seeing straight right now."

"*Both* eyes open, people. *Both* eyes." Seven pairs of eyes widen simultaneously. "Heads up. Shoulders square. Arms bent, hands together." Ron surveys the line of students aiming handguns at distant targets. "Trigger finger *free*," he yells and seven fingers relax. "Your trigger finger should not touch anywhere on the gun except for the trigger." He walks the line and reaches to a middle-aged man's hand. "Use the pad, never the joint of the finger. Do you hear that, people? Use the *pad* of the finger. And why do we do this?"

"Better trigger control."

Amy doesn't know who said it. The voice suspends in the air like a target waiting to be pinpointed. She has her own targets pinpointed. A produce stocker. A flower deliveryman. The dry cleaner clerk. Any ordinary person can be the recipient of her bullet. Because any one of them might have pulled hosiery over their face. And hosiery turns ordinary evil.

"Okay. Now your target is in sight and you're going to pull the trigger. Never yank or jerk it. Don't pull across it. Apply a steady pressure, straight back." The instructor takes a step. "*But*, before you do, be absolutely sure of not only your target, but of what's behind it, too. You're going to hit *something*. Make sure you know what the hell it is."

That's why, she knows and thanks God, that's why the armored truck workers did not discharge their weapons. Grace was behind their target. Now as she prepares to pull the trigger and shoot her weapon for the first time, her mind superimposes the concealed faces of those assailants on the target.

"Some advice as you hold your target in sight?" Ron walks along the line of students, occasionally tucking in a wayward elbow.

"Breathe with your diaphragm. Upper body breathing, when you fill your lungs, can actually move the gun, which you don't want. Practice at home. Put your open hand beneath your ribcage and force the inhale to come from there until you do it naturally. It's beneficial for you, too, bringing more oxygen into the cardiovascular system with each breath."

Amy holds her stance, gun aimed at the target, and inhales a deep breath.

"And remember, it's not so much *what* your gun is firing, as *where* you hit your target that matters. Any time you're ready, people. Ear protection in place, focus and feel free to try your hand."

Behind the headphones, sound is muffled. She flinches at the first gun being discharged. Other shots follow randomly, with no pattern to the distinct pops from both sides of her. And she finds herself pushing the soles of her feet desperately into the floor. Her diaphragm fills to capacity and slowly empties. Then again, even slower. Perspiration lines her forehead. The flashback comes quick. That seems to be the only pattern in her life right now. The speed and intensity of her flashbacks. They've grown infrequent, but hit her hard.

The kidnapper doesn't stop moving, shifting his weight back and forth, turning, surveying the armored truck, moving right and left. Her head turns to follow his erratic movements. He clutches Grace around her belly and quietly gives an order prompting the gunman near the truck to move. She feels the other gunman's hand press firmly on top of hers. A strange prickling sensation grows on her skin beneath his strong grip.

That's where it always stops. She looks first at the hand on hers before looking back over her shoulder. There is a pressure on her arms as Ron raises them. "Mrs. Trewist," he says, close and loud enough for her to hear through her headphones. "Keep your sights on the target. Try not to be lax with your aim."

Ron steps behind her but the pressure of his hands stays, lifting her arms, waiting for her to obey. Her arms tighten their position as she sees the hooded kidnapper holding her daughter on the target. She fires one shot.

"Not bad," Ron yells from behind. His voice sounds muted. "The grip was a little tight though. Is the right your dominant side?"

"Yes." It amazes her the way her mind switches back to the task at hand. As quickly as it came, the flashback has left, leaving her with a fatigued trembling in her muscles.

"Try not to choke the gun. You'll develop a quicker trigger speed that way and have more control over the weapon."

Amy raises her arms again, relaxes her right hand's grip, keeps her target in sight and continues to discharge her weapon, each bullet hitting her assailants over and over again.

"Okay, class," Ron says once they gather back in the lecture room. "Not bad for your first time. In the next few lessons, you'll improve your grips and follow-through before moving on to shooting while moving forward, as well as from a kneeling position. We'll also begin next week's class with a lesson on *verbally* challenging your assailant before firing. You have to try everything possible before resorting to using your weapon. We'll finish up now with cleaning and storage."

One of the students raises his hand and Ron checks his watch. "I'll answer questions as I move down the line."

Amy stands first in line. "Will you be covering methods for carrying a weapon in public?" She looks from the gun to his face. "All this training wouldn't have done me any good in the bank parking lot if my gun was at home in the closet."

Ron nods. "You can take one of our lecture classes on concealed carry and transportation. Think about it and I can sign you up after any lesson here. Safety and responsibility are *huge* issues once that gun leaves your house. The course makes sure the gun owner has developed a firm plan for the use of the firearm."

Amy doubts the idea of developing a firm plan. She could never have dreamed up, imagined, or planned the armored truck heist and kidnapping. Her only plan now has to be to think on her toes.

———

One thing she noticed as she held her gun with outstretched arms was the condition of her fingernails. That evening after dinner, Amy calls Celia.

"Are you busy?" she asks.

"Why?"

"Don't sound so suspicious."

"Convince me not to."

"I want you to do my nails."

"Your nails? Tonight?"

"I have a date," Amy answers in a hushed voice.

"What?"

"I'm going on my first date tomorrow night."

"What do you mean?"

"I mean I'm going on my first real date since Mark died." She fans her face with her fingers. "I can't believe how nervous I am."

"What about George?"

"George?"

"Yes. My God, who are you going out with? I can't believe you'd do this to George."

Amy smiles into the phone. "Why not? If someone asks me out, I'm free to go."

"But George is, I don't know, aren't you a couple, kind of?"

"Celia, relax. My date's *with* George. So just come over, okay? I need you to do my nails and I'll tell you all about it."

That's the delicious part about having a best friend, no matter if you are thirteen or thirty-three. That sweet anticipation of sharing a romantic story, the sharp intake of your friend's breath as the words spill out, the double entendres suggested beneath raised eyebrows.

Amy pours fresh coffee and sets two mugs on the kitchen table. She watches the bronze polish streak a line down the center of her nails, Celia's steady hand filling in the color. First she painted Grace's nails purple and Grace marched a parade through the house, waving her purple-dotted fingers like a baton in front of her, Angel bringing up the rear. Ellen directed the parade out to the shady backyard, an ice cream cone in each hand.

"But you've gone out on dates before. How about the time you went to Joel's and I stayed here with Grace?"

"That wasn't a date. That was to calm me down. This is a *date* date."

"Where's he taking you?" Celia asks, bent low over Amy's hand.

"I'm not sure. He said I should dress for somewhere formal where we can dance all night."

"You should wear that black dress with the flowers on it. And the pretty star necklace I gave you."

"I will."

Celia sets the polish aside and cups her mug of coffee close. "For a while, anyway."

Amy kicks her lightly and smiles. "I actually get butterflies when I think about it."

"Butterflies are good." Celia caps the polish bottle and gives it a shake. "Whatever happened with those flowers you got?"

"What an ordeal, Cee. We know which flower shop they came from. According to Hayes, the guy walked in and picked out the biggest display in the case with a rush delivery. But it was a cash order, so no record of identity. Another dead-end. Then I threw the whole bouquet out."

"I don't blame you. How frightening," Celia says.

"I've got all the flowers I need right here." Amy slides her white vase with the pale pink rose to the center of the table. "George gave this to me, and it says it all."

"What do you mean?"

"Each color of a rose means something different. Pale pink? It symbolizes grace."

Celia pulls the nail brush from the bottle, beginning Amy's second coat. "He's so sweet, Amy. Tomorrow night will be good for you two."

"I know."

"A date, dancing," Celia says quietly. "It'll be just like a fairy tale."

Twenty-Seven

W HEN DOES IT HAPPEN? AT what point does that invisible shift occur? When does a relationship depend on one to inhale, the other exhale? George glances out his living room window. The soft wash of evening sunlight casts a rich depth to the green grass, to the dappled colors in the flowerbeds, to the cool shadows beneath the maples. It is the depth of color recalled in memory. With a touch of summer nostalgia, he goes to his bedroom and clasps on his leather watchband before leaving to pick up Amy for their first date. As he turns away from the dresser, a glimmer catches his eye. He turns back and lifts the gold ring from the black valet on the dresser top and when he does, his father is in the mirror, adjusting crisp white shirt cuffs before putting on a tailored suit jacket, the ring, ruby set in gold, on his finger. The colors in George's memory of his father are liquid, soft gold enveloping the deep red stone as though it is wet to the touch.

So he slips on the ring and watches his father reflected back at him. Tall, dark hair, brown understanding eyes, strong chin. George adjusts his own thin black tie, then tugs his black sport coat sleeves into place over his pale gray shirt and black pants. In the ruby stone on his own finger he sees what his father always saw: a sweet night opening before him. And so he leaves the ring on, finally feeling a long-awaited approval from the past.

He has given the summer to Amy, slow and easy. What she doesn't know is that he's also given himself the summer to turn himself in, with or without Nate. *Life is like a ship tossing on the sea*, the priest had told him. *Your duty is not to abandon it, but to keep her on her course.* Turning himself in is the only way to steer his life through these seas. Coming to that decision unleashes something—he's grown older, somehow, with the knowledge of what is soon to come. At some point this summer, he'll tell Amy the truth.

But not yet. Because though his father would be proud when he does, he's still afraid. Afraid to lay his cards down for her, for Amy to see his hand. She'll know, then, and he's not sure where that truth will take them. If he'll lose her with it.

———

"Where are we going?" Amy asks.

George glances at her sitting beside him in the pickup truck. She turns toward him with a curious smile. A black silky wrap drapes loosely around her shoulders. "It's not far," he answers.

They drive through the center of Olde Addison, along Main Street's mix of historic homes, storefront boutiques including Amy's bridal shop, a coffee café and a hardware store. Beyond are streets lined with old estates, their sloping manicured lawns overlooking the cove. At this dusky hour, the sky is nature's watercolor. Hues of pinks and dark blues shimmer, fluid. Sailboats dock in the cove, fishermen cast off a long pier. George drives past as the sun sinks below the horizon. They follow a country road that takes them alongside a wide expanse of the river. It flows south, a shiny gray ribbon glimmering against the dark evening sky. Above the distant silhouette of trees, stars emerge.

While waiting at the local railroad crossing, the gates lowered, lights flashing, George looks over at her. "I'm going to ask you to do something," he says as the train rumbles past.

"Okay."

"Close your eyes."

"Close my eyes?"

"Just for a few minutes." The gates lift and George continues on, driving over the tracks.

Amy turns in her seat and faces forward as they pass early ship captains' waterside homes at the river's edge. "All right. I can do that." She closes her eyes and smiles.

"Don't peek."

"I won't." She rests her head on the seat.

Now he backtracks to get the vehicle headed in the right direction. He'd been taking random turns to keep her guessing their destination, steering her away from the road signs for Riverdale Park. He pulls into the gravel parking lot.

"Can I look?" she asks.

"No," he answers quickly. "Not until I say so." He parks in the front row of spaces at the far end. "I'm going to come around and help you out, but no matter what, *do not* open your eyes." He watches her waiting for a moment, sees the anticipation on her face, in the pretty black and floral wrap dress she'd chosen, in the sterling star necklace around her neck, then steps out of the truck and takes in the view. It couldn't be better.

———

George's footsteps move around to her side of the truck. She hears the click of the door handle being pulled, feels the evening air sweep in, and feels his hand take hers. All her senses come alive behind closed eyes. She reaches her other hand out to him and he helps her step down; the silky folds of her dress fall easily along her legs.

"I'm going to put my arm around you." His voice is close as he lets go of one hand to slip his arm around her waist and she loves the unspoken promise of a sweet time. Violins are playing, and a saxophone, a trumpet, drums. Waves of sound rise as the band's warm-up lengthens. George walks a few steps forward. "Okay." One violin grows increasingly insistent. "You can look."

Amy opens her eyes and looks down the gentle hill of Riverdale Park. The bandshell sits at the bottom looking like a big scalloped seashell open over a stage. The outside of the shell is pastel blue, its inside a creamy white. From the hilltop where they stand, the stage illumination, along with the pale moonlight, give the effect of stardust shimmering from the skies.

"George, this is so beautiful." A small orchestra fills the stage, the lone singer dressed in a black tuxedo and shuffling through sheet music, the dance floor spread out beneath a canopy of stars. Sudden tears blur the sight before her, making it all the more magical.

"Shall we?" George asks, taking her arm and waiting for two families to pass by with their coolers and folding chairs before leading her down a narrow paved walkway. Blankets and lawn chairs cover a wide expanse of grass around the stage area. Off to the side, they find an open space and Amy helps him spread out a blanket. He brought along a basket of cheese and crackers and tucked a bottle of wine with two wine glasses in beside the food. As they settle on the blanket, the band plays snippets of the love standards they'll perform that night, teasing the audience with hints of what is yet to come.

"What a perfect first date," Amy says, sitting with her legs folded beneath her, her wrap hanging low on her arms. She looks from the band to George. He sits close, an arm wrapped around a bent knee, taking in the sight.

"I'm glad you like it."

And it's apparent how he thought of everything, every detail. The basket is opened, the crackers and cheese squares set out on a small plate.

But it's when the stage lights dim, the band quiets and the bandleader takes his position that the magic takes over. Applause rises from the dark lawn behind them and the soft strain of violins plays the opening notes of *Moon River*. George hands her a glass of wine as couples walk past to the dance floor. "To summer," he says. "And to my hopeless romantic."

Amy cups the glass and looks out at the orchestra about to serenade the night with old love songs. The cool evening air touches her shoulders as she sits beside this man who came so unexpectedly into her life. *Just like a fairy tale*, she remembers Celia saying. "And to our own Stardust Ballroom," she adds, touching her glass to his.

———

Later, Amy glances at the black velvet sky dotted with glimmering sparkles. The stars above seem endless tonight. If only the evening were endless, too. When George holds her close dancing, sometimes singing to her softly, she feels his breath, his smile, the deep vibration of his voice against her ear. She feels the kiss he presses on the side of her head. His hand never leaves the small of her back.

If she can just keep a piece of this in her life, she would be no happier. That's all it would take. Every time one of the old standards plays on the radio, it'll bring her here, behind her closed eyes, into the shelter of George's arms.

"You're making my return to dating very easy, Mr. Carbone," she says. Her one hand rests on his shoulder, the other lays in his upturned palm.

George looks past her shoulder, then leans in, his hand sliding down to her wrist and folding their arms between them. "So long as I'm your only date." He pulls her in a little closer, the soft folds of her dress catching up with their steps.

"George." She smiles lightly, she can't help it, really. It's that kind of night, he'd seen to it.

He steps back and watches her, never taking his eyes from hers, dipping his head closer. "What is it, sweetheart?" The song ends as he speaks and his arm slips around her waist, leading her to the dark shadows just past the dance floor, away from the other couples milling about. "What's the matter?"

"I just love this," she says as he bends to hear her words. "The music, that beautiful sky filled with summer stars. You're too good to me."

He nods and tips her chin up. "So you're having a nice time?"

"Wonderful." Amy looks at the softly illuminated stage from the shadows, feeling his presence alongside her body. The thing is, he has stood beside her ever since she invited him to dinner months ago. She needn't fear loving him. "I love you so much," she whispers, turning to him, taking his hands in hers and kissing him tenderly. His hands pull away from hers though, and he raises them to cup her face, deepening their kiss in the shadows. A breeze lifts off the distant river; the moon rises over the treetops.

When the bandleader's voice begins singing the next song, his voice a little husky as the evening goes on, George kisses her a moment longer, then steps back, still cradling her face. "That's our song," he says.

Amy glances to the stage. "Your dedication that night."

He hitches his head toward the music. "Come on, dance with me." As he takes her in his arms on the dance floor, she lays her hand in his, squeezing his fingers gently.

And the bandleader sings about finding just the right someone to be true to.

Amy closes her eyes, remembering George's dedication sent over the radio love lines. Now, beneath July starlight, the piano and bandleader perform in duet until the violins sweep quietly in, the brushes grazing the drums. If ever real stardust might fall from the summer sky, wouldn't this be the moment?

The music continues like a dream, the lyrics suggesting that even thinking of George makes her glad.

Couples crowd the dance area knowing this is the last song of the set. Amy's head rests on George's shoulder, her eyes still closed, feeling the length of him pressed close, his arm holding her near. Her fingers fold around George's and their arms curl between them now. Close, so close. She caresses his hand as he presses his face against her hair.

And the song goes on, the lovers thrilling each other in verse.

But her eyes open then. And her heart, it beats faster as she shifts her head slightly.

In the song, lovers are loving each other still.

George turns her gently, his step leading her still. Her fingers close tighter around his hand, feeling his gold ring press against her skin.

The saxophone, like a wisp of fog, leads the musical interlude between verses. Amy looks at George's hand, at glimpses of his ring. And what she's seeing is page after page after page of frustrated sketches filling a pad on her blue kitchen table. From every angle, sideways, above, right side, left side. Line sketched, cross-hatched, shaded and not. Pages and pages of pencil strokes stemming from deep memory. And from one question.

His hand on hers, and what ... *What?* What is always missing? She steps back.

The piano joins the sax, its ivory keys waltzing lightly in their own dance together. Amy shifts her fingers, prompting George to take them within his hand. Her skin feels the ruby ring. It is warm, from her hand being wrapped around it. The gold shimmers.

And she can't breathe. Her lungs don't want to inhale; her mind doesn't want to admit. George's hand covers hers now and she feels every bit of his calloused skin. The knot of his scar presses against her hand just like on that morning when she felt Grace's shoe beneath it, his scarred hand on top. Just like when he looked her in the eye and told her to be strong.

It can't be. *He* can't be. George would never hurt her. Time stands still as she watches his hand through tears, just like then, immersed with this very man in a battle of wills over her daughter.

The bandleader reaches for the microphone.

She closes her eyes, remembering being on the pavement, her knees scraped raw, fear stealing her breath. But she's not flashbacking. This is pure truth coming to her.

She knows it as she opens her eyes and sees the ruby ring through her tears the exact same way she saw that ring through her tears the morning Grace was taken. The moment her world stopped spinning. It makes her, this truth, it makes her step back from George.

"It's you," she whispers.

"What?"

They still dance, but like a shifting kaleidoscope, the pieces of his identity spin randomly, coming together as one. The word *cripe*, the way he double-tied Grace's shoelaces one recent morning, the candy wrapper in her daughter's pocket, his deep voice and scarred hand, and the painfully missing detail on her sketches. That one detail in clear focus now. She shakes her head, trying to rid the picture from her mind. Wanting desperately to deny it. Her eyes shift from the ruby ring to his eyes. Eyes that had been hooded, that have haunted her endlessly. Hosiery had been pulled over his face, compressing his features, his nose pulled to the side beneath the hosiery strain, his eyebrows splayed disparately. But the ruby ring was clear as day. "No, oh God, no." She pulls further back and struggles to get a breath. "Say it," she says.

"Say what? Amy, what's wrong?"

Their step slows, but still his hand is on her back, resisting as she pulls away. She had never looked down the barrel of a gun until he held one on her. Until George had.

It's not possible to dance; her body stops moving.

"Be strong." Her voice shakes. When he closes his eyes for a long moment, she has her answer. Her body tenses and she twists her hand out of his. "Say it, George." She looks away briefly, not *wanting* to see the truth, before returning her gaze to his one last time. "*Be strong*. Say it, damn it. Just *say* it for me."

George reaches for her hands but she continues to back away, her eyes never leaving his, gauging his next move. She knows it'll crush every last bit of love from her heart. A love she finally gave herself over to, trusting him completely. The truth constricts already, and she whips her hands back out of his reach.

"Amy. Please."

She whispers as she inches away. "You bastard."

And the song works toward its end, the lovers finding true love through all their faults.

"Amy, it's not what you're thinking." George moves around a couple dancing close by, trying to stay within her reach. But she keeps the other couples between them now. "Amy, listen," he insists, taking a young man by the arms and moving him aside, losing momentary sight of her, she sees that in his panicked searching her out.

It all takes new meaning now, the entire night, the dark, the music, the stars mocking her. She turns away and bumps into a woman, then sidesteps to get by. Her pace quickens as she looks back, seeing George on the dance floor, heading in her direction. "No, no," she cries. There is some evil on her skin, on her arms, that her hands try to rub off as she moves past people out onto the expanse of lawn. A man grabs her arm and steadies her when her feet stumble. And in her rush, the night all blurs: blankets and lawn chairs, couples lounging and laughing, concerned looks. Pale moonlight pools ahead, far from the stage lights. She needs to get away. To warn her mother and to protect Grace.

And the band plays on, its melody fanning out through the park softly beneath the summer sky, an aural shimmering. The sound grows vast and distant. The last notes of the sax and piano wind their way to her as she bolts through darkness. Truth is there, too, in the song. The crowd thins farther back on the lawn and she hears her name. George's voice calls out one last time, "Amy!" She makes it to a stand of trees, trees that against the night are only tall black shadows hiding her, giving her a second, only a second, to catch her breath and steal a look back.

And the final notes from their song, from *It Had to Be You*, rise up the hill.

It seems another world from which she is now suspended, that illuminated bandshell, the orchestra, the lights glittering. Her fairy tale.

Moonglow dapples the cluster of trees where she pauses without her purse, without her cell phone, without her wallet. She looks back toward their blanket, then turns in the other direction. Fighting a sob, finally, finally she runs.

Twenty-Eight

George's life closes in on him as he loosens the knot of his tie. Running across the lawn, he scans the sloping hill for any sign of her. "Sorry," he says distractedly to a young family when he trips on their small cooler in his rush to detect even a trace of her, her blonde hair lifting as she runs, the sweep of her floral dress. Moonlight casts vague shadows on the hill that fool his eye with their indistinct shapes. He rights a webbed lawn chair his foot catches, righting it again when he overcompensates and tips it the other way. "Jesus Christ," he says as he stops and wipes off his forehead.

Behind him, in front of him, Amy is nowhere in sight. "Where are you?" he asks quietly. It doesn't help that people are idling about: couples visiting neighboring blankets, families relaxing in lawn chairs, snacking, laughing. He drops at the waist, pressing his hands onto his knees and exhaling a long breath. The night does him no favors, every shadow mocking him. George heads back to their blanket knowing it is all over and feeling the weight of her pain. All he wants to do is take some of it from her, to try to explain. She doesn't deserve any of this. He opens her handbag and is alarmed to see her cell phone. So there's that now, too. She has no way of reaching help. He snatches their blanket off the ground before climbing up the dark hill to the pickup. Some of the band members return to the stage and snippets of music coil through the air. The crowd thins further back and it occurs to him that Amy could be waiting at the truck. "Just be there," he whispers, knowing in his heart the last place she'll be is waiting for him.

When he reaches the parking lot, there are no silhouettes standing near the truck, no Amy slowly approaching him, her head tipped in terrible sadness, wanting to talk, her eyes not understanding, searching for the mistake in all of this.

Her worst nightmare came true at his hands. He drops the blanket and basket into the truck bed and tosses her purse on the passenger seat. His eyes return once to the sloping lawn below. Couples dance again, leaning close, talking softly. Like he and Amy did, moments before, in some terrible prelude. But it was supposed to be a good prelude, the beginning, leading to the truth. With his hand on the door handle, he stops. Just stops. Is she still in the park, waiting for him to leave before emerging from the shadows? He yanks his door open. Not the Amy he knows. She would be running as far from him as possible, trying to get to only one place, safely back to her daughter.

———

Once out of the park, Amy slips off her slingback sandals and slowly runs, glancing over her shoulder often as sidewalk grit presses into her bare soles. All that matters is getting away. When headlights approach, she steps quickly off the sidewalk behind shrubs, thinking it is George looking for her. Her black wrap slips from her shoulders and drags behind her and so she pulls it into a soft bundle and presses it against her tears while waiting for the vehicle to pass. After catching her breath, she steps back out, unsure of which way to go. Home is miles away and she left her cell phone behind. "Damn you, George," she says. "Damn you to hell."

Ahead, the indistinct outline of the elementary school takes a low familiar shape in the night. Fear keeps her moving past it, hurrying as she makes out a realtor's square For Sale sign a few houses away. "Oh God, yes, yes," she cries. She stops in front of the ranch house Celia had shown her weeks ago, aware that its owners have since moved out. The house stands empty and dark. Thick shrubs and trees conceal it well. Amy hurries up the front flagstone walkway, squinting in the darkness to be sure it is unoccupied. George will never find her here.

The key is inside that lock box. Celia's words rush back to her. *Just punch my code into the keypad.*

Amy jiggles the lock box. The code, what is the God damn code? Has her capacity to even think been taken along with everything else? Her fingers trace over the keypad, her hand trembling while she tries to remember. "Right," she whispers finally. "One-two-one-five, one-two-one-five." She repeats Celia's birth date over and over like a mantra while groping in the dark. The mere thought of safety on the other side of the door taunts her. She tugs the lock box and when it doesn't give, shakes it harder. "Come on!" she cries, bent over in the dark and carefully hitting one single digit at a time with a breath between each. On the second try, it works. She carefully lifts out the key, unlocks the front door, steps inside and closes the door quickly. It's automatic, the instinct then to stand stock-still in the vacant house to be sure no one came up the front step behind her, jiggling the doorknob, knocking, saying her name. In the silence, the sound of her trembling breath is amplified. Her eyes adjust to the darkness, squinting through it to the walls and doorways around her. And the way it sometimes will, sadness seeps into her then, too. A sensation that just keeps coming.

Amy turns the deadbolt cylinder and leans her back and her sadness against the heavy wooden door, sinking to the floor, her hands coming to rest over her face.

George circles the blocks surrounding Riverdale Park. At each stop sign, he scans the side streets for any sign of her. Pools of lamplight and pockets of shadow come alive, tricking his eyes with suggestions of movement. His heart jumps when he spots someone, but it is only an elderly man walking his dog. And so the night turns into a game of decisions playing him a fool—which way, left or right, go back to the park, head home—until he slams his open palm on the steering wheel and stops at the curb. "Jesus, where are you?" Tears come to his eyes and he pulls his hand over his face, taking a long breath. "I'm sorry, Amy. Let me tell you I'm sorry." Little traffic passes at this late hour. He wonders if she is walking home, or used someone's cell phone to get help, or called a taxi from the grocery store. It's open all night and only a few blocks further. He heads there first.

"Did you notice a woman come in to use the store phone?" he asks a cashier, glancing to the courtesy counter where Amy might do just that. The light inside is garish and he walks closer to the young cashier. "Pretty, black dress?"

"No. Sorry," she shrugs.

George walks past her to the produce aisle, then hurries across the width of the store, stopping at the beginning of each aisle, grabbing large display racks to slow himself only briefly, swinging past before rushing to the next aisle looking for Amy. At the last aisle, he sprints down its length past yogurts and orange juice and frozen pizzas and walks back across the store via the rear aisle. Finally he pulls his cell phone from his jacket and gets the number for the local cab company.

"Have you dispatched a cab to Save-Rite?" he asks, walking past carrots and potatoes and raspberries toward the Exit. "Sometime in the past hour?" He drags a hand back through his hair while Dispatch checks the log. The passing moments infuriate him as they distance him further from Amy. Time is ticking, ticking. "No. You're sure?" he asks. So she hadn't phoned a cab.

She has to be home, somehow. George backs out of his parking space and drives to her farmhouse. It's her own fortress with the acre of land surrounded by ancient stone walls. If she'd gotten a ride from someone, she'd be there already. Maybe she called Celia and her friend knows now, the story poured out in these minutes.

Soft light shines through the living room windows. The truck barely stops before he jumps out and runs up the front porch steps. His fist bangs the door insistently until the porch light comes on. Ellen cautiously opens the door. "George." She pushes the door further, looking through the screen briefly past him. "What's happened to Amy?"

George lets out a relieved breath. Amy may be distraught, but at least she's home and now her mother is upset with him, too. "Can I see her please? Tell her it's only for a minute."

Ellen's brow knits and she steps back. "What's the matter with you? Are you drunk?" she asks. "And is that Amy's purse?"

George looks at the straw handbag he's been holding and sets it on the porch table beside a flowerpot of geraniums. "Drunk? No. No, I'm just relieved she's here. Please, I have to see her."

Ellen grips the door edge. "She's not here. Hasn't been for hours. Why? What's happened?"

He realizes at that moment, first, that Amy has *not* come home, and second, that Ellen must think she is dead. Here he is alone at her doorstep, his suit disheveled, his tie loosened, his hair a mess. Perspiration lines his brow and he is visibly shaken. "Ellen," he begins. "We had an argument. She hasn't been here at all?"

"What do you mean, *here*? She's supposed to be with you."

"I'm sure she's fine. We were at the bandshell, dancing. And there was a misunderstanding."

"A misunderstanding?" Ellen latches the screen door. "Well how would she get home without a car?" She looks past him to the street.

George leans closer. "Is there anywhere she might have gone that you know of? It's important that I find her."

Ellen frowns. "Well this is her home. She would come here." Her expression changes, then. It blames him now. "Just how bad was this argument?"

"Very bad," George admits, dragging a hand through his hair. "I'm worried about her, Ellen. You haven't heard from her? Not even a phone call?"

"Nothing." Her voice turns suspicious. "Should I call the police?"

"No," he insists, pulling his loosened tie from his collar. "Give her a little time."

"Well where could she be?" Her eyes follow the dark shadows lining the farm lane.

George shakes his head and exhales deeply. "I don't know. If she calls, if she needs help or a ride or anything, please have her call me." He pulls his keys from his pocket and starts down the steps.

"I don't think I like this, George," Ellen calls out from the other side of the screen door.

And her words stop him. "Well neither do I," he yells, spinning back toward her. He is tired of being blamed. If Amy had just stopped, if she'd just given him five lousy minutes, he could have eased some of this. He could have brought her safely home. "Do you hear me?" he asks before climbing the porch stairs two at a time. The rope has come to its end. He stands inches away from the screen and his voice is ragged. "We argued and she stormed off. I've looked everywhere for her." His fist, with the necktie hanging from it, punches the doorframe in frustration. "I've driven up and down every damn street in this town worried sick. I don't know where she went or what she's doing and I pray to God she's okay." He turns and sinks onto the top step, sitting and facing the distant stretch of cornfields. Everything seems worse in the night: pain and danger and heartbreak. It all looms closer. They say darkness is a nightmare's playground, and the woman he loves is in the throes of one. He drops his head into his hands and after a long moment, stands again. Ellen still waits silent at the door. "I'm sorry." His voice drops. "I'm really sorry. Please. Just let me know if you hear from her."

Ellen doesn't answer as he walks down the wooden steps and leaves. He takes a right out of the driveway and slowly drives the length of the country lane, past Amy's beloved cornfields and lone red barn, exhausting every avenue she might have taken. When he finally returns home, he picks up the cordless phone base with its empty, unblinking answering system and moves to throw it across the kitchen, wanting to smash it against Nate's newly-tiled wall. Against Nate, for doing this to his life. But he stops himself, just in case he'll hear her voice on it in the next few days. He sets it back down on the countertop with care, thinking of Amy trying to reach him, straightening the wires and checking the connections.

"Where did you go?" Not knowing will drive him either mad, or to drink. At least downing a drink will stop him from throwing answering machines or coffee mugs, stop him from calling Ellen again and again, stop him from driving through town slow enough to draw attention. Drunk is the only way to stay safe. He throws his suit jacket and tie on the sofa and moves to the dining room, looking out the sliding glass door onto the dark patio, remembering the other night when they lingered outside. Eventually he turns and faces the dining room chair on which Amy sat that evening.

If I lose you, George, if you stop loving me, or leave me, or die, I don't think I would be able to breathe.

He pours himself a glass of Scotch knowing damn well that he has more to worry about; her stalker could very well be right behind Amy, cutting in on their dance. This could be the moment some lunatic has been waiting for. He tosses down a mouthful of the liquor. Everything he worked to prevent has come to pass.

The cordless phone sits quiet. "Ring, damn it." He moves to his living room sofa, sets his glass and bottle of Scotch on the coffee table and drags both hands back through his hair. His hands itch to grab up the phone, his heart aches to hear Amy say his name. "Just fucking ring."

—

"I'm okay, Mom." Amy's voice is empty when she calls Ellen an hour later.

"Amy. I'm about ready to call the police. What is going on with you two?"

"Please believe that I'm safe. I'll get a ride home in the morning from Celia." Amy had groped her way through the dark house, feeling her way along walls, bumping light switches, skimming wallpaper to the kitchen in the back, not visible from the street. It is only here that she dared try a light switch and the pendant lights illuminated the room, the stainless steel appliances softly shining silver. No one would notice a light on here. No one would see her pass in front of the rear window or pace alongside the concrete countertops, stepping around a few cabinet doors left open. Life was suspended, like her own. She found a rag beneath the sink and wiped off her dirty feet, leaning against the sink to keep her balance as she did. A vintage corded phone still hung on the wall at the breakfast bar. She rushed to it and picked up the receiver, crying when she heard a dial tone.

But several minutes passed before she could dial anyone, minutes when her hand rested still on the phone. What did you do in this type of situation? Should she call Detective Hayes? Turn George in? Run?

"He wants you to call him, Amy."

"He was there?"

"Yes. And very upset. Call him, please."

"I can't. It's complicated, Mom."

"Do you want me to call him?"

"No." Amy shakes her head quickly. "And don't tell him I called if you hear from him. Please don't."

"But I don't like not knowing what happened." Her mother hesitates. "How do I really know you're safe, Amy?"

Amy closes her eyes. Exhaustion slows every move, every thought. Except the thought that her mother is referring to the stalking. "Listen Mom. If I'm not home by morning, then you call the police, okay? But I'm fine. Please believe me. I need time to think right now, that's all."

"Will you stay on the line with me then? So I know you're okay?"

"I can't." Amy leans against the wall. Her dress hangs limp, her shoes are scraped and ruined. "Mom," she half whispers, longing for someone to tell her what to do. Longing for George's arms around her, for his words insisting she is so wrong. Longing to wake up and have it be yesterday. To never live this day.

"You have to speak up, Amy. I can't hear you."

She pauses. "Mom. I need you to do something for me. Would you call Dad? Ask him to come and pick up you and Grace tomorrow? It's probably better for you to be away from here."

"*What?* What's going on, for God's sake? We're not leaving you by yourself. I'm calling the police."

"No! Please don't." Amy takes a long breath. Oh the fatigue, even that hurts. "Just trust me, and I'll explain when I can. For now, lock up tight and I'll call you very first thing. Early. Tell Grace I'll see her in the morning. Goodnight, Mom. I love you."

"Amy. Wait."

Amy hangs up the phone before her mother can continue. She walks to the kitchen sink and opens the faucet, letting cold water spit out. Her eyes close as it flows over her hands like a cool salve. Any relief, any ease, is fleeting. She leans her arms into the stream, wetting down her sweating skin before cupping her hands beneath it and burying her face in the liquid. She presses the water on her neck and chest before drying her face with the folds of her dress.

There's no stopping it then, no stopping how her mind returns to the thought of George in the bank parking lot. To see the breadth of *his* grip on her hand, and the ruby ring. Her one distressing memory lapse—oh how it bothered her all summer—it filled in with only a touch tonight. She moves to the living room and curls her legs beneath her on the sofa Celia brought in for staging. Sleep comes easily, because once you find an escape hatch, it's easy, so easy to slip in. It's the only way she can finally stop crying.

Twenty-Nine

MY GOD, WHAT HAPPENED?" CELIA asks. She takes Amy into her arms in the ranch's small foyer and holds her for a long moment before stepping back and looking closely at her. "How could such a perfect date go so wrong?"

Amy turns and glances out the front door. Rain threatens; the morning sky hangs low and gray. She closes the door behind them. "I really can't get into it now." Spending the night curled on the living room sofa left her body hurting today. "Things just aren't going to work with me and George."

"But Amy—"

"I'm fine. That's what matters. Thank you for picking me up here." She slips her feet into her scraped and dirty shoes. "I need to get home to Grace."

"But how did you ever end up *here*? I couldn't believe it when you called me, it's not like you to be breaking and entering."

If only Celia knew, she'd understand. Amy walks down the hall to the kitchen, pressing out the wrinkles in the front of her dress, aware of how bad this looks and aware, too, that Celia can't know yet who George really is.

"You were running from him, weren't you? He said he was taking you dancing." Celia rushes to catch up to her in the kitchen and grabs her arm. "Wait a minute. Just wait. Were you guys at the bandshell?"

Amy turns to her and nods.

"You walked all the way here from Riverdale Park?"

"I had to."

"Wow. What kind of bomb went off?" Celia asks, looking her up and down. "Are you hurt?"

"No, I'm not." She looks out the kitchen window and pictures the small yard as her own. "Is this house still on the market?"

"Amy." There is a silence then, one saying *Let's take care of you first*, one telling Amy her friend is so worried that her next words come quietly. "I can take you to the hospital, you know, if you need to see a doctor."

Amy presses the fabric of her dress against her leg. "He didn't hurt me that way." She turns to Celia. "Please, I really have to get home."

"Well have you even glanced in a mirror? You can't face Grace and your mother looking like that. Let's get some makeup on you. Where's your purse?"

"I don't have it."

"No purse?" Celia looks at her, puzzled. "How'd you call me, if you don't have your cell?"

When Amy hitches her head toward the wall phone, Celia picks it up, listening for a dial tone. She hangs it up slowly as though the seriousness of the last evening is finally hitting her. "Come on, hon, let's fix you up." They go into the bathroom where Celia digs in her handbag and pulls out a lipstick. "Here, put this on."

Amy leans close to the mirror, her hand shaking as she touches the creamy color to her lips. Her other hand steadies her balance on the vanity top.

"Let me." Celia takes the lipstick from her. She pulls a piece of toilet paper from the roll, wipes off the smear Amy applied and starts over. "Open a little," she says, tracing a line over her lips. "Okay." Then she pinches Amy's cheeks. "That's better."

In her reflection, Amy sees her pale pink lips and remembers George kissing her when they danced close last night. Her eyes tear again.

"Jesus, how bad was it?" Celia asks.

"We had a terrible falling out," Amy answers. "He's just not the person I thought he was."

"George isn't? Are we talking about the same wonderful guy?"

Amy nods. "I really have to get home, Celia."

"Well. Okay." Again she rummages through her bag and hands Amy a small hairbrush. "Fix your hair first."

Celia's reflection watches her every move as she runs the brush through her blonde hair and presses a strand behind her ear. "What am I going to do, Cee?" she whispers.

"I've never seen you like this, Amy. Are you sure you're okay?"

Amy nods slightly.

"George must have said or done something awful. What is it? You can trust me, you know that, right?"

Though Celia moves right beside her, searching her face, Amy talks to her reflection. "I can't see him again, that's all I can say right now."

"Maybe you can. You'll patch things up. You'll have something good to eat, get some sleep and feel better in a day or two. Come on." Celia takes the brush. "First let's get you out of here before someone shows up." She checks the kitchen, closes the open cabinets, then leads Amy through the empty house and returns the key to the lock box. They walk down the flagstone path to her sedan. "Can I buy you a coffee at least?" Celia asks while unlocking the doors.

Amy gets in and looks out the car window. The tree branches bow heavy under humidity. This ranch house might be nice for her and Grace. It's small and contained and manageable. Safe. "No thanks. Grace is waiting for me."

"But maybe it'll help to talk about things." Celia drives through town, slowing in front of their favorite coffee shop, Whole Latte Life. "You're sure? I can stop here for a quick cup."

"I'm sure." Because Amy knows damn well she can't keep coffee or much of anything else down this morning. Her body threatens to rebel against the very idea of George's identity. She sits up straight and pulls the silky wrap around her arms. Getting Grace to safety is all that matters.

"Did you sleep at all in that house?" Celia asks, glancing up from the road.

"A little. I'll rest better at home."

"How about some company? I can spend the night with you and Grace. We'll watch a movie, talk about things."

"That's okay. We'll be fine." By this evening, she plans on Grace being far from here, tucked into bed in her parents' home up north, away from kidnappings and therapists and guns and George. Her father should be arriving from New Hampshire soon.

"Do you want me to come in?" Celia asks when she pulls into Amy's driveway.

"No." Amy drops down the visor and checks her face in the mirror. "Thank you, Celia. For everything. But I have to talk to my mom. I'll be okay now."

"Well you let me know if you need anything." She leans over and gives Amy a hug. "Take care of yourself. And talk to George, you hear me?"

Amy steps out of the car as the gray sky begins to mist. Home, home, home, never has it taken so long to get home. She holds the shawl aloft over her head and hurries toward her front porch.

———

Every time the bell at the door rings, George sets down the carving knife, stops laying out a platter of chicken cutlets or filling a tray of ground beef, his fingers hovering over the fresh meat, stills, and listens for Amy's voice.

"Is George here by any chance?" Celia asks Dean. She pulls her umbrella shut and sets it dripping near the door.

George hears it all and steps closer.

"He's in the back. Can I help you with something?"

"I really need to talk to George. Could you tell him that Celia's here? I'm a friend."

Every sound, every syllable, is heard. Every step, every gesture pictured in his mind.

"Why don't you have a seat?" Dean motions to the tables in the corner.

George hears Celia's footsteps, hears her chair scrape. It's why Sinatra isn't singing, it's why the radio talk station is off, the voices that usually bring him updates on crime leads and heist statistics and an expanding manhunt silenced. He walks out from behind the counter wearing his black apron, black pants, white shirt, but feeling like a different man. Furious worry keeping him up all night exhausted him.

"You look like something the cat dragged in," Celia says when he takes a seat.

"That's what I feel like." George hesitates, pressing his open hand to the back of his neck. "How is she, Celia?" he finally asks. "Have you seen her?"

"I have. What the hell happened yesterday?"

George turns to Dean. "Hey guy, how about some coffee over here?"

"Right away," Dean says, disappearing into the back.

"She's okay?" George asks Celia.

"That's subjective."

"Subjective." He looks down at his hands. "Which means she's not."

"No. It means I'm not sure how she is. Amy's not saying much."

Dean sets two steaming cups of coffee before them when the bell above the door rings. George glances over at two customers walking in before sipping his coffee. "How'd she look then?"

"Shell-shocked, to say the least. Which is why I'm here." She stirs cream into her cup. "Maybe it's none of my business, but Amy's my best friend. She's been through so much and I'm worried about her."

"What did she tell you?"

"You were at the bandshell, something happened, an argument or disagreement or something, and she walked out."

George looks into the coffee in front of him. "That about sums it up," he says, raising his eyes to hers. "No details?"

"Not really."

"Do you know where she spent the night?"

"Yes I do. In an empty house I recently staged. One I wanted her to buy, actually." Celia lifts her cup and takes a sip. "She let herself in with my lock box code."

He leans back and looks away, trying to compose himself.

"What the hell was she hiding from, George?"

"She's got nothing to hide from. Could you tell her that for me?"

"Me? You've got to tell her yourself. You've got to talk to her. Can't you go and see her?"

"She's home?"

Celia squints at him. "Yes. Yes, okay? I just brought her there. What's the big secret? She's there, you're here and you should be together. Go see her, George."

"Believe me, it's not good right now."

"You won't tell me what happened, will you?"

"I'm sorry, Celia." He shakes his head.

Celia slides her coffee away. "Well I can't believe that you would intentionally hurt her. I really can't."

"It wasn't intentional."

"But it was bad." She watches him carefully.

"Just tell her I'm here all day. Whenever she wants to talk, I'm here."

The good thing about having people around is that they are a distraction. When she folded Grace's clothes into the suitcase, she knew it was only a matter of minutes before the house would be empty. Before she would turn on the steaming shower to wash the remnants of yesterday down the drain. But she can't yet. She has to stay calm and get Grace out of this house, out of this town, away from the madness.

"Where the hell is that cat?" Amy says under her breath. The suitcases are in the driveway, Grace is strapped into her parents' car and her mother just walked out carrying a cooler of sandwiches and juice boxes for the road. Amy moves the cat carrier onto a kitchen chair; Angel's dish and food are packed inside a brown bag. She leans out the screen door. "Did you look upstairs for her, Mom?"

"Yes I did," Ellen calls back. "I haven't seen her all day."

"All day?" Dr. Brina always told her not to separate Grace from the kitten, so Amy checks Angel's favorite sleeping places: the end of her bed, the bath mat, on Grace's windowsill. Outside below, she sees her father loading the trunk.

"This time you're coming with us," he said earlier when they had coffee together. "You should have moved back home after Mark died. None of this would have happened then. Did George hurt you? Are you in trouble?"

"No and no." She tried to reassure her father on the front porch. "There's just been a misunderstanding, and it's serious. I told Mom I'll fill you in as soon as I can. But in the meantime, it's easier if Grace stays with you while I straighten things out here. Because on top of all this, I'm crazy busy with my bridal fashion show next week." She takes a deep breath and hugs her father. "After the show, I'll close the shop for a few days, stop the mail and head up to stay awhile."

But she figures he knew it was more than she let on; it was about George. She looks out at her father from the window. He aged over the past few years. How many nights' sleep did he lose worrying about her? Deep wrinkles cut into his cheeks and feather from his eyes. And now this.

"Kitty, kitty," she calls softly, turning away and lifting Grace's bedspread. A little black and white paw shoots out at her bare foot, making her jump, the folds of her limp dress brushing her legs. She gets down on her knees and pulls Angel out. Any other day, the kitten hunt would have made her laugh, but not today.

"I'll be up soon, when this is through," she says to her mother when she brings the cat carrier out to the driveway.

"When *what* is through?" Her mother stands outside the car, watching her. "With the stalking going on, I'm afraid for you."

"Mom, don't worry. What happened with George isn't about the stalking, I told you that already. What I really need to do is set up Wedding Wishes for the fashion show next week, so let me take care of that first and I'll be up tomorrow night, okay? To stay a couple days."

"And then what? Come back for the bridal show? Amy, it's too much. I don't want you running back and forth on the highway with all that's on your mind. You'll be so distracted you'll get in an accident."

"Mom. Come on, I'll be fine. And I need to be with Grace."

"No, I'm serious. Grace is perfectly safe with us. She'll be out in the yard, playing in the garden and getting plenty of fresh air and good food. I won't let her out of my sight. You just take care of things here, and we'll see you later next week. It's better this way." She reaches over and touches Amy's cheek. "Maybe you can fix things with George, too," she adds softly.

Amy's eyes tear up. "Okay," she whispers. "We'll see." She gives her mother a quick hug, then opens the rear door and leans in to her daughter. "You give Mommy a hug too," she says. "And be a good girl for Grandma and Grandpa, now. I'll see you soon, okay honey?"

"Where's Angel?" Grace asks, her eyes wide with worry.

Amy touches the tip of her beautiful daughter's nose, still relishing that innocent voice. "Right here, looking for you!" She sets the carrier on the seat beside Grace.

Grace reaches her arms up to Amy. "Want to stay home." She starts to twist in her car seat.

"Shhh." Amy leans in and hugs her again. "When I come to Grandma's, we'll look in the pretty gazing ball, okay? And you'll show me how big the sunflowers grew. Remember when we put the seeds in the dirt?"

Grace pouts around a thumb in her mouth and nods solemnly.

"Love you." Amy straightens and closes the car door. Her father starts the engine and she waves to Grace in the back seat. "Bye, sweetie." Grace waggles her fingers while sucking her thumb. "Bye Mom, Dad. I'll call you."

Her mother squeezes her hand through the open window. "Every day."

The car backs away carrying her daughter to safety in the New Hampshire hills. She follows it to the end of the driveway, walking slowly and keeping it in her sights as long as possible in order to delay what comes next.

She knows it is just a matter of time before it happens, before George seeks her out.

———

It begins again in the shower. Deep within her arms, there's a tremor. At the same time, her vision narrows, darkening at the edges until there is only tunnel vision. Her eyes glance about, orienting herself in the bathroom. She has enough wits about her to get herself out of the shower and into her robe. It started last night, this tingling, the worry, but sheer will kept it at bay until she was home and her daughter safe. Now, no amount of pacing and thinking and splashes of cold water can deflect it.

Amy sits on the edge of her bed and tightens the sash of her robe as the full-blown anxiety attack comes now. Dr. Berg warned her that this is the worst of PTSD symptoms. Anxiety. This time, she gives her body over to it completely. Sound and vision grow distorted. The morning clouds open, releasing a gentle shower of rain outside her window; birdsong fades in and out as her ears ring. She reaches one hand quickly to her nightstand, drops her head and closes her eyes. If she even loosens her grip, the room spins. Perspiration trickles down her face, along her neck, and the sound of her breathing blazes in her head. She talks herself through it, whispering over and over that she is okay. She is on her bed, Grace is safe, the symptoms can't hurt her. When they subside, when she lifts her head and the room is stable, her body gives in to the exhaustion. And again, sleep comes quickly, deeply, stifling the thought that it wasn't danger that brought on the panic. It was heartbreak.

———

George lifts a towel soaking in a bucket of sterilizing solution and wipes down the tabletops and stainless steel sink used for meat washing. He usually likes this late hour when the outside door is locked, the display room lights dimmed and Sinatra plays uninter-rupted. Every surface in the workroom needs a thorough sanitiz-ing at the end of each day.

He sent Dean home early this afternoon, at three, shut off the shop lights and listened only for the phone to ring. Because there is nothing to do but stay where Amy would expect him to be all day. He waits to hear her voice on the shop telephone, or his cell phone. To see her standing at the door, looking in. He doesn't dare alter his routine lest she not find him and turn to leave. He also knows damn well that it might be Detective Hayes knocking at the door, holding a warrant for his arrest if Amy decides to turn him in.

Now he pulls the cutting boards from the hot water and bleach solution, rinses them and leaves them to dry. Going through the motions keeps his hands busy, restraining him from pouring a drink or throwing something or calling her. All parts of the meat grinders, including the auger housing, have been disassembled, cleaned and sanitized. George picks up the wrench and methodically, silently, reassembles the auger housing to the grinders, working his way through the neat row of nuts and bolts he lined on the countertop.

He does the same with the slicing machines, then wipes off the refrigerator shelving until all possibility of cross-contamination is eliminated. Finally there is nothing left. Nothing to do but stand there. He checks his watch again, hangs clean towels in the workroom for the next day, shuts off the lights and heads home. If there is no word from Amy on his answering machine, if she hasn't left questions, words, breaths and pauses there rather than interrupt him at work, then he will go to her.

Thirty

Wᴇʜᴇɴ ᴀᴍʏ ᴡᴀᴋᴇs ᴜᴘ, sʜᴇ knows exactly what is going to happen as though she has clearly done this before. It isn't a flashback. This is simply a knowledge of what is to come because it happened already, over and over, in her mind. She showers again, dresses in faded jeans and a black tunic, straightens up the kitchen and stands at the window over the sink. The cornfield at the farm down the street is the gauge by which she judges summer's passing. Early on, she could never see the tiny plants. Now they grow tall and green beside the red barn, heavy with corn inside the curling leaves. The plants stretch to the steady rain falling from the low, gray sky. This is the time of summer when she might spot deer as she walks along the street; the corn lures them close to human life. Her own life feels emptied.

She knew he'd come. Looking out at the greens of the cornfield as vast as the sea, she steels herself upon hearing his truck door close. His footsteps sound muffled through the paned farm door, gritty on the wet stone walkway on the side of the house, leading around back to the kitchen. A surprising wave of sadness passes over her as she misses the jangling keys that often accompanied his step. He knocks on the wooden frame of the kitchen screen door and she hears him shift his position beneath the overhang to escape the rain.

Standing in the dark kitchen, she doesn't put on a light, doesn't move. She only waits at the sink, blinking back tears, unsure of what to do.

———

George stands at the back door. He knows she's home; her SUV is parked in the driveway and a lamp shines in the front window. The wait, all day, has grown interminable. When she doesn't answer his knock, his fist hammers the doorframe. "Open the door, Amy," he calls out. "Please open the door." Rainwater cascades off the overhang in sheets. He knows she's inside, listening. "Oh God, Amy. Don't do this." He takes a step into the rain, then turns back. His fist pounds twice on the door before dropping to his side. "Amy. Amy, I made a mistake," he yells, brushing rainwater off his hair. "Let me talk to you," he insists, rattling the locked screen door against its frame.

The paned wood door behind it finally opens. She stands on the other side.

"Amy." He looks through the screen at her, alarmed at the grief he sees. "Amy, we can't leave things like this."

"You want to talk now? Where were you the past two months?" she demands.

"I *wanted* to talk. There were so many times I wanted to tell you." He moves closer to the screen, his hand on the doorknob while the wind blows the rain straight at him.

Amy slips back into shadow. No lights shine in her kitchen. "Get out," she says.

George tries the latched door again, then raises his eyes to hers, squinting into the dark room. Rain drips off his hair onto his forehead. "God damn it. I couldn't tell you."

She watches him. "But you could take my daughter?" A cool mist of rain blows through the screen and she backs further away. "You played me really well, didn't you? I never even suspected you were one of them. How could you? Jesus, how could you do it?"

He tries opening the screen door again. "Just let me in, Amy. Let me explain."

"Explain what? How you planned it all?" She hugs herself, stepping further back into the kitchen, away from him. "Don't you get it? I don't want to see you."

"But you're wrong," he insists. "You're confused by what you saw that morning. I wasn't one of them. I *helped* Grace, damn it. I kept her safe."

"You had the chance to help us in the parking lot." She takes a long breath. "You had a gun," she contends, pausing between each word, the hiss of rain sounding too. "You could have stopped it." They watch each other, patient until she edges closer and begins to shut the inside door.

"Amy," he says, his fist hitting the screen doorframe desperately, a side wind blowing the rain at his face. "Don't." In her moment's hesitation, he speaks quickly. "They had three guns. Don't you understand?"

"No." She shakes her head.

He pulls his hand over his wet face. "They had Grace."

Like he knew they would, his words inflame her. "And *helped* them. Get out of here before I turn you in." He doesn't move. "Leave, George," she cries.

"I had the money," George answers, his voice controlled. "That's all I had."

"What?"

"A million dollars. That was my weapon. Not the gun." He raises his voice over the steady downpour. "The others knew that if they hurt Grace, I'd use that money to pay to have the same done to them."

"You're lying. You took Grace from me. I can't deal with you anymore."

"Then turn me in," he yells, "because I am not leaving here." When the kitchen phone rings, they both stop. "Answer it," he says on the third ring. "Answer it and tell them to call the police." When she moves toward the phone, he wrenches the locked screen door open, rushes in and grabs her arm. His hair lays wet and flat, rainwater drips from his face and hands, his clothes are soaked. Nothing could have prepared them for this moment as he pulls her to him and locks her in his arms. Her face presses against his chest and he feels her struggle to escape, to breathe. If this is how it has to be done, how an absolution is reached, he hates it. His grip gets tighter when he hears her cries.

"You bastard," she sobs, trying to punch his chest. "You God damn bastard." He quells her energy, taking the blows and holding her against him until all she can do is weep.

———

George's body folds around hers, his hand embracing her head against him. When she raises her arms to strike him, he overpowers her efforts and tightens his embrace. Their bodies stand close. He bows his head to hers, his mouth near her ear as he whispers, "Don't leave me, Amy." She feels him breathing, his chest rising. "It's not what you're thinking. It's *not*, I swear to you."

"No, George." She struggles to twist out of his hold. "No. No!" She pushes back with a terrifying thought. How easy it would be to raise her face to his, to let him kiss away her tears, to let love wash over the pain. But reality stops her with the picture of him armed with a weapon while Grace was carried away.

The telephone rings again and she manages to pull out of his arms. "Hello?" She has to press the mouthpiece against her head to stop her hand from shaking. Her legs threaten to give out, forcing her to turn and lean against the wall for support. She watches George while she listens, watches him cuff his wet shirt sleeves. "Yes, Celia." She sucks in a breath. "He's here."

George walks to the blue kitchen farm table and pulls out a chair, sitting with his elbows on his knees, watching her too. The dark, overcast sky keeps the kitchen in shadow; the rain whispers down.

"No. No, I'm fine, really." Her eyes follow his every move. A red plaid dishtowel hangs on the back of the chair beside him. He pulls it off and drags it over his face, blotting rainwater from his skin, then leaves it crumpled on the table beside the white vase holding his solitary pink rose before looking steady at her again.

Finally she turns away from George's gaze, tipping her head into the call and speaking softly. "Thank you, Celia. Yes. I'll call you later." Once Celia hangs up, Amy holds the silent phone to her ear for several seconds, collecting herself in slow breaths behind closed eyes. There is so much she wants answered. But the air refuses to take shape in her mouth, her lips refuse to form the words. She muffles a sob with the realization that this is precisely what happened to Grace. She couldn't say anything.

George picks up the dishtowel and wipes off his face again, pressing it at his wet hairline and along the side of his face before drying his neck. The air in the room is close and when he speaks without inflection, Amy raises her eyes to his. "I'm not sorry for what I did," he says. "It was the only way to help. My regret is that I couldn't stop that crime. But I can tell you I never knew about it until that day. That I got in a car that morning thinking I was going to the casino with my brother."

"Nate?" Amy stares at him for a quiet second. "I put Grace right back into both your hands?"

The distant cornfield is visible through the kitchen window, the plants tall, leaves cascading. A painted barn star hangs on the wall beside the blue and white checked curtains. George goes to the sink and looks out. "My brother tried to force me into it. But I walked away. I told him he was crazy. You didn't see that part. You didn't see me turn my back and leave the gun and everything behind in his car. I had nothing to do with it until I saw you. You and Grace walking toward the bank." He turns to face her. "Those men were ruthless, Amy. *I* wasn't going to stop them. So I made a choice."

"Well aren't you lucky." Amy paces back and forth barefoot across the kitchen's wide-plank wood floor. "You had a choice. Tell me something. What was my choice begging on my knees on that filthy pavement? Do you remember, George? I had *no* choices. Nothing." She jabs her finger at the air, pointing harshly at him. "*You* took that away from me. You."

"No. No, don't you see? I'd left. But when I saw you and Grace go into the bank, I just knew. Something was going down and I had to keep that child safe. If I kept walking away and called the police, things could have escalated and she might have been seriously hurt. I had one second to decide. One second. To call the police, or to help. Do you think either of those choices were bearable?" He waits, watching her pace past the painted hutch with lace-trimmed shelves, the potato bin with the red ceramic rooster on top of it. "Do you know who made it bearable?"

Amy circles around the farm table then, her hand lighting on each chair top. Her voice comes in a whisper. "Don't say it, George."

George moves toward her. Outside the rain starts to thunder down. "Grace did."

She turns and runs at him, raising an arm to strike, but he catches it in his grip, twisting her around and rendering her immobile. From behind, his arms lock over hers and they nearly fall over.

"Listen to me!" he whispers fiercely, scraping a chair aside with his foot and sitting her in it. "Just listen," he insists, crouching in front of her. "I had to do something to let myself live with that day. If I didn't help, I couldn't get up in the morning and go on. And the only thing I *could* do was keep your daughter safe. If I interfered with that heist, she'd be at even more risk. I understood that she was their hostage and I had to make them think I was *in*." He stands, then sits across from her at the table, moving a white coffee cup aside and leaning close. "I didn't want the money. I wanted to walk away from the whole morning. But I saw your face, Amy. I saw your pain. And then I looked at Grace sitting in the back of that truck."

"Damn you," she says, crying, her hands limp in her lap. "Damn you to hell."

"Amy. I saw what you didn't. I saw Grace's fear, I saw her eyes squeezed shut, I saw one of the men nearly accost her." When she starts to stand, he stands quicker and she sinks back down into the chair. George looks away, then right at her again. He doesn't know how to get through her pain. It might not be possible. All the while, the kitchen grows darker with the rainstorm surging outside.

"I continued to participate in the crime *just to keep her safe.* You've got to believe me."

"And why would I believe you?" She looks up at him standing close. "How do I know you didn't plan the whole thing?"

"I don't know what to say to convince you, Amy. I guess *this* is your choice, now. To believe me or not. To believe that once they secured that truck and I was in on it, I told them that if Grace wasn't given back to you right away, if she was harmed in any way, my money would hunt them down. I'd pay someone to do it."

"And then what? You became our bodyguard?"

"No. No, I never thought I'd see you again. I just wanted to get Grace safely home to you that day. And I *did.*" He sits in the chair beside her. "I did. But *you* came into my shop the next week, wanting to thank me. Jesus, Amy, I saw your state of mind. How could I turn my back on you? So I agreed to dinner. And then," he leans closer, his elbows on his knees, looking up at her face. "I fell in love with you."

"You're lying."

"What?"

"How many times did you see me cry? Or flashback? You saw Grace withdraw, you saw what I put her through to help her and you still didn't tell me?" She stands quickly, toppling her chair. "That's love? You lied to me the whole time. You looked straight at me and lied. You could be lying right now."

George shakes his head as she speaks. "No, I didn't lie. I just couldn't tell you the story. I wanted to. And I swear I planned to this summer, when you were stronger." He stands and takes her hand in his, but she yanks it away. "I wanted to marry you, Amy," he says. "But I thought you had to know me, know everything, if you'd ever agree to it."

Amy walks to the counter, her arms wrapped around herself. "Beautiful," she says through her tears, looking to the ceiling, then back to him. "A marriage proposal now."

"No. I just thought, oh God, how can I tell you what I thought?" He watches her pacing near the counter. "Everything's changed now. Everything fell apart."

"I let you hold me. I let you *touch* me." Her hand covers her mouth. "And all the while, it was you. Why didn't you just go to the authorities, George? Why didn't you *do* something?" After a second, she whispers, "Why didn't you just leave me alone?"

His eyes gauge her, judging how much more she can take. "I don't know where the others are, okay? Now listen. Before they disappeared, when they gave me Grace in the parking lot, one of them threatened you. So if I went to Hayes to report what I knew, and what I did, your life was on the line. I'm damned if I do, damned if I don't."

"*My* life?"

"What do you think the stalking is about? It's them, Amy. They don't want you near me. The stalking is a tactic to get you away from me. To get you to leave Addison for good. They're afraid *this* would happen, that you would find out who I am and turn me in."

Amy pulls open the kitchen drawer where she keeps a sketch pad and pencils and Grace's crayons. She lifts out a gun. "I'm not afraid anymore."

"Jesus, Amy." George approaches cautiously, his hand open, wanting the weapon. She backs away, still crying. She has never stopped crying, not since he broke through her screen door. He steps closer. "Just let me stay with you then. Believe *me*, Amy, and you won't need that. We'll go to Hayes together. We'll tell him everything. Whatever happens, we can get through it."

"That's enough." She waves the gun as though she might be able to bring him into her aim. "I want you and your crime and your stalking and your money *out of here*." Her hand wavers and she sets the gun back in the drawer, then blocks the drawer with her body as she leans against it, nearly knocking over a floral pitcher filled with serving utensils.

George looks around, frantic to get through to her. She won't listen. Why had he thought she would? He is the bullet that hit her daughter, her self, her life. In his panic, he sees her suitcases in the hallway. "Where are you going?" he asks abruptly.

"What I do doesn't concern you."

He motions to the luggage. "You can't leave without knowing everything. You're just confused and you don't need to leave your home. Listen to me."

"George." Amy doesn't move from the drawer. Their voices quiet, their breathing slows, but the rain still falls. "I know enough. I know that it was you in the parking lot. That you followed that bastard holding my daughter onto the truck. That you didn't turn your gun on him instead of me. Grace is safe with my parents. And as soon as I take care of a few things, I'm leaving to be with her."

"Before you go ..." He takes a quick breath, looks away and returns his gaze to her. It becomes a physical struggle to think straight and keep her in his life. "Come away with me."

"What are you talking about?"

"Away from here. Where there are no reminders." He takes a step closer. "We'll go to the cottage at the beach. Just for a couple days." He walks to her and takes her hands again in his. "We need to get away from here. At the sea, Amy. We'll fix this at the sea. I don't want to lose what we have, not for the wrong reasons."

"What we *had*, George." She doesn't try to stop her tears. "It's over. You deceived me all summer. It'll never work."

"No, it's not like that. I'll go to Hayes. Anything, Amy. I'll do anything. Let's just go to the cottage with nobody around. We'll walk on the beach, in that sweet salt air. We'll sit on the porch, we'll feed the swans in the lagoon." His eyes lock onto hers as his hands pull her close. "Let me tell you everything there, at Stony Point, in good time."

"I'll never understand."

He fights his own burning tears. "You will. You just need time."

She shakes her head. "I want you to leave now. Leave us alone." She steps back in her jeans and tunic, as casual and beautiful as can be, and ruined. "It's over," she says quietly.

George moves closer and takes her face in his hands. "Don't cry, sweetheart. Come with me, for only a day then. One day, at that little cottage. I did everything that day for your Grace. Just for Grace. For nothing else. You have to know me, to believe me." They just look at each other as she shakes her head, no.

This is the end. One day has beaten them down. If these have to be his last words, he'll make them tender. He won't leave her any other way. "I'm so sorry that I hurt you, Amy, but I'll never stop loving you."

"*Stop it*. Please." She backs up a step, her eyes never leaving his. "You have to go now. Get out, George."

He drops his hands and turns then, pushing open the screen door and pressing it closed behind him. The rain hasn't let up.

Thirty-One

EVERYTHING IS BITTER WITH THE new day, tinged somehow: his coffee, the sunrise, a long shower. It all sours. On the dining room table, an old newspaper lays folded open to the movie page, the weekend listings circled in blue ink. George brushes it aside rather than drop it in the trash. Nothing is worth the effort; it is all he can do to go through the motions. He stops mid-task, leaving a cup of coffee unfinished, the bed unmade, his face unshaven. By six-thirty, he leaves his condominium and rattles around The Main Course. Still, nothing helps, not putting on another pot of coffee, not turning on the stereo, not straightening a pile of paperwork on his desk, not turning off the stereo, and finally not walking to the work area to set out the knives and prepare equipment for the morning's orders.

The first thing he notices there is the red light shining on one of the meat grinders, a unit he meticulously cleaned and shut off the day before. "Dean?" he calls out, leaning into the main showroom. But Dean's not there; no lights are on. For the two steps closer he takes, the view meeting his eyes sets him back one. He pulls an old knife from a drawer and lifts a large piece of lace from the grinder. It hangs tattered on the blade.

"What the hell?" he says. There is no mistaking that the fabric is a veil, or part of a wedding gown. Whatever it is, a cloud of it fills the feed pan and the rest had been pushed through the grinder, leaving pieces of the white fabric hopelessly shredded and tangled in the auger and cutting blade while other pieces of the antique lace are partially intact, the intricate pattern untouched and beautiful. "Jesus Christ," he whispers. Hitting the reverse switch to try to unjam the lace only further knots it and locks up the unit.

Using the same knife, he lifts thin, opaque shreds of the tattered white lace hanging from the feed assembly and falling to the table at its base, knowing damn well it came from Amy's shop. "Mother fuckers," he says before grabbing his car keys and closing up The Main Course behind him.

—

Nate never changed the lock on the back door of the old Cape Cod where he and George grew up. He told George it's his home too, always, no matter what. So George uses his key, rushes through the kitchen and takes the stairs two at a time to his brother's bedroom. The room is thick with drawn blinds and a tangle of clothes and sheets. He hauls his sleeping brother up by the arms and shoves him back into the headboard.

"Where are they?" he demands. "Where the fuck are they? I'll kill them, Nate."

"George. Whoa." Nate pushes himself up into a sitting position. "Calm down, guy."

"Reid. Elliott. You're going to tell me. Where are they?"

Nate glances at George's hands holding him against the headboard. "Back off," he warns and George releases his grip. His brother gets out of bed and steps into a pair of jeans, clearly irritated with being pulled from sleep. He looks over at George. "I'm going to wash up. Give me a minute, would you? I'll meet you downstairs."

George walks around the kitchen table over and over, glancing toward the stairs time and again. Nate finally comes down and fills the coffee decanter with water. "Now start from the beginning," he says over his shoulder. He had pulled on a clean T-shirt and ran a wet comb through his hair. "What happened? Is it Amy again?"

"I don't have time for God damn coffee, Nate."

"What the hell's gotten into you?" His brother sets the decanter on the counter.

"They got into her shop."

"Who? What shop? What are you talking about?"

"Wedding Wishes. Amy's bridal shop. They broke in and stole one of her antique gowns, or veils, I can't tell which."

"How do you know?" He pours the water into the coffee-maker and it starts to gurgle.

"I *found* it." George pushes past his brother, yanks the coffee plug and turns to him. "I found it in shreds in the God damn grinder."

Nate backs up a step. "What? In your meat grinder? Are you sure?"

"Yeah I'm sure. Where are they? I've had enough already."

"Wait a minute." Nate turns around and plugs the coffeepot back in. "What the hell do they want with a lousy veil?"

"Oh I don't know, Nate. Maybe the fact that I wanted to marry her has something to do with it?"

"What? Marry her?"

"Listen, the point is that this time, they're fucking with *my* head."

"What about Amy? She must be upset."

"You don't know the half of it." George thinks of Amy and everything he lost with her and with that anger he shoves Nate up against the wall. "Now," he orders. "Because I can't take this anymore. You tell me where they are. Right now."

"All right, all right," Nate answers, brushing off his grip. "All I have is a number. They go back and forth between Vegas and Atlantic City. I'll give you the number, but you'll just get his voice-mail. Reid never answers."

"Reid?"

"Yeah, it's Reid's phone."

Nate shuffles through a drawer filled with take-out menus and old receipts. He flips open a black address book and scribbles down a number on a scrap of paper. Every minute matters now. As soon as he sets the pencil down, George grabs the paper, turns and walks out of the house.

"Hey!" Nate calls after him. "Hey, be careful, would you?"

George keeps walking. He doesn't see if Nate watches from the door. He doesn't see the sun shining on the dewy lawns, the flowers opening to the light. It's all he can do to wait behind the flashing railroad crossing for the train to pass, car after car after car. Stop signs are barely visible on the drive back to The Main Course where he folds Reid's number into his shirt pocket. He isn't thinking straight enough to call yet, not with the thought of one of Amy's cherished bridal pieces ruined. It's difficult pulling the tangled fabric from the grinder, difficult watching a plastic garbage bag fill with the remnants. Some of the lace is still intact; detailed stitches shape a vine pattern with small hearts blended in the leaves. "Okay, you win already. Leave her alone."

He turns to go into his office and sees one of Nate's denim work shirts draped over a chair near the refrigerator. Its long sleeves hang close to the floor. George throws it over his arm to bring into his office when something falls out of the pocket.

A placard, folded in half, is on the floor near the chair. It opens to a brief description of the lace veil Amy's grandmother had made. The lace told a love story in the vines and hearts entwined together. Her grandmother's photo appears beneath the text, the aged image an old wedding portrait of her wearing that very same veil, her blonde hair pulled back in a twist, her face looking so much like Amy. And his heart drops with the awareness of exactly which deeply sentimental piece someone has cruelly targeted.

He looks down at the denim shirt folded over his other arm, then at the placard again.

"No."

It can't be. His eyes glance around the room, searching for some explanation. For some evidence exonerating his brother from the realization sinking in.

He looks again at the shirt, holds it at arm's length and slips the folded placard in and out of the pocket. And his mind denies the image of Nate lifting a veil off a mannequin in the dark of night. No, because what his mind sees is Nate pedaling furiously after him on hot summer days, their baseball cards rat-a-tat-tatting against the spokes as they fly through the neighborhood. And there's Nate crouched on the rocks at Stony Point, a sand pail at his feet as he's bent over watching his crabbing line next to George, settling it into the seaweed and stones in the shallow water, the sun hot on their backs. And Nate, yes, there's another image, Nate sitting beside him in the driver's seat at fourteen, when George took their parents' car out on the winding country back roads and let him take the wheel. Nate in Christmas photos, always grinning with George, the decorated tree strung with gold beads beside them, frost on the windowpanes. Nate jumping onto the toboggan behind George, his mittened hands holding on tight, his head tipped back in laughter, powdered snow rising in a cloud around them.

Nate. His tag-along brother.

"No," George says as he goes to the grinder and yanks off a length of lace hanging from it. He gave his brother a key to The Main Course a year ago, a spare in case of emergency so he can let himself in whenever. Nate's watched him cleave and carve, debone and grind, the same way he used to watch him pitch and bat, skateboard and swim out to the raft. Brothers, man, through and through. Nate can probably run the shop himself, in a pinch, and certainly knows the basics of a meat grinder.

George finishes cleaning that grinder, putting unending tatters and shreds of lace into the bag he'll toss in the dumpster. Each delicate piece holds a piece of Amy's life in it, too. Then he drops the cover on the grinder and leaves a note for Dean telling him it is out of commission.

With the placard carefully set back in the pocket, George hangs the denim shirt on the chair where he found it. Because still there's a part of him denying it. Still seeking to clear his brother from this.

There's only one way to know. He leaves his shop and drives to Nate's house again. If he can just feel him out without letting on about the shirt and his suspicions. Maybe it's all a misunderstanding. Maybe someone's setting up Nate. That's got to be it. Someone's framing his brother.

It doesn't take long to pull his pickup truck into Nate's driveway, get out and ring the doorbell this time. When there's no answer, he walks over to the garage window. The Harley is parked in one bay, but the car is gone. So he goes around to the back of the house and lets himself in again, unsure of exactly what he is looking for. His eyes scan the kitchen, he brushes through the receipt drawer, thumbs through pages of the address book, looking for anything, any hint even, to clear this up.

Nate can't be Amy's stalker. It's just not possible that his brother would go this damn far. So he takes his cell from his pocket and pulls out the folded paper with Reid's number on it and dials while pacing the kitchen. Reid's got to be behind all this. When the voicemail picks up, he disconnects. After a moment, he dials the number again, listening to the ring at his ear and to something else. Something that doesn't belong. He moves quietly out of the kitchen toward the staircase until the automated voicemail answers again, prompting him to disconnect and redial, impatiently now. He climbs the stairs quickly and stops at the top, waiting for the connection to go through and the phone to ring.

As it does, George walks to his brother's room, listening to the ring in his cell. Slats of morning sunlight reach through the window blinds. And a cell phone on Nate's dresser top rings, stopping at the same time the voicemail answers George's call. He disconnects and redials. The phone on Nate's dresser rings again.

"Holy shit," George says, sitting on the edge of the bed shaking his head. It all sinks slowly in, with each thought he considers.

A framed photograph sits on a bookshelf across the room. He walks over to it, picking up the picture of him and Nate both dressed in their Little League uniforms ages ago. It was a hot day and they'd just finished a game, their knees grass-stained, their hair sweating and matted, their faces lit up.

George! The day baseball finally ended for them, that day at the cottage when George told Nate he wasn't going back to the minors, was the day Nate's anguish began. He knows it now. Feels it as sure as feeling the weight of a line drive caught in his mitt. His hand brushes dust off the glass covering the Little League picture, off Nate leaning into him, George's arm over his brother's shoulder, mitts hanging from their hands.

Years of Nate trying desperately to rectify the guilt he carried, the crushing blame he felt for their father's death and the death of his big brother's dream—it all crystallizes for George now. The lunches and car shows and ski trips and plans and dreams that never let up. The armored truck heist intended to restore the major league money and glory George had sacrificed all those years ago when their father died.

Nate was the mastermind. Not Reid. The heist was all for his brother, all to pay him back after a death that changed everything. Nate did it for him. And now Amy threatens it.

George! Nate had cried out that afternoon at the beach, one day after burying their father. His voice carried through the cottage on the sea breeze and kept going, grief reaching out over the breaking waves, echoing up to the skies above the sea. And still, it carries still.

Thirty-Two

HER REPUTATION ALONE EASES HIS nerves. She is tough, can go head-to-head with any federal prosecutor, effectively presents her case and is eminently fair. But most importantly, Attorney Claire Jensen believes him.

George looks at the clock Monday and waits for her call, answering the phone on the first ring minutes later.

"It looks good," Claire tells him.

"Good? They agreed to immunity?"

"Not yet. Sit tight."

"What'd you say to them?"

"George, for now let's just say they all know. The U.S. Attorney's office knows. And the Federal Bureau of Investigation knows. As does Detective Hayes. They all know I've got a confidential informant who has come forward with information that may be of substantial assistance to them in the apprehension of those involved in a serious crime still under active investigation. I presented, too, that my client is ready, willing and able to wear a wire to assist the government and authorities in this process. Are you still good with that?"

"Whatever it takes, Claire."

"All right then. I'll continue pushing for complete immunity from prosecution, George, but for now, no signed agreements, no talking client. So stay near the phone, okay? They know they've got to move quickly. As far as they're concerned, my client can change his mind, or try another tactic, or even disappear at any moment."

As far as *he's* concerned, Nate has to be stopped and George isn't capable of stopping him alone. So he called Attorney Jensen and, given the circumstances, she met with him over the weekend. If all goes as planned, Nate will be facing criminal charges later this week. His brother will be handcuffed and led to a cruiser, taken off the streets and tied up in the legal system for a good, long time. And if George stays away from Amy in the meantime, he thinks she'll be safe. It is their very relationship that provokes Nate.

The morning unfolds outside the slider in his dining room. Landscapers mow the expanse of lawn, a neighbor stains his deck and George begins playing the very last hand with his brother.

And it plays out quickly. By midweek, he sits with Claire in a tense conference room at the U.S. Attorney's office. She was right. The authorities didn't waste any time negotiating the terms and conditions of his immunity agreement in exchange for his assistance in resolving the crime and convicting the people involved. Papers were signed, pens and notebooks are poised now, recorders at the ready. They want to close the books on this one.

"Your attorney says you can crack this case, Carbone." Detective Hayes leans back in his chair, eyeing him.

George shifts in his seat, unbuttons the jacket of his navy blue suit and doesn't break eye contact with Hayes. "That's right. I can." And so it finally begins. Without Amy knowing, he seeks her absolution fully, starting with those four simple words.

The faces lining the table, faces that can bring her justice, listen to him describe the morning he waited for his brother to pick him up to go to the casino. When he gets to the part about returning to Nate's car after seeing Amy and Grace enter the bank, a rush of questions interrupts him until the room falls silent again, waiting for his answers. Each person leans forward as his voice, a low monotone, empties out the story. He is conscious of his breathing, his dry mouth, and requests a glass of water.

An Assistant U.S. Attorney, the FBI agents, even Hayes, they continue asking questions seeking clarification, reasoning, belief, and he pauses with each, carefully arranging his answers word by word, aware of his tongue forming each syllable. Nothing is left out, including the stalking. This is the day he always knew would come, though he never dreamt the impetus that would bring him to it would be his kid brother.

"I don't know the whereabouts of Reid and Elliott," George concludes. "But I'm sure my brother knows. He's going to be key to any unanswered questions."

Two of the federal agents conferred throughout the entire testimony. One of them speaks now. "Mr. Carbone. If we bring Nate in on your word alone, too much can go wrong, from his refusal to answer questions, to sending us on a wild goose chase, to withholding evidence. One of the terms of the immunity agreement negotiated by your attorney was that you'd assist in the apprehension of your brother through wearing a recording device. We need you to fulfill that obligation."

George glances at Claire beside him, then back to the agent. Right now he's worried about only one obligation, to Amy and her daughter. "You want him framed."

"We want Nate to talk. But if he catches wind of our scent, he can slip away too easily, especially with the cash he's sitting on. If he hasn't skipped out already. He may even know you're here."

"I understand," George says. He takes a long swallow of water.

"We need an insurance policy securing his participation in the heist. So it's necessary for him to discuss his criminal involvement without his being aware of a set-up."

"And another thing, George," Attorney Jensen interrupts, turning to him. "Once this goes down, the news will hit fast and the media will be relentless, you know that. They're going to want to draw the line between your brother and the fact that it was you who returned Grace."

George only nods.

"As a confidential informant," she continues, "your actual participation in the crime will remain undisclosed. The media won't be aware of *that*, but they'll be aware of *you* because of your connection to Grace. So keep yourself scarce. Lay low and refuse comment while this plays out."

"Got it."

Attorney Jensen turns back to the table. "We're prepared to move forward," she says.

George will do anything. His brother is ruthless. The only way he'll be stopped is by someone, with good reason, just as intent. "Name the time and place," he adds.

———

Amy lies on her living room sofa, having just talked on the phone with Grace and her parents. They still don't know of George's involvement in the truck heist, thinking only that she broke things off with him, that too much is going on in her life to leave room for a relationship. It's dinnertime now but she hasn't eaten. Because it's happened again—the inability to eat is stronger than her appetite. Since her confrontation with George, memories of him have moved like shadows through her mind: hazy, vague, but very real. Her living room windows are thrown open, the midsummer evening sweet with birdsong and cicadas. She hears the rhythmic footsteps of someone jogging past her house and turns her head, listening until the sound fades. No breeze stirs outside; the air is clear and dry, settling on her like a cool white sheet, summer noises floating on its ethereal lightness.

So she jumps when there is a knock at the kitchen screen door. It comes suddenly, not preceded by a vehicle pulling into the driveway or a car door slamming. She sits up and looks out the window before going to the kitchen.

"Hello?" Celia calls through the screen just as Amy turns the corner.

"Hi," Amy answers, seeing Celia and some luggage on the other side of the door. "Going somewhere?"

"Uh-huh. Can I come in?"

Amy pushes the screen door open. "The lock's broken."

Celia glances at the lock before walking in cool and casual in her frayed denim skirt and green tank, setting a grocery bag on the blue table. She goes back out to the stoop and returns with a duffel bag in one arm and her pillow beneath the other, which also holds a leash connected to Sasha.

"What's going on?" Amy asks as her kitchen fills up with Celia and her things.

"Well, it's kind of like a pajama party, minus the party." She turns to the dog. "Sit, Sasha." The golden retriever obeys, waggling with happiness as she does so. "Will Angel mind the dog?"

Amy shakes her head. "She's still with Grace at my parents'."

"Oh, I thought they'd be back by now."

"No, they're staying up north till after the fashion show. I'll close up Wedding Wishes for a few days afterward and head up there then."

"All right. And I'm keeping you company in the meantime." She pulls two containers of ice cream from the first bag and shoves them into the freezer.

"That's really nice of you, but I actually have to stop in at my shop."

"Now? Why?"

"The fashion show's tomorrow and twenty-two people reserved a seat. Everything's ready except for the seating and a few finishing touches."

"Perfect. I'll help."

"Wait. I thought you were going somewhere?"

"I am." Celia reaches into the second bag for two new pairs of terry cloth flip-flop slippers. They are thick and bright, one pair lime green, one hot pink. She hands Amy the pink pair. "And I've just arrived."

———

George dials the number, but upon hearing Nate's voice, hesitates. Can he end his brother's life like this, with him not even seeing it coming? Can't they settle this another way? Can't they sit down with a deck of cards and play out a very private hand?

"I've been thinking about something you said, Nate." He sits on the sofa, leaning his elbows on his knees.

"What's that?"

"Taking advantage of the situation."

"Okay, like how?"

"Like finding that bike with my name on it."

"What brings this on? I thought you were tight with Amy."

Come on, Nate, George thinks, standing then. *Ante up.* "She wants to cool things down, you know? She's still a new widow and that day at the bank shook her up. Too much shit like that's on her mind. Maybe now would be a good time to take that road trip. Give her some space."

"You serious?"

"Yeah, I'm serious."

"But you said you wouldn't touch the money."

"I'll put it back. I just need the bike for the trip, then I can sell it after." He walks to the slider and looks out while talking. "Or hell, maybe we'll make this an annual thing."

"No shit. What'd you have in mind?"

"I don't know. Maybe a few weeks out on the west coast?"

"I don't believe you."

"Why? Jesus, we've planned this since we were kids." George opens the slider and pulls out a chair at the patio table.

"And you've always shot it down. Why the sudden change of heart?"

"Sudden, Nate? You've been talking me into this since you clipped those baseball cards on my bike spokes." George squeezes his eyes shut for a long moment.

"I don't know, man. I'm pretty busy with work."

He's not sure if Nate's on to him and playing him right back, and so George keeps pressing. "Well we're not getting any younger. And it's Amy, too. We need some space, you know what I mean? It's a good time for me."

"What about The Main Course?"

"Dean will cover it." George pauses and sits at the outdoor table. "Hey, if you'd rather wait, that's fine. I just thought it'd be good now." A drink would be good now, too. He stands just as quickly and heads back inside. "And you kind of owe me one."

"When?"

"August? Mid-August."

"I've got a few jobs lined up, but I guess I can rearrange them."

"As long as I can get my hands on a bike. I'll have to do a little shopping. Let's have lunch tomorrow and we'll talk."

"At your shop?"

"No. Let's go out." George told the authorities about Nate's dream of the two brothers taking a cross-country road trip and of their talks at Joel's over the years. So that's where they want it to happen. He's sure the bar is being scoped out as they speak. George takes a long breath. This is it. His next words will frame his brother and end any semblance of a relationship. Nate will hate him. Their family will be finished. He thinks of Amy and Grace and realizes that he has no family. "Meet me at Joel's about one."

"Maybe it's true?"

Amy looks back over her shoulder, her arms raised to the top of the portable archway. Clouds of tulle spill from her hands as she wraps it on the frame.

"No, listen," Celia says as she opens another folding chair and sets it in line with the others in Wedding Wishes' showroom. "George saw what was going down in the parking lot. And I'm just saying, what if he really did put himself on that truck just for the child's sake? It sounds like something he might do, don't you think?"

Amy finishes wrapping the tulle around the arch and reaches for the string of twinkling lights, entwining them in the fabric. "Do *you* think it's true? That someone could commit a crime for honorable reasons?"

Celia shrugs and opens the last chair. "Anything's possible, I guess. You know what they say, truth is stranger than fiction."

"No kidding. And you swear you and Ben won't tell anyone about George, right? I need to trust you guys on this."

"You've got my word, don't worry. And Ben's word is good as gold."

"So you promise?"

"Promise."

"Okay." Amy steps back from the archway. "Hit that light switch, Cee."

Celia flicks the wall switch and the lights sparkle. "Oh, beautiful. They look like tiny stars floating in clouds."

"Perfect," Amy says, seeing her bridal shop magically illuminated so that the brides picture themselves in the celestial wonder. Twinkling lights are strung around the display window and checkout counter and along the top of the gown racks. "I've just got to line up the gowns for the models so they wear them in the right order." She moves to the wall rack and pulls off a tea-length dress.

"Who's doing the modeling?" Celia takes the dress from her and hangs it on the empty rolling rack near the dressing area. A silver room divider separates the fashion show dressing area from the viewers' chairs.

"A few girls from the high school and, if you can believe it, I talked Sara Beth into modeling too."

"No way! Oh she'll have lots of fun, definitely. She's game for anything antique."

"She already dibbed wearing the Jackie Onassis dress. Except that one's not for sale."

"No surprise there. It looks amazing in your window with Jackie's photo."

"I'm showing seven decades of gowns tomorrow, imagine?" She hands Celia a peplum gown of shadow organza, the fabric airy and soft. "This one's the oldest, from 1944."

"Can you picture the first bride's story? It was probably war time, maybe she married a soldier."

"That's what I love about these, their story. I wanted to pair that one with my grandmother's veil, which now I can't find. I thought I brought it in last week but it must be at home. Hang that one first on the rack; they'll be wearing them in order of the decades."

Celia slides over the other gown and sets the organza first.

"This one's always been a favorite of mine." Amy hands her another, satin with a fitted bodice overlaid in lace and pearl ribbons. "It's mid-seventies. So it goes fourth in line."

Celia takes the gown and drapes it over her arm. "Amy," she says softly.

The shop is quiet, with just the rustle of gowns sounding as Amy brushes through them lined on the wall. "Celia, don't," she finally says. "I can't talk about it anymore and I've got to get this done."

"But it's only one thing. Because honestly? I'll bet George never took his eyes off Grace that day." She pauses and Amy stops looking at the dresses, closing her eyes against her tears. She knows, oh she knows darn well that Celia won't finish her thought until she turns and looks at her. Silently, she does. "I really can't believe that he wasn't helping you," Celia says then. "You just never knew it."

Amy takes a long breath. It's so hard to admit something, when it feels like admitting it is an affront. When something is right, but you want it to be right a *different* way, a way when George stopped the day from happening. "So what do you think I should do?"

"Listen. It boils down to two things. Either you're going to pack your bags and uproot your home and work and move your whole life to New Hampshire and be done with the situation here."

"Or?" Amy asks.

Celia lifts the satin and lace gown and holds it up to Amy, draping it along the front of her body. "Or you're going to marry him."

Thirty-Three

GEORGE GOES IN TO WORK early on Friday, like he does every morning, opens up the shop, pulls a black apron over his head, ties up two roasts, checks on the weekend's special orders and waits on several customers. Tom Riley tells him about the Yankees game he and his family went to the Sunday before while George weighs two pounds of chicken cutlets.

"Great seats," Tom says. "Left field, main box. In the shade, so it was good."

Does he know how lucky, how God-awful lucky he is? George glances up from the scale at the middle-aged man talking about spending a Sunday at the stadium. It is all George wants, that kind of luck, that kind of life.

"It was hot in the Bronx," Tom is saying. "But you know, a couple ice cold beers, hot dog on the side and the day was perfect. There's nothing like it, you know what I mean, George?"

Lillian March mentions that her car needs tires. "What do you think I should buy?" she asks as George wraps a prepared meatloaf.

"I don't know, Lil. Depends on how long you're going to hold on to your car."

"A year or two, that's about it."

"Well put on decent tires, you want to be safe." Amy's SUV is a couple years old. Has she checked her tires recently? Is the tread good? The tire pressure right? He wants to check her tires, that's all he wants. That's it. He can hardly believe how he aches to be able to do only that for her. Inspect the tires, walk around her vehicle, crouch down and run his open hand over the tread, hold a pressure gauge to the valve stem, maybe check the oil, too. "You can probably pick up something good on sale to get you by."

The Houghs are throwing a Jack and Jill wedding shower for their daughter beneath a tent in their backyard, and they want to barbecue afterward. A barbecue beneath a tent, that's as intense as their lives are right now. George wants only to be blessed with that type of fortune, to sit at a picnic table and have a cheeseburger. They order the hamburger and sausage patties, chicken and side salads for the shower the following weekend. George can't imagine the following weekend. He is about to be wired to help convict his brother. It's getting closer to lunchtime and his hands tremble while writing down their order. It gets so bad he has to set the pencil down and wipe his damp palms on his apron.

"When's the wedding?" George asks without looking up.

"Second week in August. Jennifer's teaching over at the middle school and has to be back for September."

September seems worlds away. Another lifetime when all this—the heist, his affair with Amy, his last thread of family— when it will all be a dream he'll try to remember. What will he do then? Will the Marches, the Houghs and Rileys still frequent his butcher shop if they learn what he has done? Will they trust him to provide their meals, respect him still?

By the time Dean takes over at the shop and he settles in at Joel's, it doesn't much matter. This is the most difficult day yet, being wired to cull the damning words out of his brother. But Nate is dangerous, and brother or not, George has to stop him.

So for now, he acts normal. That's the irony of all this. The normalcy of two brothers meeting for lunch and a beer, talking up a bike trip. No one will look twice. It is normalcy that started it all in a bank parking lot two months ago when Nate insisted— hosiery over their heads, a two-year-old hostage in the back of the armored truck—that they resume their normal lives, that blending in provided the best cover. Nate became expert at keeping up that ordinary front, and now George manipulates normalcy's cover to hang him.

He orders a pitcher of beer. Let them try to stop him. He's wired and ready to relay Nate's incriminating words to an under-cover van parked close by. Let them say he needs to be stone straight for this to stick. He pours a tall glass and takes a slow drink, looking around the bar. Even he doesn't know who is who—who came in off the street for a sandwich and who flew in to help take down his brother. They all look alike: regular guys working for the town, a family lawyer with an office down the street, federal law enforcement agents, a couple guys from the hardware store, a local electrician. On a hot summer afternoon, the character lines delineating identity blur. They all sweat the same.

He wipes his brow and sits back for a long moment. It is a moment when he wonders if undercover eyes are on him; a moment when law enforcement officials sit in that van tuned to hear his every word; when special agents wait, armed to stop any resistance as his brother is restrained; when Miranda rights swim through the officials' minds, ready to be recited to the man behind Addison's most notorious crime; when a press conference is only a phone call away. A moment when Amy and her daughter are still at risk.

He turns in his seat and is surprised to see Hayes standing in the open doorway. Bright sunshine glares outside behind him, but the bar is dark and cool. And everyone knows something's up; anyone who matters watches Hayes walk over to George.

"Change of plans." Hayes stands at the end of the table and fills Nate's glass with beer. He takes a quick swallow. "We've got a problem, George. Got to move the venue. Let's go."

"What are you talking about?"

"Sorry to say there's been an accident. From what I hear, it's a bad wreck."

"What?"

"Apparently your brother was on his way here. He was at the train tracks and witnesses say he hesitated, like he was weighing the odds. Then he gunned it. I guess he swerved at the last second, right before the impact, but he miscalculated."

"Shit, a train hit him?" George stands then and they hurry to the door. "Are you serious?"

"I'm sorry, George. They're doing everything they can for him as we speak."

"Was he on his bike?"

Hayes pulls his keys from his pocket. "No. His car."

George stops on the sidewalk—in the sunshine, traffic driving past, a pedestrian's cell phone ringing—and takes a deep breath. "Wait. But he's alive?"

"So far." Hayes looks back at him. "Let's move it, George."

"Was someone following him?"

"He's been tailed since you talked. All night, all morning, every minute."

"You think he was on to us?"

"Don't know."

The way Nate's body is carefully laid out, you'd never guess the maiming a freight train inflicts at a railroad crossing. George stands just inside the hospital room and watches his brother. Aggressive life support fought a losing battle with internal hemorrhaging.

There is a chair near the bed, a place for a family member to sit and wait, to whisper strength to the patient. George sits with his brother's body. He doesn't doubt the possibility that Nate sensed a tail. He would notice anything out of the ordinary in the normal, regimented life he had returned to. That was his radar, the way he read his opponents' hands. And if he suspected something was amiss, he'd never let George know. Nate never once showed his cards, all his life.

So maybe Nate won. Maybe he was on to George and refused to lose. There would be no handcuffs, no shoves into cruisers or leg shackles in his game. This way, he'd never been stopped. He escaped the guilty verdict.

George inches his chair closer. Death erases the years on Nate's face. It looks as though Nate saw his life pass before him in those imminent seconds. When everything was a breath away— the train's screaming halt, Nate's own wrenching swerve, tons of metal meeting and launching his car, the earth cradling his pain— the process began. Nate's mind recanted the years, reeling him back in time. When he'd died, Nate had somehow time travelled to his younger days, baseball cards clipped on the spokes, the wind in his hair. This is what George sees on Nate's face: his mind's age at death.

It is too soon to forgive or understand. Maybe both will never happen. All he knows is this: In his own way, Nate is finally free.

George takes his brother's limp hand in his, clasps it, then stands and walks out of the room.

———

The initial news story is small. A local man perished in a car-train collision. The roads were dry, the weather clear. It looked like a case of driver error, an unfortunate decision. If you drive that strip of road, crash remnants are visible: patches of the pavement burned, the grass torn up, the curb smashed.

So Amy thinks that while models wearing tulle and lace walked an illuminated aisle in Wedding Wishes, and while brides-to-be sat close to a friend or mother murmuring to each other and picturing themselves in cascading white gowns, their hair put up beneath pretty veils, at that very moment, Nate's life came to an end.

She reads his obituary and thinks about him on Monday, the morning of his funeral. Will there be flowers there, beautiful arrangements bidding him farewell? The thought moves her to lift George's single rose from the vase, its pink color fading now, the petals beginning to curl. She snaps the stem in her hand while reading the obituary saying the service will begin at nine o'clock in the funeral home, not in a church. But still, he'll have a service. The man who orchestrated an armed robbery and Grace's kidnapping will be honorably laid to rest. George must have planned the memorial. Death freed his brother from all charges: no one knew, there were no deathbed confessions, no final statements. He died free and it upsets Amy to know this.

She stays home that morning, organizing the small inventory in her gown room, hanging two recently acquired ones out on the clothesline. One dress is cut lace over sheer silk with a V-neck, the other chiffon. They hang still in the heavy July heat and she thinks it fitting that there is no breeze making them waltz today.

By midafternoon, hours after Nate's funeral is done, she closes up Wedding Wishes for the next few days. Changing a gown on a window mannequin, setting out vintage necklaces with autumn-colored stones for upcoming weddings and shifting summer gowns to the back room, all are mere motions giving her time to think. To consider staying or going. Digging in for the long haul in Addison, or moving all she has here to a new storefront somewhere up north. Though she plans to leave tomorrow for New Hampshire to get Grace, a surprising number of requests for gowns have come in since her fashion show. Their stay up north will be cut short.

And all the while, Celia never stops calling. She uses the weather, the news, a magazine recipe, any reason to pick up the phone. If Sara Beth hadn't taken her to the antique show on The Green yesterday, Celia would have. Since Amy told her about George's identity, Celia has become her bodyguard, soul-guard and emotion-guard.

After dinner, she turns on her laptop in the living room to search for a client's request. Journeying virtually to circa 1970 for a vintage gown with a quilted waistband and waterfall frill skirt is as good a way as any to deny the present. A neighbor the next street over wants that gown for her late-September beach wedding.

Oh, she's become expert at denying the present. At denying everything about this summer. Everything about one person. Grace and Wedding Wishes and Celia and antiques on The Green and New Hampshire and fashion shows, well, well they're all a bluff, aren't they? Because sudden tears fill her eyes when one email cuts right through it all. The way it takes her breath, the way the sight of his name alone brings those tears, there's no denying the truth that it is George she has been denying with everything else.

Dear Amy,

I didn't think you'd take a phone call from me, and I only hope that wherever you are, you'll read this instead. It's only fair that you know what I'm about to tell you before the news hits. Because what's most important to know is that you're safe now. You and Grace are safe. You can rest easy. The men involved in Grace's kidnapping have been taken into police custody.

I won't go on too long, but want to tell you that I've worked closely with my attorney to accomplish this. I'm sure you've seen the reports of Nate's death. He died during his takedown and when that happened, we lost our connection to the others involved. We had no recourse but to go forward with a funeral, among other things, anticipating they'd show up there.

Rest assured it's done. You don't have to worry about them. I did what I could to right any pain, any wrong inflicted on your life, and on Grace's. If nothing else, I'm hoping that a sense of peace comes with this knowledge for you, a peace you so immensely deserve.

If you ever find it in your heart to talk to me, to know my thoughts, I'll be where I always have been, in the familiar places, at work, at home. I'll be here.

George

———

The news broke quickly and the next morning, Celia knocks at Amy's back door at six-thirty, newspaper in hand.

"I know already," Amy tells her through the screen, cupping a white coffee mug close.

"You do?"

She nods. "I heard from George. Yesterday."

Celia walks in and opens the paper on the kitchen table. "You're kidding. But I guess I'm not surprised. In the article, he's only mentioned as the one who returned Grace. There's nothing about all the other stuff, except that he couldn't be reached for comment. So they arrested the others but didn't charge George?"

"Apparently not. And I'm not sure why, but I guess they have their reasons." Amy sits with her friend and they glance at the front page.

"Hey," Celia says, reaching over and moving a strand of hair off her face. "You okay?"

"Oh Celia. It's just so ... I don't know. Surreal. Detective Hayes left me a couple messages, too."

"What did he say?"

Amy checks her watch. "I didn't call him back yet, it's early. I was going to, right before I leave for New Hampshire."

"Well did George say how it happened?"

"I didn't actually talk to him either. He sent an email with a few details, something about working with his attorney to turn in the others. I suppose it'll all come out sooner or later. But this past week must've been intense."

"Amy?"

"No, no, no." She stands and rinses out her coffee cup at the sink. "Don't go there, Cee."

"Why not?" She drops her voice and turns in her chair, facing Amy. "Come on, George was telling you the truth."

"Two months too late."

"Yeah, but the guy stood by you all summer, trying to handle *everything*. Do you think you'll go see him?"

"I don't know."

"He does love you. And you told me you felt the same at one time."

"That was before. And I really can't think about it today. I'm on my way to get Grace, so that's that." She dries out the cup and stacks it in another on the table. "Would you mind if I keep the newspaper? My parents would like to see it, I'm sure."

"Absolutely." Celia stands and hugs her. "And you think about things, okay? Take long walks with your daughter, get some fresh air up there." She holds Amy at arm's length. "You'll be okay, don't worry."

Amy's not so sure. Already her mind is in two places. Her suitcase is packed and she is ready to go. But she hesitates and makes another cup of coffee. Alone, she sits with the newspaper and reads the article slowly, looking up every few sentences as she correlates the story to what George told her, his hair matted with rain, the kitchen dark, the rainfall pouring outside that evening. Afterward she washes the coffee cup, the spoons and the tabletop. The red plaid dishtowel hangs squarely over a chair back. Each chair is pushed neatly to the table.

And still, still. She opens the refrigerator and empties the top two shelves onto the counter: milk, orange juice, bottled water, butter, yogurts. After scrubbing those two shelves with soapy dishwater, she bends to the lower shelf and empties the vegetable bins. No one's refrigerator sparkles more than hers. No refrigerated food is more meticulously organized.

And no matter what she does, no matter how many times she wipes off the counter, the tears don't stop. No matter that she retrieves the wilting pink rose from the kitchen trash can, clips the bent stem short and stands the flower in the two white coffee cups stacked on the blue table. No matter that she sets her overnight bag at the back door. No matter that she sits herself at that blue table, at all its memories, and lets herself have a good cry. Because there's no way she can get on the highway north with these darn tears blurring her vision. Like a watercolor painting, those tears blur everything: the blue of the table becomes the marsh water behind a little cottage; the white cups, the swans swimming past; the pale pink rose, the sea sky at dusk one quiet June evening. The sea, the sea. He gave them that. She pulls the plaid dishtowel off the chair and presses it into her sobs, presses until it is enough.

Until she deciphers the true blend of one summer's days.

Until the scent of damp rain comes to her, pressed against her face, and she realizes why she hasn't washed the dishtowel all week.

Thirty-Four

Rather than feeling like he's been away, it feels, walking into The Main Course the morning after Nate's funeral, like a place George once visited. He turns the key in the lock. A lifetime has passed since he's last been here. It's like turning the pages in an old photo album: touching the glass showcases, straightening the spice rack, remembering when. In the back room, he switches on the light and sees that Dean set up the new grinder in place of the old one heaved into the dumpster out back. The knives are razor sharp, the meat cases gleaming. In his office, a backlog of paperwork waits, enough to keep him holed up for several hours, away from the reporters sure to come looking for him. Now that the news of Nate's involvement in the heist broke, there'll be no keeping them away as they try to snag an exclusive.

Reacquainting with his life, George sits at his desk and thumbs through orders and invoices. So this is what it will be now, his life. It's only a reflection of what used to be; the difference is there, nearly indecipherable, quiet. No one will see it but him. All he has, all he amounts to, is each day as it comes.

He starts a pot of coffee but leaves the stereo off. Somehow it doesn't seem right to listen to music. Maybe that characterizes what he lost, the desire to whistle along, to hum the songs and hear the melodies. When he puts on his black apron and goes into the walk-in cooler to check on the inventory, only the drone of the refrigeration sounds in the insulated space. It seems to take up all the air around him.

———

Sunlight glances off the large window, fooling the eye with harsh shadows and glare. The reflections in the window are so pure, they are difficult to decipher from reality. As she lifts off her sunglasses, Amy realizes one reflection is of herself. It had first looked like the shadow of someone on the other side of the glass. A customer, maybe, ordering cutlets or fish. But when she squints and raises her hand to her eyes, shielding the sunlight, her reflection disappears and she sees it is dark inside The Main Course. No customers are having a coffee yet, waiting for their porterhouse steaks to be wrapped. A Closed sign hangs in the door. It is enough for her breath to catch, seeing the empty shop. It just isn't right, how lonely it looks, how lonely she feels, how desperately she wants to be inside that shop. Life is so open to interpretation, with its deceptions and all its illusions. Her eyes look through the glass at the details with an aching familiarity, as though for a place she once visited. Maybe he's behind the counter, working a substantial slicing knife through a cut of meat. She steps sideways, looking, but the lights are off and she turns away.

It is early still, not yet nine o'clock at Sycamore Square. Amy glances around at the other specialty stores: a clock shop with decorative potted shrubs at the doorway, a clothing boutique and a coffee shop. None are open yet. Her fingers tighten their hold on a small gift bag and she turns around, back toward The Main Course, mad at herself more than anything that it came to this. That she didn't listen to George, that she didn't see past her own immense pain. That she contributed at all to his life's undoing is unbearable. And if it's so unbearable, well, it wouldn't hurt so much if it wasn't twisted up in love. She stands right against the door, cupping her eyes, the bag hanging beside her face, and sees a light deep inside.

Her eyes close for one moment, a moment when she feels the sun on her shoulders, hears summer birdsong and distant traffic, a moment when life comes rushing back. She presses her ear to the glass door, listening intently for muffled Sinatra, for a whistle, for the drone of a voice on the telephone. Her hand presses against her other ear, blocking out everything but a sign of George.

Someone is in the back; lights are on. She can see that now through the glare of morning sunlight. Her hand reaches for the handle and she rattles the door, hard, all the while staring, watching for a motion in the shadows, for George looking up from his work.

"George," she says, breathless, and shakes the door again. When no one comes, she knocks hard, rapping her knuckles on the glass. "George!" Her hand burns, her knuckles too, from her insistent knocking. She shifts over to the display window, trying to see in at a better angle. The gift bag falls to the ground when she cups her face against the glass. "Come *on*," she whispers. "Damn it." She scoops up the bag and returns to the door in one quick motion, grabs the handle and shakes it, tears streaking her face. "George! Please God, open the door."

———

George pauses in the freezer while immediately considering if it is his imagination. He's craved her voice often enough in the past week, wanting to hear it on the phone, wanting it to call after him as he gets into his pickup, wanting to look up in a grocery store aisle or at a gas station pump and see her. He knows, too, what it feels like to turn at a desire so strong and find nothing. It's something he'll have to live with, have to get used to, especially with the reporters coming around. The immunity agreement keeps his name out of the crime, but Nate's is front and center and already they're looking for him, knocking on the door, wanting his take on his brother's story. What else could it be? Maybe it's better if they don't even know he's here.

The knocking comes again—once more, strong—then it is quiet. Dean will have to fend off the media when he opens up later. He closes the freezer and heads into the dimness of the shop. Okay, he imagined hearing her call his name all the past week, turning at illusions, squinting into shadows. It's almost expected now. So routine is good. Checking stock and placing orders will get him through the morning.

But there is an unmistakable difference between imagination and reality, and the distinction is right in front of him.

Amy stands pressed against the door, her hands cupping her eyes, straining to see into the dark shop. When he takes a step, still in shadow but watching her closely, tears are visible on her face. Her eyes search the room and when he moves closer, they stop on him.

George he sees her mouth say, a slow hopeful smile coming as she knocks rapidly on the glass and rises on her toes, as though he can't see her there. She wears a long, brown crochet sundress and clutches a gift bag. "George," she says louder with another quick few raps. He still doesn't stir. She is smiling. She is okay. The sun shines from behind her, casting her in silhouette. He relishes these quiet seconds he thought would never, ever come.

She reaches over and twists the door handle. "Please open up?" Her voice is muffled through the glass.

In a few quick steps he is at the door, turning the lock and pushing it open. Her demeanor changes then; she moves back and presses the folds of her dress. Their eyes lock while everything between them wavers, and finally dissipates. He asks her, gently, "Was that you making all that noise?"

"Oh George," she says quietly. "Can I talk to you? Please?"

"Come on," he says, stepping back to let her through and locking the door behind her. "Would you like to sit down? I'll get you a coffee."

She shakes her head quickly. "No. I don't think so, George. George."

When he turns back, she stands near the register, in front of the case of cheeses, the shelf of fresh bakery bread nearly empty beside her. Both her hands clutch the bag and she is looking straight at him. What confuses him, though, is the way she keeps saying his name.

"I read the paper this morning," Amy begins. "George."

"Listen, are you sure you don't want to sit?"

"I'm sure."

It is amazing how when you know someone, really know someone, every nuance carries a message: the way one blinks, shifts their gaze, sets their mouth. Talk almost becomes unnecessary. He sees this in a moment when her expression changes, when though she seems glad to be here, there is something else. All week he wanted to only know that she was safe. There were so many small things, *just this*, he'd pray, *just this*, that he'd wanted in the past days. But mostly to know that she and Grace were okay. Now, in this moment, he wonders if they are, if something happened.

"What's wrong, Amy?" he asks.

She turns away, takes a step, and turns back, facing him.

"Is Grace okay?" he asks, waiting for her to talk. To say why she's here.

Amy nods. "Are you staying here, George? Keeping the shop?"

"For now," he answers, folding his arms across his chest. "I really haven't thought too far ahead. Haven't made any plans. Why?"

"Oh," she says, wiping her cheek with the back of her hand. "I was afraid you'd leave."

George watches her eyes move from him, looking vaguely past him to the outdoors. "Is there a reason I shouldn't?" he asks.

Slowly, her gaze comes back to him and she is serious. "So many. I'd like to think, well. It hasn't been easy this summer. For either of us."

"No, it hasn't."

"And I'd like to think that it takes time to understand everything. More time. Somehow."

"Amy."

"I know. It's just that I came here not knowing what I would say, George. And, well, what I'm trying to say is that I'm sorry. I'm so sorry."

"Don't be sorry, Amy. This was the farthest thing from being your fault."

"No." She walks closer, shifting the gift bag she is holding from one hand to the other. Her dress clings in soft brown folds. "That's not what I mean. What I'm saying is that I'm sorry for not believing you, that day in my kitchen, George. In the rain." She presses a lock of blonde hair behind her ear and watches him intently. "I'm sorry that I didn't accept what you were saying, what you did."

He doesn't move. They stand facing each other in shadow. Pedestrians pass by outside the door. The telephone rings. Still George doesn't move, waiting with arms crossed, waiting to see if this is goodbye, if this is condolences, if this is gratitude.

"I'm sorry that I denied your life like that, denied how you cared for me. Because that's what I did. I denied your actual life when I turned away and I was wrong." She looks up with a long breath. "Okay," she whispers. "Okay." She takes a step closer. "So here's the deal." Her hand reaches out and takes his. "If you can find some way to forgive me for not seeing through all my troubles to you, to you keeping me afloat all summer, and holding me up, well if you can somehow forgive me that, I wonder if we can have another chance."

"A chance."

"Yes." She pulls her hand away. "Here." She opens the bag she'd been holding and lifts out a book. "It's an agenda planner. You know. A date book." She offers it to him hesitantly and he takes it, watching her. "You promised me something a few weeks ago, remember?"

He shakes his head no, glancing down at the date book. It is bound in black leather and is new, its pages stiff.

"It's a gift. I wanted to bring you something. Something for you. I didn't have time to wrap it, I'm sorry. Open it," she whispers. "To the marked page."

George flips the black date book to the page where she left a bookmark. It falls open to the week ahead of them. The days are blank except for Thursday, where her easy cursive fills the square. It's noted for seven o'clock, something about the movies and popcorn and lemonade. He looks up at her silently.

"Turn the page," she whispers again.

He does and sees a week later that Friday evening is blocked off, filled with plans for take-out seafood on the river, watching the boats while the moon comes up. When he hears her voice, soft, his throat tightens.

"You promised me an easy summer. We were going to date, remember? To take our time, kind of lazy-like. When you told me that, that we should just date, well I really liked that. It was so old-fashioned and I'd like to do that, George. Oh God, I miss you so much."

He glances at the leather planner and then looks back at her. "You know it's not over yet for me. Part of the deal was that I won't be prosecuted, but a lot comes with that. My attorney says we have a long road ahead and it won't be easy."

"We'll get through it," she answers, stepping closer. "You and me. Just like we did the first time around. Except this time, well, this time *we're* in control. Please, George."

He looks at her still, then down at the planner and thumbs through a few pages. A week is blocked off in late August. "What's this?" he asks, his voice hoarse.

She tries to smile, he sees that, smile against tears and sadness and hope. "I was being a little presumptuous. But if maybe you could get away from all this for a few days, well Grace and I are free that week. She really loved that beach of yours, George. That pretty boardwalk, her seashells. That little cottage at Stony Point. You told me once that you could explain everything. In good time, I think was how you put it, in good time walking on the beach, in the sweet salt air. And I want to hear it, there, at your cottage at the sea, the whole story." She pauses, the room quiet. "So that's the deal. I love you, George. I trust you, always have."

JOANNE DeMAIO

George sets the date book on the counter and walks to her. With one arm, he hugs her, pressing a kiss to the side of her head. She backs up a little, to see him and he touches his forehead to hers. "Are you asking me out, Amy?"

She nods and he leans closer, kissing her once, lightly, before embracing her in his arms and kissing her again, once, twice, each kiss deeper and sweeter with the promise it holds.

"I didn't know if you'd be here," she says, smiling and crying at once when he pulls back. "I'm sorry, so sorry if I hurt you."

"Don't be sorry." His thumb catches a tear. "It's all done. It'll be okay."

"I missed you, missed everything we had."

"Shh." George tips his head down and kisses her again. "I missed you, too. And Grace. She's okay?"

"She's beautiful. She's really coming along."

"How about you?" he asks, lifting her chin with his finger, drawing it across her cheek, touching her gold hoop earring, her neck, her hair. "Are you okay?"

She shrugs and tells him, "I've been home, you know? Going a little crazy with all this," she says softly. "Let's just say my kitchen is really shining now."

"You look thin." His hands move to her shoulders. "Have you eaten anything today?"

"No."

He presses her hair back off her face, cradling her neck. "Let me take you out to breakfast. We'll walk over to the coffee shop and talk more there."

Amy nods, leaning her face into his hand. "I'm going to my parents' today, too. Grace is waiting. Come with me?"

George looks closely at her, seeing not just this summer, but the past year in her eyes. "No, sweetheart. You go. Spend some time with your daughter." He picks up the date book and flips it open. "I'll see you Thursday night, though. That'll give you a couple days." He knows how delicate her house of cards is, how she struggles with each one, each moment, each relationship, day, event. It can't be a struggle anymore.

Amy follows him to the back room where he lays the agenda planner open on his desk, takes a pen and boldly circles Thursday. He lifts off his apron, closes up the office and they walk through the dark shop out into the summer sunshine. There is a tentativeness there, when her hand links with his, her fingers moving gently. He feels it.

"I have to leave right after breakfast," Amy tells him. "And I'm missing you already."

He leans over and kisses the side of her head as they walk through the outdoor plaza. The sun is hot, rising high in late-July's sky. He notices it, just like he does the potted barrels of yellow marigolds and red geraniums along the cobblestone walkway, vinca vines trailing down the sides. Shop doors are propped open to the summer day now, to the easy talk of passersby, and to warmth. Store clerks wheel racks of sale merchandise outside the doors.

"Do you need to get gas for the trip?" he asks.

"I filled my tank last night," she says.

"Okay. Good. Call me when you get there?"

"I will. Promise."

"I'll be waiting." He turns toward the parking lot. "Where are you parked?"

"Over there." She points to a further corner of the lot. "Why?"

Ahead, a maintenance crew is repainting the shopping plaza's colonial-style lampposts and up above, a vapor trail from a jet lays white lines across the blue sky. Deep green umbrellas are being cranked open at patio tables outside the coffee shop, clicking as they rise.

"It's a long drive on the highway. I want to check your tires before you go."

Acknowledgments

I'D LIKE TO OFFER MY gratitude to those who have helped bring this story to light.

Thank you to my publishing team, an array of talented and dedicated individuals, all of whom I'm fortunate to have on my side. The care and attention you give to my work means so much.

I'd like to acknowledge the Wethersfield Historical Society's museum exhibit "Wethersfield Weddings: Tying the Knot." The collection of antique wedding gowns on display captured a delicate visual history that was instrumental in forging my vision for Amy's vintage bridal shop.

For answering my questions about legal procedures, I turned to criminal defense attorney Brian J. Woolf, who clearly and patiently explained what George's options might be upon seeking legal counsel. Your help was invaluable, and I am deeply grateful. Any mistakes are mine.

Two special places are worth noting for their influence on the story. The sparkling fountain in my hometown opens *True Blend*, so I'm tossing in a coin of thanks for the hopes and wishes it inspires. Point O' Woods Beach, a peaceful stretch of sand and sea along the Connecticut coast, is close to my heart and finds its way into all my books. Because answers can always be found beside the sea.

Finally, to my husband Tony, and to my daughters Jena and Mary. You're truly the best.

Also by

JOANNE DEMAIO

Snowflakes and Coffee Cakes

Blue Jeans and Coffee Beans

Whole Latte Life

For a complete list of books by *New York Times* bestselling author Joanne DeMaio, visit:

www.joannedemaio.com

About the Author

JOANNE DEMAIO is a *New York Times* and *USA Today* bestselling author of contemporary fiction. She enjoys writing about friendship, family, love and choices, while setting her stories in New England towns or by the sea. Her previous novels include *Snowflakes and Coffee Cakes*, *Blue Jeans and Coffee Beans*, and *Whole Latte Life*. Currently at work on her next novel, Joanne resides with her family in Connecticut.

For a complete list of books and for news on upcoming releases, please visit Joanne's website. She also enjoys hearing from readers on Facebook.

Author Website:
www.joannedemaio.com

Facebook:
www.facebook.com/JoanneDeMaioAuthor